The Second Sister

The Second Sister

by Leslie O'Grady

St. Martin's Press
New York

Design by Laura Hough

Library of Congress Cataloging in Publication Data

O'Grady, Leslie.
    The second sister.

    I. Title.
PS3565.G68S4   1984   813′ .54   84-13255
ISBN 0-312-70845-9

First Edition
10 9 8 7 6 5 4 3 2 1

To Espa and John O'Grady

Chapter One

I knew the man was following me. I had first noticed him seated by the potted palms in the lobby
of my cousin's hotel, his golden head bent over a newspaper
as he tried to look as if he belonged here. He failed, of
course, because it is my responsibility to know each and
every one of our guests by name, and I knew at a glance that
this man was not registered with us.

At the time, I felt no apprehension or fear—that was to
come later, in another country far from Egypt—but merely
mild curiosity, for he was good-looking in a cool, Nordic
way, and woefully out of place in his heavy, brown tweed
suit. Finally, I decided he was at our establishment solely to
dine, for the Clark's Hotel boasts the finest French chef in
Cairo, and guests at other hotels often come just for dinner,
then return to their own accommodations. Without a second
thought for the man in the brown tweed suit, I crossed the
lobby and went about my duties of introducing travelers to
the exotic city that is Cairo.

The next day, however, as I was escorting a small group of
English people through the narrow, noisy streets of the Old
City's bazaar, I saw the man again. My party of five had
slowly wound its way past stalls offering leather goods, cop-
per work, and carpets, and was stopped in front of a jew-
eler's booth, where the tempting variety of necklaces and
scarab amulets instantly lured all the women. While one of
them was examining a faience bead necklace, I happened to

glance up and there the man was, not ten feet away, blatantly staring at me.

In the light and color of the bazaar—hot blue sky, ochre buildings, natives robed in vivid blue or white—he was a figure of darkness in that brown tweed suit. At a glance, I could see he was tall, with the trim body of an athlete, and, though a wide-brimmed hat shadowed part of his clean-shaven face, I could discern a thin, cruel mouth. When our gazes locked for just an instant, I felt eyes as dark as a pharaoh's tomb drill right through me, and my heart quickened at the intimacy of it.

Then the woman distracted me by asking if I thought the blue beads were really thousands of years old, and when I turned again, the man was gone.

Just a coincidence, I thought, and dismissed him with a shrug. But, the next day, when he appeared at Giza, where I was escorting the Worthington party on a tour of the Great Pyramid, I began to think our meetings more than mere coincidence.

Riding sturdy white donkeys with such grandiose names as "Benjamin Disraeli" and "Lillie Langtry," we had left just as the hazy blue light of dawn was turning gold and the narrow streets were not yet filled with people hurrying to market. My dragoman, Hassam, an Egyptian who serves as my guide, translator, and watchdog, headed our little procession. The ride took over an hour, and when we arrived at the sparse, rocky plateau on which the pyramids have stood for centuries, the party was still cheerful, undaunted, and properly in awe at the magnificent sight that greeted their eyes.

The strong morning sun, filtered through the pervasive dust, gave the Great Pyramid a ghostly, shimmering quality as it towered majestically before us, filling the horizon and making everything around it dwindle into insignificance by comparison. There were other sights to intrigue the eye on the vista spread before us—several smaller pyramids, and, of course, the enigmatic sphinx holding its head proudly above the shifting, encroaching sands—but all eyes remained fixed on the Great Pyramid and all, save the bothersome flies that buzzed about us and our donkeys, were moved to respectful silence.

Our party that morning included Mr. and Mrs. Worthington, who fancied themselves amateur archaeologists; their morbid daughter, Agnes; and their maid, all touring Egypt for the first time. Since their arrival several days ago, they had plunged into all activities with an enthusiasm that was contagious, whether visiting the ancient al-Azhar mosque, the antiquities of the Egyptian Museum, or the Citadel, with its panoramic view of Cairo.

Now as we urged our donkeys forward and trotted up to the base of the pyramid, it became even more apparent that the face of the massive structure was not a seamless triangle, as it appeared from a distance; it was, rather, constructed of large limestone blocks positioned one atop the other to form steps to the summit. I noticed with satisfaction that we were the first group of tourists to have arrived this morning, though a horde of beggars and peddlers had already stationed itself here and eagerly awaited our arrival.

As we dismounted, the Worthingtons were making plans to ascend to the top, while their maid seemed eager to descend into the Pharaoh Cheops' burial chamber. However, Agnes, still sulking because she hadn't been consulted about the day's activities, adamantly refused to join either party despite her parents' disappointed protestations to the effect that she would be missing the experience of a lifetime. The child could not be swayed, and I, ever the peacemaker, agreed to wait with her at the base of the pyramid while she watched her parents being pulled and pushed up the large blocks by three strong Bedouins.

As we stood there, our fly switches ready and our faces shaded by broad-brimmed hats and heavy, utilitarian umbrellas, Agnes squinted through steel-rimmed spectacles at her parents' leisurely progress. She was such a gangly, awkward child of twelve and reminded me so much of myself at her age that my heart had gone out to her the moment she arrived at our hotel.

She moistened her lips nervously, as she always did before asking one of her morbid questions, and said, "Miss Clark, is it true that, when the pharaohs died, they had all their servants put to death and buried with them?"

"Agnes, wherever did you get that idea?" I chided her gently. "No, they made tiny pottery figures, called *ushabtis*, to be buried with them. They believed that in the hereafter these pottery servants would come to life to serve them."

"What utter nonsense!" she exclaimed with true Christian arrogance. "Everyone knows you either go to heaven or—or the other place when you die." Then she kicked at the soft sand with her toe and ran her tongue over her lips. "Miss Clark, is it true that the air inside the pharaoh's tomb is poisonous?"

"Oh, dear," I said with mock seriousness. "If that is the case, then I fear we've just lost your maid." When the child looked sheepish and tittered at her own silliness, I said, "It's so tiresome just standing here, waiting for the others. Why don't we go for a walk?"

With my long skirt trailing in the sand, and Hassam following at a discreet distance to ward off persistent peddlers and beggars, Agnes Worthington and I slowly strolled around the base of the Great Pyramid.

I kept asking her questions about herself and her home back in England, mainly to give her the attention she craved, and she responded with enthusiasm, as will almost anyone in whom a little interest is shown. Her plain cabbage face actually glowed prettily as she described her home in Yorkshire, populated with cheery servants and scores of dogs, cats, and ponies.

Suddenly, Agnes squinted up at me and said, "Miss Clark, is it true that you and Mr. Clark are cousins?"

"Yes, Agnes."

"I was just wondering. I heard Mama say she thought it odd that a beauty such as yourself should be running a hotel in Cairo with her cousin. Mama said she suspected he was keeping you."

I felt the blood rush to my cheeks, but before I could make further comment, Agnes went on ingenuously, "I wouldn't like to be kept here against my will." Again the morbid reasserted itself and she said, in a hushed voice, "Is it true Mr. Clark is keeping you here against your will? Because if he is, I'm sure my parents could help you to escape."

I squeezed her hand and tried not to laugh. "No, Agnes, Mr. Clark is not keeping me here against my will. We really are cousins, and as close as brother and sister. While I appreciate your concern, I must tell you I am here with him because I wish to be."

Dismayed and annoyed as such speculation makes me, I could not blame Agnes's mother for thinking Cyrus and I are not what we seem. There are always a few raised eyebrows when we are introduced as cousins. Perhaps people disbelieve us because there is scant physical resemblance. Cyrus is a large Viking of a man, with coloring so fair his brows and lashes are almost invisible, while I am of average height, with hair the color of a raven's wing and pale green eyes that are described as either bewitching or shy. Adding to the confusion is the fact that our personalities are as dissimilar as Egypt and England. My cousin tends to be loud and impulsive, while I am quiet and cautious. But, people will think what they will, and I am long past taking offense when a guest assumes I am Cyrus's mistress.

"As long as people keep coming to the Clark's Hotel," Cyrus says gleefully, "let them think what they please."

And they do keep coming, year after year, enough to fill our small hotel to capacity during the winter months when Egypt's hot, dry climate, like a lodestone draws Europeans out of their own cold, gray countries. In all due modesty, I like to think that my duties as hostess have something to do with our success. While we'll never replace Shepheard's as the premiere hotel in Cairo, we receive a fair number of guests. I serve as go-between for the European traveler and the Egyptian native, smoothing the way so that the experience of their meeting contains a minimum of unpleasantness for both. With the invaluable assistance of Hassam, I can escort our guests to the pyramids, the bazaars, any number of mosques, and even hire shallow, two-masted boats called *dahabeyah*s for them so they can sail down the Nile to the Temple of Karnak and the city of Luxor. I have become so indispensable Cyrus calls me his Right Arm.

However no situation is perfect. Since coming to Cairo, I have had to stave off the unwelcome advances of certain gentlemen. While this was most embarrassing in the beginning, I have learned to refuse them skillfully so their dignity remains intact and they don't take their patronage elsewhere.

"You can't blame a man for trying, coz," Cyrus would always say to me. "You're such a gentle little thing, and those great green eyes of yours just make a man want to protect you."

Thinking about unwanted masculine attention made me recall the man who had been following me. Was he like all the others, I wondered, seeking a diversion with an Englishwoman while away from home?

I was soon to find out.

Just as Agnes and I rounded a corner, the object of my thoughts seemed to appear out of nowhere and came walking right toward us.

The shock was so great I stopped with a gasp and clutched at Agnes's hand, causing her to look up at me in alarm. But I ignored her, my eyes fixed on the man effortlessly making his way toward us over the sand.

I was mesmerized as if by a cobra slithering toward me, unable to move, let alone run, to save my own life. The man looked even taller today, still out of place in the brown tweed suit that must have been suffocating in this heat. The wide-brimmed hat gave him scant protection against the fierce sun's reflected light, for the part of his face I could see was already beginning to burn. As he walked closer, I could feel his dark eyes again watching me.

When he was only a few feet away, I finally got a close look at him, and was quite unprepared for him being even more handsome than I had originally supposed, with craggy features in a face filled with humor and intelligence. I could see now that his eyes were a peculiar dark gray and heavily lidded, giving him a languid look, but I read wariness in their smoky depths, and I doubted if those sleepy eyes missed anything.

Then he grinned, revealing perfect white teeth, and his mouth softened, no longer thin and cruel.

"Good morning, Miss Clark."

Dumbfounded that he knew my name, I could only open my mouth in a vain attempt to say something as he went striding by. Agnes began tugging at my hand. "Oh, look, Miss Clark. Mama and Papa have reached the top. I think they're waving to me."

I turned and threw my head back to look up at the summit, and by the time I had turned once again, the man was far away. I couldn't very well run after him without appearing undignified.

I knew I had to discuss this matter with Cyrus. He is a perceptive man, and usually knows what I'm thinking and feeling even before I do, except when his mind is occupied by his hotel, a most demanding mistress. By the time my exuberant party finally returned to the hotel, it was already lunchtime and my cousin was preoccupied with feeding his guests.

As I walked into his neat, spacious office, he merely glanced up from his desk and said, "Oh, there you are, coz. Mr. Blanch—?"

Cyrus and I know each other so well, all he generally has to do is utter a few words, and I know instantly what he is talking about. "Mr. Blanch requested a picnic luncheon today," I replied. "I told Henri this morning to prepare one for him."

"Well, our esteemed chef forgot to pack it. Will you smooth some ruffled feathers?" I barely had enough time to nod before Cyrus added, "And the Dickens party—?"

I had promised the Dickens party of four I would help them rent a *dahabeyah* this afternoon, and had totally forgotten about it. I winced. "I'm sorry, Cyrus. I forgot."

His nearly invisible blond brows came together in a frown of reproach. "Now, now, Cassandra, you are my Right Arm and I depend on you not to forget anything. You know the Dickenses favor us with their patronage every year, and glowingly recommend us to their many wealthy friends when they return to England. We must always go out of our way for them."

"Yes, Cyrus, I know. I'll attend to them at once and apologize profusely for having inconvenienced them."

As I watched him rise hurriedly, I said, "Cyrus, there is something very important I must discuss with you."

"Later, Cassa, later," he replied, slipping into his jacket and dashing out the door before I could utter another word.

Since what I had to tell him would have to wait, I went to the kitchen to have a sumptuous picnic prepared for Mr. Blanch. Then I ate a quick luncheon myself, met the Dickens party in the lobby, and accompanied them to the wharves of Bulaq, where hundreds of *dahabeyah*s were docked, their tall masts a forest of poles rising from the water. After looking at one boat after another all afternoon and haggling with their captains over a fair price, we finally found the Dickenses a suitable craft, and returned to the hotel, exhausted but satisfied. Leaving them, I cornered Cyrus in his office once again.

"Cyrus," I said, as I stood before his desk, "I must speak with you. Now. Immediately."

He sat back, his round face alight with curiosity, since all catastrophes had been dealt with and tea time was not yet upon us. Once his guests were content, Cyrus always had time for me. "What is it, dear Cassa? Why the belligerent look on your lovely face?"

I sat opposite him and mopped my brow with my handkerchief, for the office was stifling, despite the fact that the shutters were closed against the relentless sun. "A strange man has been following me."

He smiled indulgently. "Why does that surprise you? You are a beautiful woman, though, Lord knows, at twenty-six, you're far from an ingenue. But," he added in his teasing voice, "you're still quite lovely."

"Thank you, Cyrus," I retorted. Then I told him about the gray-eyed stranger and how I had seen him first in our lobby, then at the bazaar, and today at the pyramids.

Cyrus shrugged and gave me his standard excuse. "He's probably a European traveling alone who thinks you'll provide him with a diversion while he's away from his wife and children. It's happened before, you'll recall. That German prince, the French artist . . ."

I rolled my eyes at the memory of those most persistent examples. "But this is different somehow, Cyrus," I replied, feeling a sense of dread descend on me for no apparent reason.

"Well, now, you're certainly safe here, and as long as you take Hassam with you wherever you go . . . No one would harm you with Hassam around."

"But Cyrus, the man knew my name."

Now he rose and came around the desk to put his huge hand on my shoulder. "I wouldn't worry about it, Cassa. He's probably some chap just playing at being mysterious to catch your attention. It wouldn't be difficult to find out your name, you know. All he'd have to do is ask the desk clerk. Why don't you go to your room, and I'll have one of the *safragi*s bring you some lemonade? Then you can rest before dinner."

I smiled wanly, nodded, though his words did not reassure me, and went upstairs to refresh myself after my long day outdoors.

Once inside my modest chamber on the second floor, I flung my straw hat on the bed, then went to the washstand to refresh myself, hot and sticky from an afternoon in the merciless Egyptian sun. After sponging the dust from my face, which looked so tan despite the almond oil I use in an attempt to keep it fashionably pale, I took a seat under the window and calmly fanned myself, trying to relax.

My room had one of the best views in the hotel, overlooking the terrace and the rooftops of Cairo beyond, and it was a scene I usually found tranquil and refreshing, despite its exotic appearance.

Tall green palms swayed in an afternoon breeze so blistering it felt like the blast from a potter's kiln, while narrow white stone minarets shimmered against the milky sky. On that afternoon, there was no sound to break the serenity. Small iron chairs scattered across the terrace below were all empty of the usual Europeans chatting over drinks, and the road beyond, usually congested with donkey boys, beggars, snake charmers, and other Egyptians who eked out a living from the tourists, was now nearly deserted as everyone fled the heat. It was not even time for the high reedy call of the muezzin to float over the city, as he summoned faithful Moslems to prayer.

My enjoyment of the scene was interrupted only once, by a *safragi* bearing the promised lemonade on a tray, and when he departed, I returned to my seat and my thoughts.

As I sat there, sipping cold lemonade and fanning myself, the dark-eyed man boldly invaded my thoughts, persistently reappearing even as I sought to banish him by thinking of tomorrow's schedule that was sure to keep me busy. Who was he, I wondered, and why had he been following me? I could not accept Cyrus's reason, for I had learned to recognize the soulful looks, the flattering words, and the rapt attention of a gentleman bent on seduction. This man had not demonstrated such tell-tale signs. No, he had another reason for seeking me out, and I wasn't sure I wanted to know what it was.

Suddenly, I felt exhausted, so I went to my bed, parted the filmy mosquito netting, and crawled inside its protective cocoon to take a nap. I closed my eyes and soon fell into a light sleep haunted by the dark-eyed stranger.

Later, I rose feeling curiously unrefreshed and irritable, as though I hadn't slept at all, but I dressed for dinner anyway, donning a gown of Nile green silk that buoyed my spirits somewhat. Then, once my hair was brushed and arranged in a simple knot at the nape of my neck, I was ready to go downstairs and mingle with our dinner guests.

As I descended the staircase, however, I stopped in surprise when my gaze fell on the very man who had been following me.

In the crowded lobby, he was standing alone at the reception desk, watching everyone who walked by as though looking for someone in particular. His brown tweed suit had been replaced by elegant black evening attire, and he blended in with all the other guests passing through on their way to the dining room.

Just then, he glanced up, saw me, and came striding toward the foot of the stairs. His eyes gleamed with amusement as he looked up and said, "Good evening, Miss Clark. I've been waiting for you."

I looked down at him and tried to keep from blushing. "You have me at a disadvantage, sir. You seem to know who I am, and yet I can't recall ever having been introduced to you."

He inclined his head slightly. "My name is Geoffrey

Lester, and I would like to speak to you in private, if I may."

So, Cyrus had been right all along. This man was like all the others. "I'm sorry, Mr. Lester," I said, descending the few remaining steps. "That would be most improper."

His face fell, and as I sought to walk past him, he made a detaining gesture. "I assure you, Miss Clark, that my intentions are not at all improper, though what I have to say may shock and upset you. I would rather we spoke alone than in this lobby, where anyone could overhear."

I stopped and regarded him with mild reproof. "That is certainly the most original approach I've ever received from a gentleman, Mr. Lester. You are to be congratulated."

He looked a bit exasperated with me. "I can assure you I am most sincere, Miss Clark, but sorely lacking in patience. I fully intend to speak to you, either now, or at some later date. The choice is yours."

His mouth had hardened into a stubborn line, and I could tell he meant what he said; so I surrendered with a sigh. "I suppose no harm would come of speaking with you. My cousin's office will afford us some privacy."

I knew Cyrus would be busy playing the jovial hôtelier with his guests, and his office would be quiet and empty. So I led the persistent Mr. Lester through the lobby, down a winding corridor, and into Cyrus's deserted office.

"Now," I said, closing the door behind us, "what have you to say to me that will be so shocking and upsetting?"

"I would advise you to sit down, Miss Clark."

He was so very somber, I felt a shaft of fear jab at the pit of my stomach. "What is it, Mr. Lester? Has something happened to Aunt Venetia or Uncle Harry?"

He shook his head. "No, Miss Clark. As far as I know, they are both in good health. The reason I have come to Cairo is that your mother sent me to find you."

I felt the blood rush from my head and heard a ringing in my ears just as my legs turned to water and refused to support me. Mr. Lester moved fast, and before I could collapse, he had assisted me to the nearest chair, where I quickly sat.

"I know this has been a great shock to you, Miss Clark," he said kindly. "May I get you a glass of lemonade, perhaps, or a cold compress?"

"Some lemonade would be most appreciated," I replied, and watched as he nodded and left the office.

I didn't really want the drink, simply an excuse to be rid of Geoffrey Lester for a few moments so I could collect myself. The mere mention of my mother had opened a wound I had thought long since healed, and the hurt was excruciating. I wanted to rush outside into the pink and blue twilight, past palm trees and into the endless desert, until my lungs had burst and I had collapsed into oblivion. I closed my eyes and leaned my head against the back of the chair, trying to compose myself.

I don't know how long I had been sitting that way, when a voice startled me by saying, "Miss Clark?" and I opened my eyes to find Mr. Lester standing there, proffering a glass of lemonade.

I thanked him and sipped it slowly while he strode around Cyrus's office, studying some sketches of Egyptian scenes that were grouped together on one wall.

I needed time to think, time to settle the tumultuous thoughts that chased each other through my brain, and time to decide just what I was going to say to this man.

Finally, I set my glass down and addressed him. "You were wise to insist we speak alone, Mr. Lester. The news you bring has been something of a shock to me. I don't know quite what to say."

His smile was warm and persuasive as he crossed the room and sat down next to me. "Say you'll return to London with me and stay with your mother for a while."

My brows rose in surprise. "My mother actually wants to see me?" I twisted my hands together to keep them from trembling. "I don't know how much you know about my mother, Mr. Lester. She abandoned my father and me when I was barely four years old, and in the last twenty-two years, I've never seen her, never received so much as a note from her, never learned whether she was alive or dead. And she certainly never cared to know about me. Now, after all this time, she wants to see me? You must forgive me if I seem less than enthusiastic."

"But she has tried to contact you over the years," he insisted. At my look of disbelief, he went on with, "First, your aunt and uncle deliberately withheld her letters to you, and later, when your mother tried to see you, she was told you were traveling abroad with your father."

I shook my head stubbornly. "Aunt Venetia and Uncle Harry would never, ever, have done that, but, quite frankly, Mr. Lester, I wouldn't blame them if they had." Feeling much stronger now, I rose to put distance between us, because this man's penetrating stare was disconcerting. "My mother deserted her husband and daughter for the kind of life she thought she deserved, one of ease and plenty, not the hard life of a soldier's wife. Aunt Venetia told me all about how my mother had divorced my father so she could marry that Earl of Whatever." I couldn't keep the bitterness out of my voice as I added, "She got everything she wanted, didn't she? A huge estate crawling with servants to see to her every whim, jewels, carriages. . . . Everything my poor father couldn't give her. I suppose losing me was the price she had to pay, but she paid it willingly enough."

"She didn't get everything she wanted," was his reply. "No one ever does in life."

I looked at him, but said nothing, then turned away to stare through the shutter's slats at a conjurer performing his sleight-of-hand for a group of tourists. I waited until the show was over and the tourists dispersed before speaking, and even then it was as though I were standing outside myself, listening to someone else.

"When I first learned that my mother wasn't really dead,

as I had previously thought, but that she had abandoned my father and me, I hated her for what she had done. That hatred threatened to consume me, until the people I loved helped me to realize that hatred is a wasted emotion. I felt great bitterness and resentment for a long, long time, Mr. Lester. Now, I honestly don't think of my mother very much, because there are others who do care about me. I feel nothing toward her, neither love nor hatred, just . . . indifference." I turned to him now. "Do you understand?"

His smile was sympathetic. "Of course, Miss Clark. When your mother first asked me to help find you, I was concerned about the type of young woman I'd find. If you were still bitter, I knew I could never persuade you to return to England with me. But indifference? Now, that gives me hope."

"Oh? And why is that?"

"If you're indifferent, then at least you no longer hate your mother. And if that's the case, perhaps you wouldn't be averse to seeing her."

"Perhaps," was my noncommittal reply. Then, as if to prove that there was no animosity left in me, I returned to my chair, smoothed my skirts, and said congenially, "Now, will you tell me how you came to know my mother?"

His craggy face softened, as though he had just had a pleasant thought. "A friend from my Oxford days lived near your mother in Northumberland, and she and her husband would often entertain us when we were out of school. Now, of course, I am married to their daughter."

The room seemed to teeter, and I had to grasp the arms of my chair and breathe deeply before the feeling passed. All I could do was stare and babble, "Daughter? I have a *sister?*"

He saw my pain and confusion at once and looked put out with himself. "I see you didn't know. Forgive my being such a callous fool and breaking the news so abruptly."

After an eternity, I murmured, "So, I have a sister. Imagine, after all these years, to discover I have a sister." I shook my head, still bewildered and overcome. I was being inundated with one revelation after another, and could barely sort out everything this man had said to me.

"They had only one child," he explained, reaching into his pocket. "She's twenty years old, and her name is Leonie. As you can see from this photograph, she favors your mother."

I jumped up and whirled away, refusing to look at it. Striding over to the window again, I hugged myself to make sure I wasn't trapped in some nightmare.

Although I could feel Geoffrey Lester's eyes on me, he made no attempt to speak, as though he knew I needed time to accept what he had told me, and I appreciated his sensitivity and tact.

When I finally turned to face him, I was shaking and there were tears stinging my eyes. "Why should Mother want to see me now, when she already has another daughter?"

"She wants to learn to know you, Miss Clark, and to perhaps make you understand why she did what she did all those years ago."

This astounding revelation rankled, and I had to lash out at someone in my frustration. "What is there to understand? My mother was an immoral woman who left her husband for another man. It's quite simple, really."

Geoffrey Lester's face darkened, and he looked as though he were about to say something, then changed his mind. Instead, he placed his fingertips together and regarded me with that unswerving, contemplative look. "While in Cairo, I have heard not one unkind word spoken about you, Miss Clark. The donkey boys adore you for your kindness and generosity with tips—*baksheesh*, I think they call it—and your guests praise your sunny disposition, patience, and indefatigability. One of your waiters even told me you helped obtain medical care for his sick wife. I would have thought such a paragon would have a forgiving nature as well."

"You expect too much, Mr. Lester."

"You're a grown woman, Miss Clark, not a child," he retorted, "and I would have hoped you had learned by now that nothing is black or white in life. There are many shades of gray to any situation."

I hung my head at his rebuke. Then, overcome with curiosity, I asked, "Does my mother still live in Northumberland?"

Mr. Lester shook his head. "After I married her daughter, she came to live with us. My sister also lives with us in London." At my puzzled look, he added. "Your mother's husband died suddenly three years ago, before he could adequately provide for his wife and daughter. Because there was no male heir, ownership of the estate passed to a cousin of the earl. There was no question of your mother and Leonie staying on, of course, under those circumstances."

So, my mother was now a widow, and the man for whom she had forsaken my father was now dead. In spite of myself, I felt a twinge of sympathy for her.

Geoffrey Lester, who had been watching me in silence, suddenly said, "Are you afraid to come to England?"

"Afraid? Of what?"

"Afraid that you might actually come to know and admire your mother. I do."

I could see what he was attempting, and I refused to be baited. "I have made a good life for myself out here, Mr. Lester. After I learned my mother had abandoned me, I became painfully shy and withdrawn because I felt no one could love me. My cousin Cyrus urged me to come to Cairo with him, and working here has restored my confidence somewhat. I'm engaged in satisfying, productive labor, and I don't know if I'm willing to give it up just because my mother has had a change of heart and now wishes to see me."

I blushed, wishing I hadn't revealed so much of myself to this stranger, but there was something about Geoffrey Lester that made one want to tell him things one would tell no one else.

My speech seemed to chasten him into silence, but not for long. He smiled. "Ah, an independent woman, I see. You remind me of my elder sister, Maud, in that respect. She, too, is a modern, independent woman." Then his voice became quieter, more reflective. "Productive labor is all well and good, Miss Clark, but don't you ever get lonely? I'm sure you long for those things other women crave, a husband, a home, and children of your own. Surely some fine, upstanding young man will one day take you back to England as his bride anyway, so why not come a little sooner?"

I raised my head proudly, resenting his patronizing tone. "I am never lonely, Mr. Lester. I have Cyrus, our many affable guests, and the splendors of Cairo to fill my days. Unlike my mother, I don't need a man to define my existence. Perhaps I shall escort travelers to the Great Pyramid until the day I'm too old to ride a donkey."

"And then what will you do?"

"Take a carriage."

His eyes crinkled at the corners as he laughed heartily and reached into his pocket again to take out more papers. "At the risk of offending you once more, I've taken the liberty of paying in advance for your passage to England. Regrettably, I have lingered in Egypt too long already and must sail tomorrow."

I was most annoyed by the man's presumption, but I held myself in check. All I said was, "You shouldn't have wasted your money, Mr. Lester. Should I decide to come to England, I shall pay my own way, thank you."

"You will come, you know."

"You're very certain of that, aren't you?" was my sharp retort.

He nodded. "I can see you are a good, decent person, Miss Clark, and I doubt if you'll be able to resist going to your mother's aid, regardless of what she did to you in the past."

That left me speechless.

Then he invited me to dine with him, but I was still agitated, and I refused. After Mr. Lester left Cyrus's office, I remained for a few minutes to compose myself in the soothing silence. Then, just as I was leaving, I noticed the photograph of my sister lying on the edge of the desk. I picked it up without looking at it and returned to my room.

Once upstairs, I sat for some time in the dwindling light before I could gather enough courage to turn over the photograph I held, face down, against my skirt. And even then, I didn't actually look straight at it until curiosity finally overcame my reluctance.

Was this what my mother looked like? If so, she had golden hair and huge, expressive eyes that were either green, like my own, or some other pale color, such as blue. They dominated a delicate, heart-shaped face that suddenly looked familiar to me through the mists of time and caused a lump to form in my throat.

Overcome, I had to close my eyes for a minute or two, and when I opened them, I stopped thinking of my mother and instead searched for similarities between my sister and me. We weren't alike at all. Leonie's mouth was a perfect, voluptuous pout, while mine was too generous for my face. At least I could boast a straight, slender nose, while my sister's was short and upturned, a definite flaw in those perfect features. But who would ever notice such a minor imperfection when there was so much else to admire?

As I continued to study the photograph, feeling both curiosity and a touch of envy, I could tell Leonie possessed enough confidence and poise for both of us. I seriously doubted if Leonie Lester had ever known a moment of uncertainty in her life.

I sighed dismally and set the photograph aside.

I thought about my discussion with Geoffrey Lester earlier that evening, and certain things he had said provoked and puzzled me. He had intimated that Cyrus's parents, my

Aunt Venetia and Uncle Harry, had somehow conspired to keep my mother and me apart. Could that be true, I wondered incredulously.

I will admit that, throughout my life, people have lied to me about my mother, an Englishwoman with the incongruous name of Persia. When she abandoned me, I was merely told she had gone away, which I, being so very young, readily accepted. When I was a little older, I was told she had died while following my father on one of his regiment's military campaigns halfway round the world. By that time, I had been living with the large family of my father's brother for several years.

The Clarks lived at the Grange, a modest manor house tucked away in the rolling Cotswold hills of Gloucester. The house itself was of mellow limestone, the same soft yellow as the pyramids, though nestled against lush green fields and wooded hills rather than arid desert. It was the only home I had ever known.

But, as much as I loved the Clarks, it was my father I eagerly awaited, marking time from one visit to the next.

My father was a younger son, and, since there were no funds to buy him a commission, he enlisted in the army as a common soldier. I had understood at an early age that I could not accompany him to the places whose names I could barely pronounce, but his very absence made me love and appreciate him even more on those occasions when he did visit me, his pockets bulging with gifts. I remember a warm, loving man, as tall as Mr. Lester, with melancholy eyes, rosy cheeks, and grand mustaches waxed into points that I feared would prick me when I hugged and kissed him. Despite his bluff manner and ready laughter, I always sensed an air of sadness about him that made me sad for him, but I could never bring myself to question him about that private pain. Ten years ago, in 1879, when he was killed during the Zulu War, I wished I had. But not even my father's death moved Aunt Venetia to reveal to me the truth about my mother.

She left that for my sixteenth birthday, a day I shall never forget.

I had just returned, hot and flushed, from a long, leisurely gallop across the countryside on my cousin Bill's new hunter, which I had been allowed to ride as a special birthday treat. When I returned to the house, I was told Aunt Venetia wanted to see me at once in her sitting room, and I remember being very surprised by this. A summons to my aunt's upstairs sitting room was akin to a summons to Buckingham Palace, for that room was my aunt's sanctuary where no one, not even her beloved husband, dared intrude without an express invitation.

That day, as I timidly entered that snuggery, and my eyes adjusted to the dimness, I could see that it hadn't changed since the last time I had been summoned here, years before, because of some long-forgotten transgression. It was still kept dark, perhaps to hide the fact that it contained so few pieces of furniture, and those that remained "date from the Norman Conquest," as Cyrus liked to say. There were just a few chairs and a table draped with a faded cloth to keep its legs modestly covered. It was topped with several photographs of the Clarks' ten children. As I crossed the room, I could smell the pervasive scent of lavender and spice pot-pourri set out in open dishes to sweeten the air.

"Do come in and sit down, dear Cassandra," Aunt Venetia commanded from her seat across the room. When I seated myself in a chair next to her own, she came right to the point, as was her custom. "You've just turned sixteen, my dear, and there is something I must tell you."

With her plump, diminutive figure dressed in black bombazine, and with a frilly lace cap on her graying head, she looked for all the world like the Queen herself, but Aunt Venetia was not so dour, and she smiled kindly at me.

"What is that?" I demanded uneasily.

She took a deep breath and folded her plump hands in her

lap. She did not look at me as she replied, "The truth about your mother."

I swallowed hard and stared at a photograph of Cyrus and his youngest sister, my cousin Peg, mounted on a fat bay pony. "My mother is dead. Father told me so years ago, when I was just a child."

Aunt Venetia closed her eyes and gave an imperceptible shake of her head. "No, Cassandra, that is not true. We had to tell you that monstrous lie because you were too young to understand the truth. I'm sure God has forgiven us for it."

I shrank back in my chair, a numbness beginning to creep over me. In a moment, I would be frozen in my seat, unable to move or talk, so I said, in a high, querulous voice, "What are you saying, Aunt Ven? That my mother isn't dead after all? That she's alive?"

My aunt sniffed in disapproval. "For all intents and purposes, she might as well be dead."

"You're not making any sense, Aunt!" I cried, resisting the disrespectful urge to reach over and shake her.

She looked at me, her blue eyes filled with compassion and understanding, and she began, in her gentle voice that had banished many a nightmare, "I know of no other way to tell you, Cassandra. I've been dreading this day for years, but Harry says I must tell you." She hesitated, then said, "Your mother abandoned both you and your father when you were just a child, my dear. She bolted with another man, a wealthy peer who could give her the material possessions she wanted. Later, she brought further shame and scandal to our family when she divorced your father and married this other man."

I fainted for the first time in my life. One moment I was shaking my head wildly, mouthing refutations, and the next I was looking up at my aunt, who was waving smelling salts under my nose. When I was revived and sitting up again, a worried-looking Aunt Venetia asked me if I wanted to go to my room and postpone our conversation until later. I refused.

"Why didn't you tell me this sooner, Aunt?" I demanded. "Why did you let me go on believing all these years that she was dead?"

"We thought it best you didn't know," she replied sincerely. Then her face radiated warmth and contentment. "Even though we had a brood of our own, and it's been a struggle to feed and clothe them all, we took you into our home and raised you as if you had been one of our own. You were so happy here with all your cousins, it seemed as though it would be a sin to spoil life for you."

As I stared balefully at my aunt, trying to hate her for this cruel deception, I could see that she had acted out of love and in what she believed were my best interests. How could I hold it against her?

She seemed to read my mind. "And how would you have felt all these years if we had told you about your mother before you were old enough to understand? I think you would have become a bitter, hostile young woman, Cassandra."

I couldn't refute her.

"Has—has my mother ever tried to contact me?" I asked instead.

Aunt Venetia's gaze slipped away, and she spoke so softly I had to strain to catch her words. "Painful as the truth may be, I won't lie to you. She has never displayed any curiosity about you whatsoever. She has never attempted to write to you, never requested to see you." My religious, moralistic aunt couldn't resist adding an emphatic, "She is an evil, sinful woman, and you would do best to forget her."

But how could I, now that I knew the truth?

Needless to say, after that unexpected revelation, I was in a stupor for weeks, wandering aimlessly through the hills behind the house, trying to piece together the fragments of a comfortable life suddenly shattered, attempting to sweep away the web of deception that had been spun about me for years. It was as if I had awakened to discover that some malevolent magician had turned me into another person, one totally different from the Cassandra Clark I once had been.

I went through a long period of blaming everyone for the circumstances that had drastically reshaped my life. I blamed my dead father, Aunt Venetia, and Uncle Harry, for not having told me the truth sooner, and even more I blamed my mother for deserting me, the child of her blood. I became a surly, rebellious young woman—contrary, quick to find fault, disrespectful—and, in retrospect, I wondered how the Clark family ever tolerated me with such kindness and forbearance.

If it hadn't been for Cyrus . . .

A pounding on the door aroused me from contemplation, and when I said, "Come in," Cyrus himself loomed in the doorway.

"Coz, whatever are you doing sitting here in the dark?" he asked, setting his lamp down. "Agnes Worthington was asking for you at dinner tonight. Gruesome child. She wanted to know if it was true that Egyptians allow flies to infest their babies' eyes."

"She only affects a morbid mind to attract attention," I said absently, still staring out at the dark sky. "Cyrus, do you remember when I first learned my mother wasn't dead?"

He frowned as he eased his large frame into the chair next to mine. "Can't say that I do. Was I home from Hong Kong then?"

"Yes. You had come home before leaving for South America."

"Ah, yes, I remember now. You were most eager to go to your mother, if I recall."

I nodded. "And you took me by the shoulders and shook me, saying, 'Cassa, don't you realize that if your mother had *wanted* to see you all these years, she would have done so?'"

"You remember the exact words?" he asked, amazed.

"Yes, because you made me accept the fact that she didn't want me, and I could put my resentment behind me and begin to heal." I looked over at him. "You've always known just what to say to help me. And I can never thank you enough for bringing me to Cairo with you."

Such emotional displays usually embarrass Cyrus, and now he fidgeted in his seat. "I couldn't see leaving you to rot at the Grange, with no life of your own, playing aunt to all my sisters' children, living their lives instead of your own. You were such a meek little thing then, always blushing and turning away whenever a man so much as looked at you." He shook his head. "How my mother fought to keep you with her, once I told her of my plans."

I reached out to pat him on the hand. "And I'll always be in your debt for that." Then I was silent for a moment. "Tell me, Cyrus, did you ever know I had a sister?"

He hesitated and turned as pale as his brows, as though debating whether to lie to me. "Ah, you've been talking to Mr. Lester, I see."

I looked over at him sharply, trying to read his face by the lamplight. "You've met him?"

"When you declined to dine with him tonight, he came up to me and introduced himself. I take it the identity of your mysterious stranger has been revealed."

"Did he tell you why he was in Cairo?"

Cyrus nodded.

I rose, too agitated to remain still. "A sister! I never even knew I had one!" Suddenly, an unpleasant suspicion presented itself to me, and I turned on Cyrus. "Have you known about this all along, Cyrus? Is this just one more matter your parents have conspired to keep from me all these years?"

Cyrus can be a smooth and accomplished liar when the occasion warrants, but he cannot lie to me. If he attempts it, his pale face turns red, his cheeks puff out, and he sputters, as though he just can't get the untruthful words out. He made a few sputtering noises now, then realized attempts at prevarication were useless. "I learned it just before we left for Egypt," he admitted, his voice low. "Mother told me."

"You've known for the past three years and you never *told* me?" I cried. "Cyrus, how *could* you?"

"Now, now, Cassa, what good would it have done? We were all set to leave for Egypt, remember?"

"And how long had Aunt Ven known?" I demanded.

Cyrus shrugged and tried to make light of the situation. "Oh, ever since the child was born, I suppose. Mother knows everything. She's like Horus of the all-seeing eye." He was silent for a moment. "What is all the point to this, coz? You know Mother loves you as one of her own, and the greatest sin a woman can commit in her eyes is to desert her own child. Mother just tried to protect you from what she thought was an evil influence. No time to go blaming her for keeping secrets again, is it?"

As usual, Cyrus made a world of sense, and I felt my anger evaporate. "No, it isn't. Your family has been like my own, Cyrus, and I certainly can't blame your mother for doing what she thought was right."

"That's my Cassa," he said with a warm smile.

"Did Mr. Lester tell you why he came all the way to Egypt to find me?"

"He said your mother tried to contact you when your sister was getting married, but you and I had already left for Cairo. According to this Mr. Lester, my mother refused to tell him where we had gone, so he set about doing some investigating on his own. He said he's been looking for you for about a year."

That astonished me.

"So," Cyrus said with great finality, "what are you going to do now? Are you going to desert me, my Right Arm?"

I pressed my fingers to my eyes, sore after an afternoon in the Egyptian sun, and searched for an answer. I thought of Geoffrey Lester's hooded gray eyes looking right through me, and I wondered whether he was satisfied with what he found there.

"I just don't know," I said to Cyrus. "I just don't know."

Chapter Two

When I awoke the next morning after a restless night, my head was bursting with unanswered questions. Why, I wondered, as I washed and dressed, had Geoffrey Lester come all the way from England just to tell me my mother wished to see me, when she could have simply written me a letter? Better still, why hadn't she just come herself?

After breakfast, I had to escort a small group to the Blue Mosque, but when we returned later in the morning, I rushed over to Shepheard's Hotel to find Mr. Lester, who was the only one who could answer those questions and put my mind to rest. I was chagrined to learn he had checked out early that morning to return to England, and was probably in Alexandria by now. I departed Shepheard's feeling rather like a boat cut loose from its moorings, drifting aimlessly on an open sea.

He was very clever, I decided as I ate my luncheon alone in my room. First, he opened a Pandora's box filled with tantalizing images of my past, of a mother I hardly knew, and of a half-sister I knew not at all. Then he quickly withdrew, leaving me hungry for more.

I stared at Leonie Lester's picture, which I had tucked beneath my mirror's frame so I could study it at my leisure. I should have just torn it in two and forgotten about the Lesters and my mother, but something always restrained me.

In the days to come, I found myself overwhelmed with curiosity about these three people who had suddenly intruded on my contented, orderly life, and I thought about them every waking hour. Little did I realize that my days of contentment in Egypt were over, and that these three people were to blame.

Change was bearing down on me as relentlessly as the winds that sweep down off the desert. Several weeks after Geoffrey Lester's visit, I found my attitude changing toward Egypt. Suddenly, what had once been endlessly fascinating to me seemed primitive, barbaric, even frightening. When I took a group out to the Great Pyramid, I no longer envisioned the people who had built these majestic monuments so long ago. Instead, I became irritated with the beggars and peddlers always swarming around me, their eager, whining voices grating on my nerves. Now, all mosques looked alike, with their minarets, domes, and latticed windows casting filigree shadows on their cool stone floors, and I repeatedly stifled yawns of boredom as I rushed my tourists along.

Even more reprehensible was my attitude toward the Egyptian people themselves. The veiled women, only their dark eyes visible, had once seemed mysterious and exotic, but now I pitied them because they lacked my freedom. And all Egyptian men, whether they were donkey boys or soldiers, with their swarthy faces, fierce black beards, and eyes that followed one without appearing to move, had become sinister. I no longer trusted these people, and found myself constantly looking over my shoulder, peering into shadows, straining to hear footsteps behind me.

The land itself turned hostile as well. The blistering heat gave me a throbbing headache every afternoon, and the swirling dust irritated my eyes, making them red and watery. I could no longer tolerate the flies, the dirt, the pungent odors of mules, camels, and unwashed human skin.

As my disenchantment grew, my duties at the hotel suffered. I ate every meal in my room, where I could stare at Leonie's picture, rather than make forced conversation with our guests in the dining room. I found myself offering elaborate excuses to explain why I couldn't tour the Citadel or arrange for a trip to the Saqqarah Pyramids farther south. Finally, Cyrus called me into his office, and I could tell by the serious set of his mouth that this was not going to be pleasant for me.

"Close the door behind you and sit down, coz," he ordered. "We have to have a long talk, you and I."

I felt a flush of embarrassment travel up my neck and diffuse through my cheeks, for I knew my work was not up to my own usual standards, let alone Cyrus's exacting ones.

My cousin, never one to be evasive, said, "What's wrong, Cassa? And don't tell me, 'Nothing,' because I know you too well to accept such an answer. Something is preying on your mind."

I can never sit still when I'm agitated, so I rose and went to the window. Running my hands along my upper arms, I murmured, "I don't know, Cyrus. All of a sudden, I've become so—so *bored* with Egypt."

"The guests are beginning to notice," he remarked. "Frau Gruber complained she has missed your company at lunch for the past week, and Count Alba is in a lather because you were supposed to accompany him and his wife to some mosque, and you begged off at the last minute."

"I'm so sorry, Cyrus."

"Bad for the hotel, coz," he said.

Then he fell silent, though I could feel his eyes watching me in puzzlement. I did not turn to meet his gaze, but continued to stare through the slats at a snake charmer entertaining some Europeans, who stayed at a prudent distance and squealed as the cobra's hooded head rose from its basket and weaved hypnotically from side to side.

Now Cyrus stood up and crossed the room. "I think I know what's wrong," he said softly. "I can pinpoint the exact moment when this boredom began to occur. You haven't been the same since that Lester fellow came here and told you about your mother."

I stared at the floor and murmured, "You may be right."

"I know I'm right." Then Cyrus inhaled deeply, as though girding himself for some unpleasantness. "Perhaps it's time you went back to England and saw your mother."

My head swung around, and I stared at him, aghast. "Leave the hotel? But Cyrus, we've both worked like slaves to make it a success. I am your Right Arm."

A pained expression flitted across his colorless face, and his tone was lightly teasing as he said, "My dear coz, you must admit that your contributions to the running of this hotel have been negligible as of late. I spend half my day covering up your mistakes. You'd probably do yourself, and me, a world of good if you went back to England and faced your past." Then he grinned, to take the sting out of his words. "You could always come back, you know."

"I wouldn't dare leave if I thought you wouldn't have me back," I retorted. "But I haven't decided what to do." I looked out the window again, but the snake charmer and his audience had vanished. "If I go, do you realize that half the fortune teller's prophecy will have come true?"

"Prophecy? What are you talking about?"

"Don't you remember that day last spring when a group of French tourists wanted their fortunes told, and I took them to the old woman who sits near the entrance to the bazaar? They insisted I take a turn, and the fortune teller said I would travel across a large body of water only to meet my death in water."

"Pleasant thought." Cyrus laughed, as I knew he would. "Do you mean to stand before me and tell me that my cousin, sober, level-headed Cassandra Clark, actually believes someone can foretell the future by swilling down a vile concoction made with dried spiders and snakes' tongues? My girl, you constantly amaze me."

"Of course I don't believe it!" I retorted indignantly. "But, in light of the fact that I never learned to swim, don't you think that prediction is a trifle too close to the bone for comfort? If I were superstitious, which I'm not . . . Anyway, it's enough to make one think twice before embarking on an ocean voyage, don't you think?"

That gave him pause, then he just shrugged and dismissed it with, "It's just coincidence, coz, pure coincidence. Years ago, in my reckless youth, a Chinese fortune teller told me I'd become prime minister, and, as you can see. . . ." He grinned and spread his hands apologetically.

"Believe me, Cyrus, if I really want to go to England, no fortune teller's prophecy is going to stop me."

His blue eyes twinkled mischievously, and he said with great conviction, "Oh, if I know you, you'll go."

"Perhaps," was the only commitment I would make.

But then came the evening I was introduced to Lady Quartermain.

I always think of evenings in Egypt as a reward for having endured the blistering heat of the day, and that night was no exception. It was a beautiful night, clear and serene, with a spray of stars overhead and the moon suspended between two palm trees like a crystal ball held in a gypsy's hands. The cool night air blowing in from the desert picked up delicate scents of mimosa, jasmine, and bougainvillaea from some unseen gardens before gently wafting over the crowded terrace.

Here, wealthy, beautiful women in floating gauzes and silks sat sipping cool drinks and chatting idly with their handsome escorts, enjoying the brief respite from the heat of the day. The air crackled with voices and laughter.

I was moving among them, inquiring about their day, when Cyrus suddenly loomed out of nowhere and whispered, "There is someone you must meet. She knows your mother and the Lesters." Before I could express my surprise, he was steering me around tables, and adding, "I'd pretend I wasn't related, if I were you. The old gossip will tell you more that way."

As we approached a lady and gentleman seated toward the farthest corner of the terrace, Cyrus grinned broadly and became once again the congenial host.

"Good evening, Lord and Lady Quartermain. May I present my cousin, Cassandra Clark?" When the introductions were acknowledged, he continued with, "As I mentioned, Lady Quartermain, Cassandra knew Persia Knighton quite well when she was in England." Cyrus turned to me, his face deadpan. "Did you say she was a friend of your mother's?"

I felt myself blushing, but realized it was too late to withdraw gracefully, thanks to my cousin's glib tongue. The only thing to do was play along with this charade. "No," I said, "I met Persia through a mutual friend."

Lord Quartermain, a lanky man with a pained expression, rose and wished me good evening, then turned to his wife. "If you'll excuse me, I'll leave you two ladies to chat while I smoke my cigar." He obviously knew his wife too well.

"Dear Ferdy," she said with an indulgent shake of her head as she watched him depart. "He knows how much I love to talk, especially when I meet someone who is a friend of a friend. Do sit down, Miss Clark," and she indicated the chair her husband had just vacated.

When I thanked her and took my seat, Cyrus quietly disappeared after Lord Quartermain, leaving me at the mercy of "the old gossip."

I guessed Lady Quartermain to be in her early fifties judging from her thickening figure, graying hair, and jowls so cruelly visible by the light of the lamp. Her dark eyes gleamed expectantly, and I knew at once that she was one of those people who relish gossip the way some relish a good meal.

"What a small world this is," she declared, and the diamonds around her neck sparkled like a collar of stars. "Fancy coming halfway round the world only to meet someone who knows Persia Knighton, of all people." Before I could open my mouth to comment, she went on with, "You know, Miss Clark, at first Ferdy and I weren't going to come to Egypt, but—" And I sat there for ten minutes listening to why the Quartermains had decided to winter in Egypt instead of Italy.

I've seen two types of traveler come through the portals of the Clark's Hotel. The first usually becomes quite giddy with freedom, shuns his fellow travelers, and will often "go native" for the duration of his stay, wearing a red tarboosh and even keeping an Egyptian woman. The other, more typical, is like Lady Quartermain, always seeking out the familiar, gravitating toward his countrymen at the slightest provocation, telling them things he'd never dream of revealing under normal circumstances, and isolating himself from the natives at every opportunity.

"Mr. Clark and I were talking about England," she went on, "and people we both might know, when Persia Knighton's name was mentioned."

On purpose, no doubt, I thought, thinking of Cyrus and his well-developed sense of mischief. "And how is Lady Knighton?" I asked. "It's been years since I've seen her."

Lady Quartermain regarded me with a quizzical expression. "Then you didn't know?"

"Know what?"

"Why, that she's a widow, of course."

"No, I didn't," I lied, trying my best to look shocked. "I've been out of touch with so many people since coming to Cairo. How sad for her."

The older woman gave me a self-satisfied smile. "I can see that I have much to tell you, Miss Clark." And with a creak of whalebone stays she settled her thick figure firmly in the chair as though intending to be there a long, long time. "It was such a pity about the earl," she began, "but he always had a reputation as a hard-riding man, and it didn't come as a surprise to anyone when he broke his neck trying to train a green hunter." The diamonds winked and sparkled as she leaned forward and lowered her voice so the people at the neighboring table couldn't hear. "But I think it was a blessing for poor Persia."

She dangled her bait skillfully, and I jumped at it. "Blessing? Why, I thought they had an ideal marriage."

Lady Quartermain laughed, a loud, braying sound that caused heads to turn. "Oh, their marriage was far from ideal, Miss Clark, let me assure you. Knighton was never an easy man to live with, especially when the best poor Persia could do was present him with a daughter. I have it on good authority that their relationship was never the same after that. First, to be closed out of society, and then to have one's husband turn against one . . ."

I knew I was being manipulated, but I couldn't resist saying, "Closed out of society? But I thought she was a well-known hostess."

Lady Quartermain's smile was just a trifle malicious. "My dear Miss Clark, no one with any social connections whatever would receive a divorced woman in her home. It simply isn't done."

I sat back in my chair, stunned. So, for all those years during which I had pictured my mother as the center of glittering society, in reality, she was never received. Had that been what Geoffrey Lester meant when he said she didn't get everything she'd wanted out of life? But I had no time to dwell on the question, for my indiscreet confidante was speaking again.

She reached out and took hold of my arm as if to keep me from leaving, though, to tell the truth, I'd have been hard-pressed to do so at this point. "Did you know that Knighton always dined with a loaded pistol by his plate, and that if guests asked why, he would reply, 'Why, in case I ever want to shoot my wife, of course!'"

An unwitting gasp of horror and disbelief escaped my lips as Lady Quartermain released me and sat back in satisfaction, now that she had done her worst. "Of course, Knighton knew that if he died without a male heir, his entailed estate would go to a grasping cousin he detested. Perhaps that galling thought was what soured him against his lovely wife, but to die without providing for her or their daughter . . . Why, if that upstart hadn't married poor Leonie, Persia would probably be sewing dresses somewhere right now."

"How very interesting," I declared.

"Oh, a very wealthy upstart," Lady Quartermain admitted with a disdainful sniff, "but an upstart all the same. His name is Geoffrey Lester. His father was a financier of sorts and made his fortune on the stock exchange. An odd fish: He had a penchant for all things Indian and even built himself a house down in Kent the likes of which no one has ever seen in England. Quartermain and I were invited there once. It's a replica of some maharajah's palace, we were told. I found it quite odd." Then my confidante's eyes narrowed as though she were debating whether to reveal something further. Finally, she threw caution to the winds, grasped my arm again, and whispered, "I have it on the best authority that Lester and Persia were once lovers, and the only reason he married the daughter was because the mother wouldn't have him!"

Disgust welled up inside me, even as I marveled at the extent of Lady Quartermain's knowledge, and I just wanted to get away from the malicious old crow. I forced myself to say, "How utterly shocking!" Then I added, "I never had the opportunity to meet the daughter. What is she like?"

Lady Quartermain gave a dismissive shrug. "Oh, she's quite beautiful and cuts a dashing figure in society. Quartermain seemed quite taken with her. It's said that her husband adores her, but she treats him as though he's not fit to kiss her skirt. And she is quick to remind everyone she is *Lady* Leonie Lester, too. I don't think Geoffrey Lester is a happy man, but what can he expect, marrying above his station like that?"

"What indeed?" I murmured, wishing now that I hadn't encouraged her to be so free with her gossip, and grateful to see her husband come sauntering across the terrace toward us. "Well, Celestine," he said, "have you talked enough for one night? If so, we had best be going. We'll have to rise with the rooster if we're to take that boat trip down the Nile tomorrow. It was a pleasure meeting you, Miss Clark." Then he bowed, and I knew I was dismissed.

I rose, thanked Lady Quartermain for her conversation, wished them a good holiday, and went off to my room to mull over what I had just been told.

As I sat there in the darkness, listening to sporadic hoof-beats in the road below, I recalled what Mr. Lester had said about life not being black or white, but many shades of gray. Throughout the years, I had had a notion of my mother, and it was decidedly black. But now, thanks to Lady Quartermain's galloping tongue, the shades of gray were becoming more distinct, taking form and giving that picture a totally different dimension.

Whenever I had thought of my mother, I had pictured her as the beautiful, smiling countess, being presented at Court, attending balls and galas, entertaining guests at her Northumberland estate in the fall, when the London season was over. She was always happy, never sad, and her life was as perfect as my childish imagination could make it. Perhaps I needed to convince myself she was happy because it justified my keeping my distance and not thrusting myself upon her. If I had known before what I now knew, I probably would have gone to her immediately.

Sitting in my chair, watching the palm fronds tremble in the breeze, I felt only deep pity for my mother and the price she had paid for what she did. While I could not quite bring myself to forgive her, I could at least feel sorry for her now.

I rose and looked down at the terrace. It was late, and there were just two people left now, newlyweds named Walters, a young solicitor and his bride. They were so absorbed in each other, they had failed to notice that everyone else had long gone inside. Their hands were touching across the table as they leaned toward each other, their faces glowing in the soft lamplight with shared hopes and dreams.

I had never felt so lonely as I suddenly did watching that couple on the terrace below. All my life, I had never really belonged, never fit in. While Aunt Venetia and Uncle Harry had always treated me like a member of their large, loving family, a little part of me always felt like the child who sits at the top of the stairs watching a party going on below, yearning to join in, yet realizing the adults would not welcome him. Though Cyrus was as close as a brother to me, it still wasn't the same as having a real brother. Or sister.

But now, my mother wanted me to come to London and become a member of her new family. She was reaching out, seeking to make up for the past and forge some bonds again. Perhaps I could finally belong, if I could just bring myself to take the first step.

I knew it was Cyrus even before his shadow filled the doorway and he said, "So, when will you be leaving for England, coz?"

I left the following day.

Cyrus even entrusted his precious hotel to someone else and made the railway journey with me to Alexandria, where I sent a telegram to the address Geoffrey Lester had given me and booked passage on a steamship bound for England. Two elderly sisters, returning to England after having served three quarters of their lives as missionaries in China, agreed to chaperone me, then discreetly withdrew so Cyrus and I could say our goodbyes.

As we embraced and bade each other a tearful farewell, words were unnecessary, for Cyrus and I each knew exactly what the other was thinking and feeling at this moment. But when we finally drew apart, he smiled and said, "You can always come back, you know."

"I know," I replied as my face crumpled and I dissolved into tears.

Then I boarded the ship and stood at the rail, waving to Cyrus. He cupped his hands to his mouth and yelled something up at me that sounded like, "Don't forget to stay away from water."

"I'll try not to fall overboard," I shouted back.

As the ship moved off, drifting farther and farther away, Cyrus grew smaller and smaller, until he was a mere speck on the dock. Then Alexandria, its white buildings golden in the morning light, dipped behind the horizon, and I was on my way.

I finally arrived in London from Southampton on the 20th of May. A cold, steady rain was falling as I left Waterloo Station, and this put a damper on my spirits. All around me, people milled about, clustered in the shelter of doorways, or raced down the pavement in search of an omnibus or hansom cab.

Luckily, a cab stopped for me, and while I sat huddled in a corner, arms crossed for warmth, I cursed myself for forgetting how unpredictable English weather can be and for not having put on the warm, waterproof ulster that was packed away in a case atop the cab. As I stared out my window through a heavy wall of water, my optimism for this venture was quickly disappearing, and I found myself longing for the searing heat of Cairo and the familiarity of Cyrus and his hotel. London was dismal, gritty, and gray. All around me, horses and carriages were jockeying for position. I seemed to spend more time stopped in traffic than moving, and my patience soon became frayed. Although I craned my neck, I couldn't get a good look at the shops we passed, and even the houses seemed cold and aloof, their windows closed and draperies drawn. My despondency deepened.

Finally, my cab stopped. Now that I was here, my heart thudded wildly, and my hands shook at the prospect of what I was about to do.

I must have been sitting there too long, for I heard the cabbie's trapdoor open and his gruff voice say, "This is where you wanted to go, ain't it, miss?"

When I blushed and stammered some excuse, he said, "Well, it's pourin' out and I got more fares to collect, so be off with you."

I could see I wasn't going to get any sympathy from him, so, when he reached his hand down through the opening, I paid him and then struggled with the door myself. When I stepped down onto the curb, where my bags had been unceremoniously thrown from above, I barely had time to shut the door before the cabbie cracked his whip over his horse's head, and the animal started off, leaving me standing there in the pouring rain, with three heavy bags at my feet.

I had been let off before a gray, forbidding house the size of the Grange, only much more elegant, with its graceful arched windows and lacy wrought-iron balconies. A high stone wall running around the property discouraged passersby from peering in, plainly proclaiming to the world that the people who lived here treasured their privacy and no doubt resented intruders such as I.

Did I really belong here, I wondered with some trepidation. Well, I thought, as I felt the cold rain run off the rim of my hat and trickle down my neck, if I stayed out here any longer, I would soon be soaked to the skin, so I had better act. My three bags posed something of a problem, since I could manage only two of them at once. One of them would just have to sit there until someone could come for it, I decided, as I pushed open the iron gate. I grasped a bag in each hand and lugged them down a flagstone path, then up several steps.

No sooner had I lifted the heavy brass knocker and let it fall than the door swung open to reveal a tall, imposing man

I assumed was the butler. He looked down his long, acquiline nose at me as though I were some parlormaid without sense enough to use the servants' entrance. "Yes?" he said, in a tone that would freeze water.

My cheeks burned, but I managed to hold my head up high and say, "Would you please be so good as to tell Mr. Lester that Miss Clark has arrived?"

The butler was obviously not impressed. "Is he expecting you, miss?"

"Yes. He should have received my telegram from Alexandria long ago."

"I wasn't told to expect anyone today, miss."

I scowled at him. "Well, if you would allow me to step in out of the rain, and go tell Mr. Lester that Miss Clark has arrived from Egypt, I'm sure that he'll confirm that I am expected."

Without another word, the butler stepped aside, and I swept into the foyer with as much dignity as I could muster. By his black look, I could see he expected me to pick up my own bags, but I realized if I did that, I would be permitting this man to intimidate me from then on. I smiled and murmured, "Oh, yes. There's a third bag outside," and pretended not to see his look of consternation.

I tried not to gape when I was admitted, for the foyer was a feast for the eye, with an ornate plastered ceiling, papered walls in muted tones, and a parquet floor waxed to a high gloss. A quick glance into an antique mirror hanging to my right confirmed my worst suspicions about my appearance. The sodden rim of my hat drooped, and lank tendrils of wet hair stuck to my face like seaweed. No wonder the butler hadn't wanted to admit me.

"If you'll wait," he said, as he set my bags down and glared at a puddle on the floor, "I'll tell the master you're here and send someone to retrieve your other bag." He proceeded down the hall at a measured pace, designed, I was sure, to prolong my agony.

I didn't have to wait long. As I stood before the mirror, desperately trying to stick limp, sodden strands of hair back into their pins, I heard footsteps coming down the hall.

"Why, Miss Clark . . ." Geoffrey Lester said in a cold, daunting voice that held surprise, but no hint of welcome. I stared at him. There was a line of displeasure between his scowling brows, and he was regarding me with barely concealed annoyance. The thin mouth was set in an uncompromising line, and I was beginning to wonder if I had imagined the warm, solicitous man in Cairo and his invitation to come to London.

I may have looked like a half-drowned kitten, with my dress soaked and clinging to me, but I was not going to be made to feel like some gauche, unwanted guest. As I shivered from the cold, my cheeks were warm with anger, and I raised my head proudly to say, "As I recall, you told me in Cairo several months ago that my mother wished me to come to England. As you can see, I've decided to accept your invitation. I'm assuming you received the telegram I sent from Alexandria before leaving?"

"We never received such a telegram," he said, still unsmiling, without making a move to see to my comfort.

I was so cold, my teeth began chattering quite audibly, and suddenly Geoffrey Lester snapped to attention as though he had awakened from a dream, and managed to look mortified. "Do forgive me for my atrocious lapse of manners, Miss Clark," he said, smiling broadly now. "You must be exhausted after your journey. Heffer," he said, addressing the haughty butler, "will you have someone take Miss Clark's bags up to the Green Glass Room and make sure one of the maids attends her?" After Heffer mumbled something and ambled off, Geoffrey Lester smiled at me again. "I'm pleased you decided to come after all, and I know your mother will be so pleased as well."

I looked around nervously, as if she would suddenly walk out of the doorway and confront me. "Where is she?"

"I regret to say that both she and your sister are out at the moment, but I expect them shortly. I'll have some luncheon sent up to you right away, and you can change into some dry clothes. Then, whenever you are ready, I'll be waiting in the study."

"That sounds splendid," I said, between chattering teeth, for the cold and nervousness had both finally got the best of me, and I felt as though I'd never be warm again.

Before I knew what was happening, Mr. Lester had taken off his coat and draped it round my shoulders. "That should warm you," he said with his solicitous smile. "I believe it is a typical reaction to feel the cold more acutely when one returns from a hot climate such as Egypt. I know it took me days to get warm when I returned. Now, if you'll follow me . . ."

As we walked through the foyer and up a staircase of dark, polished wood, my brother-in-law asked me all about my trip from Alexandria, and we compared voyages. When we reached the top of the stairs, we took a right turn and proceeded down a corridor of closed doors. Finally, we stopped before one of them and he flung it open.

"This is the Green Glass Room," he said. "It will be yours for as long as you decide to stay with us. If it is not to your liking—"

"I'm sure it will be fine. Thank you for the use of your coat," I said, taking it off and handing it back to him.

For just a second, those heavily lidded eyes flicked over my form, which I'm sure was outlined perfectly by my wet dress, but before I could even blush, Geoffrey Lester smiled and left me.

The source of the room's name was apparent the moment I entered and saw the pair of magnificent bay windows fitted with cushioned window seats. The topmost panes of each window were squares of green stained glass, and this color was repeated in the wallpaper, though the plush Aubusson carpet was in deep shades of wine.

The Green Glass Room was welcoming and cheerful, reminding me of the bedroom at the Grange I had shared with two of Cyrus's sisters. It was spacious, yet cozy, with a carved mahogany bed large enough for three people, a cavernous armoire, several smaller chests, and a lady's writing desk over against another wall.

I walked in and barely had time to set my sodden hat down before a light knock sounded. It was a young, rosy-cheeked maid followed by a footman with my bags. She smiled at me and said she was here to light a fire and draw a bath for me.

After she helped me out of my wet clothes and wrapped me in a warm throw, she went about her duties and I went to a window seat for a leisurely look at my new surroundings. The heavy, dark rain clouds scudding across the sky fascinated me. Beneath them stretched a vast sea of slick, steeply pitched roofs and a forest of chimneys that extended to the very horizon, and, in the large yard below was a charming walled garden filled with flowers and a tree right in the center, a full, leafy oak tree, not some tall, skinny date palm. It was a homey, welcoming scene, yet I could not banish my uneasiness.

"Your bath is ready, miss," the maid announced, and I went into the little dressing room where a tub of steaming water awaited. I gratefully stepped into it, letting the hot water take the chill from my bones, and when I was through, I dried myself and went back into the bedchamber, where a cosy fire was now burning in the grate and a tray of food had been left on a small table.

After luncheon, as I sat sipping a glass of sherry, I found myself wondering whatever had happened to the telegram I had sent from Alexandria. Then I shrugged aside my misgivings. Perhaps it hadn't been delivered, or was mislaid by that oh-so-efficient butler.

Yet a vague sense of discomfort gripped me. I couldn't explain why, but Geoffrey Lester was not the same man I

had met in Cairo. There was something very different about
him now, a coldness and reserve that had not been there
before. I shivered when I recalled his frosty reception that
plainly told me he hadn't wanted me to come to England
after all.

Well, Cassa, I said to myself as I drained my glass and
rose, you're here now and had better make the best of it.

I went to the armoire and was not surprised to find that my
dresses barely filled half of it. I selected a visiting dress of
pale gold striped silk trimmed demurely at the cuffs with
guipure lace, and I was confident this would serve me well
whatever the occasion. I took it out, put it on, and, after
studying myself in the cheval glass to make sure there wasn't
a hair out of place this time, I went in search of Geoffrey
Lester.

Just as I reached the head of the stairs, he came trotting
up, and stopped when he saw me. I could see him taking in
every detail of my appearance, and felt myself blush in spite
of my best efforts not to. He smiled at me. "That dress is
very becoming, Miss Clark." After I thanked him, he said,
"Your mother has just returned and is most anxious to see
you. Would you care to wait for her in the drawing room?"

My heart seemed to stop, and my throat constricted. The
moment I had been obsessed with for weeks was now at
hand, and I found myself losing my nerve at the last minute.

Geoffrey Lester seemed to sense my rising panic, and
said, "It will be all right, Miss Clark. Don't be frightened of
your mother. She is the gentlest person I know."

I managed a shaky smile in return. "I've never been so
frightened in all my life."

He extended his hand to take my cold, stiff fingers and
led me downstairs to yet another closed door, through which
he ushered me into the drawing room, then left me to con-
template my meeting with my mother.

After the warmth and cheeriness of the Green Glass
Room, I found the drawing room most oppressive and

gloomy, with its heavy, modern furniture and dark damask curtains closing out what little light was available on such a cloudy day. Every table top was cluttered with photographs or expensive bibelots set so closely together, they touched. There were Staffordshire dogs, Parian busts, Dresden shepherds and shepherdesses, and delicate bowls that looked Chinese to me.

I stopped to examine a dainty enameled egg that probably cost enough to feed an Egyptian peasant family for several years, and I found myself wondering for the thousandth time how my mother and I would react to each other after all that had happened, after all the years that had passed.

"Cassandra?"

I froze, unable to turn toward that hesitant voice both unfamiliar and yet somehow familiar. Behind me, I heard doors close softly and muffled footsteps cross the room. Then they stopped several yards away and waited.

Finally, I set the egg down with trembling fingers, turned slowly, as one would in a trance, and came face-to-face with the woman who had abandoned Father and me.

Over the years, she had gradually faded into a shadow figure, an impression light and fleeting that became increasingly harder to visualize. But now, as I faced her, that blurred image suddenly snapped into sharp focus.

My work at the hotel had taught me how to size up people quickly, and now I sought to determine what kind of woman my mother was. She was tall, slender, and striking, with dark gold hair put up in a dignified style, and her skin was as delicate as a white rose petal. The years had barely touched her, leaving only deep lines engraved into the corners of eyes that were as green as my own.

What was I looking for as I studied her with my probing, critical eye? I was seeking someone heartless and calculating, whom I could dislike at once. So, I was taken aback to discover a nervous, expectant woman, with a warm, hesitant smile and a gentle demeanor.

"Mother," I croaked, thrown off balance by a reality so at odds with what my imagination had created over the years.

She kept staring, her eyes roving over me as though she couldn't believe I was here in her drawing room. Finally, she nodded in mute approval and said, "Why, you've grown into such a beauty, Cassandra," then broke into tears.

I know I should have run to her and flung myself into her arms, but the memory of my melancholy father held me back. There was still so much that had to be said before I could bridge the gap of time and hurt that yawned between Mother and me.

She started and seemed poised to take a step toward me, but hesitated at the last moment. With a soft sigh of resignation, she seated herself in one corner of a velvet upholstered divan and motioned for me to join her.

I tucked myself into the other corner, leaving an expanse of sofa as wide as the emotional gulf between us.

"I couldn't believe it when I returned from shopping today and Geoffrey told me you had decided to come after all," she said conversationally, dabbing at her eyes with a handkerchief. Her voice was soft and pleasant, with a musical quality.

"I sent a telegram the day I left Alexandria to warn you I was on my way," I explained, "but Mr. Lester said it was never received. I'm afraid I quite startled him with my unexpected arrival."

My mother looked puzzled for a moment, then just smiled and said, "Yes, he told me. But what matters is that you're here at last. When Geoffrey returned from Egypt, he was not very encouraging and warned me not to be disappointed if you didn't accept his invitation to visit. He told me what a spirited, independent lady you had become, working with your cousin Cyrus in that hotel." She stared out into space for a moment, as though searching her memory for some lost thought. "I remember Cyrus best of all Venetia's children, though he was only ten when I—" She caught herself for a moment, then went on. "I remember him as such a large, fearless boy, enterprising even at such a young age." Mother's face actually glowed as she said, "Why, I remember once he even sold some of his toys to his sisters for a handsome profit. Venetia was furious when she discovered what he had done and made him give the money back."

I had to laugh at that, in spite of myself. "That sounds like Cyrus. We were always very close, and when he invited me to go to Egypt with him and run a hotel, I couldn't refuse. We arrived about a year after General Gordon died at Khartoum, and we've been there for three years now. The hotel is almost as well known as Shepheard's," I added proudly.

"So Geoffrey tells me."

An awkward silence descended, as though we had both run out of mundane things to say, yet couldn't say what really mattered to us. The words, "Why did you abandon Father and me?" formed in my mind, but I just couldn't say them. Not yet.

Then my mother cleared her throat and said, "How was your voyage from Egypt?"

"Very pleasant."

Again, the quiet stretched out and filled the room, as vast and bleak as the Egyptian desert.

Finally, when Mother saw that I wasn't going to make the first move, she took a deep breath and cleared her throat again. "I know I have behaved abominably to you and your father, Cassandra, and I wouldn't blame you if you never found it in your heart to forgive me. I'm not sure I'm worthy of it. But I did have my reasons for what I did, though you may find them difficult to understand."

My mother was so overcome with emotion that, for a moment, her shoulders shook uncontrollably. When she composed herself, she apologized and continued. "You must know that you've always been in my thoughts throughout the years, and a day has never gone by when I didn't think of you."

"Then why didn't you ever try to see me, or even write me a few words?" I demanded sharply. "Why didn't you ever come for me, instead of leaving me with relatives?"

Her mouth twisted into a small, self-deprecating smile. "Despite what you must think of me, Cassandra, I am not an unfeeling woman. I knew when I—when I gave you away— I forfeited all rights to call you my daughter. Yet how could I forget my own child? I did write, as Geoffrey said he told you, but Venetia always returned my unopened letters with a scathing enclosure of her own, reviling me for daring to want to become a part of your life again." My mother's voice became low and regretful. "She had every right to make me feel ashamed of what I had done, and she finally convinced me it would be in your best interests if I never attempted to contact you again. She said you were so happy with your new family that it would be too cruel for you to learn the truth."

I sat there in silence, strangely moved by the ring of sincerity in her voice.

Finally, Mother arched one brow and said, "Well? Aren't you going to tell me what you think of me?" She sat up very straight, as though bracing herself for a barrage of verbal abuse.

I must say I grudgingly respected her just then. She made no excuses for what she had done and didn't deliver any maudlin speeches designed to play on my sympathies or make me feel guilty. She also fully expected to pay by taking any punishment I cared to mete out.

I shook my head. "As I told Mr. Lester in Cairo, I am long past hating you, Mother. At best, I am indifferent."

Now a look of pain twisted her face, and I suspect indifference hurt her more than hatred. When she spoke again, she said, "You are more generous than I deserve." She was silent once more, then closed her eyes, as though preparing herself for some further ordeal. "Geoffrey told you about Leonie."

I nodded. "It was something of a shock to discover I had a half-sister."

"She only learned of your existence a short while ago herself and was furious with me for never having told her about you. I—I hope you'll like each other and be friends."

"I hope so, too, Mother."

"I also hope you won't envy her, Cassandra."

Now I gave my mother a cool, indignant look. "And why should I envy Leonie?"

A faint blush colored her pale cheeks. "She had such a far different life from yours, Cassandra, one with many more advantages."

"I don't envy anyone, Mother," I said firmly. "While the Clarks weren't wealthy in material goods, they had an abundance of warmth and love, which they willingly shared with me. Aunt Venetia was like a mother to me, and Uncle Harry a father." From what I had heard from Lady Quartermain about life in the Knighton household, I needn't have envied Leonie at all, but I didn't say this to my mother.

"I didn't mean to imply that your upbringing was deficient in any way, Cassandra," she said hastily. "I shall always be grateful to Venetia and Harry for all they did for you." Then she began asking me about my life at the Grange, and I sensed in her a desperate hunger to know what she had missed by giving me up. As I started talking about my life with the Clark brood, I watched my mother carefully. My childhood tales of days spent roaming the Cotswold hills caused her face to glow and her eyes to mist, so I made her chuckle with my humorous character sketches of the string of governesses who had tried to tame us, usually failing. Mother was so charming and attentive, I found myself warming to her in spite of my initial reservations.

When I came to the day Cyrus and I arrived in Cairo and stood in the dusty street, looking up at the run-down building that was soon to become our hotel, Mother clasped her hands in pure delight. "So, you just left the staid drawing rooms of England behind you to start a hotel in Egypt, of all places. How you do remind me of your father, with his adventurous spirit!" When she saw my accusatory look, her smile faded. "Ah, your father . . . There is much I have to tell you about him, Cassandra."

I thought of my father, with his melancholy eyes and air of sadness, and felt the old bitterness well up inside of me for the first time in years. It was as though he were here in this room, sitting between us, asking me to choose, and I felt the tenuous bond of closeness to my mother evaporate.

I rose and walked over to one of the floor-length windows that looked out into the downpour. "You do know that he is dead."

"Oh, yes. I read it in the papers. He died in the Zulu War." Then her voice softened. "I am so, so sorry, Cassandra."

"It was the Battle of Isandlwhana, to be precise," I went on, as if I hadn't heard her. "He was one of the first to die. The men who retreated were hunted down, one by one, by the Zulus. At least Father was spared the horror of waiting for death and knowing it was coming."

Suddenly, I didn't want to discuss my father any longer, didn't want to stay to hear what my mother had to say about him. "I've had a rather long journey, and am quite fatigued. If you don't mind, I'd like to go back to my room and take a nap. We'll have plenty of time to discuss Father later."

And I rushed out of the room before Mother could utter a word to stop me.

Chapter Three

When I returned to my room, I flung myself onto a window seat, drew up my knees in a most unladylike fashion, and sat huddled there, my emotions in a turmoil. A mental image of my father haunted me, and it was not a very pretty picture. I saw him dying alone, stretched out flat on his back, a Zulu *assagai* sticking out of his chest, his sightless eyes staring up as if in horror and disbelief, at the hot blue African sky. What had been his last thoughts as the life seeped out of him in a pool of blood? Betrayal by his wife, his commander, his God?

Unable to sit still a moment longer, I jumped up and paced the room, wondering what I was even doing here in this cold, rainy country. I now belonged to the bright, healing heat of Africa, where my father had died, where Cyrus depended on me, where all the heartache Mother had caused could be banished and forgotten.

As I recalled that awkward reunion downstairs, I wondered about those many things she said she had to tell me about my father. Was she going to try to turn me against his memory with lies and try to convince me that she was the wronged party? Well, if that was her plan, she would find me unreceptive and rebellious.

I was just making my fourth turn around the room, wondering what to do next, when a knock sounded at my door. Opening it, I was startled to find, not the maid I expected, but an auburn-haired Amazon wearing a high-waisted dress with a decidedly medieval look to it.

"How do you do?" she greeted me with a warm, friendly smile. "You must be Cassandra. I am Maud, Geoffrey's sister."

"Why, how do you do?" I said, tilting my head back to stare up at her. "Won't you come in?"

She thanked me, and, as she entered the room, I noticed she was slightly stoop-shouldered, as though she had spent years leaning over to hear what others had to say.

As she turned to smile at me again, she said, "Geoff was right. You are a beauty, aren't you? Our Leo won't be pleased with that at all, I guarantee it." Then she walked over to the window seat I had just vacated, and sat down. "I'll just sit here, if you don't mind. I adore window seats. They encourage reflection." Seeing my rather startled and bemused expression, she said, "Oh, don't pay me any mind, Cassa. You don't object to my calling you that, do you? I know I tend to overwhelm people until they know me better."

"Pardon me for asking," I said as I sat down next to her, "but why do you consider yourself overwhelming?"

She laughed, a deep, throaty chuckle that seemed to bubble up from some well deep within her. "Can a woman be nearly six feet tall and not be overwhelming? I'm also painfully honest, and most people take their truth sweetened with a bit of treacle."

Her eyes, heavily lidded like her brother's, were a lively hazel color that twinkled with mirth, and I found myself warming to her immediately. Maud Lester had welcomed me as though she had known me forever, and I appreciated it.

"Geoff has told me all about you," she continued, "and I must confess I'm fascinated by your hotel in Cairo. But more about that later. Right now, I am here to welcome you to Upper Brook Street and to issue a warning."

My good mood evaporated, and I felt myself draw away from this odd young woman who spoke so candidly. "A warning? I'm not sure I understand."

"You will, once you meet your sister. I may as well tell you right now that Leo and I do not get along at all, and make no pretense of being friends. I think she's a vain, grasping, self-centered—well, I'm sure I make myself plain enough. There is a great deal of animosity between us, but I've never been the sort to pretend I like someone when I don't. So hypocritical, don't you agree?"

"Oh, yes," I murmured, still somewhat daunted by Maud Lester.

"Good," she said with an approving nod. "I knew we were alike the moment I set eyes on you." Then she leaned forward, an earnest look on her face. "You must be on your guard, Cassa. Leo must always hold center stage, and she won't relinquish it to anyone. If she perceives you as a threat in any way, she will not make your stay pleasant."

I realized Maud was only trying to give me some helpful advice, but I found myself resenting her unabashed criticism of my sister, even before I had met her. I wanted to form my own impression of Leonie, uncolored by other people's prejudices.

Those sharp hazel eyes saw this at once. "You're put out with me."

"No, I—"

"Don't deny it. You think I'm being unfair to poor Leo and you want to form your own opinion of her." When I blushed, Maud just smiled and said, "You needn't worry about offending me. I'm a tough old horse."

"Well, I do like to make up my own mind about people," I admitted.

Maud chuckled again. She was not conventionally beautiful, for her lips were too thin and her skin liberally dusted with freckles, which she made no attempt to conceal with powder or paint. But her face had a marvelous ingenuousness and mobility that made her appear more attractive.

"Well," she said, "then you'll have to discover for yourself just what kind of person your sister is."

Tiring of discussing Leonie, I asked, "And what do you think of my mother, Maud?"

"I like her," she replied without hesitation. "Granted, what she did to you was odious, but she has always struck me as a kind, gentle person. Whenever we have a problem, she always offers us sage, level-headed advice, and, in many respects, I've come to think of her as my own mother, since mine died when I was just a child. She's certainly never given Geoff or me any cause to distrust her, and with a daughter like Leo . . ." Maud just shrugged.

So, both the Lesters liked my mother, but I had my own reasons for reserving judgment.

Instead of pressing me, Maud said, "Do you have any questions about my family?"

I couldn't tell Maud I already knew a great deal about her family, thanks to Lady Quartermain, so I said, "I'm afraid all I know is that your brother is married to my sister."

"Then I shall enlighten you," she said, propping one elbow against the windowsill and cradling her chin in her hand. While I listened, she corroborated nearly everything Lady Quartermain had told me.

When she finished, Maud added, "You're probably thinking we Lesters are a spoiled and pampered lot, but let me assure you, nothing could be further from the truth. Even though we were well off, Papa never forgot his humble beginnings and insisted that his children learn some skill in case we lost our fortune and had to fend for ourselves. Geoff took a degree in engineering and was sent off to build railroads in the wilds of Canada, 'to make a man of him,' I remember Papa saying. But I didn't escape, either. Papa insisted I attend lectures at Cambridge, though, of course, I couldn't read for a degree."

I was impressed and even a little envious. For most women, myself included, education meant learning how to sew, play the piano, and conduct oneself in polite society. The men were given the meat, and the women had to settle for trifle.

Maud turned her attention to the rain being whipped against the glass, and her voice took on a faraway quality. "I know my father had advanced ideas for our times. When he died five years ago, he didn't leave his fortune to his son, but divided it equally between the two of us."

This surprised me, and I blurted out, "Your brother didn't resent that?"

"I'm sure most men would have, but Geoff isn't most men. He's always been honest and fair." Suddenly, her voice chilled and her face grew set and angry. "Then he married Leo and everything changed."

"How?" I asked, intrigued.

Maud looked at me. "Your sister is the antithesis of the kind of woman that Papa would have wanted for Geoff. She is like the china doll a little girl dresses up and sits in the corner of the nursery, doing nothing except looking beautiful." She appeared wistful as she murmured, "Geoff's wife could do so much . . . so much." Then she shook herself, smiled at me, and said, "But I suppose common sense goes out the window when love is involved. At least, that's what I've heard." She looked at her watch, which hung from her neck on a thin gold chain. "I have a little time before I'm due at my commercial school, so why don't we go downstairs and I'll show you the rest of the mausoleum and introduce you to the servants? You've already met Sally. She is to be your personal maid for as long as you stay."

"I've never had a personal maid before."

"However have you dressed yourself all these years?"

"I've usually managed."

Maud gave me a look of approval. "I'll wager you have."

As we left the room and started back down the corridor toward the stairs, I suspected that Maud had a blind spot when it came to Geoffrey for she seemed eager to defend him, while she was unduly harsh on his wife.

I said, "Did you say you ran a commercial school?"

Maud nodded and her face brightened with enthusiasm. "It's called the Lester Commercial School, named quite modestly after my own family, of course, and I recruit working class girls to study there. We train them to use a typewriting machine, do accounts, that sort of thing, so they can work in offices instead of factories or the streets. Most of them can't afford the tuition, so I finance it for them."

"Why, that's very generous of you."

She shrugged off my praise. "My father taught us we have a responsibility to those less fortunate than ourselves, especially since we've been blessed with so much."

We had come to the head of the stairs, and as we descended to the landing, the sounds of hurrying footsteps and voices floated up from the foyer below. Maud put out her hand and motioned for me to be still.

Three footmen with boxes piled to their chins came trooping through the foyer.

As we watched them, Maud whispered to me, "I see our dear Leo has been buying out Bond Street again. At the rate she's going, Geoff will be bankrupt before he realizes what has happened."

My eyes followed the packages borne by the footmen, and I counted at least seven large dress boxes and numerous small ones that must have contained hats, shawls, gloves, slippers, and other accoutrements of an elegant lady of fashion.

Then two figures strolled into view, the harassed one obviously a maid, and the other my sister Leonie, nonchalantly sifting through some calling cards while the maid bustled about her. As the maid assisted her with her ulster, it was as though she were unwrapping a parcel that promised some exquisite delight inside. Off came the wet garment to reveal a confection in elegant pink.

I took an eager step forward to go down to greet her, when Maud's hand restrained me once again. In a moment, I saw why, for her brother had suddenly emerged from the drawing room and approached his wife.

I expected him to smile in greeting and perhaps kiss her

cheek, so I was surprised when he merely bowed stiffly and said, "Madam, I would like a word with you in the drawing room, if you can possibly spare me just a moment in your hectic schedule." Leonie hesitated, and, for a moment, I thought she was going to refuse. Then she merely shrugged those slender shoulders and murmured something I could not hear. Geoffrey stood aside, she swept past him into the drawing room, and the doors closed behind them.

"Hmmm," Maud mused, her face alight with curiosity. "I wonder what that was all about? I suppose I shall find out eventually. But come. I promised to show you the rest of the house."

We went down to the cavernous, immaculate kitchen, where I was introduced to an army of faceless servants, and just as we came back upstairs, the drawing room doors flew open and Geoffrey came storming out, his handsome face twisted into a livid mask. As he glanced up and saw us standing there, watching him, his expression softened somewhat, but his eyes remained as black as the scudding clouds outside.

"Miss Clark," he said, unsmiling, "I see you've met Maud."

"Yes," I replied. "She very kindly volunteered to show me the house."

"Perhaps now would be the perfect time to introduce Cassa to Leo," Maud suggested. Her words must have displeased her brother, for he gave her a quick, sharp look. "Would you like to do the honors, brother, or shall I?"

"I wouldn't advise interrupting Leonie just yet," he said, "but do whatever you wish, Maud. You know you always do." Then he bowed and left us.

"He's right, you know," she murmured without a trace of guilt as we approached those closed doors. "I _do_ usually do as I please, so I suppose I'm no better than Leo, in my fashion."

Maud flung open the doors without even knocking, to reveal my sister standing in the middle of the room, the very air around her still crackling and vibrating with rage. Framed photographs were strewn about the carpet, the glass shattered.

Leonie Lester was so breathtaking, I couldn't tear my eyes away, though I knew I was gaping like some country bumpkin seeing the squire's wife for the first time. No photograph could do justice to her magnificent violet eyes and the lush, softly curved figure with its tiny waist and generous hips. Even her hair was distinctive, parted in the middle, brought down over her ears, and caught up in a small knot at the back of her head.

"Oh, Leo," Maud murmured, feigning surprise at finding the room occupied. "I didn't realize someone was in here. I was just showing your sister, Cassandra, the house, but since you are here, I shall introduce you." She stepped back away from me so that Leonie and I were face to face.

I had lost count of the times I had dreamed of this meeting between myself and the sister I had never known. In those dreams, we both usually gave a cry of pleasure and surprise, then ran into each other's arms, tears streaming down our faces, caught up in the emotion of the moment. The reality was nothing like that.

My long-lost sister just stared at me out of those violet eyes that raked me over mercilessly from the top of my head to the hem of my gown, and then a little self-satisfied smile touched her mouth, as though she was pleased with what she saw. This scrutiny took only seconds, but it made me wither inside, my self-confidence gone.

Rather than turn and flee, my first inclination, I pretended I was greeting one of Cyrus's formidable *grande dames*, smiled warmly, and stepped forward. "How do you do, Leonie? I've been so looking forward to meeting you."

She returned my smile, but the warmth never reached her eyes, as she fastidiously stepped around the pictures and came toward me with both hands extended. "Cassandra, how delightful to meet you at long last." Her hands were cold, but her cheek warm and silky as she touched it briefly to my own, and the faint, spicy aroma of geraniums enveloped me. Then she held me at arm's length. "You don't look anything like Mama or me. Well, perhaps you have more of your father in you, but that can't be helped, I suppose."

I blushed, stung by her cruel, careless words, for she was acting more the lady of the manor hiring a new parlormaid than the affectionate sister greeting a long-lost sibling.

Before I could regain my composure, Leonie continued with, "Well, you must excuse me, ladies. I've had the most fatiguing morning, and do want to rest a bit before tea. I'm sure you understand, Cassandra."

"Of course."

"We'll have plenty of time to get acquainted later, when I've rested. I'm sure we have so much to talk about." Then she went gliding off in a cloud of geranium scent, but when she reached the door, she turned to Maud and said, "Will you be a dear and have one of the maids clean up that accident?" And before Maud had the chance to refuse, she was gone.

When the doors were closed and we were alone, I fully expected the outspoken Maud to tell me exactly what she thought of my sister, but all she said was, "That's Leo. Now, shall we continue our tour?"

I nodded numbly and followed her, trying to conceal my bitter disappointment and keep treacherous tears from falling.

I'm afraid I couldn't give my undivided attention to Maud as she took me through one opulent, overstuffed room after another, for my thoughts were on my short first meeting with my sister, a meeting that had left me disappointed and confused.

Leonie had treated me as though I were some momentary interruption in her hectic, well-ordered life, and without a word, she had told me that having a sister meant absolutely nothing to her at all.

"Now we have the library," Maud was saying as we entered a large, quiet room redolent with the smells of beeswax, paper, and old leather bindings. Then she glanced at me. "Are you really feeling up to this? I know you've been trying to be attentive, but I can read your face like one of these books, and I can see that you're disappointed by your meeting with Leo."

"She wasn't exactly overjoyed to see me, was she?" I muttered ruefully.

"What did you expect?" Maud demanded, leading me over to a chintz-covered chair and indicating that I should sit down. "Don't answer that. I can see by the look on your face that you thought your reunion would have all the emotional impact of Stanley's finding Dr. Livingston in Africa."

I burst out laughing and nodded my assent.

Maud settled her flowing skirts about her and flopped down beside me, regarding me with a quizzical expression. "Well, I've told you once what I think of your sister, and I'm not going to waste my breath repeating myself. You've seen for yourself the truth of my words."

Vain, grasping, self-centered . . .

"But, to be fair, perhaps my sister-in-law was still smarting from another set-to with Geoff; that may have been why she was so brusque with you."

I raised my brows in surprise. "They had a row?"

"Didn't you notice the photographs at Leonie's feet? They must have had quite a battle, and she must have started throwing things. Our Leo always throws things for effect, but she is very careful not to break something really valuable." Maud opened her mouth as if to elaborate on Leonie's relationship with her husband, then looked suddenly reticent, as though she had thought better of it. She glanced at a clock on the table, rose rather abruptly, and said, "Well, I must be off; I'm due at the school. Would you care to come with me?"

"I've only just arrived, and it has been rather an eventful day for me. I'm exhausted. I think I'll take a nap before tea, if you don't mind."

"It was thoughtless of me even to suggest it. Well, perhaps some other time."

We left the library and parted company.

As soon as I had entered my room and curled up on one of the window seats, I noticed that the storm clouds, which earlier seemed low enough to scrape chimneys, had now thinned out, and the sun was fighting for supremacy over the sky.

I wished I could banish my sense of foreboding just as easily, but I couldn't. The memory of Leonie and her brusque dismissal of me still smarted.

But something else puzzled me even more. I recalled Geoffrey's meeting with his wife in the foyer, the peremptory, cold manner in which he had requested she join him, and I felt confused. What had happened to the warm, loving husband who had showed me his wife's photograph with such pride and deep affection? Maud confessed that her brother and his beautiful wife often argued, and, again, I couldn't reconcile the Geoffrey Lester I had met in Cairo with the man who had greeted me so coldly today.

What had caused him to change since he had returned to London?

With a sigh, I went to the desk and rummaged for paper and a pen, for I wanted to write to Cyrus to let him know I had arrived safely. By the time I was finished, I had filled both sides of two sheets with details of my journey and included brief sketches of Maud and Mother. When I came to Leonie, I hesitated and finally decided not to worry Cyrus by telling him the truth. I wrote about my sister in glowing terms.

Then, since prevarication exhausts me, I lay down and slept until a knock on the door awoke me. It was Sally with a tea tray, explaining that since everyone else had gone out, she thought I would like tea in my room. After devouring the cucumber sandwiches, I went downstairs to the library, selected a book, and read until it was time to dress for dinner.

Later, after Sally helped me dress in one of my better gowns, I went downstairs to the drawing room, where, I was told, everyone congregated before dinner.

I hesitated before those closed doors, assailed by a sudden attack of nervousness that put a fluttery feeling in my stomach and dried out my mouth.

Just pretend you're back in Cairo, I told myself, getting ready to address a group of guests about today's itinerary. Immediately, the flutterings stopped, and I felt calm and poised once again.

The footman opened the doors for me, and I swept inside, my head held high. "Good evening, everyone," I said with my brightest smile.

I barely had had time to scan the room when Leonie, looking like a cool raspberry ice, rose from the chaise longue and glided toward me.

"Cassandra, you look charming, simply charming," she said, her tone so friendly that I wondered if I had imagined the petulant young woman I met earlier. She took my arm and drew me over to where a woman and a man were seated together on the divan. "There are some people I'd like you to meet. Edith and Edgar Wickes, may I present my sister, Cassandra Clark? Cassandra, this is Edith, who used to be an instructor at the French school I attended, and her brother, Edgar. They are dear, dear family friends."

There was no mistaking the Wickeses for anything but brother and sister, for they both shared the same light brown hair, dark brown eyes, and high forehead. But there any resemblance ended. Edgar was slight of build, very handsome, with a shy smile and "little boy lost" air about him guaranteed to bring out maternal feelings in any woman. Edith, on the other hand, was not as well favored. She was more hand-some than pretty, with decidedly masculine hands that were large and bony, with short, blunt fingers. She sat up very straight, never letting her back touch the back of her chair, and her manner was more direct than her brother's. I found myself thinking that nature should have given Edith more of her brother's looks and him more of her forthrightness.

Edgar rose to his feet at once and seemed just about to speak, when his sister suddenly thrust her hand out and took mine in her forceful grip. "We've heard so much about you, Miss Clark," she said. "It's a pleasure to meet you at long last."

Edith's hand may have been bony and cold, but her smile was warm and her voice strangely hypnotic. She had a certain presence that drew one to her at once, and I found myself warming toward her.

Edgar seemed to fade away under the force of his sister's personality. All he said was, "Yes, Miss Clark, it is a pleasure to meet you"; his handshake was limp and lifeless.

After I had murmured something appropriate, Leonie turned me around to face the others, and said, "You know everyone else here, of course."

The rest of the family was scattered around the room. No one was smiling. Tension filled the air again, and I had the uncomfortable feeling I had just interrupted an argument of some kind.

"Why don't you come sit next to me, Cassandra?" my mother said, breaking the tension.

She was seated on the other divan, embroidering a green velvet garment that covered her lap, and when I sat down and asked her what she was embroidering, she replied, "It's a coat for Maud."

Suddenly, Edith said to Maud, "Do you think any teaching positions will be available at the school soon?"

Maud, who looked like a wild woman with her auburn

mane worn loose and free, shook her head. "Not yet, I'm afraid."

"I've been looking for a teaching position ever since leaving Paris six months ago," Edith explained to me, "but so far, I haven't had any luck."

I said something conciliatory, aware that Leonie was flicking her critical gaze over me from the chaise longue.

"I can't understand it, Cassandra," she said.

"Understand what?" I said, turning toward her.

"How a pretty woman such as yourself is not married."

I felt myself turn red, and Maud glared at Leonie, but it was the voluble Edith who put Leonie in her place. "Perhaps some of us haven't met the right man, Leonie. We can't all be fortunate enough to find a man like Geoffrey."

"I couldn't have said it better myself, Edith," Maud said, with a satisfied smile.

Leonie just made a face, but said nothing.

Then Geoffrey, who had been leaning against the mantel, staring into the cold fireplace, broke the tension by asking me if I wanted something to drink before dinner.

"Some sherry, please," I replied. While he went to the sideboard to pour, I said to the quiet Edgar, "Are you engaged in finance like Geoffrey, Mr. Wickes?"

Before he could speak for himself, his sister guffawed. "Edgar, a financier like Geoffrey? Heavens, no, Miss Clark! Tell her what you do, Edgar."

He blushed and said, "I'm merely a clerk, Miss Clark, at the Westminster Bank in Victoria's Gate."

I have a soft spot for the downtrodden and oppressed, and now I felt anger toward Edith Wickes. "That's nothing to be ashamed of," I said with a smile I hoped was reassuring. "Everyone has to start somewhere."

Edith quickly sprang to her own defense. "Oh, I'm not disparaging my brother, Miss Clark. He's an excellent clerk, but he's not sufficiently challenged at Westminster. In fact, all he needs to do is to prove himself, and I'm sure he'd be a bank president in no time."

Edgar looked as though he wanted to fall through a crack in the floor. "Edith, please . . ."

Just as Geoffrey handed me my glass of sherry, he said, "Did you know that Cassandra just today came from Egypt?"

Edgar, grateful for the diversion, said, "Leonie did say something about your having lived in Egypt awhile, Miss Clark."

Before I could open my mouth, Leonie cut in with, "Why, can't you tell? Cassandra's so brown and healthy looking, not pale as a ghost like the rest of us."

Why did I have the uneasy feeling that Leonie's compliments were not really compliments at all? I just ignored her and said to Edgar, "Yes, Mr. Wickes, for the past three years, I've been helping my cousin Cyrus to run a hotel there."

While they all listened attentively, I told them the story of how Cyrus came to own his own hotel.

"But whatever did you _do_ there, Cassandra?" Leonie inquired. "Beguile some pasha into adding you to his harem?"

Edith's voice was stern and reproachful. "Leonie . . ."

To my astonishment, Leonie once again deferred to her and murmured, "Forgive me, sister dear. I do apologize."

From over by the fireplace, Geoffrey said, "Cassandra saw to it that their guests lacked for nothing and were pleased with their holiday in Egypt." By the time he finished reciting a list of my accomplishments, I sounded as though I had run the hotel single-handedly.

Everyone bombarded me with questions about my life in Cairo, and gradually, the focus shifted away from Leonie to me. I could see her violet eyes harden in pique, so I was not surprised when she announced it was time for us to go into dinner.

Much later, after the sumptuous meal was over, Edith suggested a game of charades, but Edgar begged Leonie to play the piano, and she agreed at once. So, while everyone drifted into the music room, I slipped out into the garden unnoticed.

The flowers were closed tightly for the night, but their rich, intoxicating perfume lingered, as did a trace of twilight in the sky. When I reached the center of the yard, I stopped and turned.

In the brightly lit music room, I could see Leonie was the center of attention at the piano, with Edgar diligently turning the pages of her music. My sister played expertly, and the sweet strains of some popular tune reached me with the sound of their voices harmonizing. Mother sat on the sofa doing her embroidery, with Edith next to her, but neither Maud nor Geoffrey was to be seen.

Suddenly, Maud appeared in the doorway and came walking outside toward me.

"Geoffrey asked me to bring you this," she said when she reached me, draping a cashmere shawl over my shoulders. "He said you were probably still feeling the cold."

I shivered suddenly, grateful for the shawl's warmth against the night's chill. "Thank you. That was very considerate of him."

"He usually is," Maud replied. Then she said, "So, what do you think of our Leo now?"

I wanted to say something polite and noncommittal about my sister, but I knew Maud prized honesty, so I said, "She's everything you said she was."

She nodded in mute agreement. "Those thinly veiled insults are your sister's specialty. On the surface, they seem like compliments, but think about them for a while. . . . It's rather like turning over a beautiful stone and finding a slug underneath."

"Aptly put."

Maud grinned, and her hazel eyes danced. "Papa always said I was gifted with a fine turn of phrase." Then she became solemn once more. "What do you think of the Wickeses?"

"Edith is so . . . so magnetic. She seems to draw you to her as soon as you enter a room. But Edgar . . ." I shrugged. "It seems so unfair that such a personable young man has to tolerate his sister's bullying."

"Edith does tend to trample him," Maud agreed, "but then, he does allow her to get away with it. No backbone, that one. He could take a few lessons from Geoffrey."

Inside the house, Geoffrey himself sauntered into view, but he still stood well apart from the others and seemed to be staring out into space.

I decided a direct attack was best if I were ever to get the answers that would ease my sense of foreboding. So I took a deep breath and said, "Maud, is something wrong here?"

I sensed her grow tense, and in the dim light, I could still discern the wary expression on her face as she hurriedly said, "What do you mean?"

"I've sensed a certain tension in this house ever since I arrived, and it was especially apparent at dinner tonight. Your brother was quiet and withdrawn, and Mother looked distressed about something. Even you seemed on edge. The only people who appeared unaffected by it all were Leonie and the Wickeses. Is my presence here in some way responsible?"

Maud was quiet for a moment, and I wondered if she were debating whether to tell me the truth. "Geoffrey and Leonie have been having some . . . difficulties lately, that's all. Most married people have them now and then, as I understand. I'm sure things will be back to normal shortly."

But somehow there was a hollow ring to her words that made me uneasy, and I had a feeling there was much more that Maud wasn't telling me.

Through the glass doors, which were open just a crack, the piano music crescendoed, and Edgar's deep voice filled the night.

"Leonie plays well," I said, "and Mr. Wickes has a beautiful voice."

Maud seemed relieved that I had dropped my questions. "Yes, they make a handsome couple, don't they?"

"But isn't it rather strange that my sister socializes with a former instructor? Although I've only known her for a day, I would say Leonie isn't the sort to entertain people she sees as her social inferiors."

"How perceptive of you," Maud said. "Leo and Edith first met four or five years ago at the Ecôle Lafarge in Paris. From what Persia has told me, it was a particularly difficult period in Leo's life—something to do with her father—and Edith became a sort of second mother to her, as well as her teacher. They are very close. Perhaps that is why Leo feels responsible for her. Ever since Edith arrived here, your sister insists she and Edgar dine with us every evening. I know the Wickeses are not well off, and I suppose it's one meal they don't have to buy. They live in a dingy terraced house in Kensington, and, between Edgar's meager salary and Edith's savings, I suppose they just scrape by."

I couldn't help but notice that the cuffs of Edgar's dark suit were frayed and had been darned repeatedly, and that Edith had worn a plain black skirt and white blouse instead of a dinner gown.

"Leo constantly badgers me to find a position for Edith at my school, but we are completely staffed at the moment. When she's not asking for herself, Edith constantly promotes her brother. She makes rather broad hints that she thinks Geoff should use his influence to get Edgar a better position."

So that was why Edith had given Geoffrey such a pointed look in the drawing room.

"I think Leo feels sorry for them," Maud said. Then she gave a little snort. "Now, that seems rather out of character for our Leo, doesn't it?"

Before I could reply, Mother appeared at the door and summoned us back inside. Soon, the guests departed, and I went upstairs to bed.

*   *   *

Later, I was sitting at the dressing table and brushing my hair for the night, when a soft knock sounded at my door. I was a little taken aback to see it was Leonie herself. In a voluminous white lawn night shift, with her pale straight hair flowing down her back, all she lacked was a halo to resemble the perfect angel. But when she came to stand before me, her arms crossed and violet eyes flashing, that illusion was immediately destroyed, for there was nothing holy about her anger.

Before I had a chance to greet her, she said, "I want to know why you came here, Cassandra."

As I brushed my hair over one shoulder and secured it with a ribbon, I replied, "I am here because Mother wants me."

"And is that your only reason?"

"No, it is not. I came to London because I was curious about the sister I never knew I had. I was hoping we could get to know each other and perhaps even become friends."

"Oh, I see," she said, nodding her head vigorously as though the truth had dawned upon her. "You expected me to welcome you into this family and share my life with you just because we are related by blood."

"The thought had crossed my mind that perhaps you were as curious about me as I was about you."

She dropped her arms rigidly to her sides. "Well, I'm sorry to destroy your illusions, sister dear, but I am not the least bit interested in you. As far as I'm concerned, you can just go back to your little hotel in Egypt and leave us to our lives."

My heart was pounding wildly, but I imagined myself being scolded by an irate traveler for coming to the defense of a donkey boy suspected of stealing, and my self-control returned.

"Why am I such a threat to you?" I demanded.

My sister threw back her head and laughed, a harsh, brittle sound. "You? A common soldier's daughter, who works in a *hotel* like one of those poor wretches Maud is always trying to save? My dear, dear Cassandra, you flatter yourself. I am a nobleman's daughter," she stated haughtily, "and I'm afraid you'll never fit into my world, no matter how hard you try."

I clutched my hair brush on my lap with both hands so she wouldn't see them trembling. "You may not want me here, but Mother does, and I'm staying, Leonie."

She waved her hand in a dismissive gesture. "Oh, Mother . . . She's just feeling remorseful for having abandoned you, and now she's trying to assuage her guilt. But she'll soon tire of you. I think it's rather cruel of her, actually, to show you a life you can never have and then send you back to your little hotel."

I could sense she was just trying to undermine my confidence again. I forced myself to remain calm and ignore her spiteful words. "What have I done to deserve your animosity, Leonie? I would really like to know, so I could change myself, and we can be friends."

"We can never be friends," she said.

"But why? We've only just met today. You don't even know me."

She shrugged and like a petulant child said, "I don't wish to know you, that's all," as if that were reason enough.

Then she whirled on her heel and padded off toward the door. When she reached it, she stopped, looked back at me, and said, "There's nothing for you here, Cassandra. I can be a formidable enemy, so I would suggest you take my advice and leave for Egypt as soon as possible."

And she left me alone, wondering what I had done to cause her to dislike me so.

Chapter Four

The next morning, I awoke to a cacophony of bird-song rather than the muezzin's wail, and wondered in confusion where I was. But, as I washed and dressed for breakfast, I felt as though I hadn't slept at all. Leonie's blatant hostility and words of warning had preyed on my mind all night, like scavenger jackals, and whenever I was on the verge of drifting off, they would attack and awake me anew.

When I looked at the clock on the mantel and saw in dismay it was already ten o'clock, I panicked, for I did not want the Lester family to think I was a sluggard who made a habit of sleeping until noon. I breathed a sigh of relief when Sally appeared, chided me gently for not having rung for her assistance with my morning toilette, and told me that breakfast was always an informal buffet served until eleven o'clock.

After dressing, I followed the tantalizing aromas of coffee and bacon to the dining room, deserted now except for Mother, seated at the end of the long mahogany table and sipping her lemon-grass tisane. When she saw me, she smiled and said, "Good morning, Cassandra. Did you sleep well?"

"Yes," I murmured, trying to stifle a yawn as I went to the sideboard for a plate, "I slept very well, thank you."

After peeking under a bewildering array of covered dishes set out on the sideboard, I decided on a sugared rusk. Then I sat down next to Mother, but said nothing, waiting for her to make the first move.

"I must apologize for Leonie," she began, her eyes troubled. "She was most rude to you last night."

"I know it must be difficult for her to welcome an intruder into her home."

"You are not an intruder. You are also my daughter, and her sister. I am at fault for not telling her about you years ago, but that is still no excuse for her behavior. I know you were expecting quite a different reception from her, but I beg you to give her a little more time to adjust. I'm sure she'll come to like you eventually."

My mother's expression was so hopeful, I could not bring myself to tell her of the sharp words my sister and I had exchanged last night in my room. "I'm sure she will."

Her brow clouded over and she stared out into space. "I'm going to tell you something about your sister that few people know, and I wish you'd keep it in strictest confidence."

"Why, of course."

She sipped the tisane, and her voice became soft and sad. "It was the year Leonie was eighteen, her first season. Although I couldn't present her to the Queen myself because I was a divorced woman, one of Knighton's sisters sponsored her. Leonie was such a success at the presentation. After her first ball, many handsome young men, Guardsmen and wealthy noblemen, vied for her hand. It looked for a while that she could take her pick and make a brilliant marriage.

"But, then her father died, and her world collapsed. When word spread that Lady Leonie Butler was no longer an heiress, her suitors vanished. In the meantime, she had fallen in love with the most ardent one, a handsome viscount. When his engagement to a plain, but wealthy, daughter of some baronet was announced, Leonie was devastated. She cried for weeks, and I despaired for her sanity."

This, to me, did not seem such a catastrophe. "But surely, if he only wanted to marry her for her wealth, isn't it better she discovered this before the wedding?"

"The aristocracy are a practical lot," Mother said gently. "Love is often the last consideration in a marriage."

I wondered if she were speaking of herself, as I went back for another rusk. "But Leonie is married to Geoffrey now. I should think she's happy and content."

"I'm sure she is," Mother said hastily, "but there's a part of her that still mourns her first love." She turned in her seat so she could look over at me. "I'm telling you this because I want you to understand your sister and try to be patient with her when she is curt with you. She's always been at the center of things and resents anyone else's trying to usurp her place."

"Mother, I'm not here to take any attention away from Leonie."

"I realize that, my dear, but perhaps your sister doesn't."

I returned to the table and sat down. "I shall try my best to be friends with her, but I must honestly say she doesn't make it easy."

"I know. She's always been a bit headstrong." Suddenly, her face brightened. "I just had a thought. Would you like to go shopping today, just the two of us?" Her eyes darted a critical glance at my dress, a serviceable brown serge that even I admitted made me look rather like an impoverished governess. "We could visit my dressmaker, order you some new clothes, and—"

I bristled at any hint of criticism. "My dresses may not be as fashionable as Leonie's, Mother, but they will do for me."

She looked stricken, as though I had just slapped her. "I didn't mean to imply that there's anything wrong with your clothes, Cassandra. I thought the gold striped silk you wore yesterday was most flattering. But I'm not sure you fully understand this family's position in society. Geoffrey and Leonie attend a great many social events—balls, dinners, receptions—and you wouldn't want to discredit Geoffrey, would you?" When I didn't answer, she said softly, "Besides, it would give me a great deal of pleasure to buy you some new clothes."

"I can't be bought, Mother."

"Believe me, Cassandra, that was not my intention!"

I rose hurriedly, torn and indecisive. I realized Mother was just making an attempt to reach out to me, but there was still a part of me that held back. Perhaps I was just a common soldier's daughter who would never find a place among these wealthy, fashionable people, or maybe it was my stubborn loyalty to my father. Maybe I really did fear being seduced by my mother's gifts and congenial manner.

"Perhaps some other time, Mother," I said, and went back upstairs to my own room.

I stayed there for the better part of an hour, curled up on the window seat and watching the gardener below carefully pruning the white roses that climbed in profusion along one wall. I eventually became restless, and, deciding I couldn't spend the entire day shut away in my room, I went downstairs to the library in hopes of finding something to read.

I was delighted to find the room empty, so I went to a shelf and started scanning the many volumes. I was so engrossed in my task that I failed to hear the door open and light footsteps cross the room.

Just as I stood on tiptoe to reach a volume on the top shelf, a deep voice said, "Let me get that for you," and I whirled around to find Geoffrey standing behind me.

I breathed a sigh of relief. "You startled me."

"I'm sorry. I thought you heard me come in."

As he reached up, he was so close I could discern the clean, citrus scent of his shaving cologne and became intensely aware of his masculinity. I stepped back quickly and turned away, lest he see how disconcerted he had made me.

He didn't seem to notice, for he retrieved the book and said, *"King Solomon's Mines* . . . It's set in Africa, so I'm sure you'll enjoy it." He handed me the book and began scanning the shelves himself. "There's something else I think you would enjoy. Ah, here it is." He added a magazine to the book. "It's called *A Study in Scarlet.*"

I thanked him for his recommendations and started to

leave, when he said, "Cassandra, please wait. I'd like to ask a favor of you."

I stopped, my curiosity aroused. "Of course."

"I understand your mother invited you to go shopping with her this afternoon."

My heart sank. "Yes, and I refused."

"Might I ask why?"

I couldn't meet his eyes as I said, "I don't feel quite up to it. Perhaps the fatigue of the voyage hasn't worn off."

"I think there is another reason for your refusal."

Now I did look at him. "Well, there isn't."

His heavy lids drooped, giving him that deceptively sleepy look. "Are you sure you're not trying to punish her?"

I felt my cheeks grow warm, and I knew I was blushing profusely. "I can assure you, Mr. Lester—"

"Geoffrey, please. We can dispense with such formalities. I am, after all, your brother-in-law."

"I can assure you, Geoffrey, that I didn't intend to punish Mother for anything. I merely refused to go shopping with her. My clothes are more than adequate, so why should I go shopping for something new? Besides, I haven't the money for such extravagances."

"But your mother does."

"And that is precisely my point."

He understood at once. "You think she's trying to buy your good graces with gifts, is that it?"

I nodded and stared at the floor.

"I don't think that was her intention at all. I think she wanted to do something for you without asking anything in return." When I made no comment, he continued with, "I passed her in the hall a short while ago and noticed she seemed very upset. Though she didn't want to tell me the reason, I finally pulled it out of her. She thought this shopping excursion would give you some time to be alone together and to get to know each other. What could be the harm?" His eyes narrowed and grew cold. "Or are you afraid you'll fall under her spell like the rest of us?"

I knew he was baiting me again, but his words did make sense. "Are you ordering me to accompany my mother?"

His brows rose, and a mocking smile touched his mouth. "Order? Such a strong term, Cassandra. Let's just say I respect your mother and don't enjoy seeing her upset."

Put in such terms, there was no room for refusal. I was, after all, a guest in this man's house. "All right. I'll go with her."

Geoffrey's dazzling smile transformed his entire face, softening his stern features and making him look more like the man I had met in Egypt.

"Thank you, Cassandra," he said earnestly, and before I knew what he was doing, he quickly took my hand and kissed it. Lips that were so often drawn into a cold, hard line felt surprisingly warm to the touch.

Then he left me.

Tears of gratitude welled up in my mother's eyes when I told her I had changed my mind and would go with her that afternoon. She thanked me with a humility that made me feel guilty for having refused her in the first place.

As I dressed for our excursion, I found myself looking forward to being alone with my mother.

She was waiting for me in the foyer, looking demure and half her age in a day dress of dove gray. And her pleased expression as I descended the stairs made me feel welcome and happy for the first time since arriving. But it was not to last.

"We're going to have a wonderful time," she assured me, squeezing my hand. "First, we'll go to Madame deBrisse's in Regent Street, and—"

"Splendid!" a familiar voice said behind us, and as we turned, Leonie glided down the stairs, tugging on her kid gloves as she walked. "I've got to go to Madame deBrisse's myself for some new yachting clothes."

I hadn't known my mother's invitation included Leonie, and when I glanced at her, I saw Mother was not pleased. She looked chagrined, and the corners of her mouth were turned down in irritation.

"I wasn't aware that I had invited you to come with us, Leonie," Mother said.

"You didn't. But I overheard one of the maids discussing your little outing, and I thought I'd just invite myself along." Leonie looked like a cat that had just devoured a dish of cream right under the cook's nose. "No use in taking two carriages, is there?"

Mother stood her ground. "Weren't you supposed to be at home today, receiving? I noticed the Duchess of Manchester called yesterday and left her card, so she's sure to call again today."

"Everyone knows I am only at home on Thursdays, Mother. The duchess can call then, if she wants to see me so desperately," was my sister's blithe reply.

Mother still didn't move. "I had wanted to spend some time alone with your sister."

Leonie glanced at me as if I were a piece of furniture. "Oh, Mother, you can be alone with Cassandra at any time, and I don't see why you're making such a fuss of this. Do be a dear and come along. I can see Fred is waiting with the brougham." And without another word, she swept toward the door, determined to have her way.

Mother just sighed in defeat, and murmured, "Come along, Cassandra."

As I followed the two women out the door, I found myself wondering why Mother allowed Leonie to order her about as if she were a maid. If one of the Clark girls had tried such tactics with Aunt Venetia, she would have been sent to her room, even though she was married with children of her own. I decided my mother had probably spoiled and indulged Leonie so much when she was growing up that my sister knew she could get her own way no matter how much

Mother protested. So Leonie just did what she pleased because she knew Mother would always capitulate in the end.

Once we three were seated and the carriage moved off, Leonie said, "I need some new gowns, and Cassandra"—she glanced at my dress with blatant distaste—"could certainly do with some stylish clothes. Wherever did you get that dress, my dear? Some little seamstress in Egypt, no doubt, who made a living by copying the clothes of her betters."

That was exactly how I obtained all my clothes, and I blushed in mortification. Mother saw I was embarrassed, and sought to divert Leonie. "I don't see why you need more dresses, Leonie. You just bought a dozen for Ascot Week alone." She shook her head. "Your clothing bills are so outrageous, I'm surprised Geoffrey hasn't cut your allowance by now."

"Oh, Mother, he could afford three times what he gives me. Besides, a man in his position needs a stylish wife who is a credit to him."

"And are you a credit to him?" Mother snapped.

Leonie smiled sweetly. "Why, of course. In every way."

Once again, I sensed those undercurrents that were running last night at dinner, hiding some deep, dark secret just beneath the surface.

Mother said, "Still, I'm going to suggest to Geoffrey that he cut your allowance."

Leonie just laughed, that tinkling sound that could be so charming or so cold. "Are you threatening me again, Mother?"

"Geoffrey adores you. The least you could do is show your appreciation and act like a real wife to him!"

"He may not be as rich as the Rothschilds, but if he adored me, as you claim, he'd take me to Paris in the spring and rent a villa in Biarritz or Cannes for the winter," my sister retorted, her violet eyes flashing.

Mother's face turned bright red, and her lips pursed in anger. "Biarritz! Cannes! So you can flaunt your—"

"Mother!" Leonie snapped. "That will be quite enough. You're embarrassing Cassandra, not to mention me." Then she turned to look at me. "Oh, don't look so uncomfortable, sister dear. Mother and I have had this argument countless times. It's nothing new."

"You don't owe me any explanations," I said.

"Oh, but we do," she countered smoothly. "Since you've charged your way into our cozy family circle and want so desperately to be a part of our family, then you must learn of our family skeletons. But not now, of course. At a more appropriate time." After uttering that tantalizing morsel, Leonie abruptly said, "Tell me, what do you think of Geoffrey?"

She caught me by surprise, and for a moment, I just stared at her blankly. Then I said, "He seems to be a kind, considerate man."

My sister's eyes took on the coquettish gleam so apparent in the photograph Geoffrey had given me in Cairo. "Kind? Considerate? But you make him sound so deadly dull! Don't you find him dashing! Handsome? Romantic? Most women do."

I refused to play her little game. "What is the point of this conversation, Leonie?"

She made a mocking face. "You sound like the typical older sister, so pompous and serious. You and Geoffrey would make a good pair."

Finally, Leonie fell silent, and I leaned forward to look out the window at passing buildings and a muffin man with his pan balanced on his head like an Egyptian woman carrying her water jug up from the river.

"You know," I said to Mother, "until I went to Cairo with Cyrus, I had never set foot outside Gloucester."

"That's obvious," Leonie muttered under her breath.

I ignored her as I would a complaining tourist. "Now I find myself in the unique position of being a traveler dependent on someone else to be *my* guide. Tell me, what would you recommend I see and do while I'm in London?"

"Oh, there's just so much . . ." Mother murmured, appearing to rack her brain. "Coming from Egypt, you'd probably enjoy seeing Cleopatra's Needle, and the Egyptian Hall in Piccadilly. Then there's Madame Tussaud's—"

"But those wax figures are so gruesome!" Leonie exclaimed, wrinkling her upturned nose. "I think Cassandra would much rather go to the Savoy some evening to see *The Yeoman of the Guard*. I've already seen it, but I suppose I could sit through it again."

Soon both Mother and Leonie were so absorbed in choosing the sights for me to see in London that their altercations were soon forgotten and, before we knew it, the driver announced that we were approaching Regent Street.

As I poked my head out the window for my first glimpse of Regent Street, Leonie said, "Of course, Bond Street is eminently more fashionable, but I'm sure the shops here will be adequate for your needs."

"I'm sure they will," I replied, refusing to let her make me feel slighted.

The gently curved thoroughfare was lined with shops, their fronts shaded from the fierce afternoon sun by green awnings. It was also more congested than the Cairo bazaar, and when our carriage stopped and we alighted, I noticed other hansoms and broughams were parked three deep along the street, forcing other traffic to come to a halt or to try to find some way of going around.

"Our carriage seems to be adding to the obstruction of traffic," I said to Leonie, as we wove our way through the crush.

She gave me her best condescending look and replied, "Where else is a lady supposed to park her carriage while she shops, if not in the street? And we certainly can't be expected to go wandering around searching for it later."

I just followed without another word, past loitering footmen and pages waiting patiently for their mistresses, into Madame deBrisse's dress shop.

I felt like royalty the moment we stepped inside. Though it was crowded with other fashionable patrons, all falling silent as we walked in, a haughty shop assistant dressed in severe black bombazine came up to us immediately, greeted Mother and Leonie by name, and ushered us into another room obviously reserved for favored patrons. After we were seated on tiny ivory chairs upholstered in purple velvet, another young woman came in bearing a silver tray laden with tea and cakes, which we refused, and still another presented us with a selection of fashion plates to study while we waited. Leafing through all the colored pictures of such beautiful dresses, I felt my head begin to spin.

At just the right moment, Madame deBrisse herself appeared, a short woman with the top-heavy figure of a pouter pigeon and an obsequious air. She escorted us to a dressing room, where my measurements were taken and discreetly recorded, and then a line of assistants trooped in carrying bolts of the finest silks, taffetas, tartans, and brocades for our selection.

Finally, Mother decided I would order seven day dresses, seven tea gowns, three walking dresses, and one magnificent ball gown. I protested that I couldn't allow her to buy me that many clothes, but she would not listen to me much the same way Leonie hadn't listened to her earlier. I resigned myself to having a new wardrobe.

Leonie watched for a while in thinly disguised amusement, then went off to another dressing room to be fitted for the yachting clothes she professed so desperately to need. I felt more comfortable without her around.

We remained at Madame deBrisse's for several hours, and when we piled back into the carriage, which was among those still parked three deep outside the door, I was looking forward to returning to Upper Brook Street. But I was soon to discover there were many more shops yet to patronize.

Wherever we went, Leonie couldn't resist commenting on everything I selected. If only this hat weren't so large, it would make me look younger. . . . If only this shawl were more subdued, it wouldn't overpower me so. And on, and on, and on.

What was supposed to have been a quiet, pleasurable afternoon for Mother and me turned into an unpleasant, trying time filled with Leonie's dubious compliments. By the time we left the last shop and piled back into the carriage with my boxes, I wished I had never agreed to come along. Mother's face was as gray as her dress, and she sighed often, but Leonie blithely paid her no mind and acted as though nothing were amiss.

When we finally arrived back at the house, I had such a headache and my confidence was in such shreds that I just couldn't face anyone at tea, least of all Geoffrey. When I made my excuses, Mother just smiled apologetically and patted me on the shoulder in mute understanding.

As I sat on my window seat, staring out over the rooftops of Mayfair, I found myself feeling sorry for my mother for the first time, in spite of my best efforts to resist it. I recalled what Lady Quartermain had told me about her, and, thinking about how Mother had been treated by her own daughter today, I felt myself mellowing toward her. Perhaps having a spoiled, disrespectful daughter who did not take your feelings into consideration was payment enough for what she had done to Father and me. I had seen little regard between Leonie and my mother since arriving. They always seemed angry and at odds, like wary pit dogs circling each other. Ironically, my mother seemed more at ease with me, the child she hadn't seen in more than twenty years, than with the daughter she had raised.

A knock at the door interrupted my thoughts, and when I called for the visitor to enter, Maud came marching in, bearing a tray.

"When you didn't come down for tea, I thought you'd be hungry, so I brought you something," she said, setting the tray down and arranging her long limbs on the seat.

"That's very kind of you," I said, pouring myself a cup of tea. "We've been shopping all day, so I haven't even had luncheon. I am famished."

"Feeling a bit fatigued after your afternoon with our Leo?" Maud asked, smoothing the patterned silk of her dress.

I rolled my eyes as I nodded and wolfed down a cucumber sandwich.

"Persia told me all about it. She was very upset that Leo invited herself along and spoiled your afternoon." Maud pulled the pins out of her hair and shook it free. "Leo and Geoff are taking their daily carriage ride through the park now. Leo insists they join the rest of fashionable society as they all parade around like peacocks for one another." There was no mistaking the sarcasm in her voice. "I'm surprised they didn't invite you along. On second thought, I'm not. Leo resents competition."

I swallowed my food, then scoffed at that. "Me? An old spinster, competition for Leonie? Oh, come now, Maud."

Her hazel eyes danced. "I can see compliments make you uncomfortable. But, I wouldn't underestimate myself if I were you. Leo may be a rose, but you're a—an orchid."

I chuckled at that, and kept silent while I ate the rest of the tiny sandwiches. Then I said, "With such an age difference between Leonie and your brother—"

"Twelve years," Maud said. "Geoffrey's thirty-two."

"Then he must have known Leonie as a child."

Maud nodded. "Leonie was only ten years old when he first began visiting them. I remember his coming home from school for the summer and praising Persia as a charming, witty woman. But his only comment about Leo was that she was a winsome child." A dreamy smile touched her mouth. "I think my brother was infatuated with Persia and feeling protective, considering the way old Knighton treated his wife."

I looked down into my teacup and said nothing of Lady Quartermain's insinuations that they had been lovers.

"Geoff visited them whenever he could," Maud went on, "but after he took his degree and left for Canada, that ended that. I understand that during the time he was away, Persia kept up a correspondence of sorts with him. Then Papa died, and Geoff was summoned home. I had just finished my studies at Cambridge and was involved in improving factory conditions, and I recall quite clearly that one of the first things he did upon returning home was to go up to Northumberland and see the Knightons." She shook her head. "And what a surprise he found waiting for him."

"What do you mean?"

"The 'winsome child' to whom he hadn't given a second thought was now a ravishing young woman of eighteen on the verge of her first season. He was smitten hard, but, of course, only a wealthy nobleman would do for our Leo, and she wouldn't give him the time of day. Perhaps it was her revenge for his never having paid any attention to her when she was little. Or some other reason . . . Then her father died, and you know the rest." Maud smiled bitterly. "Suddenly, Geoffrey Lester didn't look like such a poor prospect any longer."

"I can imagine it must have been hard for her," I said.

Maud nodded. "In a way, I can understand why Leo is so spoiled. To have everything one day, and then to lose it all the next . . ." She shrugged.

I said something conciliatory, and the old iconoclastic Maud asserted herself. "Oh, while I understand, I can't really bring myself to feel too sorry for her. Leo should be grateful she has her looks and a husband who dotes on her. I wonder how she would feel if she had to carry baskets of white lead on her head all day, until she died of lead poisoning? Or what if she were forced to sleep in a shelter for destitute women, night after night, in a bed as narrow as a coffin? She should count herself fortunate, but she doesn't. All she can see is what she's lost, not what she's gained."

"I think we're all guilty of that at one time or another."

Maud stared at me until I squirmed. "You are so different. If only Geoff had met you first."

I felt myself coloring, but said briskly, "Oh, Maud, I'm sure Leonie loves your brother."

Her eyes hardened into deep gold. "In her fashion, I suppose. But I suspect she's more in love with Geoff's money than him. How can someone who loves only herself love anyone else?" Then she rose abruptly and announced, "Well, I'm afraid I must leave you now. As president of the London Society for Housing, I have some architects' proposals to read over. Geoff and Leo are going to the Duchess of Manchester's for dinner tonight." Then she wished me good night and left.

Later, I was coming down the stairs just as Leonie and Geoffrey were getting ready to depart for their dinner engagement, and they made such an arresting couple I stopped on the landing just to admire them. Geoffrey was handsome and distinguished in black evening attire, and Leonie more beautiful than ever in a gown of soft rose taffeta, cut low, but decorously. A long strand of pearls graced her slender neck, and a simple fillet of gold was set low on her forehead, just above her brows, making her look like a medieval princess.

As I watched in silence, Geoffrey slipped Leonie's wrap over her shoulders and let his hands linger there in a gentle caress. Leonie gave a brief shrug and stepped away, as though she couldn't bear his touch, and Geoffrey's arms fell to his sides. Then he turned suddenly and caught me watching.

He stared at me and knew that I had witnessed the little scene. Then he turned and left.

Chapter Five

T he next morning, I rose late, ate a bowl of hot por-
ridge alone, then went to the library in search of
another good book. When I entered, only a maid was there,
dusting, but she bobbed a curtsey and left, leaving the quiet
room all to me.

But not for long.

I had spent a good fifteen minutes browsing among the
books on the free-standing oak bookcase that partitioned the
far end of the room, when suddenly, I heard the faint creak
of the library door, followed by the tapping of boots and the
jingling of spurs. Peering between the shelves, over a row of
books, I saw Geoffrey come striding in, dressed for riding
this morning in well-tailored clothes that fit his tall form to
perfection, making him every inch the proud country squire.
Glossy black Wellington boots and tight blue trousers accentuated his long legs and slender hips, and the dark blue riding coat, with an immaculate white stock at his throat, was a
perfect foil for his fair coloring.

Since I was hidden behind the shelves, Geoffrey thought
he was alone. Suddenly, his face contorted in anger, and before I knew what was happening, he strode over to the reading table and smashed his fist down on it with such force that
a vase of roses actually jumped.

"Damn her!" he roared, and I jumped as well.

At any moment, he would turn his head and see me, so I
thought it best to make my presence known before he caught
me watching him as he had last night. Clutching a book for

support, I stepped out from my hiding place, cleared my throat, and said, "Geoffrey, is something wrong?"

He whirled around, his brow still furrowed and his face flushed in rage, but when he saw me, the anger seemed to dissipate even as I approached him.

"Cassandra . . . I thought I was alone." He stared at the floor and rubbed the tip of his riding crop against his boot. "No, nothing is wrong."

I did not press the issue, for he obviously did not wish to discuss what had caused such a violent outburst. "I was just returning *A Study in Scarlet*. It was most engrossing."

"I'm glad you enjoyed it," he said absently.

We grew quiet, and the only sound was of flower petals falling, a surprising noise in the contrasting stillness. Finally, for want of anything better, I said, "I seem to be on my own this morning, so I thought I'd find another book to occupy my time."

He looked toward the tall windows, through which the sun was trying in vain to cast its light into the farthest recesses of the room. "I hope you don't intend to spend all your time reading. It's too beautiful a day to be imprisoned inside." He hesitated. "I have a suggestion. Why don't you come riding with me?"

"Now?"

He nodded. "I go for a morning ride in Hyde Park whenever I can, and would dearly love some company today." He sounded bitter as he said, "Unfortunately, my wife is still sleeping and can't come."

"But—but I don't have anything suitable to wear," I protested. "My riding habit won't be arriving until the beginning of next week."

The gray eyes sparkled. "Oh, I'm sure your mother would be more than willing to lend you one of hers. She may be taller, but you're almost the same size."

Geoffrey seemed so eager for my company, I found myself relenting. Whatever Leonie had done to enrage him so, perhaps I could cool his anger a little. It was the least I could do for his graciously opening his home to me.

"Well," I said, with mock seriousness, "I haven't ridden a horse in some time, but if you can find me a suitable donkey, I shall be happy to ride with you."

That caused Geoffrey to laugh, and the humor that I had once seen in his face returned, however briefly.

"I know just the horse," he said, matching my light-hearted mood, as we walked out of the library together.

That suitable mount turned out to be a dainty white mare named Bittersweet, and she, along with another horse, was waiting in the drive when I emerged from the house.

Except for the fact that the skirt of my borrowed habit trailed on the ground when I walked, my attire seemed made for me. The jacket fit comfortably, without binding, and the tall hat with its spotted veil covering my face made me feel quite fashionable and mysterious.

"I'm afraid it's not the donkey you requested," Geoffrey said, as I patted Bittersweet on her velvety muzzle to get acquainted, "but at least she *is* white like the donkeys of Cairo."

I smiled up at him. "She is just beautiful."

"Well, if you like her so much, she's yours to keep," he said. "Call her my way of thanking you for coming."

"I—I couldn't possibly accept such a gift," I stammered.

"Nonsense. A horse is a necessity in London. Besides," he added gravely, "I will be offended if you don't accept her."

"Geoffrey—"

"Please. I detest arguing."

I saw the prudence of surrendering to this man, who was frowning at me in annoyance. "All right. I'll accept her, but only as a loan. She'll stay when I return to Cairo."

"As you wish," he said brusquely, and I had the feeling not many people dared refuse Geoffrey Lester's gifts. "Come. Let me give you a hand."

As I took the reins and prepared to mount, he grasped my ankle in his strong hands, and I fancied I could feel their warmth through the leather boot, my heart quickening at his touch. In a moment, I was settled in the sidesaddle and watched Geoffrey prepare to mount his horse, a huge, fiery thoroughbred named Westwind.

I held my breath as Geoffrey vaulted into the saddle. The moment the animal felt his master's weight on his back, his ears flattened and he tried to sidestep, but Geoffrey was too experienced a rider to let such a trick unseat him. Using his voice and hands to soothe, he soon calmed the horse, and he moved down the drive, with me in his wake.

As we waited for a barouche to pass before we walked our horses into the street, Geoffrey said, "Is everything to your satisfaction? Your room, your maid . . . ?"

"Oh, yes, and everyone has made me feel so welcome, especially Maud."

Geoffrey smiled. "My sister can be exasperating at times with her obsession for honesty, but she has a heart of gold."

"I know," I replied, smiling at a young street sweeper who doffed his hat to me and winked insolently. "She told me about her commercial school and housing for the poor she's financing."

"Oh, she's done much more than that," he said. "She's worked to reform fallen women, improve working conditions in factories . . . many charitable projects."

"Then I take it you approve?"

"And why wouldn't I approve?" he asked, appearing surprised that I could even ask such a question. Before I had time to make a comment, he went on with, "The only time I did object was several years ago, the Queen's Jubilee Year, to be exact, when she joined a group protesting the banning of public meetings in Trafalgar Square. The overzealous police called in the Guards, and in the ensuing confrontation, Maud was one of those barely escaping with their lives."

I shuddered. "I don't think I would have the courage to do that."

"Well, I finally persuaded her to channel her considerable energies into a less hazardous cause, but my sister is such a firebrand, at first she refused. Finally, she agreed, and now the school and her housing project don't leave her time for such dangerous activities." He smiled as he shook his head. "Dear Maud . . . one couldn't have a more decent sister, or friend."

"She's never married?"

"Regrettably, no. She says she hasn't the time, but I rather suspect it's because she hasn't yet met a man whose zeal for causes matches her own. Maud has very exacting standards for friends." Then he asked me how Bittersweet rode.

"Oh, like a dream," I replied, ecstatic. "Her gait is so smooth, I barely move." I don't know what came over me, but suddenly, I found myself saying, "I've never had a horse of my own before. Uncle Harry could only afford mounts for the boys, and we girls had to beg rides from them whenever we could."

"In spite of that, you ride very well."

"One learns quickly on the donkeys of Cairo," was my reply, and Geoffrey smiled again.

We rode in companionable silence until we reached the end of Upper Brook Street, then turned into a street Geoffrey called Park Lane, which was lined with grand houses, freshly painted, with colorful window boxes beneath the windows on the ground floor. He pointed out that we were actually just across from the park itself, and I turned in the saddle to look at the green expanse of parkland.

Finally, we reached Hyde Park corner, and, as we rode beneath the arched entrance, the expectant Westwind began prancing, for he knew where he was and was eager to run.

"Would you like to put Bittersweet through her paces?" Geoffrey asked, keeping his horse on a tight rein.

I nodded, touched my heel to the mare's side, and we started off together at a sedate trot.

As we moved down Rotten Row, I noticed that there were

mostly gentlemen out this morning, probably because their ladies followed Leonie's example of not rising before noon. The women that were here were all dressed in gaudy habits of red, purple, or green and were mounted on magnificent, spirited horses, with hides so glossy they could almost reflect the sun. These women seemed intent on attracting attention to themselves, for I noticed one or two approach a gentleman riding alone, smile, and boldly engage him in conversation. They were most persistent, for if one gentleman shook his head and rode away, they rode on to the next, and the next. I didn't need anyone to tell me what kind of women these were.

Then Geoffrey began cantering his mettlesome stallion, so I had to concentrate on keeping up. I did notice, however, that everyone seemed to know Geoffrey, for men were constantly saluting him, and he nodded in return.

Finally out of breath, I called to Geoffrey, "You go on ahead. I must stop and rest for a minute."

He slowed Westwind. "Are you sure you don't mind?"

When I shook my head, he rode off.

As I stood on the sidelines, watching Geoffrey canter down the path, I was aware of two horsemen stopping a little off to my right.

One of the men leaned over to adjust his stirrup and said to his companion, "Have you heard Lester's got a new *chère amie?* She's quite a stunner."

"No!" came the disbelieving reply. "I wonder what the Divine de Vigne will have to say about that."

I had been mistaken for Cyrus's *chère amie* often enough to know it was a term for mistress. I turned in the saddle to stare at the two men, but they rode off, leaving me to stare at their backs in stunned silence.

Could it possibly be true that my brother-in-law kept a woman as his mistress? Why, he and Leonie had been married only two years! Yet, why would those men make such a statement if it weren't true? I felt suddenly sick inside at my new discovery.

Geoffrey, meanwhile, had turned Westwind and was galloping back, letting his horse extend himself to the limit of his endurance. They made an awesome sight, the powerful stallion's muscles rippling as he ran, his rider leaning forward, ever in control, seeming a part of the animal, like some mythical centaur. I could feel the ground shake as they approached at a breakneck speed.

"Cassandra," Geoffrey said, his face stern as he reined in Westwind on his haunches in a dramatic display of horsemanship. "Is something wrong? You look frightened."

I smiled brightly and thought fast. "It's just that I feared you weren't going to stop in time."

He threw back his head and laughed. "I credit myself with being able to control my horse, even one as spirited as this. Come. Let's go back to the house."

We rode to the park entrance, about to leave, when another horseman approached us, and I am ashamed to say I disliked him on sight.

Perhaps it was the heavy-handed way he controlled his horse, a skittish chestnut who appeared to be no stranger to crop and spur, judging from the thin sheen of nervous sweat that glazed its coat.

The rider looked like some wild gypsy prince. He had black, curly hair, a thick mustache, and swarthy skin, and I noticed many female eyes riveted on this broad-shouldered specimen, astride his horse like some god. But I was not of the admiring sisterhood, for there was something distasteful about him despite his good looks.

The first words out of his mouth did nothing to dispel my negative first impression. "Why, Lester, you rogue! Found a pretty horsebreaker for yourself at last, eh! 'She walks in beauty, like the night.'" He was unctuous, like an Egyptian merchant seeking to wheedle one into buying something one didn't need, and he even made Byron's poetry sound somehow tawdry.

I darted a quick glance at Geoffrey, and saw that his expression was as stormy as it had been in the library this morning.

His emotions communicated themselves to his horse, who pawed the ground menacingly and shook his head until his bit jingled.

"This is my sister-in-law," Geoffrey said, biting off each word. "Miss Cassandra Clark, may I present Lord Adam Rushton. Rushton, this is Leonie's sister, newly arrived from Egypt."

"Ah, yes. Leonie has mentioned you. Miss Clark, the pleasure is all mine. I must say that you are far too beautiful to be anyone's sister-in-law."

He held his reins in one hand so he could extend his other one to me, but I was so furious with him that I wasn't going to give him the satisfaction. I tugged Bittersweet's reins, causing the startled mare to step back away from Lord Rushton.

"You must forgive me for not taking your hand, Lord Rushton," I murmured, "but I am not so skillful a rider as you."

The man was so full of himself he never imagined I had cut him deliberately. "Well, Lester here is an expert rider— aren't you, old boy?—" he said, with a ribald wink at Geoffrey, "and I'm sure he'll impart his secrets to you."

I tried to pretend I was back in Cairo, fending off the unwanted advances of some boor, but this time, it didn't help. Lord Rushton was too blatant, and I felt myself blushing again.

"I'm sure," I murmured.

"If you'll excuse us . . ." Geoffrey said coldly, sensing my discomfort, and started to walk his horse away.

Just as he passed, Lord Rushton reached out to touch Geoffrey's arm. "Sorry, old boy. It was an honest mistake."

Geoffrey mumbled something unintelligible, and Rushton grinned insolently and tipped his hat to me as we rode out of the park.

"Who *was* that horrid man?" I demanded, glancing back over my shoulder in time to see Lord Rushton ride up to one of the gaudy women and start talking to her.

"I must apologize for Rushton," Geoffrey said, "but he fancies himself another Lord Byron, quotations and all. Ever since someone unwisely called attention to the fact that he vaguely resembled Byron, Rushton has tried to emulate his hero—at least where women are concerned." He shook his head. "Poor fool. He doesn't realize he's a bore, so one tends to excuse him." Geoffrey added as an afterthought, "For some inexplicable reason, Leonie likes him."

"But I take it you don't."

"I don't trust a man who mistreats his horses," was all Geoffrey would say. "Incidentally, I noticed the way you cut him. Most skillfully done."

"He was rude, and he deserved it," I declared heartily, causing Geoffrey to laugh.

But as we rode in silence back to the house, and I had time to think about all that had happened in the park, I realized I had glimpsed another side to my brother-in-law, one I hadn't suspected. One just had to recall all the greetings he had received this morning to know he was well known and respected by his equals. And he was powerful enough to do as he pleased in this man's world. He could take a mistress without regard for his wife's feelings and still expect faithfulness from her. What did it matter if her sister knew? She could learn to tolerate the situation as well.

True, it took a warm, compassionate man to travel thousands of miles just to bring my mother and me together after all these years. And it was more than generous of him to have given me the mare. But now I had seen his cold, unfeeling side, and it left me disappointed, uncomfortable, and decidedly wary. I found myself hoping I would never have to clash with Geoffrey Lester, because I sensed that he was a strong-willed man who would make a remorseless opponent.

Before too long, we were back at the house, and grooms came rushing out to hold our mounts. Geoffrey dismounted first and then reached up for me. As I placed my hands on his broad shoulders, he was smiling, but as I swung lightly to the ground, he stared up at something beyond my head, and his face clouded over and grew somber. I turned and looked up at the house. Standing in an upstairs window, watching us, was Leonie.

"Thank you for riding with me, Cassandra," he said formally. "I'll be leaving for my club now, should anyone ask for me."

And before I could say a word, he remounted Westwind and cantered off down the drive. Why did I have the feeling he had changed his plans only after seeing his wife in the window?

After changing and returning my borrowed habit to my mother, I went back to my room to find Leonie waiting for me. She was wearing a dress of pale violet crepe that made her eyes look enormous. A spray of fresh violets was pinned to her dress, but it did not dispel her geranium perfume.

"Where did Geoffrey go off to in such a rush?" she demanded, without a word of greeting.

"He said he was going to his club," I replied.

"Did you go riding with him in the park?"

I nodded. "He let me ride Bittersweet." I decided it would not be prudent to tell her the mare was a gift to me from her husband.

Leonie's smile was condescending. "Yes, she's a nice little mare—for an inexperienced rider, of course." Before I could comment, she said, "Did you meet anyone special in the park today?"

"Just a man named Adam Rushton," I replied.

Mere mention of his name caused her pouting mouth to curl in a smile. "He is so very charming and gallant, don't you think? I once saw a portrait of the poet Byron, and I thought the resemblance was just uncanny. Half the women I know would give their most precious possessions to establish a liaison with him, but his wife, Lady Fiona, is such an eagle-eyed harridan. I, quite frankly, don't see why he ever married a woman so much older than himself, but that is neither here nor there. Adam and I are close friends, and I'm sure you'll be seeing more of him."

I tried to hide my disappointment, for I was not looking forward to enduring Lord Rushton's bold looks again.

To avoid saying something complimentary about the man, I said, "Leonie, can you tell me what a 'pretty horsebreaker' is?"

She put her fingertips to her lips to conceal a smirk. "My, my, wherever did you hear such a term?"

I wasn't going to tell her that Lord Rushton had mistaken me for one, so all I said was, "In the park this morning."

"You're such an innocent," Leonie declared with a worldly sigh, "so I suppose I must be the one to tell you. Mother certainly wouldn't, and Maud would be sure to sermonize. Pretty horsebreakers, my dear, are women of easy virtue who exercise a stable owner's best mounts in the hopes of being seen and acquiring a, er—protector for themselves. They usually display their wares in the morning, when all the gentleman are out, but leave by the afternoon, when we *respectable* ladies ride."

So, Lord Rushton had suspected me of being such a creature. That was just one more black mark against him in my estimation. "Thank you, Leonie. Now I know."

Then she strolled over to my dressing table and stared at her reflection for a moment in the glass. Suddenly, she stood up and said, "I think I should warn you not to be deceived by Geoffrey's charming manner, Cassandra. He has the devil's own sweetness about him, but he can be quite hateful, as I know only too well."

I sat myself down on the window seat. "Why, Leonie, whatever do you mean?"

She shook her golden head as though I were beyond belief. "Congratulations, my dear sister. Such a performance would put even Ellen Terry to shame. That's an engaging trick you have of widening your green eyes so innocently, but it shan't work with me, I'm afraid."

"Leonie, whatever are you talking about?"

She shrugged. "I was watching from the window, and I saw the look on Geoffrey's face when he helped you to dismount. Then, when you turned and caught my eye, you looked so guilty, I found myself wondering what my husband could have said, or done, to make you look like that. A few pretty compliments, perhaps?"

I couldn't very well tell her that it was Geoffrey's touch as he swung me out of the saddle that caused me to blush. "I really can't remember what we had been discussing."

Leonie plucked a violet from the spray on her dress and absently twirled it between her fingers. "You wouldn't be the first woman to be attracted to my husband. One direct look from those stormy eyes of his tends to make one melt inside. And he is so forceful and strong, with that feeling of violence bubbling just beneath the surface." She stared at me as though her gaze alone could transfix me to the spot. "Haven't you ever sensed that violence about Geoffrey, Cassandra?"

I knew she wasn't speaking of violence in an ordinary sense of the word, so I rose to break her spell and faced her squarely. "You're being foolish and melodramatic, Leonie. I am not attracted to your husband, despite what fancies you may have to the contrary."

"Oh, fancies, are they?"

"Yes, fancies. Nothing more."

Now she reached out to touch my arm, as though to reassure me. "Oh, don't misunderstand, Cassandra. If you and Geoffrey . . . Well, if you decide to become his next *chère amie*, I shan't oppose you. But I beg of you, please be discreet. We have what my great-grandmother—on my father's side, of course—would have called a marriage of convenience. Geoffrey goes his way and does what he wishes, and I go mine, doing what I wish. It's simple, really."

"And sad."

She laughed, that light, tinkling sound that could be amused or mocking. Now it was both. "I don't really expect you to understand, little provincial that you are. I'm merely trying to give you a bit of sisterly advice."

Then she walked over to the window seat and knelt on it, her hands propped against the sill, as though she were looking out at something in the yard below. "When I married Geoffrey, I loved him dearly, but my love meant nothing to him. He tossed it aside like a wilted rose."

And then she burst into tears.

For a moment, I was taken aback to see my witty, brittle sister softly weeping, and I suddenly felt oddly touched. So, the bright, sparkling society flirt was vulnerable after all, and I wanted to protect her from any more hurt.

"Don't cry, Leonie," I murmured, making her sit on the window seat, so I could sit next to her, my arm around her.

She leaned against me gratefully, her slender shoulders shaking with sobs. "We weren't married a year when he took a mistress."

I was startled that such a sheltered, well-bred young woman would know of such things, but then, Leonie was married.

"If you suspect Geoffrey of having a mistress—"

"Oh, I don't suspect, I *know*. She's an actress friend of Maud's named Marietta de Vigne, and he keeps her in a little secluded villa in St. John's Wood. I've seen it."

I was silent for a moment, as I rocked her gently, not knowing quite what to say. "What do you intend to do about it?"

"Do?" She took out a handkerchief and dried her eyes. "There's nothing I can do. For the longest time, I tried every wile imaginable to win my husband back, but he was cold and unresponsive. Now, I don't think it matters to me any more. As long as Geoffrey is discreet, that's all I can ask for. He will tire of her eventually, just as he would tire of you."

I stiffened and drew away from her. "You needn't concern yourself, because I have no intention of replacing this Miss de Vigne or anyone else."

Now Leonie rose, looking desperate and wild-eyed. "Innocent Cassandra. If Geoffrey makes up his mind to have you, there is nothing you will be able to do about it."

And before I could say another word, she went running from my room.

We dined early that evening, for Geoffrey and Leonie were attending the opera and their carriage would be ready at eight o'clock. Mother and I had not been invited. I realized Leonie wouldn't want me to embarrass her in my outmoded clothes, but I couldn't understand why she hadn't asked Mother to join them, for I was sure she would have enjoyed an evening away from her interminable embroidery.

When we went in to dinner, Leonie flirted shamelessly with Edgar Wickes, who stared at her in ill-concealed adoration, while Geoffrey spoke to everyone at the table except his wife. As I ate my buttered crab and watched the two of them pointedly ignore each other, I couldn't stop thinking of what Leonie had told me that afternoon, her tears, and her deep, deep unhappiness. I began to wonder if perhaps I had misjudged her. It must have been devastating to see the man you loved callously turn to other women, especially when you yourself were all any man could desire.

I didn't know what to think, as I watched Geoffrey laugh at something Mother had said. Was he the cold, unfeeling monster Leonie depicted, or merely the unsuspecting victim of her lies?

Soon, the endless meal was over, and the Wickeses accepted Geoffrey's offer of a ride home, leaving with him and Leonie. Maud disappeared on a recruiting mission, leaving Mother and me alone in the music room with the evening stretching out before us.

When Heffer brought Mother her tisane, then left, she sighed deeply and seemed to unwind, like a coiled spring. Her lovely face lost its pinched look, and she set aside her embroidery as though she were finally tired of stitching vines and leaves.

"Do open the doors, Cassandra, if you would," she said to me, fanning herself with her hand. "It's a bit close in here, don't you think?"

Though I still hadn't grown accustomed to the cold, I did as she bade me, standing in the doorway for a moment in the cool night air and trying not to shiver. "A fog is rolling in," I said, as the faint lowing of the foghorn could be heard in the distance, a mournful sound that made me sad.

"London is notorious for its fogs," she replied. "They're so thick you can't see your hand in front of your face. Street arabs often make a few shillings escorting lost pedestrians home at night, did you know that?"

I shook my head as I stared out into the thick, yellowish mist that had already blotted out the stars, the sky, and half the yard. It lingered at the edge of the path and I shut the doors against it, suddenly fearful, as though it were a dangerous, physical entity, stalking me.

"Do you have such fogs in Cairo?" Mother asked.

"Occasionally there's a light mist in the morning, off the Nile," I replied, trying to gather my courage to ask her what I wanted.

"Do you miss living there?"

I stared at my reflection in the dark glass and read the fear in my own eyes. "I do miss Cyrus. He calls me his Right Arm, you know. I find myself wondering who's soothing some irate guest when something doesn't go as planned, and who's accompanying the tourists to all of the sights."

Now she rose, cup in hand, and strolled over to Leonie's piano. "Do you play?" she asked, running her fingers lightly over the keys. "I imagine Venetia insisted you learn. It's quite necessary for a young woman. It's so—so intimate to sit there while some handsome young gentleman turns the pages for you."

I thought of Edgar last night, doing just that for my sister. "I did have some training, but I'm not very good. Aunt Venetia and Uncle Harry could only afford piano lessons for Marian, the eldest girl, and she in turn had to teach her six sisters, so when it came to me, she was rather tired of it, and my lessons were often neglected." At my mother's silence, I turned to her. "I'm afraid I'm quite deficient in the domestic arts, Mother." I hadn't meant it to sound like an accusation, but somehow, it came out that way, for Mother looked away and returned to her seat.

"And you blame me for that," she said.

"No, I don't. The failure was mine. My watercolor sketches were always a blur, the seams I sewed were never straight, and I haven't an ear for music. It's not your fault at all."

She picked up her needlework again, and I could see she was very upset. The easy camaraderie of a few moments ago was rapidly becoming frayed around the edges, perhaps because I reminded her too much of how she had failed me in so many little ways.

Now was the time to broach what had been on my mind all evening. "Mother," I said, clasping my hands firmly in front of me, "I want you to know that I know all about your life with the Earl of Whatever."

The needle stopped, poised above fabric, and my mother gave me a long, level look. "Everything?"

"Everything."

"Who told you? Geoffrey? Leonie?"

I shook my head. "No. A Lady Quartermain in Cairo."

Two spots of high color appeared on Mother's face, and her mouth tightened in an expression of disgust. "Celestine Quartermain . . . She makes it a point to know everyone else's business and spreads it around London." Then a wry smile touched her mouth. "It must have given you some satisfaction to learn how much I've suffered for leaving your father."

Those words stung me like angry wasps. "Mother! How can you say such a thing! I'll have you know that, after Lady Quartermain was through with her vile gossip, I found myself feeling sorry for you. In a way, she was responsible for my coming to London."

Mother gave a long, drawn-out sigh. "Well, I'm glad it brought you to me, but I don't need, or want, your pity, Cassandra," she said, her voice tight and controlled.

I found myself admiring her for that, in spite of myself. "But if you were so miserable with the Earl of . . ."

"Knighton. The Earl of Knighton, Cassandra. He was my husband once, and I'll thank you to be respectful to his memory."

But I could not say the name of the man who had taken my mother away from Father and me. "Why didn't you leave him and return to Father?"

This so startled her, she actually jumped. "Go back to Jason?" Then her eyes filled with tears. "My dear, dear child . . . after what I had done to him? That was out of the question."

"He needed you, Mother. I needed you. He would have forgiven you and taken you back."

She shook her head and turned her attention back to her task. "I just couldn't, Cassandra. No, I made my choice and had to abide by it."

I am ashamed to say that resentment threatened to overwhelm me at that moment.

"Even if you couldn't have returned to Father, you could have found some way to have *me* with you, especially after he died, couldn't you?"

"Ah, so that's what this is all about." Mother rose now, quite out of sorts with me. "I've explained all that to you already, Cassandra, and I'm sorry if you can't understand. I think this conversation is fruitless, don't you?"

And she bade me good night and left me alone with the swirling fog beckoning to me from behind the doors.

Much, much later, when the house was dark and hushed, and I had long been abed, a sound awakened me. It was Leonie's light, trilling laughter, followed by a man's low voice. I knew it wasn't Geoffrey.

Soon they passed by my door, their voices faded, and I rolled over onto my side and fell asleep.

It could have been my confrontation with Mother that gnawed at me, or perhaps I finally did wonder what Leonie was doing passing by my door with a strange man at two o'clock in the morning. Whatever, I suddenly found myself wide awake once again.

I tried everything to get back to sleep, but nothing worked. The beating of my own heart seemed to be keeping time with the clock on the night stand, and I knew I was fighting a losing battle. Perhaps something to eat would calm me, so I lit my lamp and crept downstairs.

I knew all the servants were in bed, and the fires in the stoves had been put out long ago, but perhaps by rummaging about the kitchen, I could find a biscuit tin.

I tiptoed down the darkened hall so I wouldn't waken anyone. Suddenly, I saw a light at the end of the corridor, and as I approached the stairs, I realized that someone had left the gaslights on in the stairwell. I thought this most odd, for usually Heffer himself or one of the footmen stayed up until the master of the house returned, then turned out the lights and went to bed.

Well, I decided as I started down the stairs, I would turn them off on my return trip and do Heffer a favor.

I found my way down to the kitchen without mishap, and after searching, found the biscuits. I helped myself to several, wrapped my treasures in a napkin, and started back upstairs.

Suddenly, just as I stole down the main hall, I heard the stairs creak with heavy, leisurely footsteps, and a sense of panic caused me to extinguish my lamp and shrink back into the shadows. I was, after all, in my nightdress, and even though it was a modest garment, I still did not want Geoffrey to find me roaming the halls in it. I stood against the wall and held my breath, praying he wouldn't discover me.

But it was not Geoffrey who descended the stairs.

The man was of average height, but stout, and because I stood hidden below, and a little behind him, all I could see of his face was a profile and a neatly trimmed beard. Smoke from a thick cigar enveloped him in a haze with each puff, and, as the strong odor of tobacco tickled my nose, I feared I would sneeze and give myself away.

As I stood frozen against the wall, holding my breath, he strolled through the foyer as if he were quite familiar with the Lester house. Then something amazing happened. The man let himself out, and after he closed the door quietly behind him, I heard the unmistakable sound of a key turning in the lock. I could feel my jaw drop in surprise, and when I regained my composure and thought it was safe to come out of hiding, I hurried through the foyer and into the drawing room, which overlooked the street, and peered out from behind the curtains.

All I could see over the top of the wall was a driver seated in his hansom cab, his chin to his chest as though he had been dozing for a long, long time. Suddenly, the driver snapped to attention, flicked his whip, and moved off. I stood there for a moment, watching the horse move down the street.

Then I went back upstairs to ponder this strange event, turning out the gaslights.

I made up my mind to ask someone about the man the next day.

Chapter Six

W hen I went down to breakfast the following morning, I was surprised to discover Mother, Geoffrey, and Leonie dining together, but again, the strain among them was palpable.

Mother and Leonie wished me good morning, and Geoffrey rose with a brief smile. Then the silence returned. It was as though I had walked in on a conversation I was not supposed to hear, and everyone was waiting for me to leave before resuming it.

As I helped myself to eggs and toast, I decided to engage them in conversation whether they liked it or not. When I seated myself, I said, "Is there some member of the family I haven't met yet?"

Three pairs of eyes regarded me in bewilderment, and Mother said, "Why, Cassandra, whatever do you mean? You've met everyone who lives here."

"Well, late last night, I couldn't sleep, so I went down to the kitchen for something to eat. I thought it quite odd that the gaslights in the foyer had been left on, and then I saw a strange man come down the stairs, let himself out, and lock the door behind him. I watched from the drawing room window as he got into a waiting cab and drove away." I scanned their faces. "He acted as though he was quite at home here. I was just wondering who he was, that's all."

Suddenly, Geoffrey glared at Leonie, then rose so quickly his chair tipped over and went crashing to the floor. Without a word, he flung his napkin down and went storming out of the dining room, leaving me to stare after him.

I turned to Mother and Leonie in astonishment. "Whatever did I say to upset him so?"

"Don't look so stricken, sister dear," Leonie said, dabbing at her lips with her napkin as though nothing out of the ordinary had happened. "Geoffrey is just in a singularly black mood this morning, that's all."

One look at Mother's tragic countenance confirmed my own suspicions that there was indeed more to Geoffrey's outburst than a disagreeable mood.

I faced Leonie squarely, trying to keep my temper in check. "I'm sorry, but I can't accept that. Something I said upset Geoffrey very much, and I think I deserve an explanation."

My sister's pouting mouth turned up into a mocking smile. Ever cool, ever confident, she replied, "Cassandra, mind your own affairs. Geoffrey's behavior should be of no concern to you."

Her dismissal angered me further. "It was the man I saw last night, wasn't it? That's what upset Geoffrey so."

Out of the corner of my eye, I saw Mother reach for her teacup, but her hand was shaking so badly, it rattled in its saucer, and she had to set it down before it spilled.

Leonie rose. "I'm having my portrait painted and am due at the artist's studio for a sitting this morning. I don't want to be late, so if you'll excuse me . . ."

I watched helplessly as Leonie glided out of the dining room, and when the door closed behind her, I turned to my mother for answers.

"Mother, will you please tell me what in God's name is going on in this house?"

She was very pale and shaking so badly, I feared she would collapse. "I'm—I'm—sorry, Cassandra, but I just can't discuss it right now." And she, too, rose.

"Mother, please! Don't you go running off on me, too!"

"I'm sorry," she muttered, as she started to leave.

And then the answer came to me with such a startling flash of clarity and force, it took my breath away.

"That man I saw last night . . . ," I called after her as she reached the door. "He's Leonie's lover, isn't he?"

The ensuing silence was hard as glass. Mother stopped and whirled around, an agonized expression on her face. "Oh, he's much more than that."

And before I could question her about such a mysterious statement, she fled the room, like everyone else.

I knew it would be futile to follow, so I just sat there in silence, drumming my fingertips against the tabletop, while my breakfast cooled on my plate. So, Leonie had a lover. That would certainly account for Geoffrey's remoteness since my arrival, the air of brittle tension in this household.

"How could Leonie do such a thing to her own husband?" I murmured aloud, and as soon as the words were out of my mouth, I answered my own question. She was retaliating for Geoffrey's divine actress.

I scowled, for some piece of this riddle continued to nag at me like an aching tooth. Geoffrey's mistress was kept hidden away in a place called St. John's Wood, but I had seen Leonie's lover here, in Geoffrey's own house, while he was out for the evening. My sister had kept an assignation with another man right under her husband's roof.

Rising and righting Geoffrey's chair, I proceeded to pace the room, my brow furrowed in thought. Mother's words about the man being more than Leonie's lover came floating back, puzzling me and teasing my curiosity even further. It was obvious that no one wanted to talk about him, especially Geoffrey and Leonie. Perhaps this was just natural reticence on their part, but I had the feeling there was something more to it.

In spite of Leonie's declaration yesterday that she and Geoffrey went their separate ways, and that she gave the impression that neither cared for the other, I could see that his wife's lover upset Geoffrey. What I could not understand is why he tolerated it.

Well, I was going to find out.

A quick search of the house revealed that no one was around to answer my questions. Leonie had indeed gone for her portrait sitting, Geoffrey was at his club, and Mother was locked in her room, guarded zealously by her maid, who told me in no uncertain terms that the countess could not be disturbed. That left only Maud, and she was at her school.

"Heffer," I said to the butler, "I'd like a carriage brought round to take me to Miss Lester's school."

"The carriages are all out at the moment, miss," he informed me.

"Then hail me a cab," I said. "I shall be ready in five minutes."

A half hour later, my cab stopped before a new red-brick building situated in a neighborhood of old, shabby houses. A shiny brass plate beside the front door proclaimed it "The Lester Commercial School," so I asked the driver to wait and I went inside.

There I found an efficient-looking young woman who asked if she could be of assistance, and when I told her my name and asked to see Miss Lester, she rose from her desk and disappeared down the hall. When she returned, she said Miss Lester would be delighted to see me and directed me to Maud's office.

As I walked in, Maud rose from her huge oak desk at the far end of the room. "Why, good morning, Cassandra. How delightful to see you. So, you finally decided to come visit my school after all."

Maud's appearance was so startling that for a moment I forgot my reason for coming. Her loose, comfortable Liberty dress had been replaced by a day dress any lady would wear, complete with stays that nipped Maud's Amazonian proportions down to size.

"Why, Maud," I said, "whatever happened to your Liberty dress? You look quite . . . conventional."

She chuckled at that. "Have you ever heard the expression, 'When in Rome, do as the Romans do?' Well, I've found the girls' parents are less intimidated if I look like everyone else rather than some Aesthetic creature. I'd rather endure this damned creaking corset—" She grimaced and massaged her ribs. "—if it means one more girl will enroll. But come, let me show you the school."

I didn't move as she came around her desk toward me. "Maud, I didn't come here to see your school." Seeing her crestfallen look, I amended, "Well, I did, but there's something else we must discuss as well."

"This must be serious, for you look so grim," she mused, indicating a bobbin-turned chair for me, while she returned to her desk and slouched down in her chair.

"It is," I replied, sitting down. Then I moistened my lips and plunged right in. "Maud, ever since I arrived in London, I've sensed that something is very wrong in your house. Whenever Geoffrey and Leonie are together, sparks of animosity fly between them."

Maud said nothing, but her eyes narrowed warily, as though she were trying to anticipate what I was going to say next. Then, when I told her about seeing that strange man the night before, she became visibly agitated, rising quickly to turn her back to me and stare out the window at the alley beyond.

"What was even stranger was everyone's reaction this morning at breakfast," I said. "Geoffrey went storming out of the room like a man possessed, and Leonie just refused to discuss it. I confronted Mother and finally forced her to admit that the man was Leonie's lover. But then she said something very odd." And I repeated what my mother had said about the man being "more than" Leonie's lover.

"What did she mean, Maud?" I demanded.

Maud turned to face me, a nervous, placating smile on her

face, and I thought she had turned quite pale beneath her freckles. "Why . . . nothing."

I exploded. "Oh, please, Maud! Credit me with some intelligence! I thought I could at least get an honest answer from you, of all people." I rose and placed my hands on her desk and leaned toward her. "Will you please tell me what all the mystery is about? Who is this man, and why does he have a key to your house, coming and going in the middle of the night? And why does Geoffrey allow it, especially when he strikes me as a man who would never tolerate his wife's taking a lover under his own roof?"

Maud regarded me for the longest time, then she capitulated. "All right," she said with a sigh. "You're going to find out about it sooner or later, so I may as well be the one to tell you." She took a deep breath and clutched at her desk until her knuckles turned white. "The man you saw last night . . . Leonie's lover, is—"

She hesitated.

"Maud, please!"

"He's Edward, the Prince of Wales."

I burst out laughing. "Oh, Maud, surely you're jesting with me."

She didn't return my smile, just stared at me.

In the room above, the staccato tap-tap-tap of the type-writing machines sounded like gunshots, and the beating of my own heart seemed to fill the room.

I swallowed several times. "Leonie's lover is the future King of England?"

"The same."

I had to sit down quickly, before I toppled over.

It was common knowledge that the prince had favorites, the most public one being Lillie Langtry, a dean's beautiful daughter from the Isle of Jersey, who became an actress after she and the prince had parted. I could still remember Aunt Venetia roundly scolding anyone who dared mention Mrs. Langtry's name in her presence, and in Cairo, Cyrus would make me turn scarlet by saying, "Look, coz, I'm mounting Lillie Langtry!" whenever he rode one of the hundreds of donkeys named in her honor, so great was her fame. But to learn that my own sister had joined the ranks of such a courtesan . . .

I looked up at Maud, and my own voice sounded foreign to me. "However in the world did this happen?"

She propped her elbow on the desk and cradled her chin in her hands. "While Geoffrey was in Cairo, searching for you, his pretty wife couldn't bear to be excluded from the social whirl she craves like an opium addict craves his pipe. One day, she was riding through the park with some friends when the prince noticed her and asked to be introduced. Your mother and I were a little uneasy when she was invited to Marlborough House, for the members of the prince's set have a reputation for being very fast. Leo assured us it was all very respectable, for her friends were there to chaperone. What fools we were to believe her."

Now Maud began tugging her hair from its pins, a sure sign of her nervousness. "Then one day, I returned home from a committee meeting to find all the servants had been ordered to remain below stairs, and Leo was locked in the drawing room alone with the prince, who had come to call. One doesn't need to be brilliant to guess what had happened." Her voice faltered. "It was only a matter of time before the prince's rented hansom started appearing at the front door just about every night."

"Couldn't you or Mother have stopped her?" I demanded.

"We tried to talk some sense into her," Maud said, somewhat defensively, "but do you know what the cunning little minx said?"

"Dare I ask?"

"She said, 'You must ask Edward if he will break off with me, and if he agrees, I shall.'" Maud's ironic laughter filled the office. "Can you imagine my going up to the son of my sovereign and saying, 'Pardon me, Your Royal Highness, but

I really wish you would find another favorite and leave my brother's wife alone'?" She shook her head at the absurdity of it. "All I could do was wait until Geoff returned from Egypt." Maud's voice grew wistful. "Telling him about Leo was even harder than writing to him about our father's death."

"What did he say when you told him?"

"I've never seen him so hurt or so furious. Then, when he calmed down, he was determined to take Leo away, but several of the prince's friends had a long, heart-to-heart talk with him and made him see the wisdom of accepting the situation."

My eyes widened in indignation. "Accept the situation! How can a man stand by and watch another man carry on with his wife?"

Maud regarded me with the long, hard look that always made me squirm. "Everything is always black and white to you, isn't it, Cassa?"

At first, I blushed, then I grew angry. "And I can't believe you're defending the man."

"At first, I felt as you do, that Geoffrey should stand up to the prince and put a stop to the liaison. But then I met the prince, and . . ." Maud groped for the right words. "I found him likable, congenial, charming . . . Words just can't express the feeling that comes over you in his presence. He shows such a sincere interest in you, you find yourself not wanting to deny him anything."

"He sounds rather depraved to me, using his position to seduce other men's wives."

"Actually, I would say he's more like a naughty little boy than a depraved person," Maud said, with her fine turn of phrase.

"Oh, Maud, you make it sound as though every subject should willingly sacrifice his wife for the good of the realm."

Now it was her turn to look embarrassed. "I don't mean that at all. But, after meeting His Royal Highness, I could understand why so many husbands have looked the other way when the prince fancied their wives." She had pulled out so much hair she looked like a madwoman. "I'm not condoning Leo's behavior, Cassa, and my brother certainly isn't blameless, either. There must be something lacking in their marriage for his wife to seek out another man, though I don't know what it could be. But I'm trying not to judge. Hopefully, Leo will fall out of favor, and we'll be able to get on with our lives again, though I seriously wonder if they'll ever be the same."

Feeling suddenly drained, I sighed and rose. "Well, thank you for talking to me, Maud. I think I'll be on my way now."

"Won't you let me show you the school before you go?"

I hated to disappoint her, so I let her take me on a tour of the school, then got in my waiting cab and left.

On my ride back to Upper Brook Street, I felt as though one of the columns from the Temple of Karnak had fallen on me. My sister was the Prince of Wales's latest diversion, and the entire Lester family seemed to condone it.

No, that really wasn't fair. I had seen Geoffrey's look of anguish and helplessness as he bolted from the dining room this morning, and Mother looked as though she could barely hold herself together. Somehow, I doubted if any of them had remained unscathed by Leonie's scandalous behavior.

His wife's situation would certainly explain the sudden change in Geoffrey. I could imagine how he must have felt, returning after some months' absence to find his wife had become the prince's mistress. No wonder Geoffrey always looked so haunted and miserable, so stiff and unyielding toward Leonie.

I sighed as I leaned back against the cushions. The truth of Maud's accusation—that I only saw situations in black and white—hurt me, so I tried to overcome my prejudices and to understand why Leonie had ever agreed to such a liaison.

I'm afraid Aunt Venetia's strict, moralistic upbringing had shaped me more than I cared to admit, for I found it difficult to excuse my sister's behavior.

How could Leonie let herself be taken advantage of? The prince had engaged her emotions as surely as the Earl of Knighton had engaged our mother's, and, in the end, he would just cast her off for someone else and ruin her life as well as the lives of the people who loved her.

"Cassa," I warned myself, "it's really none of your concern. What Leonie does with her life is her own affair."

My thoughts were soon dispelled, for the cab had turned into Upper Brook Street, and I was astounded to find it as clogged with carriages as Regent Street had been yesterday. Broughams, victorias, and hansoms lined both sides of the street, most with impressive crests on their doors and liveried drivers and footmen standing in attendance. I could tell we had august company.

After paying the cabbie and going inside, I said to Heffer, "What are all these people doing here?"

He replied, "Madame is always at home to callers on Thursdays, miss. Would you care to join them?"

"No, thank you," I said, and scurried upstairs unnoticed.

I wondered if Mother were in her room, and when I went down the hall, I found the door no longer guarded by her zealous maid. When I knocked softly, a weak voice called, "Come in."

The drapes had been drawn against the strong daylight, and Mother lay on her bed, a compress across her forehead and her tisane within reach on the nightstand.

"Cassandra . . ." she murmured.

"Aren't you feeling well, Mother?" I asked, sitting on the edge of her bed.

"My head feels as though it's been split by an axe, but other than that, I'm fine." She looked at me pointedly. "And how are you?"

I looked around her room, surprisingly spare and austerely

furnished, considering the opulence of the rest of the house. "I went to see Maud at her school. She told me everything."

"I imagine you were appalled."

"I was shocked at first," I admitted, looking at her, "but I'm trying to understand and not to judge. However, I am curious as to how you could have allowed this to happen. You are Leonie's mother. Surely you have some influence."

She turned the compress over and closed her eyes. "Cassandra, my dear, you must know by now that I have no influence with my daughter. Leonie does what she pleases, when she pleases. She always has. We are powerless to stop her."

"Doesn't she realize how much she's hurting her own husband and family?"

A look of profound sadness crossed her face. "Poor Geoffrey. I suppose she realizes what she's doing to him, but I don't know if she really cares at all. Leonie doesn't confide in me anymore, or ask my advice. If she did, I'd warn her she was embarking on a path that will only lead to her destruction."

"She seems doomed to repeat your mistake, Mother," I said rather tartly.

Now she sat up and glared at me, her headache forgotten for a moment. "If by mistake you mean bolting with Knighton, that wasn't a mistake. One of the reasons I left your father was that I had fallen head over heels in love with Knighton. He just enchanted me so, I couldn't help myself and had to have him, no matter what the cost. And the cost was dear, Cassandra, very dear."

"Was it worth it?" I demanded coldly, rising.

"I would like to tell you it wasn't, because that's what you need to hear," she said, "but I'm afraid that would be lying. Even though he never forgave me for not having given him a son, even though he mistreated me terribly toward the end, I loved him and would do it all over again."

She was right. This was not what I wanted to hear, and suddenly, thoughts of my melancholy father filled my mind, and I couldn't stand being in the same room with my mother any longer. Without a word, I turned to go.

"Cassandra, please don't be angry with me," she called. "One day, you shall fall in love and then perhaps you'll understand."

Now I stopped and turned to face her. "Oh, no, Mother. If falling in love means having my emotions played upon by some man so that I become his—his slave, without concern for the feelings of others, then I don't ever want to fall in love."

And I left her to her compress and tisane.

I rang for Sally and had her bring me luncheon on a tray, for I was not in the mood for mingling with Leonie's ardent courtiers downstairs. Then I curled up on my bed and slept.

I awoke to a hand shaking my shoulder, and opened my eyes to find Leonie's harassed-looking maid standing there.

"The mistress would like to see you in her room," the woman said timidly.

At first, I was going to refuse, then decided Leonie's wrath was not worth enduring. I would have to face her sooner or later, so I might as well get it over with.

My sister's room resembled the inside of a confection box, all pink satin, gilt, and ruffles everywhere. She herself was a vision in a mauve tea gown as she reclined on a chaise like Cleopatra, writing in a small, leather-bound book. The spicy scent of geraniums perfumed the air, making me feel as though I had entered a hothouse of rare and beautiful tropical flowers.

"Ah, there you are, sister dear," she said when I entered, closing her book and tucking it out of sight beneath a cushion. "We missed you at my at home today. Well, that is to say, Lord Rushton missed you and was so disappointed that you hadn't graced us with your presence."

I stood before her and looked down. "I *know*, Leonie."

She understood at once. "Ah. I suppose Maud told you?"

I nodded.

"What, Cassandra? No sullen looks of disapproval, no sharp words of censure? How could I commit such a despicable act as to become the royal mistress? How could I subject my poor husband to the shame, the notoriety . . ."

"Well," I said evenly, taking the chair she indicated, "how can you?"

She leaned forward, her eyes glittering with excitement, eagerness, and even hunger. "Because it is an *honor* to be Edward's love. Of all the many beautiful, desirable women in the realm, I alone captivated him, and I alone please him."

"Until someone else catches his fancy," I murmured, trying to quell her enthusiasm.

Leonie shook her head. "I am exceptional. Edward usually prefers much older women, who have been married for years and years and have produced an heir for their husbands. That he should prefer a young woman of twenty is a tribute to my beauty. Edward says he's never met anyone so enchanting, and even his most intimate friends assure me that they've never seen him so smitten, or so content."

"You really look upon this as an honor, don't you?"

My sister glowed. "But, of course! It's quite grand to be cultivated by people who would otherwise not have given me the time of day. Now they treat me with great deference, as though I were the Princess Alexandra herself, and many powerful men seek me out because of my influence with Edward. *La maîtresse du roi,* that's what I am."

"Surely the princess must resent you."

Leonie shook her head as she picked at a ruffled satin pillow. "Alix has never been anything but warm and cordial to me, even though she knows I'm her husband's new favorite. She is a rare woman. She knows what her husband needs and generously looks the other way."

So, like everyone else, even the prince's own wife sanctioned such liaisons.

Leonie stretched like a languorous cat, confident of her

power. "I wouldn't give it up for anything in the world: sitting next to the future King of England in his box at the opera, and later having a quiet midnight supper with him alone; riding through the park and seeing people standing on benches just to get a glimpse of me. Me!" She picked up a hand mirror and studied her reflection somberly, as though searching for imperfections. Satisfied that there were none, she set the mirror down. "Why, do you know women actually copy the way I arrange my hair? A *coiffure à la Lester* is all the rage in London now, though it takes a woman of exceptional beauty to wear such a simple style. Even my favorite color—pink—is in vogue. Everyone wears it."

Now she rose, glided over to her desk, and rummaged through the drawers, while muttering, "I am so well known that even the society photographer Lafayette asked me to sit for him."

She found what she was looking for, crossed the room, and thrust into my hands what looked like picture post cards of the type a tourist would send from Cairo. As I flipped through them, I noticed they were all of my sister in different ensembles and assorted poses. In one, she looked elegant and haughty in a lavish gown and enormous flowered hat, her hands resting on a balustrade. In another, she wore a sporty white yachting dress, one hand holding down her straw boater against some imaginary sea breeze. But still another of her as a demure milkmaid, seated on bales of straw, with her golden hair hanging in plaits, almost caused me to burst out laughing.

"They're sold in shops," she explained proudly, "where anyone can buy them."

I stared at her in disbelief. "You mean any chimney sweep or dock worker could have a picture of Lady Leonie Lester to gawk at? Sounds rather vulgar to me."

She dismissed my comment with a wave of her hand and a chuckle. "You're so conventional and old-fashioned, Cassandra, you'd fit in splendidly at Court with all the rest of the withering old crones. One must change with the times. I'll have you know it's an honor to become a 'Professional Beauty' and have your photograph taken for the picture post card trade."

I failed to see the glory in it, but wordlessly handed the cards back to her.

She flipped through them herself, absorbed in her own likeness. "One morning, I was strolling along the promenade in the park, when a woman suddenly accosted me. She wore grubby, vile-smelling clothes, but she thrust a grimy post card photograph of me into my hand and begged me to sign it for her."

The woman may have been old and malodorous, but I could see she had won a place in Leonie's brittle heart. "But what about Geoffrey?" I demanded softly. "Don't you care what this is doing to him?"

Leonie tossed her head and rose to put her post cards away, then turned to face me, blatant unconcern on her face. "Has Geoffrey ever once considered my feelings? No, he just took a mistress without ever stopping to consider how I would feel when I found out."

There was no use arguing with her, so I rose with a sigh. "How you conduct your life is your own affair, Leonie. I just hope you won't have cause to regret it."

"Oh, I won't, Cassandra. Believe me, I won't."

When I left her, I felt as though the walls were closing in on me, and if I remained in this stifling house a moment longer, I would go mad. But where could I go? I knew the answer in an instant.

Later, as Bittersweet was cantering down Rotten Row, I realized I had made a wise choice, for the warm sun on my back and the cool breeze whipping against my face chased away the feeling of deep oppression. There were many more horsemen crowding the lanes this afternoon, and I couldn't fail to notice the interested looks men were giving me, but I ignored them and concentrated on determining what I should do about the Lesters.

Uppermost in my mind was not the shocking news about Leonie and the prince, but my mother's revelation that she had left my father because she actually loved the Earl of Knighton. How could anyone love another man more than my father? It was incomprehensible to me. Somehow, I could forgive my mother for wanting a man who could give her the luxuries of life, but not for loving him. That upset me more than Leonie's infidelity.

And, if I couldn't forgive my mother, what was I doing here, I wondered, as I reached the end of the row? I thought of Cairo, and sensible Cyrus, and I yearned for the simplicity of Egypt, where the only intrigues that went on in the Clark's Hotel concerned who wanted to be seated next to whom at dinner. Perhaps I just should pack my bags and leave the Lesters to their profligate lives.

Suddenly, I glanced up and there was Geoffrey riding toward me, the afternoon sun burnishing his hatless head into a golden helmet. He looked as though he had just come rushing from his club without bothering to change into riding clothes. As our eyes met, I felt my heart begin to race in panic, for I dreaded facing him, and for a moment, I entertained the wild thought of turning Bittersweet around and galloping away. But it would be useless, of course, for Westwind could easily outrun my mare, and Geoffrey would only overtake me eventually. So I rode toward him.

"You shouldn't go riding without a groom," he said gently, without smiling. "Someone will mistake you for a pretty horsebreaker again."

I stared down at his strong, long-fingered hands holding the reins so effortlessly. "Why should anyone assume I am any different from my sister?"

"Cassandra, I can see that you're troubled. We must talk."

"Please. So much has happened today. I'd like to be alone."

"But you can't remain here by yourself."

I surrendered. "All right. But I really don't want to return to the house."

"We don't have to. We'll find a quiet spot in the park."

So we turned and rode slowly, in silence, both staring straight ahead, and soon, after we passed a shimmering body of water dotted with pleasure boats, the crowds thinned out, and the thunder of hoofbeats dwindled and disappeared. Trees gave way to a grassy flat, and except for a noisy group of boys playing ball, we were alone. Soon, even they raced off, and the park became as quiet as a mosque.

I swallowed hard, gathered my courage, and said, "I know why you bolted from the dining room this morning."

"Your mother told me you had gone to see Maud, and, knowing my sister as I do, I'm sure she didn't spare you any details."

"She didn't."

"And were you shocked?"

Now I did look at him. "Yes, at first. You see, I am very old-fashioned. I believe a husband and wife should be faithful to each other."

"Sometimes circumstances make that impossible," he said, plucking at Westwind's mane, and I wondered if he was thinking of his own infidelities.

"I realize that," I replied, "and have tried to see the situation from Leonie's standpoint." I told him about my conversation with her before coming to the park. "I felt very sorry for her."

"She finds the power of her situation exhilarating."

In the distance, two birds dipped and swerved against the sky. "I find my sister to be very shallow, so I'm really not surprised that she would encourage the prince. But there is one thing I don't understand." When he looked at me expectantly, I said, "How can a man who professes to love his wife as you do condone such a situation?"

At first he didn't answer me, and the only sounds were the measured clopping of our horses' hooves and the creaking of leather. Then when he did speak, he sounded far away, as though he were talking to himself.

"When I returned from Egypt, and my sister told me what had happened in my absence, I felt as any man might. Betrayed. Hurt. Angry. I was so enraged, I wanted to strangle Leonie. But when I calmed down and began thinking rationally, I saw the only possible course of action open to me was to take her as far away from the Prince of Wales as I could. I told Leonie we were taking a world tour, and, for the first time since our marriage, she didn't defy me." A bitter smile twisted his mouth. "I think she realized she had pushed me too far this time, and she feared what I would do if she refused me."

"Maud told me the prince's friends persuaded you to stay," I said.

He nodded, and we stopped our horses to give them a rest. "I never should have listened to Hartington and Knollys, but they convinced me he needed Leonie, perhaps more than I did. Nothing was said, of course, but I knew we'd be ostracized socially if we refused the prince anything. I can live without society, but I know Leonie cannot."

I just shook my head sadly.

"So, I became a *mari complaisant* and joined the ranks of all the other cuckolded husbands who avert their eyes and pretend nothing is happening when their wives return in the morning from a midnight supper with His Royal Highness. And I learned to absent myself discreetly when the prince came to call, as he did last night." He slapped his thigh in anger, causing his horse to jerk his head up and neigh. "To this day, I don't know why I ever agreed to this charade!"

I studied his face for a moment, and there was such abject misery there that my heart went out to him, and I impulsively placed a comforting hand on his arm. His eyes widened at my unexpected touch, but before I could pull away in embarrassment, his hand closed over mine, gripping it as though he were a drowning man and I his lifeline.

When he finally released me, my voice trembled slightly as I said, "But you must remember that Leonie could have just as easily rejected the prince's attentions."

He smiled briefly at my naivete. "Oh, no, that would be asking too much of her." Then he stared at me, hard. "I want you to answer something truthfully, Cassandra."

"If I can."

"Do you think me a coward for sharing my wife with another man?" When I didn't answer right away, he said, "Come, the truth. It is important to me."

I couldn't lie. "I don't think you're totally blameless, but no, I don't think you're a coward. As Maud pointed out to me, what man could refuse Edward anything?"

Geoffrey threw back his head and groaned. "But don't you see? If I truly loved my wife, it wouldn't matter who the man was. I'd wrest her away from Satan himself."

And then I understood, and the revelation left me speechless. When I regained my composure, I said, "You mean you don't really love Leonie?"

"Oh, who am I trying to fool?" he said harshly. "Maud was right. I never should have married Leonie. But did I listen? No, I was too stubborn and too blind. Now I'm imprisoned as surely as if I were in a jail."

We fell silent again, as our mounts dropped their heads and began to graze, unusually calm in the face of the turmoil their riders were experiencing.

Finally, tiring of discussing Leonie, I said, "I'm thinking of returning to Cairo."

Geoffrey turned in the saddle, startled by my news. "But, you arrived just three days ago, Cassandra. You can't leave right away."

I made a great pretense of brushing dust from my skirt so I wouldn't have to look at him as I said, "Mother and I don't seem to be able to reconcile, and I'm wondering if we ever will."

Geoffrey made an impatient sound. "As I told you in

Cairo, you've got to give yourself some time to get to know your mother. Three days is hardly enough. Besides," he added, his voice cajoling, "you haven't even seen the sights of London yet. How can you return to Egypt without even seeing the capital of the British Empire?"

I wanted to tell him how out of place I felt, like a camel at the North Pole, but I couldn't. So I just said, "London will always be here. If I don't see it this time, then another time."

Now Geoffrey was staring intently at me, his smoky eyes boring right through me. "Tell me, has learning about Leonie's lover influenced your decision to leave? Have we disgusted you with our condoning it?"

"No," I replied, shaking my head emphatically. "I realize people in society have different values, but Leonie has nothing to do with my decision. It was something Mother said to me this afternoon."

"What did she say that upset you so?"

"I prefer not to discuss it."

He didn't press me, as I feared he might. "Your mother needs you more than ever, you know. Ever since she's learned about the prince, she's often taken to her bed and has been living on those tisanes of hers. She seems to have headaches quite often, and I'm worried about her health."

Why was he telling me this, I wondered? Was he truly concerned about Mother, or merely playing on my sympathies to persuade me to stay? Leonie had already warned me that her husband was adept at getting people to do what he wanted. Suddenly, I found my sympathy for him quickly being replaced by resentment.

He went on with, "Why, just yesterday, Persia told me what a comfort it was having you here, and what a great source of strength you had become to her."

I stiffened in the saddle, causing Bittersweet to shake her head and snort. "Did she really say that?"

Geoffrey nodded. "She told me she was pleased to see

you had grown into a person of exceptional character, totally unspoiled. She was especially grateful you weren't bitter toward her."

Not far from us, a red-coated soldier strolling arm-in-arm with his lady reminded me of my father. I felt a lump rise in my throat and tears sting my eyes.

"But if you won't stay for your mother, then stay for your sister."

I turned in surprise. "My sister? Leonie doesn't even want me here, let alone need me."

"She does, whether she realizes it or not. For all her august social standing, Leonie has precious few real friends, especially among women. You look at me skeptically, Cassandra, but I think your presence will have a beneficial effect on her. Perhaps you can grow as close as sisters should be, if you remain. Besides," he added, almost as an afterthought, "I am enjoying your company."

I relented. "Well, perhaps I will stay for another week or two."

"Splendid." His grin erased all harshness from his face, and he looked young and carefree.

Whether he was pleased that I was staying, or pleased that he had gotten his own way, I couldn't tell, for Geoffrey Lester was an enigmatic man who kept his feelings to himself.

We turned our horses and started back for the house.

Chapter Seven

I wish I could say it was Geoffrey's impassioned plea that persuaded me to postpone my return to Cairo, but, in reality, it was the arrival of dozens of beautiful dresses from Madame deBrisse's that changed my mind. One day after lunch, I went upstairs and there they were, stacked on my bed halfway to the top of the bedposts. As I opened box after box, to reveal the most stunning creations in every shade of sea and sky, I realized with a sinking heart that what I feared had come to pass. After accepting such gifts, I was honor-bound to stay and repay Mother with my presence. I had sold myself for a few yards of satin and lace.

As the days went on, Geoffrey took it upon himself to see to it that I was never alone and lacking for something to do. He insisted on accompanying me on my morning rides through the park, though at first I was going to refuse him, for Leonie's accusation that he had designs on me still lingered in my mind, and if it were true, I did not want to encourage him. There was enough strain between my sister and me without giving her yet another reason for disliking me so.

But I soon discovered I really had no choice but to accept Geoffrey's company. If I refused, he would demand to know why, and then I would be forced to tell him what Leonie had said. And considering the fact that she had taken an august lover of her own, I couldn't see the harm in riding with her husband every day.

After those rides, we usually returned to the house for breakfast, changed our clothes, and went to see the sights of London. We sauntered among the graves of kings and poets in Westminster Abbey and ascended the narrow stone staircase winding its way to the Whispering Gallery in St. Paul's. Whether we fed the animals bread in the Regent's Park Zoo, or strolled through the Grosvenor Gallery's latest exhibit of paintings, Geoffrey was a knowledgeable and entertaining guide. I once caused him to burst out laughing by telling him he would always have a position at the Clark's Hotel guiding tourists should he ever grow weary of the life of a gentleman.

We were slowly becoming friends, but at the time I didn't realize what a dangerous friendship it could be.

One evening at supper, Leonie announced, "Next week is Ascot Week, and Geoffrey and I have been asked to stay with the Marquis of Wellin for the event."

Edith, who always ate as though each meal were her last, stopped long enough to look surprised. "Why, I never knew you liked horse races, Leonie. You never seemed terribly interested in them while you were in Paris."

"Who could ever escape Madame Leblanc's evil eye long enough to go!" Leonie reminded her. "Anyway, Ascot isn't just the races. It's one of the highlights of the season, with parties, balls, receptions . . . And besides, Geoffrey has a horse running this year, don't you, dearest?"

As Geoffrey sipped his wine and nodded, Mother looked perturbed. "But Leonie," she said, "Cassandra doesn't have enough new gowns for Ascot. The ones we received from Madame deBrisse's are just adequate."

Without a trace of embarrassment in her voice, Leonie declared, "I'm afraid Cassandra hasn't been included in the marquis's invitation, Mother." Then she flashed me what was supposed to be a placating smile. "You don't mind remaining behind, do you, Cassandra? You'll have Mother and Maud for company."

But Geoffrey wasn't going to allow her to treat me so shabbily. His voice was deceptively bland as he said, "Oh, I'm sure if I imposed upon the marquis, he could make arrangements to accommodate another guest. Wellin Hall must have thirty bedrooms, so there's sure to be room for one more." Then he gave his wife a look daring her to contradict him.

"But dearest, you don't know if Cassandra even wants to go to Ascot with us."

Her pointed look was my hint to refuse, or else have Leonie an enemy for the duration of my stay. I cleared my throat. "Thank you for your kind invitation, Geoffrey, but I'm afraid I would feel quite out of place at Ascot."

"Well, thank heaven's that's settled," Leonie muttered as she rose, the signal for the rest of the women to rise and leave Geoffrey and Edgar to their cigars and port.

But Geoffrey ignored his wife, remained seated, and continued addressing me. "Nonsense, Cassandra. Don't you want to see as much of England as possible while you're here?"

I could feel everyone's eyes on me as I sat there, trying desperately to think of some excuse for refusing his invitation. Finally, I rose, smiled across the table at Mother, and said, "I think I would rather spend the time getting reacquainted with my mother."

It was the only excuse I could have given that Geoffrey would accept. As Mother caught my eye and smiled in warm appreciation, Geoffrey rose in surrender.

"I'm sure the time will be well spent then," he said, inclining his head at me.

As we women filed past the table on our way to the drawing room, I risked a glance at Geoffrey. I could tell from the knowing look in his eyes that I had not fooled him at all.

Later, long after Edith and Edgar had left and the rest of

the family retired for the night, I went down to the library to return a book and was startled to find Geoffrey sitting there, his long legs stretched out before him, and an open decanter of brandy on a table within convenient reach.

His eyes were half closed, giving him that sleepy, innocuous look, but I knew he was watching me hesitate in the doorway. He glanced at the clock on the table. "Why are you still awake? It's nearly midnight. Everyone else has retired."

I crossed the room to a nearby shelf and slid the book back into its slot. "I wasn't the least bit sleepy, so I stayed up to finish this book."

"As long as you're awake, why don't you sit down and talk to me?" He indicated a chair across from him.

I stood where I was. The decanter was nearly empty, and I knew from past experience with certain of Cyrus's guests that excessive drink and a late hour usually conspire to cloud a gentleman's good judgment. A wise woman keeps her distance in such a situation.

He noticed my reluctance at once, and one corner of his mouth rose in a quirky smile. "What's the matter? Are you afraid of me?"

"Don't be silly," I replied, walking over to the chair and sitting down to prove I trusted him. "Why should I be afraid of you?"

"Leonie could tell you why," he muttered, as he reached for the decanter and emptied it with a none-too-steady hand.

I let that comment pass. "Are you looking forward to Ascot Week? It must be exciting to have a horse running."

He drew his hand through his hair and scowled, as though his thoughts kept dancing just out of reach, and when he spoke, his words were halting and slurred. "No, I am not looking forward to—to Ascot Week. I am not—not looking forward to being dragged from one damned dinner party after another, trying to pretend that I'm—I'm still in love with my wife. I am not looking forward to it at all." Then he closed his eyes with a sigh and rested his head back against the chair. "I wish you would—would change your mind and come with us, Cassandra. At least I'd have someone intelligent to—to converse with."

Suddenly, I thought I heard the faint, but unmistakable, creak of a floorboard, and I glanced sharply at the library door, which I had taken the precaution of leaving open as soon as I knew Geoffrey was alone. I listened, but there was only silence in the dark hall beyond.

"As I said at dinner," I went on, "I think with Leonie away, it would be the perfect opportunity for me to come to know my mother."

Geoffrey was staring at me through narrowed eyes, and didn't seem to be listening to me or even thinking of Ascot. "You should wear your hair down more—more often. It makes you look young and—and innocent. Younger than Leonie, in fact. And as for innocent . . . that sister of yours was born knowing just what men desire."

I reached up and, to my dismay, discovered I had unpinned my hair because I was undressing for bed when I changed my mind and decided to return the book. Even without a mirror, I knew my thick, unruly tresses were flowing down my shoulders in wild abandon.

I decided to ignore his "drunk talk," as Aunt Venetia would call it, and tried to steer his thoughts away from me. "Leonie made it very clear at dinner tonight that I would not be welcome at Ascot."

Now the expression on his face changed, and I knew I was in danger. We were alone together in the library at midnight, and he was looking at me in the same way the German prince and the French artist had once looked at me in Cairo, like a wolf gauging the helplessness of a rabbit. I found myself inching down to the edge of my seat in preparation for flight.

"Hang what Leonie wants!" Geoffrey roared, then flung his glass with all his strength into the cold fireplace, where it splashed and shattered into a million tiny shards. I jumped and cried out. When he looked at me again, his face was the picture of arrogance and raw fury. "She may be the prince's whore, but I am still master in my own house, and she will do what I say!"

I rose now and stood behind my chair for protection, grasping its back to steady myself. In his volatile frame of mind, I couldn't be sure of what Geoffrey would do next, and I became increasingly aware of my own vulnerability.

"I think you've had too much to drink, Geoffrey," I said, turning and praying he would let me leave the library with some semblance of dignity.

Before I realized what was happening, Geoffrey was on his feet with the litheness of a pouncing cat, and he caught me by the wrist, effectively preventing my escape.

I whirled around to face him, my heart pounding so rapidly, surely he could hear it in this hushed room. "Let go of me this instant! Must I remind you that you are married to my sister?"

For a moment, he loomed above me, large and threatening, those inscrutable eyes boring down into my very soul, and his tight grip didn't loosen. Then he said, "I remind myself of that fact a hundred times a day," and dropped my wrist in dejection and defeat.

Free now, I resisted my initial impulse to flee. I was moved by his pain and longed to say something comforting, but I realized that he might misinterpret my words. I tried to act as though nothing unusual had happened. "Good night, Geoffrey," I said calmly, then turned.

"Good night, Cassa."

As I walked out the door, the faint, lingering scent of geraniums tickled my nostrils. In panic, I looked up and down the dark corridor, but there was no Leonie, just a teasing remnant of her presence. How much had she seen or heard, I wondered, as I hurried to the safety of my room?

* * *

Neither Geoffrey nor I mentioned the incident again, and several days later, he and Leonie departed for Ascot.

After their carriage disappeared down the street, I strolled through the house, which seemed strangely silent and empty after the intense flurry of activity just before their departure. I decided to find Mother.

She was in the garden, sitting by herself in the shade of the oak tree. I was halfway across the yard before I realized there was a man sitting in the chair beside her, hidden from view at first. He rose at my approach.

Mother turned to me and smiled. "Ah, Cassandra, I was just about to come looking for you. There is someone I'd like you to meet."

As I came closer, I could see her companion was an elegantly dressed young man of about my age, slight of build, with curly chestnut hair and a short, clipped beard.

"Cassandra," Mother began, "I'd like you to meet Lord Horace Reeve, Marquis of Sherborne, our next-door neighbor. Horace, this is my elder daughter."

"A pleasure, my lord," I murmured.

"Miss Clark, the pleasure is all mine," he said, bowing. His eyes were a warm, friendly brown, and as they quickly appraised me, they grew even warmer with approval.

I couldn't resist adding, "Were you named after the Egyptian god or the Roman poet?"

He laughed heartily, a deep, pleasant rumble. "The Roman, of course. Horus would have been an abomination." Then he added, "Please take my chair, Miss Clark. I must be on my way."

Mother looked crestfallen. "But, Horace, you've only just called. Surely you can't be running off so quickly."

"I only came to try to persuade you to join the Lesters at Ascot, and, since you have refused, my call has been for naught. My coachman is due to drive me to the station in twenty minutes."

"And do you have a horse running, my lord?" I asked, as I

seated myself. It seemed to me that many gentlemen in Leonie's circle raced horses.

The marquis nodded, those compelling brown eyes holding mine for longer than courtesy required. He really was quite good-looking, with boldly drawn features and a mouth quick to smile. "Yes, I do, Miss Clark. As a matter of fact, my Brown Bess will be running against your brother-in-law's horse."

"Good luck to you, though I must honestly say I hope Geoffrey's horse wins."

His eyes sparkled with good humor. "Ah, loyal as well as lovely. Well, good day, ladies. It's been a pleasure meeting you, Miss Clark, but I'm sure we will be seeing each other again very soon." Then he bowed and departed.

As I watched him disappear through the gate that joined the two properties, I said, "What a charming young man."

"Yes, he is," Mother readily agreed, obviously fond of him. "Horace is a member of the Marlborough House set and close to the royal family. Even the Queen approves of her son's friendship with Horace, and she doesn't approve of many of those. He comes from a very old, very noble family. Knighton and I used to be great friends of his parents' until they were lost at sea when their yacht was lost in a storm. Horace just has one younger brother, who is already distinguishing himself in the church. The family owns half of Shropshire, and they have another seat in Sussex.

"And yet, for all that, Horace is quite unspoiled and a true gentleman. He's not dissolute, like so many of them are nowadays. I can't imagine his ever saying the wrong thing or doing anything to embarrass anyone." Mother sighed. "Three quarters of the mothers in London would love to marry off their daughters to him. I even had my hopes that he and Maud would make a match of it, but she insists he's much too young for her. She's probably right. Still, I often wonder why he hasn't married, when he could have his pick of women."

"Perhaps he hasn't met the right one," I said.

Mother gave me an odd look, then picked up Maud's velvet coat and her basket of embroidery floss. "Well, enough about Horace. You don't know how pleased I was when you decided to spend this week with me instead of going to Ascot with Leonie and Geoffrey."

"Well, with my sister around, I seldom have the opportunity just to talk with you, Mother," I said.

"I'm afraid she thinks any affection I show you somehow lessens what I give to her, but, of course, that is nonsense." When I said nothing, she just smiled. "I do so love coming out here in the garden. You can smell the roses and enjoy the sunshine, and the only sounds you hear are the jays squabbling among themselves."

She was right. It was quiet and tranquil here. But my mind wasn't on the peacefulness of the scene. I had something to ask my mother and wasn't sure how I should go about it.

Finally, I just blurted out, "Mother, there is something I must ask you, and I hope you'll answer me truthfully."

Without hesitation, she replied, "If I can."

"How did you meet the Earl of What—Leonie's father?"

A shadow passed across her face and her smile froze, but her hands continued their slow, painstaking needlework. "Why do you want to know?"

"I just need to know, that's all."

"All right then, if that's what you're sure you want."

"It is."

Her hands fell still, and she stared out into space, as though looking back across time through a cloudy glass. "Your father's regiment had been transferred to yet another godforsaken corner of the Empire, and I was staying behind in England because you had just recovered from some childhood illness and weren't yet strong enough to travel. We were to join him in the spring. That fall, some noblemen were hunting not far from our cottage, and one of them suffered a bad fall. His friends came to the door and asked if the man could recuperate in my house rather than make a painful, dangerous journey by hurdle back to his host's house. I felt I couldn't very well refuse such a request if a man's life depended on it. The injured man was Reginald Butler, the Earl of Knighton."

Mother's face softened at the memory. "So, I nursed him. Later, he told me he fell in love with me the moment he regained consciousness and saw me bending over him. He always said he thought he had died, and I was the welcoming angel."

I almost scoffed at that obvious ploy, but Mother seemed to think it had been sincere, so I decided to remain silent and leave her to her illusions.

Now she reached over and brushed a stray wisp of hair away from my cheek. "Do you remember him at all, Cassandra? Of course, you were very small, then."

I shook my head, resenting her for asking. "I don't remember that time of my life at all. I've heard people often forget such unpleasant memories."

She flushed slightly and sat back. "When Reginald regained his health, he didn't return to his estate in Northumberland, but stayed with the friend with whom he had been hunting. He called every day, courting me, even though I resisted and he knew I was married and the mother of a young daughter. But soon I fell in love with him as well. When spring came, instead of joining your father, I wrote him a letter explaining that I was in love with another man and asked his forgiveness for betraying him. Then I thought it best for all concerned if I sent you to live with your aunt and uncle. Afterward, when I knew you were safe, I bolted with Knighton to Northumberland.

"Your father was a proud man, and only met with me once, to tell me he was going to divorce me for my infidelity. If I didn't want him, he wasn't going to waste his time trying to win me back."

I sat up straight and stared at her in disbelief. "What did you say?" When she repeated herself, I said indignantly, "Don't you have that all wrong, Mother? Aunt Venetia said you divorced Father, and he tried many, many times to win you back."

Her expression was patient. "Perhaps if he had tried to win me back, I would have returned to him. And, as for my divorcing him, I had no grounds. He was the injured party, not I." Now there was pity in her green eyes. "Cassandra, I realize you revere Venetia for being the mother you never had, but I'm afraid she was less than truthful with you on many occasions. She has never liked me, right from the moment I first met her, and I'm not surprised she would try to paint me as more villainous than I was."

"Well, one of you is obviously lying," I said between clenched teeth, rose, and stormed back into the house without a backward glance.

When I returned to my room, I avoided the window seats, for they would only look out over the yard and my mother sewing patiently, so I flung myself down on the bed instead.

"She's got to be lying," I said aloud, though there was no one to hear me. "She's trying to poison my mind against Father and Aunt Venetia."

Gradually, as I lay there, my boiling anger simmered, then cooled, and I became calmer and more rational. Hadn't my aunt lied to me before? In every instance, she thought herself justified, but if she had lied about my mother's death, couldn't she have lied about many other aspects of my parents' stormy marriage?

My mind was in such a state of indecision, it was causing my head to throb, so I rose. Suddenly, the prospect of spending an entire week alone with my mother seemed unbearable. I felt like a caged tigress, prowling back and forth, back and forth. I craved activity and mental stimulation.

And then I had an idea.

*   *   *

I caught up with Maud, dressed in a tailored suit and all buttressed with whalebone, just as she was about to leave for her school or one of her many philanthropic committee meetings.

"Maud," I said, taking her arm and pulling her toward the drawing room, "I must speak to you at once."

She closed the doors behind us and turned to me. "This sounds urgent."

"It is." As I faced her, I took a deep breath and my words tumbled out in a rush. "Maud, I want to work. I've been considering this very carefully, and I've decided to go to the London office of Thomas Cook's Tours and see if they can give me some type of position."

For once, Maud seemed at a loss for words, and just stared at me, her hazel eyes wide with disbelief.

"The truth of the matter is," I continued, "I've been nearly going out of my mind here with nothing to do. In Cairo, hotel guests kept me busy from dawn until midnight, and here, all I do is go riding in the morning, see a few sights with Geoffrey, and spend the rest of the day reading. I think I must have read half the books in your library by now, and I've only been here three weeks!"

Maud sat down on the divan. "That's Leonie's fault. She hasn't properly introduced you to her set. I overheard Persia telling her that we should be having some sort of reception to introduce you into society, but Leonie always has some lame excuse for not doing it."

I made a face. "To tell you the truth, Maud, I don't consider a morning spent shopping and an afternoon making calls doing anything worthwhile."

She chuckled at that. "I can see you were wise to refuse Ascot." Then her face grew set and serious. "On the other hand, I'm afraid there's not much acceptable employment for a lady such as yourself, Cassa. I can't really see you standing on your feet all day in some dressmaker's shop, trying to persuade snooty customers to buy things they don't need. Besides, Geoff would never permit it."

At that statement, I felt my ire rise. "I really don't think this should be any of your brother's concern."

"But it is. You're a guest in his house, and for you to go out working every day would reflect badly on him." Before I could utter a few acerbic comments about domineering men, Maud rose and began strolling around the room. "Hmmm. Let me think for a moment." She became lost in thought, and suddenly, her face lit up like a bonfire on Guy Fawkes Day. "I have it!" She reached over to grasp me by the arms. "How would you like to help me recruit pupils for the school?"

This was not the kind of suggestion I had been hoping for and wrinkled my nose in reluctance. "I don't know, Maud . . ."

Her hazel eyes danced with excitement. "Oh, Cassa, you would be perfect, just perfect! It would be just like the work you did at your cousin's hotel, chatting with people, putting them at their ease. You enjoyed that, didn't you?"

"Yes, but—"

"Well, just as you explained the sights of Egypt to your guests, you would tell the girls and their families about the Lester Commercial School. You would point out the many benefits and explain how exceptional students are allowed to study without cost. I'm sure you'd find it easy." Now Maud was practically floating on air with excitement. "Oh, please say you will at least try it, Cassa. Please say yes!"

I was still skeptical. "Do you really think I'm suitable for such work?"

"Of course you are! You're pretty, intelligent, and likable. Besides, it will keep you occupied while not offending anyone's sensibilities. Charity work has always been acceptable employment for ladies, you know. And just think of all the women whose lives you'll change for the better. What more could anyone ask?"

She was very convincing, and I suddenly felt a wry touch of sympathy for all those who had to come up against the formidable Miss Maud Lester when she wanted something.

"All right, Maud. I'll try it "

"Splendid. We'll start tonight."

The carriage rolled to a halt. Maud poked her head out of the window and looked around. "It would seem we're here."

As a footman opened the door for us and we stepped down, the driver up in his box called, "You had best be careful, Miss Maud. I don't like the looks of this neighborhood."

And neither did I. The old stone houses looked grim and desolate, and I sensed curious, hostile eyes observing us, though, as I glanced around uneasily, I could not see anyone watching us from those dimly lit windows. I shivered and pulled my shawl more closely about me, wondering why I had ever agreed to this.

"We'll be careful, Fred, don't you worry," Maud called back, as she took a lantern from the footman and headed toward a doorway.

Once inside, she turned to me and said, "Unfortunately, the girls most in need of training at the school live in the poorest neighborhoods, but it can't be helped. They can't be expected to come to me, so I—we—must ferret them out and make them listen to reason."

There were no lights in the narrow, dirty hallway, and Maud's lantern cast eerie, shivering shadows on the stairs and chipped plaster walls, but she was undaunted as she bustled forward. "Watch that step, Cassa," she warned me. "It seems to be loose. We can't risk an injury now, can we?"

When we reached the top of the stairs, Maud consulted a slip of paper in her hand, then turned down a dark corridor that reeked of cooking oil, bacon, and onions, and if she hadn't had her lantern, we surely would have tripped over a gaunt old man sound asleep against one wall, his spindly legs taking up half the hall.

Maud noticed me wrinkle my nose at the man's filthy rags. "They've got to sleep somewhere, haven't they? I should have thought you had seen worse in Cairo."

"Somehow, one expects it in Cairo," I retorted, "not here."

She smiled at that as she stopped before a door, knocked briskly, then waited. No answer. She knocked again, more forcefully this time.

"Miss Falkirk, are you in there?"

In response, the door opened just a crack, and a haggard face peered out. "Who are you, and what do you want?"

"My name is Maud Lester, and this is my assistant, Miss Clark. We're from the commercial school, and we'd like to speak to your daughter, if you don't mind."

"It's all right, Ma," a squeaky voice said from within, and the door opened, revealing a slight girl of about fifteen.

"Good evening, ma'am," she said politely, sketching a brief curtsey. "Another lady from the school said you'd be callin' tonight."

Maud smiled as she sailed into the room, which, I could see, from the black iron stove in one corner and bare mattresses on the floor, served as both kitchen and bedroom for its two occupants.

"How do you do, Katie?" Maud said. "And this must be your mother. How do you do, Mrs. Falkirk?"

The older woman, a gaunt, worn version of her daughter, nervously wiped her chapped hands on her apron before shaking Maud's outstretched hand. "Won't you please sit down?" she said, indicating several chairs at a rickety table.

"So kind of you," Maud murmured and took her seat as though she were always accustomed to sitting at the kitchen table when she called.

When we were seated, she explained to Katie and her mother all about the Lester Commercial School, the subjects taught there, and what its graduates could expect once they had had their training. She was warm, enthusiastic, and most persuasive.

But, most of all, Maud stressed the economic advantages of commercial training to Katie, and showed how she would earn more money than a seamstress or factory worker, and work fewer hours in the bargain. As Katie and her mother exchanged hopeful looks, I could see that this is what interested them the most. Money. Money for food, clothing, and a decent place to live. I suddenly caught Maud's fervor and prayed Katie would agree to enroll in the school.

Maud went on for another half hour, but I suspect young Katie was already convinced. By the time we left and got back into the carriage, Katie Falkirk assured Maud she would be a new student in the fall.

"That seemed rather easy," I said as I settled my skirts around me, feeling that I had, in some small way, contributed to Maud's success tonight.

"Oh, you think so, do you? Let me assure you most of my recruits are just the opposite of Katie." Maud stopped to rub her ribs and curse her corset before saying, "Most of the girls defy me to persuade them to enroll. Most of them tell me that they can earn more money by becoming streetwalkers than by working in an office. And they're right. I won't deny it. Sometimes it takes three or four visits before I can convince them on moral grounds that I offer them a better opportunity in a respectable occupation."

My heart sank. "It sounds like a hopeless battle."

"Oh, it's not for the faint of heart," she assured me as the carriage rolled off, "but I think you're very courageous, Cassa. I don't mean to discourage you before you've even started. When a girl resists, she becomes a challenge, and if you do win her over, victory is so, so sweet, and the satisfaction of saving a fellow human being from misery and degradation is immeasurable." She added as an afterthought, "Of course, you lose some as well."

"Well, I'd certainly like to try to help you, Maud."

"Good. I knew I could count on you." And she outlined her plan for indoctrinating me, swearing, "By the time I'm finished with you, you'll be able to take my place."

I thought of Cyrus. "I'll be your Right Arm."

Maud chuckled. "I like that. Yes, you'll be my Right Arm."

By the end of the week, Maud was merely the observer, and I the leader of the recruiting mission. I was the one who presented the school's case to often reluctant girls and their suspicious parents, and I was the one who suffered if they refused. But I always went back and tried again. And again. I hadn't felt so useful since leaving Cairo.

I was so absorbed in this new task, I didn't think about Leonie or Geoffrey at all. Little did I realize how much my life would change once they returned.

Maud and I were just going out for the afternoon, when she stopped and said, "My goodness. I almost forgot. Geoff and Leo are due back from Ascot today."

"I've been so absorbed in our work, Maud, I must confess I haven't thought of them in days."

She chuckled. "Nor I. I can't say that I've missed dear Leo at all."

Almost as if on cue, the front door swung open, and the foyer was suddenly filled with harried, scurrying footmen. In moments, a radiant Leonie herself came gliding through the door, followed by Geoffrey, who looked sullen.

"Ah, the travelers return," Maud said, descending the stairs. She went up to her brother and gave him a puzzled look, followed by a sisterly kiss on the cheek. "Welcome home, Geoff." She did not kiss her sister-in-law, merely inclined her head and murmured, "Leo . . . How was Ascot?"

"Divine, just divine," Leonie gushed, as she placed her parasol on the hall table. "The balls were lavish, and we even rode in Edward's carriage for the Tuesday promenade.

You should have heard everyone cheer us!" Then she took her husband's arm and beamed at him. "And tell them the most exciting part, dearest."

Whatever this exciting news was, it didn't seem to move him at all. His face was tight and weary, and a line was between his brows again. But at the sight of me, standing off silently to one side and overshadowed by Leonie, something thawed inside, and a warmth lit up his eyes for just a second.

"You haven't yet greeted Cassa," he said to his wife.

She flicked a dismissive look in my direction and said, "Well, how could I, with her hiding off in a corner like that? How *are* you, Cassandra?"

"Just fine, Leonie," I said.

Before Geoffrey could utter a word of greeting to me, Leonie bubbled, "Black Moth came in first! Isn't that exciting? Geoffrey's horse won the Gold Cup!"

So the Marquis of Sherborne's horse had lost. After Maud and I had congratulated Geoffrey, Leonie said, "Shall we all go into the drawing room? We have so much to tell you about our week." Then she looked over her shoulder and said, "Cassa, do be a dear and go fetch Mother, will you? I don't want to have to repeat myself."

Geoffrey stopped and glared down at her. "Cassandra is not a servant, Leonie. Heffer can fetch your mother."

"I don't mind," I said quickly and went running off to find my mother before Leonie lost her temper and created a scene.

We gathered in the drawing room and listened attentively as my sister took center stage and regaled us with anecdotes about her week at the races. There was nothing about Geoffrey or his horse, just a recitation of all the women who tried to imitate her by wearing pink dresses and their hair *à la Lester,* and I found my attention wandering to yet another girl I would try to recruit that night. I grew even more restless as Leonie launched into the details of some society scandal that was the talk of the town, and as I glanced around the room, I noticed that everyone else seemed bored as well.

Finally, Maud interrupted Leonie long enough to say, "Well, Cassa hasn't been idle in your absence. Would you care to guess what she's been doing?"

"Avoiding the sun," Leonie said, plainly irritated by the interruption. "Her brown complexion has finally faded."

Maud gave her a scathing glance. "No. I've been teaching her how to recruit pupils for my school."

Leonie shuddered delicately. "How perfectly horrid! How can you bear to associate with such people, Cassandra?"

"I don't mind. In fact, it makes me feel rather useful," I replied.

From his place at the mantel, Geoffrey was regarding me with a look of approval that made me feel warm inside.

My sister sighed. "All this dreary talk of being useful is boring me to tears. I think I shall go and rest before tea."

I never realized how very shallow my sister was until that moment. She couldn't bear to share the limelight with me for one second.

Now Maud rose also. "Well, Geoff, as much as we'd love to hear what you have to say about Ascot, Cassa and I were just about to leave. We'll talk later."

He nodded, and we left, but he went out himself, and we didn't see him for the rest of the evening.

The next day, I had Sally bring me breakfast on a tray so I could finish the last few pages of a report for Maud.

As I wrote, there came a knock at the door, and I barely looked up as I called, "Come in."

The door swung open, and there stood Geoffrey, dressed for riding and frowning in displeasure.

"Well," he demanded preemptorially, before I could say a word of greeting. "Aren't you dressed yet?"

My eyes widened in surprise. "But I *am* dressed."

"I meant, why aren't you dressed for our morning ride?"

Now I understood. "I'm sorry. I haven't been riding ever since I began helping Maud. I'm afraid I quite forgot about our morning rides together."

"Well, change into your habit and be quick about it," he ordered, tapping his riding crop against his thigh. "The horses are saddled and waiting."

Then he whirled on his heel and left before I could open my mouth and decline his invitation.

After he had gone, I just stood staring at the closed door in astonishment that was quickly giving way to anger.

"The audacity of the man!" I cried, flinging down my pen and rising to go after him. No man, not even Cyrus, had ever spoken to me that way before, and I resented it. Well, I was certainly going to let him know my feelings on the subject of high-handed men.

My hand was on the doorknob, when I hesitated, overcome with second thoughts about such a rash action. I reminded myself that I was a guest in Geoffrey's house, living here through his generosity. Still, did that give him any right to order me about without so much as a by-your-leave? After all, I was not his valet or his butler. The least he could have done was to ask me politely if I would mind accompanying him on his ride.

Well, I decided, ringing for Sally to help me change from my morning dress into a riding habit, I would accompany him today without argument, but I was going to let him know in no uncertain terms that I did not appreciate his commandeering tone.

When I joined Geoffrey in the drive, his mood hadn't improved, for he still wore his scowl and he was pacing back and forth like a restless panther, his hands clasped behind him.

When he saw me, all he said was, "If you haven't ridden Bittersweet for over a week, she's sure to be frisky this morning." As he gave me a hand, he added ominously, "I hope she doesn't throw you."

I did not smile as I settled myself in the saddle and took the reins, and the testiness in my voice matched his own as I retorted, "I felt Maud's report was much more important than exercising Bittersweet."

"Oh, you did, did you now?" Geoffrey mounted Westwind effortlessly, and, for once, the stallion was rather docile.

I wish I could have said the same for my little mare. All those days of standing in her stall had taken their toll, and it was she who was dancing in place and pulling at the bit to be off. When I did touch my heel to her side, she broke straight into a canter that nearly sent me flying back over her rump, and I had all I could do to regain my balance and bring her under control.

"That's a lesson for you," Geoffrey said with something like relish as we walked our horses out into the street. "When a horse is your responsibility, you must exercise it regularly or take the consequences."

I didn't thank him for the lesson, just looked straight ahead and rode on in stony silence.

As we rode down Upper Brook Street, past housemaids washing windows, Geoffrey kept stealing glances at me, as though expecting me to smile and engage him in conversation.

Suddenly, he growled, "Are you going to spend the entire morning sulking like a child? I'd expect such behavior from Leonie, not you."

My head snapped round, and I felt the blood rush to my cheeks. "I wasn't aware that I was sulking."

"What else would you call the great, frosty silence enveloping you at this moment?" He pretended to shiver. "I detect a noticeable autumn chill in the air, but it would appear to be still summer."

When I stared straight ahead and said nothing, Geoffrey

stopped taunting me to say, "Come, come, Cassandra.
You've been furious with me ever since we started out. What
is the matter?"

I took a deep breath and vented my resentment of the way
he had treated me. "You never even asked me if I wanted to
go riding with you this morning, merely ordered me to get
dressed and join you. You sounded like one of Cyrus's insuf-
ferable guests ordering a donkey boy about."

His aristocratic chin came up, and he stared down at me
out of those inscrutable eyes, and when he spoke, his tone
was mocking. "I just assumed these morning rides were as
important to you as they were to me, but obviously, I was
wrong." Suddenly, his face became rigid and devoid of expression, as he halted his horse right in the middle of the
street. "Well, if you have more pressing matters to attend to,
miss, I suggest you go back to the house and attend to them.
I'm sorry I took you away from your precious reports."

And, with a mocking nod of his head, he set his heels to
Westwind and went galloping down the street, leaving me to
stand there and stare after him.

For a moment, I just sat there, chagrined, while carriages
rumbled past and other horsemen blatantly stared at me, a
lady alone, without even a groom for protection. At first, I
was furious with him, but as I thought about his actions, I
began to wonder what had set him off so. It was not like
Geoffrey to order me about so callously. And to gallop off,
leaving a lady alone to the mercy of passersby . . .

My own irritation dissipated in a flood of curiosity and
compassion, and I urged Bittersweet after him. I had to discover what had caused this change in him, though I was beginning to suspect it had more to do with Leonie and Ascot
than me.

When I arrived at the park, I headed immediately for Rotten Row, where I was sure Geoffrey had gone to exercise
Westwind.

As I was craning my neck for any sign of him among the crush of riders, I suddenly heard a voice call out my name, and I turned to see the Marquis of Sherborne riding toward me.

"Why, Lord Sherborne, what a pleasant surprise," I said.

I must have sounded disappointed or preoccupied, for he frowned and said sharply, "Is something the matter, Miss Clark? You seem quite distressed."

"I think I have lost Geoffrey. You haven't seen him anywhere, have you?"

The marquis smiled slightly. "No, I haven't. But perhaps we can search for him together."

Bittersweet, now more docile, fell into step beside his horse, and we walked slowly down the thoroughfare, scanning the faces for any sign of Geoffrey. My companion himself cut a dashing figure in his black cutaway coat and glossy top hat, and I noticed many women stealing longing and admiring glances at him as we rode by.

"Will you accept my condolences, my lord?" I said.

His brows rose in comic surprise. "For what, Miss Clark? Being saddled with a name like Horace?"

I laughed. "No, for losing at Ascot."

"Oh, that is no great loss, Miss Clark. My horses usually lose. They're a notoriously inept lot and a constant source of embarrassment to me." His eyes sparkled as he grinned. "I don't know why I bother racing them at all, but a gentleman must do something with all his time. Besides, my father raced horses and his father before him, so I feel honor-bound to continue the tradition. The only difference is, their horses always won."

And, as we continued, this droll, charming man, whom I was beginning to like more and more with every passing moment, regaled me with tales of his horses. Brown Bess always finished second, no matter what the race, and one named Chester II was the laughingstock of turf circles because he persisted in finishing dead last, no matter what the field.

Then there was one named Gallant Knight who had shown early promise by actually winning a race. But only one. I laughed often and soon had forgotten all about my earlier argument with Geoffrey.

Suddenly, my companion's lighthearted mood changed, and he became serious. "When I saw you come galloping into the park, Miss Clark, I could see you were very upset about something. Forgive me for my boldness, but your mother has spoken of you so often, I feel as if I know you, even though we've only just met. I hope you will think of me as a friend you can turn to, if ever the need should arise."

I was deeply touched. "Why, thank you, Lord Sherborne. I shall remember that."

His carefree mood returned. "Splendid."

Suddenly, I saw Geoffrey walking a lathered Westwind toward us, and, by the rigid set of his jaw, I could tell that his surly mood hadn't improved.

He nodded curtly at Sherborne, then said to me, "Are you ready to go home now?"

"Yes, Geoffrey." Then I smiled brightly at Lord Sherborne and said, "Good day to you, Lord Sherborne."

"Miss Clark . . . the pleasure was all mine. I look forward to seeing you again very soon."

As Bittersweet fell into step with Westwind and we were out of Lord Sherborne's hearing, Geoffrey said, "Haven't I warned you about riding alone in the park? A woman is apt to attract attention of the most unsavory kind, and I don't mean the marquis."

"But I did have an escort," I reminded him gently, "until he left me standing in the middle of the street."

A muscle twitched in Geoffrey's jaw as he continued to stare straight ahead. He was silent for the longest time, and when he finally spoke, he startled me by saying, "What was your real reason for refusing my invitation to Ascot?"

So this is what had been preying on his mind all this time.

I knew I couldn't lie to him again, so I took a deep breath, looked directly at him, and said, "I thought Leonie would resent me if I went, yet I couldn't very well say that in front of everyone at dinner."

"Ah, I suspected as much."

"But I wasn't totally untruthful," I protested. "I did want the time alone with my mother."

Now he did look at me. "But, as I told you in the library that night, Cassandra, I am master in my own home and my word is law. You have nothing to fear from Leonie."

"But I didn't wish to turn her against me!" I cried, causing Bittersweet to snort in surprise. "I want us to learn to be sisters. We've already wasted twenty years not knowing of each other's existence."

"You may desire it, but I doubt that Leonie does, so you can stop trying to curry her favor, for she will only take advantage of your generosity and mock you for it."

Deep disappointment welled up inside of me, and I had to fight back the tears.

He sensed my distress at once and reached out to cover my hand with his. "So, the next time you decide to sacrifice yourself for your sister, think again. And never, ever feel that you must make excuses to me. I am not the unfeeling ogre that Leonie would have you believe. I would have understood your reasons for declining my invitation, you know."

I apologized, then said, "I will remember that."

"See that you do."

Then we rode in silence all the way home.

Chapter Eight

The Wednesday after Leonie returned from Ascot, she finally decided to include me in her social activities.

Mother and I had declared a truce of sorts and were lunching together, when I received a summons from Leonie to join her in her rooms immediately. With an apologetic shrug for my mother, I followed my sister's maid upstairs.

Maud had told me that Leonie and Geoffrey had gone to a ball the previous night and hadn't returned until early in the morning. I was, therefore, not surprised, when I entered my sister's bedchamber, to see her reclining against dozens of pillows at the head of her huge mahogany bed.

"Ah, sister dear," she murmured in a hoarse morning voice as she poured herself a cup of tea from her breakfast tray. Her straight hair flowed down past her shoulders in a sheet of spun gold, making her look like a guileless child or a tiny doll.

I stood by her bedside. "You wished to see me, Leonie?"

She indicated a chair, and when I sat down, she said, "I've decided that, since you *are* my sister, it's time you were introduced into my circle of friends."

My friends. Weren't they Geoffrey's friends, too, I wondered?

"This afternoon, you'll start accompanying Geoffrey and me on our rides through the park. And, since tomorrow is Thursday, you may attend my at home." She sounded as though she were conferring a great honor. Then the violet eyes darted over me. "I'm sure you have something suitable to wear, now that your new clothes have arrived from Madame deBrisse's?"

"Mother will help me select something suitable," I said.

Her eyes narrowed as she scrutinized me more carefully. "If Heloise, my maid, arranges your hair, I'm sure you won't disgrace me. At least that horrid brown complexion has finally faded."

I held my temper in check as I said, "I will do my best not to disgrace you, Leonie. Will that be all?"

"Yes. Just be ready by half past four. Promptly."

"I shall." I rose, now that my interview was over. "Will Mother be accompanying us?"

She looked at me as though I were daft. "Of course not. I thought you knew by now that, as a divorced woman, Mother is not received in society."

I was learning not to be surprised by Leonie's small cruelties, yet I couldn't resist saying, "But she's your *mother*, Leonie. Surely her feelings come before any senseless social convention."

"Social conventions aren't senseless. They bring order to an otherwise chaotic world, and keep people in their place. And, unlike yourself, Mother understands why she can't accompany us, Cassandra. She wouldn't *want* to cause me embarrassment." Then, she dismissed me with a curt wave of her hand.

There was no arguing with her, so I left my sister to finish her breakfast, while I returned to the dining room and my luncheon.

At first, I hesitated to tell Maud about my sudden entry into London society, for she had always made it quite plain that she considered such activities frivolous and not worth her effort. She surprised me when I did tell her, by saying, "Well, Leo can hardly keep you hidden away in the attic like some idiot relative, can she now?"

We were in her sitting room—office, discussing our next recruiting mission, and she gathered her papers together. "I just hope you won't turn into another Leo, Cassa. You're far too valuable to me for that."

Pleasure surged through me, and I smiled in delight. "Am I really, Maud?"

Her hazel eyes sparkled. "Aren't you my Right Arm? Yes, you've been doing quite well for the school, better than I'd ever hoped, in fact. In the eight recruiting missions you've gone on, five girls have enrolled. If this keeps up, I'll have to expand the school."

I sat back in my chair, absurdly pleased with myself.

"But, before you become too cocky, my girl, I have a special assignment for you, and it's a most difficult one."

I leaned forward eagerly. "Oh?"

While looking down at the paper before her, Maud kept tugging at her hair until it sprouted every which way. "Her name is Betty Frakes. She works in a factory that manufactures matches, and is the sole support of an old blind aunt and three younger brothers. I've gone to see her six times already, and I just can't seem to make her see the wisdom of attending the school. The last time I was there, she wouldn't even open the door to me." Now Maud glanced up, and I could tell she was concerned. "I'm afraid if I don't reach her soon, she'll take to the streets. But perhaps she'll listen to you."

"Where does she live?" I asked, and as I listened, Maud recited the address while writing it on a small scrap of paper.

Suddenly, there came a knock on the door, and when Maud said, "Come in," Mother entered.

"Cassa," she said, barely able to keep the excitement out of her voice, "it's time to dress you for the promenade."

I left Maud and began preparing for my debut into London society.

An hour later, after Mother had helped me to dress and Heloise to arrange my hair into a cascade of soft curls at the back, I stood before the cheval glass to inspect their handiwork.

"Cassa, you look beautiful," Mother declared, clasping her hands together as her eyes sparkled in delight.

"That dress is most becoming, miss," Heloise agreed.

Refutations rose to my lips, but were never uttered. Although I could not bring myself to say I was beautiful, I could admit that I was perhaps pretty in a dark, exotic way, like the women of Cairo. The aqua silk of my gown flattered my complexion, and the saucy osprey plume on my hat gave me a dashing air. As I slowly turned back and forth before the glass, I found myself wondering what Geoffrey would think of me in all my finery.

"Well," Mother said, "hurry along now. I think Leonie and Geoffrey are waiting for you downstairs, and you know patience is not one of your sister's virtues."

I hurried down the hall, and when I reached the stairs and descended to the landing, I heard Leonie's exasperated voice. "Whatever can be keeping her? If we don't leave now, we'll be late."

"You know, if you keep scowling, you'll mar your considerable beauty with ugly lines, my dear," I heard Geoffrey reply. "I'll go look for her."

He turned and strode toward the stairs, and when he glanced up and saw me standing there, he stopped, with one foot on the first step. Our eyes met, and, in that instant, Geoffrey was caught completely off guard. He looked as though he were seeing me for the first time.

"Ah, at last!" Leonie called up to me impatiently. "Whatever took you so long?"

I thought this amusing, since my sister looked as though she had spent half the afternoon at her toilette, but I had eyes only for Geoffrey as he slowly came up the stairs and extended his hand to me.

"You look exquisite, Cassa," he said, his fingers tightening on mine and causing me to blush.

"Yes, yes, you look very nice, Cassandra, very nice indeed. Now, can we please be off? And, Cassandra," Leonie added as she glanced at herself in the foyer mirror one last time, "don't forget your parasol. You don't want your face to turn that common brown again."

Just at that moment, Mother came hurrying down the stairs with the requisite parasol, and the three of us were finally off to our promenade.

All during the drive to the park, Leonie was in a sullen mood, and spent the entire time staring out into space, saying little unless spoken to, but the moment our carriage turned Hyde Park corner and started down the carriage road, an astonishing change swept over her. The sulky pout she had worn since leaving the house vanished, to be replaced by a look of sheer radiance and anticipation. Her mouth was curved in a warm, inviting smile, and her eyes sparkled coquettishly. It was as though she were Sarah Bernhardt, readying herself for a command performance, and, in a moment, I could understand why.

As Fred steered the horses as close as possible to the railing that separated the lower classes from their betters, we became the center of attention.

"There she is!" I heard a boy cry as he pointed to my sister. "It's Lady Lester!"

Suddenly, hundreds of heads turned at once, and a loud hue and cry was raised, as though some lucky huntsman had sighted the elusive fox. A great wave of humanity surged forward. People jostled and elbowed one another out of the way, fighting for a glimpse of Leonie as we rode by, and those not so fortunate as to be standing close to the rail stood on painted wrought-iron benches and peered over the heads of those in front of them. Many spectators waved, reached out, and called her by name as if they knew her personally, and were granted a dazzling smile and wave in return. Geoffrey and I ceased to exist.

The pedestrians were not the only ones under Leonie's spell. In every passing carriage, men tipped their tall hats, and elegant women with spaniels in their laps nodded and smiled in our direction, hoping for some acknowledgment from the prince's favorite. Every so often, a woman would look my way, then lean forward to whisper something to her companions, and they in turn would stare boldly at me. I had never been the object of such scrutiny in my life and found panic starting to overtake me. But I breathed deeply and forced myself to think of Cairo and all of the wealthy, fashionable people with whom I had mingled there, and I was able to relax, sit back, and smile in return. I, too, played my assigned role, trying to be a credit to Geoffrey, though he seemed quite indifferent to the attention we were receiving.

The only person I did recognize was the bold, rakish Lord Rushton, sitting back in his open landau and eyeing all the lovely young women, a pasha inspecting his harem. At his side was a plain, overdressed woman with small, piercing eyes and the hooked nose of an eagle; I presumed her to be his wife Fiona. Whenever she caught her husband's eye wandering, she regarded the object of his attention with a cold, hostile stare of warning. Since Lord Rushton grinned and tipped his hat to me as our carriages passed, I, too, felt those hard eyes on me.

Suddenly, Leonie's attention was diverted from her adoring public, and her face lit up even brighter. "There's Edward's carriage," she said excitedly, placing her hand on Geoffrey's arm. "Be a dear and have Fred pull over, won't you?"

The order was given, though Geoffrey looked pained, as though steeling himself to have a tooth pulled, and our carriage eased out of the congested thoroughfare and moved onto an open space beneath some tall, shady trees. I watched out of the corner of my eye as the royal carriage followed, an open landau pulled by high-stepping horses wearing royal red browbands on their bridles.

Leonie must have seen my look of sheer fear, for she gripped my arm hard and said, "I trust you won't make a fool of yourself, Cassandra. Just bow from the waist when introduced, and don't speak until Their Highnesses address you first. Do you think you can manage that?"

Before I could reply, Geoffrey glared at her and growled, "I'm sure Cassa won't disgrace you, Leonie."

As the royal carriage drew up across from us and stopped, I couldn't resist staring at the man who was the cause of so much heartache in my family. Albert Edward, Prince of Wales, heir to the British throne, was indeed the portly, middle-aged man I had seen on the stairs that night. Now I realized why he had looked so familiar at the time. From the time I was a child, I had seen his likeness often enough in the illustrated newspapers.

"Good day to you, Lady Lester-r . . . Lester-r," he greeted us. His voice was surprisingly deep and guttural, and I noticed he had a tendency to roll the *r*'s of certain words.

By his side, the Princess Alexandra smiled graciously, and I was at once struck by her great beauty, youthfulness, and dignity. Where did she find the strength to be so charming to a woman she knew was having an affair with her husband?

"Good day to you, Your Highnesses," Leonie said. "I'd like to present my sister, Cassandra Clark, if I may."

As soon as the prince's prominent blue eyes met mine, I bowed, as Leonie had instructed.

"Miss Clar-rk," he said warmly. "What a pleasure it is to meet you at long last. Lady Lester-r has told us so much about you."

"Thank you, Your Royal Highness," I replied in a voice that trembled ever so slightly. "The honor is mine."

Then he leaned over toward the princess and repeated my name, causing me to wonder if the princess were hard of hearing. But before I could speculate further, she turned, smiled at me, and said, "How do you do, Miss Clark?" in a charming Danish accent.

I bowed once again and murmured that the pleasure was mine.

Now the prince turned his attention to Geoffrey.

"Congr-ratulations once again on your win at Ascot, Lester-r. Now I wish I had placed a substantial wager on Black Moth instead of my own horse."

Geoffrey's smile lacked any real warmth as he said, "Thank you, Your Royal Highness. I'm sure one day you'll lead your own horse into the winner's circle."

I had the feeling Geoffrey treated the prince with as much civility and courtesy as was required, but nothing more. He might have to accept his role as *mari complaisant*, but Geoffrey had set the conditions. The prince could not go so far as to expect friendship from him. Tolerance, perhaps, but not friendship. That would be too much to ask.

Evidently, the prince didn't think so, for something like consternation flared in his eyes, then vanished almost as quickly. He merely chuckled good-naturedly. "I look forward to that day."

Then Leonie complimented Princess Alexandra on her beautiful ensemble, and a few pleasantries were exchanged about the lovely weather and the huge crowd in the park. Finally, the prince said he hoped all of us would attend the many state functions planned for the Shah of Persia's visit in July. They bade us good day and drove off to parade before their other subjects.

When they were out of earshot, I turned to Leonie and said, "Is the princess deaf?"

She nodded. "Yes, she is, poor thing. She suffered from a fever some years ago that left her hard of hearing and lame in one leg. And she always wears necklaces and dresses with high collars to hide a scar on her throat, the result of yet another illness when she was a child." Leonie shook her head, and it was the first time I had ever seen her show compassion for another human being. Perhaps she was not as heartless as everyone believed.

This bit of information made me feel an aching sorrow for Alexandra, a woman who had obviously suffered so much already, but I said nothing as our carriage completed its lengthy circle round the park and we left for home.

If I had thought my entrance into London society had been harrowing, I had yet to face my first at home with Leonie the following afternoon.

Dressed in a new gown of seafoam green muslin, my hair having once again been arranged by Heloise, I joined Leonie in the drawing room at one o'clock. No sooner were we seated than callers began arriving. The gentlemen, I noticed, didn't surrender their hats and canes to Heffer, or leave them on the table in the foyer, but carried them into the drawing room and placed them on the floor to let everyone know they were not staying for any length of time, but just visiting. The conversation was always light and frothy, and callers remained for only fifteen minutes or less before wishing us good day and leaving to make other calls.

The only familiar face among the parade of lords and ladies was the Marquis of Sherborne, who gave me a conspiratorial smile from across the room before coming over to rescue me from the clutches of a deaf old duchess with a loud, screeching voice that would have deafened me if I had listened to it a moment longer.

"Miss Clark, are you aware of the sensation you caused yesterday in the park? No, I can see that you're not. Every young man of my acquaintance fancies himself in love with you already."

I blushed at his profuse compliments. "Please, my lord, you're embarrassing me."

"Believe me, Miss Clark, I wouldn't do that for the world. I am merely speaking the truth." Before he could say another word, a matronly woman interrupted us and led the marquis away to meet her daughter. They kept him in their thrall for the longest time, and, though he kept catching my eye and grimacing in consternation, he could not extricate himself without being rude. And the Marquis of Sherborne was never rude.

Just as the river of callers trickled off and I was beginning to think this interminable affair nearly over, none other than Lord Rushton himself walked in, with a woman clutching his arm as though she feared he might run off. She was the woman I had seen in his carriage yesterday, so I knew she must be his wife.

Lord Rushton's mischievous black eyes sought me across the room, and he nodded and grinned. His wife caught that smile and glared at me as though her husband's flirtatiousness were somehow my fault.

"Ah, Adam and Fiona," Leonie said, rising from the chaise to cross the room toward them. "I was beginning to think you wouldn't come today."

Lord Rushton's wife touched her lips to Leonie's cheek. "We came expressly to meet your sister," she said, her voice carrying. "How naughty of you, Leonie, to keep such a beauty hidden away all this time."

From the frozen smile on my sister's face, I sensed that she did not appreciate hearing me referred to as a beauty. I suspect Lady Rushton had used the complimentary term in a deliberate effort to irritate Leonie.

When my sister brought them to introduce me, she retaliated by saying to me, "And you've already met Lord Rushton several times, Cassandra," causing Lady Rushton to glance at her husband in suspicion.

"Yes, I've already had the pleasure," he said smoothly, bowing over my hand. Then to allay his wife's fears, he added, "I met Miss Clark riding with Geoffrey one day, my dove."

She muttered, "I see," through tightly pursed lips. I could tell that she was searching for some hidden meaning to her husband's truthful words.

All during their visit, I had the distinct impression Lady

Rushton didn't like me, and I was relieved when she left and my first at home was finally over.

Surprisingly enough, my sister seemed as relieved as I, for she sighed as she leaned back on the chaise, kicked off her slippers, and relaxed. "So, what do you think of Lady Rushton?"

I didn't know what to say. "She seems pleasant enough."

"Dear, dear Cassandra," Leonie mocked me. "Can't you ever say anything unkind about someone who so richly deserves it? Fiona Rushton is a harridan who keeps her poor husband on a leash and is jealous of any pretty young woman who looks his way. I think she would fit him with a dog collar and keep him chained to her side day and night, if she could get away with it. She loves Adam so desperately, her possessive behavior borders on the vulgar."

I suddenly felt a pang of pity for the obsessive Lady Rushton, another woman, like my mother, so consumed by love that she was doomed to act irrationally.

Now Leonie was looking at me with an odd expression on her face. "And she doesn't like you at all. I could tell that right away."

I bristled. "Why, she doesn't even know me well enough to dislike me!"

"She knows that her husband is attracted to you, and that is enough to make you her mortal enemy. I also suspect Adam enjoys teasing her with tales of his many conquests."

"How cruel!" I exclaimed, disliking Adam Rushton even more.

"I am serious, Cassandra. I would be on my guard, if I were you. Fiona may not have any style, but she can make life most unpleasant for you."

I failed to see how, for I did not plan ever to be in Lord Rushton's company again, but I knew that arguing with Leonie was an exercise in futility. I thanked her for the warning and went upstairs to prepare for my interview with Betty Frakes.

*   *   *

It was past eleven o'clock, and a thick, yellowish fog blanketed the street as I trudged out of the Frakes's house toward the carriage waiting in the warm circle of a street lamp's glow.

Bitter failure weighed heavily against my shoulders, and tears of frustration stung my eyes. I was tired, stiff, and cold, and longed to be back at Lester House.

"Is that you, miss?" I heard Fred's solid voice call down from his perch.

"Yes," I replied. "I'm sorry to keep you men waiting so late."

"We didn't mind, miss. Just doing our job. But the master is sure to be worried."

The master was the furthest thought from my mind as the footman held the door open for me, and I dragged myself inside, falling against the cushions with a disgusted moan. I had failed, and what was worse than not having convinced Betty Frakes to enroll in the school was the fact that she had convinced me it would not be in her best interests to do so. Maud had warned me that this would be my toughest case yet, but she hadn't quite prepared me for the sense of utter helplessness I would feel.

I had met the old, blind aunt whom Betty supported, as well as the young woman's three younger brothers, boisterous boys, all under the age of ten. Their father had abandoned them after the birth of the youngest, and their mother had died just months previously of injuries sustained when she had fallen into a machine at the factory where she worked, leaving young Betty with the care of the family resting on her slender shoulders. The pittance Betty earned in the match factory was far from enough, and she told me proudly that one of the supervisors wanted to set her up in a fine house of her own in a better neighborhood. She would never have to return to the factory again, and he graciously offered to support her family as well.

I tried every argument Maud had taught me and a few of my own to convince the beautiful, dark-eyed young woman to change her mind and enroll in the Lester Commercial School. I pleaded, cajoled, and even threatened her with eternal damnation, but to no avail. Betty Frakes was determined to take the course she had chosen for herself, and there was no changing her mind.

I had no choice but to admit defeat and leave.

Now, as I sat alone in the darkness of the carriage, the injustice of it all and the waste of such a promising life overwhelmed me, and I let the tears fall. It was one thing to see an Egyptian peasant condemned to lead the life of grinding poverty his ancestors had endured for centuries, and quite another to see someone with the potential of a Betty Frakes throw her future away so carelessly.

At the same time, I couldn't help but admire her for her courage and self-sacrifice. I thought of the blind aunt, who would not be reduced to begging in the streets, and the three boys, who would perhaps lead better lives than their sister, and I prayed they all appreciated what she was doing for them. Perhaps in their world, one had to be the sacrificial lamb so the others would have a chance to succeed.

I must have dozed off, for the next thing I knew, the carriage had stopped and Fred was peering in at me. "We're home, miss. I'm sorry it took so long, but the fog's so bad I couldn't even see the horse's heads half the time."

"That's fine, Fred," I murmured, stifling a yawn as I rubbed my stiff neck. Then I extended my hand so he could help me down.

I seemed to step into a goosedown comforter as the fog parted, then rushed to envelop me in its damp embrace. The Lester gate was a mere shadow, and beyond that was no house, just a rectangle of weak light from a window, floating like a disembodied ghost. Someone had waited up for me, probably Maud.

Even though the gate swung open quietly, on well-oiled

hinges, the fog picked up the sound and magnified it to a screech, and my own footsteps reverberated portentously as I trudged up the walk.

No sooner had I reached the bottom of the steps than the front door opened in a flash of light that blinded me for an instant.

"Cassa?" a voice called out.

It was not Maud.

"Yes, Geoffrey," I replied wearily, dragging myself up the steps toward the warm, welcoming light and silhouette at its heart.

Strong hands gripped my arms and drew me into the foyer. "Where in the hell have you been?" He shut the door and turned, his craggy features pinched and anxious. "It's nearly midnight, and I've been damn near out of my mind with worry about you."

I was on the verge of telling him about Betty, and how I had failed, when he suddenly reached out and drew me to him, holding me so tightly the breath was squeezed out of me and I could feel his frantic heartbeat beneath the rough twill of his coat. His cheek was hard against the top of my head, and his voice shook as he murmured, "God, I don't know what I would have done if something had happened to you tonight."

My face was burning from such sudden close contact, and I managed to step away from him. Before I had the chance to speak, his fingers dug into my shoulders, and he drew me back to him. Geoffrey's eyes burned into mine, and then with a groan of surrender, his mouth came down hard on mine. And it is not to my credit to say that I responded.

I think it was my aching disappointment over Betty that night that made me so vulnerable to warmth and human contact. Geoffrey's kiss was at once fierce and gentle, possessive yet yielding, sweeping me away on some violent tide I was quite unprepared for. In one heady, endless instant, propriety, decency, and any number of noble virtues were overwhelmed by the passion of the moment, and I responded to him, shamelessly pressing my body to his, savoring the warmth and hardness of his mouth beneath my own, reveling in the way my senses seemed to spring alive at his touch.

When we reluctantly parted, shaking and breathless, we just stared at each other, astounded at the depth of feeling each had elicited from the other. Then brutal reality rushed in, and I tried to step back, appalled that I had just kissed my sister's husband.

"Geoffrey, no!"

But he wouldn't release me, and as I saw passion darken his eyes, melding iris and pupil, I feared he was going to kiss me again and go on kissing me until he bent me to his will, and I no longer had the strength to resist.

He seemed to read my thoughts, for he gave one shuddering sigh and his arms fell to his sides. "You needn't fear me, Cassa," he said thickly and with great effort. "I've never yet taken what hasn't been freely offered by a woman, and I'm not about to start now, though, I must confess, you make it very tempting." He closed his eyes and sighed. "I was just worried half out of my mind for you, that's all."

"You needn't have been concerned," I said softly, as I stepped away from him and tried to bring my ragged breathing under control. "I had Fred and a footman to protect me."

"That still doesn't reassure me. Just last year, some maniac killed five women in Whitechapel, the area you went to tonight. They called him Jack the Ripper because of his grisly expertise with a knife, and, to this day, he's never been caught. No one even has a clue as to his identity. When the clock chimed eleven and you still weren't home, I had this wild thought that perhaps Jack had reappeared and struck again."

"Thank you for your concern," I murmured, curiously touched. "Now, if you'll excuse me . . ." And I started for the stairs, seeking to escape from this powerful man who had wreaked havoc on my emotions.

"Cassa?"

I turned and looked back. "Yes?"

"Did the girl agree to enroll in Maud's school?"

I shook my head as tears of disappointment stung my eyes. "No," I replied with a sniff, brushing away a tear. "I'm afraid I failed. Maud will be so disappointed. She so wanted to recruit Betty."

Geoffrey came toward me and said gently, "You obviously are upset by all this. Please. Come into the drawing room and we can discuss it." Then he extended his hand to me.

He must have read the mistrust and doubt in my face, for his arm fell to his side and a sardonic smile twisted his mouth, making him look like the Devil himself in the flickering gaslight of the foyer. "You needn't fear the beast in me this time. I promise you that I want conversation, nothing more."

Suddenly, I needed to talk about Betty Frakes, needed to mourn her as though she had died. Against my better judgment, I turned and followed him into the drawing room, where he lit the gaslight and we sat at opposite ends of the divan. While Geoffrey listened attentively, I poured out my heart about Betty, her blind aunt, and her three brothers, and how she was determined to let a man at the factory "take care" of her.

"She was the best one I've ever tried to recruit," I said with a dismal sigh, "intelligent, curious, quick. Why, she even had her own small collection of books piled on a table. Oh, they were old and waterstained, with the pages falling out, but just the idea that she had probably gone without food to buy some books . . ." I shrugged. "I knew right then that she had a thirst for knowledge." Now I rose and began pacing the room. "I saw so much poverty and igno-rance in Cairo, and there was nothing I could do about it, beyond giving the poor donkey boys as much baksheesh as our guests could spare. Here I did have the chance to change a person's life, and I couldn't do it." Now the hot tears fell afresh. "Please excuse me for crying, but I just feel so—so helpless!"

"Don't apologize." Geoffrey rose, drew me back to the divan, and took my tiny hand in his large, strong one. "Look at me, Cassa." When I did so, he said, "You mustn't blame yourself. I'm sure there is just so much one can do in a situation like this."

"But I can't help feeling that if I had just done something differently, or been more persuasive, I could have convinced Betty to enroll in the school."

His fingers tightened on mine. "May I offer you some advice?"

I sniffed and nodded.

"You are a kind, sensitive person, Cassa, and you're taking your work much too much to heart. You feel a great sense of personal failure when you don't succeed with one of these girls—am I right?—and it preys on your conscience for days. I've seen it. You must become resilient, like Maud, or these girls will tear your heart out. When she loses one recruit, she puts her out of her mind and looks forward to saving the next one."

"I can't help the way I am," I protested. "I care about all of them."

"I know," he said with one of those gentle, understanding smiles that touched me, "and I wouldn't want you to change. But, you can't save the entire world, now can you? There will always be people like this Betty Frakes who have set their lives on one path, and, for whatever reason, can't, or won't, deviate from it. You must do your best with those who can be helped."

Suddenly, the great weight of my disappointment vanished, and I felt uplifted by Geoffrey's counsel. "You know, you're right. I never thought of it that way before." I studied him for a second, for he had revealed to me a surprising part of himself that I hadn't suspected existed.

"I'm glad you agree."

Now he was drawing dangerously close once again, and I recognized that look in his eyes, so I rose, wished him a hasty good night, and fled from the drawing room.

Despite the bone-weariness that exhausted me, I found sleep would not come because Geoffrey haunted my thoughts.

Whenever I closed my eyes, I could imagine him watching the drawing room clock as the hours ticked away, dragging on and on, with still no sign of me. Perhaps his apprehension had become panic, then terror, as he thought of Jack the Ripper and his hapless victims. He must have been tormented by demons of his own, judging by the look of desperate relief that greeted me when I walked in the door, safe and unharmed.

His kiss had been unlike anything I had ever experienced. Oh, it was not the first time I had been kissed by a man. In Cairo, while touring a dark mosque, the French artist had kissed me when the other tourists had their backs turned, and the German prince had grabbed me in a deserted hallway and kissed me with a certain cold military precision. There was nothing cold about Geoffrey's kiss.

"You must pretend it never happened," I told myself sternly in the darkness.

And I assured myself it never would again.

Chapter Nine

In the days following my entrance into society, I was inundated with invitations from people I had met at Leonie's at home, and this turn of events delighted Mother.

"It would appear you're a spectacular success, my dear," she said proudly one morning as she set another handful of embossed vellum envelopes before me on my desk.

I grimaced as I put down my pen and turned my chair away, to avoid having to look at that growing stack of invitations. "I've spent nearly the entire morning refusing most of them."

Mother folded her hands primly in front of her and stared down at me in annoyance. "If you keep issuing refusals, you'll never be invited anywhere again. People will think you don't like them, or you're aloof."

There was such an overlay of ill-deserved censure in her voice that I found myself bristling. "I don't really care, Mother. My recruiting missions are more important to me than any ball or soirée."

"I only want you to enjoy yourself, Cassandra. What can be the harm in having a good time and making new friends?"

"There's nothing wrong with it, but socializing just takes up time that could be spent more profitably." I realized that sounded a trifle pompous, but I couldn't help myself. "Besides, I am not Leonie. I cannot be transformed into some social gadabout."

Mother's green eyes narrowed slightly, as they usually did

when something irked her. "I'm not trying to turn you into something you're not," she told me with exaggerated patience. "It's just that I'm sure you never had the opportunity to enjoy such occasions when you were living with Venetia, so I thought you'd enjoy them now."

She couldn't have chosen a more inappropriate line of reasoning, for, as usual, any intimation that my life with the Clarks was somehow lacking angered me. I rose and walked away from her. "Are you now trying to compensate me for the life I never had?"

Mother sighed, accepting the childish words with a tolerance I didn't deserve. "I can see you're determined to be difficult today, Cassandra, so I'll just leave you. By all means, feel free to refuse as many invitations as you wish, but don't come whining to me that you're bored, with nothing to do."

And she swept out of the room.

As soon as the door closed behind her, I regretted my sharp tongue and spitefulness, but I just couldn't stop myself. It seemed that when we were making giant strides toward understanding each other and bridging the gap between us, Mother would cast aspersions on Aunt Venetia or Father, and my resentment would come spilling out. Perhaps I was just too sensitive to what I imagined were slurs against my beloved aunt.

Finally, I returned to my desk and penned my regrets to a few more people, then decided I needed a change of pace. So, I put on a hat, draped a shawl across my shoulders, and went downstairs, thinking I would go for a quiet, soothing carriage ride through the city and perhaps stop at the British Museum to stroll through its Egyptian Galleries.

Just as I was about to leave, I heard Geoffrey call my name, and I turned in time to see him come skipping down the stairs. He looked quite distinguished this morning in his black frock coat and gray striped ascot secured with a plain gold pin.

"Are you going out this morning?" he asked with a smile.

I nodded. "I thought I'd go for a carriage ride."

"Then I'll accompany you as far as the stock exchange."

I had successfully avoided being alone with my brother-in-law ever since the night he had kissed me, and felt a little apprehensive about the prospect of sharing a carriage with him now.

But once we were inside and on our way, he acted as though he had put the incident out of his mind, and was most pleasant and congenial to me. He spoke about the stock exchange, and I learned that, even though Geoffrey was independently wealthy, he often increased his fortune by buying and selling stocks and bonds and making prudent investments, both for himself and to help finance many of his sister's charity projects. As I listened to him, I thought of Lady Quartermain's great disdain for "upstarts" like Geoffrey Lester, who were self-made men. I couldn't understand why a man who had inherited his fortune from a long line of ancestors was superior to a man who had made it himself, but then, I wasn't Lady Quartermain.

Suddenly, Geoffrey said, "Did you receive an invitation to Lady Oglethorp's ball next Wednesday?"

I smiled apologetically. "I've received so many invitations, I really don't remember, but I probably refused it along with all the others."

"Why? I was looking forward to escorting you—and Leonie, of course. You've yet to attend a ball, and Lady Oglethorp's are among the best. She's a lively, witty hostess with a reputation for bringing together the brightest minds of the political and artistic worlds. I'm sure you'd have a splendid time and meet some very interesting people." Then he said, with a perfectly straight face, "Besides, you could recommend the Clark's Hotel to the lot of them."

I laughed at that. "Cyrus would like that, I'm sure. Do you think it's too late to take back my refusal?"

Geoffrey shook his head. "I'm sure Lady Oglethorp wouldn't—"

He never finished the sentence. Suddenly, shouts filled

the air. I looked out the window to see what all the commotion was about. I saw a short man with a bowler hat cup his hands to his mouth and shout, "Look out!"

Before I had had time to wonder what he was warning us about, or glance at Geoffrey in puzzlement, the thundering of hoofbeats and clattering of carriage wheels filled the air, closer and closer, like a locomotive bearing down on us. The noise became deafening and there was a crash and the sickening sound of splintering wood. I was hurled forward at the same moment, toward Geoffrey, whose eyes widened as he cried out my name and reached for me.

The last sound I heard was my own voice screaming as I thrust out my arms and was whirled head over heels. Then came excruciating pain, and the world seemed to explode in a shower of stars before the welcome velvet blackness blotted them out.

When I next regained consciousness, I was lying in my own bed in the Green Glass Room, with my worried-looking mother seated by my bedside.

"Feeling a little better, dear?" she asked with a wan smile as she took a compress from my forehead and wrung it out in a basin of water.

"Ooooh, my head!" I groaned, wincing, as a blinding pain shot across my forehead. Then it all came flashing back, the carriage, Geoffrey, the crash, and I started in panic. "Mother, what am I doing here? What happened? Where's Geoffrey?" But when I tried to sit up, the pain shot through me again, causing me to see stars, and I was forced to lie back, gasping.

"You mustn't try to move," Mother admonished me, placing the soothing compress across my forehead.

I closed my eyes and savored its healing coolness. "What happened, Mother? Is Geoffrey all right?"

"There was an accident," she began, trying to sound calm, but unable to keep her voice from shaking. "A runaway carriage crashed into yours and tipped it over. You were lucky. You were only knocked unconscious. Can't you feel the bump on your head? But Geoffrey . . ." Her eyes misted over with tears and words failed her.

Using all my strength, I propped myself up on one elbow and ignored the pain. "What about Geoffrey, Mother? How badly was he hurt?" Then a thought struck me, and I fell back. "He isn't—"

"Dead?" She shook her head. "No, my dear, he isn't dead, but I won't minimize the seriousness of his injury. He has a gash on his head, and when the carriage shattered, a shaft of wood became lodged in his chest, very close to the heart. Luckily, a doctor lived in one of the houses near where the accident occurred, and he was able to treat Geoffrey right in the street. Then they took him to St. Bartholomew's Hospital, though I wish they had brought him home. Hospitals are no place for a sick man, you know. As I was saying, Fred managed to jump clear when the carriage overturned, and he insisted on bringing you home himself."

I sat up again, and this time, the pain wasn't as fierce, so I tried to swing my legs over the edge of the bed, but Mother's hand restrained me. "What do you think you're doing? The doctor has ordered you to stay in bed at least until tomorrow."

Ignoring the stiffness in my shoulders and back, I said, "Mother, there is nothing wrong with me. I must go to the hospital to see if Geoffrey is all right. You may come with me, or I'll go alone. The choice is yours."

Her cool green eyes narrowed and regarded me strangely, but before she could say a word, the door opened to reveal the Marquis of Sherborne, looking very grave.

"Do forgive me for the intrusion, Countess," he began, not looking at Mother, but directly at me. "I just heard from one of my servants the news that there's been an accident, and that Miss Clark was injured."

"Do come in, Horace," Mother replied. "Perhaps you can help me to convince my headstrong daughter that she must remain in bed for her own good." And while the marquis quietly crossed the room, Mother told him all about the accident.

The young man looked most upset, and there was concern deep in his eyes. "You're very lucky to be alive, Miss Clark."

I smiled wanly at him. "I know, Lord Sherborne. But I must go to the hospital to see how Geoffrey fared."

Mother and the marquis exchanged looks. He said, "If she tries to leave this room, Countess, I would suggest locking the door. She's too weak to resist."

Mother smiled in triumph. "Why, thank you, Horace. What a fine idea. Cassandra, you're not leaving this room until tomorrow. I have no intention of having two members of my family hospitalized."

"Traitor," I muttered to the marquis, but, in truth, my head was splitting, and I doubted my own ability to get to the hospital on my own. They had won.

Suddenly, the marquis startled me by placing his hand on mine. "I only have your best interests at heart, Miss Clark." And before I could say another word, he bowed, wished us good day, and left with best wishes for my speedy recovery.

"Such a considerate young man," Mother murmured. "And he seems to like you."

But there was something in the marquis's eyes that unsettled me, and I wondered if he was feeling a stronger emotion than friendship.

The next day, waking from a restless sleep haunted by bizarre, fathomless dreams I couldn't remember, I discovered a huge bouquet of colorful, exotic hothouse flowers standing in a vase by my bedside. I knew they were from the marquis even before reading the card he had enclosed. Feeling much better, I insisted that Mother allow me to go to St. Bartholomew's Hospital. She reluctantly agreed, but only if she accompanied me.

When we arrived, we found both Maud and Leonie there already, for they had stayed the night. Maud looked drained and exhausted. Leonie resembled a sulky child whose play has been interrupted rather than a wife whose husband could be dying. I wanted to shake her.

"Mother . . . Cassandra . . . ," she said, rising stiffly from her chair to greet us. "Whatever are you doing here? I thought Cassandra had to remain in bed."

"They've obviously come to be near Geoffrey," Maud snapped, trying to stifle a yawn. She didn't look as though she had fared too well spending so much time alone with her sister-in-law.

"What have the doctors said about his condition?" I asked, hoping my voice didn't sound too eager or desperate. I must have failed, for Leonie glanced at me suspiciously.

Maud said, "He's been recovering from surgery, where they removed the wood from his chest." Then she blinked hard, as though trying to remove a haze from her tired eyes. "Forgive me, Cassa, but how are _you?_ You're lucky you weren't seriously injured as well."

I squeezed her hands. "I was very lucky."

Suddenly, a dapper-looking gentleman with kind eyes walked into the room and said, "Lady Lester, I've good news for you."

Now Leonie became the very picture of a concerned wife, clasping her hands to her breast, her voice eager and pleading. "Dr. Dennison, how is my husband? Will he . . . will he live?"

The doctor, no doubt moved by the fresh tears clinging so prettily to her lashes, patted her hand in a fatherly gesture of reassurance and comfort. "He came through the operation like a trooper, madam, and survived the night. The gash on his head was less serious than it looked. Head wounds tend to bleed profusely, you know. Although the splinter of wood was perilously close to his heart, we removed it satisfactorily. He should be up and about in a month or so with diligent and tender nursing, which I'm sure you'll provide."

Leonie seemed to melt with relief. "Oh, thank you so

much, Dr. Dennison, thank you. My prayers have been answered."

"Now, he's regained consciousness and has been asking for someone named Cassandra. His mother, perhaps?" the doctor inquired innocently.

Leonie whirled around to stare at me with a mixture of surprise and malevolence on her face. "Cassandra? He's been asking to see Cassandra?"

"Why, yes." The doctor turned to Mother. "Would you be she, Madam?"

"I am Cassandra Clark," I said softly, stepping forward. "I was in the carriage with Mr. Lester when the accident occurred."

The doctor squinted at the bump on my forehead. "Yes, I can see you were."

Leonie added, "Cassandra is my sister."

If the doctor thought it odd that Geoffrey should want to see his sister-in-law before his own wife, he kept his composure admirably. He merely said, "Come this way, miss," and I followed him down a long corridor to a large, open ward that was surprisingly dim and cheerless for a room of its size.

Narrow iron beds lined each wall, and the ward reeked of sickness and carbolic, so that I had to suppress the urge to cover my nose and mouth with my handkerchief and fling open a window, for even the city's dirty air would seem fresh by comparison. As we walked that forbidding gauntlet, I noticed that some patients were sicker than others. A few were sitting up, wide-eyed and chipper, while others were flat on their backs, groaning in pain. In addition, there were others besides myself visiting friends or loved ones, and they chattered away as if they were in their own drawing rooms. It struck me as excessively noisy for the poor patients trying to recuperate.

When I saw Geoffrey lying on a bed like all the others, while a woman talked and laughed loudly with the man in the next bed, I turned to Dr. Dennison and snapped, "Isn't it possible for Mr. Lester to have his own room, for pity's sake? How can he get any rest with all this noise?"

The doctor was obviously used to distraught visitors, for he smiled benignly and said, "Mr. Lester is receiving the very best care, Miss Clark, and I'm sure he'll recuperate along with everyone else."

My concern for privacy vanished the moment I stood at the foot of Geoffrey's bed and stared down at him, his head and shoulders swathed in bandages. I felt such a feeling of dread tie my stomach into knots that it was all I could do to keep from flinging myself at him and crying out his name. I managed to restrain myself as the doctor offered me a chair by the bedside.

"He looks barely alive," I said to Dr. Dennison.

"It's just the effects of surgery," he assured me. "Mr. Lester is doing fine, I promise you."

And with those words, he left me.

Geoffrey's eyes were closed, his dark lashes starkly outlined against his face, as colorless as a death mask. His bandaged chest was barely rising and falling, and, for one horrifying moment, I thought he had stopped breathing, but then his head moved ever so slightly, and I sighed deeply in relief.

The shock of seeing such a large, robust man so pale and helpless touched a core of tenderness deep inside me, and I felt the tears spring to my eyes. I forgot everyone else in the ward as I blindly groped for the hand that was lying so still atop the bed covers. It was limp, but still warm with life.

As I sat there, holding Geoffrey's hand and studying his face, I suddenly thought of a life without him and was overcome by a tidal wave of black despair that was greater than anything I had ever known. Even the shock of hearing about my father's death hadn't caused me to experience such a rush of overwhelming devastation and loss.

Suddenly, the noisy woman nearby looked in my direction and said, "Anything wrong, dearie? He hasn't gone on you, has he, 'cause if he has—"

"Will you please be quiet?" I snapped, without looking at her.

"Well!" she sniffed indignantly. "Some folks just don't appreciate a little concern from their neighbor, do they, Alf?"

I didn't hear Alf's reply, for at that moment, Geoffrey stirred and groaned.

"Geoffrey," I murmured, clasping his hand as tightly as I dared.

His eyelids fluttered and opened into mere slits. He could see me, I knew, for his lips moved in the weakest of smiles. Then, with superhuman effort, he took a deep, wheezing breath and tried to speak.

I silenced him by placing my fingertips against his lips, which felt warm to my touch. "Hush. Please don't try to speak. You're still very weak and have to conserve your strength."

But when I took my hand away, he disregarded my words and managed to whisper my name, followed by, "All right?"

I smiled, nodded, and gingerly touched the lump on my forehead. "I was only bruised when the carriage over-turned." Then I explained how Fred had taken me home, but Geoffrey's injuries required hospitalization. "I'm fine now, Geoffrey, just fine. Please don't worry about me. You must rest and get well."

He tried to smile again.

"Mother and Maud are here with me, and so is Leonie. She spent the night here, anxiously awaiting any news of you."

But Leonie's self-sacrifice didn't seem to interest him, for he closed his eyes and drifted off again without mentioning her. It was at that moment that Dr. Dennison returned to escort me back to my family.

"Mr. Lester is sleeping now," the doctor told Mother, Maud, and Leonie when we rejoined them. "I would advise all of you to go home and return tomorrow. There is nothing more you can do for him."

"But can't I at least see my husband?" Leonie protested. "You allowed my sister to see him."

The doctor remained adamant. "I'm afraid not. But I'm sure he'll feel up to having more visitors tomorrow. Good day to you, ladies."

When Dr. Dennison was out of the room, Leonie sighed and exclaimed, "An entire month! We'll miss the Princess Louise's wedding to the Duke of Fife, the Shah of Persia's visit—"

Suddenly, the shock of the accident and having seen Geoffrey under less than ideal conditions overwhelmed me, and something inside me snapped. Before I could think about the consequences of my actions, my hand shot out and slapped my sister across the face. "Your husband almost died in that accident, and all you can think about are the social activities you'll miss?" My voice shook with a mixture of rage and delayed hysteria. "You are the most selfish, self-centered little whore—"

"Cassandra!" Mother cried, stepping between us and grasping me by the arms, while Maud looked ready to restrain Leonie.

"Cassa didn't mean it," Maud assured her. "She's just suffering from shock and exhaustion. We're all a bit tense. You must excuse her."

I fell silent, suddenly overwhelmed by what I had done. Leonie looked as though she wanted to claw my face to ribbons as she nursed her red cheek. But her cool, measured words did more to me than physical violence.

"Well, well, well," she mused. "I didn't know my own husband could arouse such strong feelings in my sister." Her voice was silky and soft, but with an edge of menace. "And how very interesting that the first person he calls for is not his own wife, but his sister-in-law." She turned to Mother. "Don't you think that is very interesting?"

Mother released me and turned to face her, a placating smile on her face as she sought to pour oil on troubled waters. "Cassandra was in the accident with him, and he was just concerned for her welfare, that's all. You know Geoffrey loves you, Leonie."

"I'm sure," she said. Then, without another word, she whirled about and stormed out of the room.

Much to my relief, Leonie seemed quickly to forget my outburst at the hospital and accepted my apology with good grace. She returned to her usual routine of calls, balls, and parties, acting as though her husband's injuries were no reason to forgo Princess Louise's wedding or the Shah's visit. In fact, I think she rather relished her role as the invalid's wife, visiting the hospital for a few minutes in the morning and reporting Geoffrey's progress to their friends at night. She made much of the fact that the prince and princess had sent him flowers and notes wishing him speedy recovery, though I suspect Geoffrey was more touched by the simple nosegay of violets from Edith and Edgar, who could ill afford even that, than by any ostentatious displays from royalty.

Sometimes, though, despite her insistence that any rift between us was long forgotten, I would catch Leonie staring at me when she thought I wasn't looking, and it always made me shiver and wonder what exquisite revenge she was planning.

And then came the day Geoffrey was released from the hospital.

He was still quite pale and weak but managed to walk through the front door unassisted, and seeing all the servants lined up to welcome him home cheered his spirits. There was a great deal of fight and determination left in him, and, for the first time, I felt optimistic about his recovery.

At first, the doctor confined him to his room, but later, when his strength improved, Geoffrey was allowed to go downstairs to take one meal with the family, or read quietly in the library. Within four days, however, his strength increased so rapidly he started going out into the garden to sit in the healing warmth of the July sun for a few hours each day.

As I watched him dozing in his chair like an old man of eighty, with a rug drawn across his lap, I was relieved to find that I felt nothing for him beyond a certain maternal tenderness that women often feel for a helpless, injured man. My own good sense was rapidly returning. I told myself that I had responded to Geoffrey's embrace that night because I had been so crushed by my failure to win over Betty Frakes, not because I desired him. I was not like Mother or Leonie, to be swept away by blond good looks, broad shoulders, and a sardonic smile. I thought myself so much more sensible and independent. How could any woman possibly be attracted to an arrogant, willful man who had so little respect for his wife that he took a mistress so soon after their marriage?

Yet, in the hospital, when I thought that he might die . . . I pushed that heretical thought out of my head, turned away from the window, and went in search of Maud.

As Dr. Dennison had promised, about a month after the accident, Geoffrey was fully recovered, and life returned to some semblance of normality in the Lester household.

But then something happened that was to affect our lives more than any of us could imagine.

One evening, we were all gathered for dinner when Leonie suddenly announced, "The prince has invited us to dine at Marlborough House the day after tomorrow, to celebrate your recovery, Geoffrey." Then she turned to me. "And you've been invited as well, Cassandra. Edward was quite impressed with you that day you met him in the park. He was going to invite you sooner, but then there was the carriage accident, and we couldn't go anywhere." She glanced at her husband as if it had been his fault.

My mouth suddenly went dry. "Must I go?"

Leonie rolled her eyes toward the ceiling. "Of course you must, you goose. It's a royal command."

Edith, seated at my left, patted my arm. "This will be a

great honor for you, Cassandra. Not everyone is invited to dine with our future king, you know."

Geoffrey didn't smile and was strangely silent as he ran his fingertip along the rim of his wine glass. I sensed he didn't relish socializing with his wife's paramour, even if he was the Prince of Wales.

"Well, Geoffrey," Leonie said with a touch of impatience, "are we going to accept the invitation or not?"

He glanced over at her. "You know we shall."

"Splendid."

Mother seemed positively delighted with the honor that was about to be bestowed on me, for her face glowed with maternal pride. I could tell she was pleased that I was finally going to a social event, and with such august company.

"You can wear one of your new dinner dresses," she said. "I'm sure you'll look enchanting."

Before I had the chance to comment, Heffer came into the dining room. He handed Leonie an envelope. She glared up at him as she set down her fork to take it. "A letter? Couldn't this have waited until we finished dinner?"

"I'm sorry, madam, but the boy who brought it to the door said it was very important and should be delivered to you at once."

"Oh, very well . . ." she muttered with some asperity and tore open the envelope right there. Suddenly, her eyes grew as round as saucers, and she uttered a shrill cry.

"What is it?" Geoffrey demanded, alert, from the opposite end of the table. He was on his feet in an instant and by her side.

"Bad news?" Maud inquired.

Leonie had turned a ghastly, chalk white. "Who would do such a thing?" she muttered, thrusting the paper at her husband as though it were poison.

"Whatever is it, Geoffrey?" Mother demanded, as he scowled at the paper in his hands.

He turned it over and held it up so all of us could read it. The word WHORE was scrawled in bright red letters that seemed to leap from the page. A startled ripple of surprise passed among those assembled, and we exchanged horrified looks.

"Whoever could have sent that?" Edgar said, his dark eyes enormous as he shuddered delicately. "It looks as though it's written in blood."

"It's just paint," Geoffrey replied, squinting as he studied it further.

Leonie, meanwhile, gave me a long, lingering look, then said, "I want the police notified this instant. I want the—the maniac who did this caught and punished."

"Heffer," Geoffrey said, turning to the butler, "is the messenger still here?"

"No, sir. He went running off the moment he handed me the envelope. He was just a common street urchin who was probably paid a sixpence to deliver it. I doubt he could be found now."

Geoffrey dismissed the butler and turned to his wife. "It's probably some high-minded individual or religious faction that disapproves of your relationship with the prince," he said, his voice soft and surprisingly concerned.

Two angry red spots stained Leonie's fair cheeks. "When Edward hears about this, he'll have all of Scotland Yard working to find them, and when they do . . ."

As Geoffrey walked back to his seat at the head of the table, he said, "I don't think you should tell anyone about it."

Leonie reared back in her chair, incensed, her eyes blazing. "Not tell anyone! I want the people who sent it caught and punished! Of course I'm going to tell someone."

Maud said, "I think Geoff is right, Leo. The police would have a devil of a time trying to catch the culprit, and besides, I doubt that the prince would appreciate the scandal a story of this sort would generate. You know yourself that certain newspapers in this city would give such an item front page coverage."

It was just the argument needed to convince Leonie. She

relented, though reluctantly. "Well, I suppose you're right. But it just galls me to think that anyone would dare to do this to *me!*"

Geoffrey seated himself. "I think the less said about it, the better. The person who sent it would obviously get great satisfaction out of knowing he had rattled you."

Leonie rose, and placed her hand to her forehead. "My evening has been thoroughly spoiled. If there is a lunatic out there capable of sending me such a note, I'm not safe anywhere, even in my own home. Geoffrey, I've decided I don't want to go to the Havershams' soirée tonight. If you'll all excuse me . . .."

As she glided out of the room, Geoffrey crumpled the paper into a tight ball and left it beside his plate, where it stayed as a grim reminder throughout the rest of the meal.

The mysterious note cast a pall on the entire evening, and, after dinner, when we gathered in the drawing room, everyone had a different opinion about the best course of action. Mother and Edgar seemed the most upset by what had happened, and, for once, Maud was strangely silent on the subject. Edith, however, was her usual voluble self and challenged Geoffrey about the wisdom of his decision not to inform the police. He, in turn, seemed to be annoyed with her, patiently explaining that, since the messenger had disappeared into the night, it would be almost impossible for the police even to question the lad, let alone discover who had hired him.

I soon grew tired of all the speculation, and excused myself. I went into the library, where I could be alone to think. I hadn't been there five minutes when the door opened and Edgar appeared.

"Am I disturbing you, Miss Clark?" he asked, hesitating shyly in the doorway.

"Not at all, Edgar. Please come in." When he crossed the room and sat in the chair opposite me, I said, "I just needed to get away for a few minutes. This has been quite a surprising evening for all of us."

He nodded, his eyes darting nervously around the room, while he toyed with his shirt cuff, which, I noticed, was newly darned. "Who would want to do such a thing to Lady Leonie?"

"Some deranged person, no doubt?"

Now his soulful eyes widened, and he looked like a frightened puppy. "You don't think she's in any danger, do you, Miss Clark?"

There was something in the tone of his voice that caught me by surprise, and I looked at Edgar quizzically, but did not voice what I was thinking, for I really didn't know him that well yet and didn't want to be presumptuous. Besides, what if I were wrong?

So I said, "Cassandra, please."

"Cassandra, then."

"As I was about to say, I don't think Leonie is in any real danger. Whoever sent that note just wants to frighten her, that's all."

This seemed to reassure him a bit, for he smiled shyly. "I'm relieved. I wouldn't want anything to happen to her."

Then an awkward silence fell, for Edgar didn't really seem to know what to talk about, and I knew from past experience with reserved hotel guests I would have to bear the burden of conversation.

So I said, "Tell me, Edgar, do you have any other brothers or sisters?" just for something to talk about.

"No."

I tried again. "Then Edith and you must be very close."

He seemed to relax and open up a little. "Yes, we are. My mother died when we were only children, and my father could never manage to hold any job long enough to support us properly. Edith became father and mother to the three of us. She worked as a companion to an old woman and, when she wasn't nursing her, she studied the books in the lady's extensive library. Finally, Edith was able to attend a very fine school in our town. My sister is brilliant, Miss—Cassandra. She studied day and night and soon was able to become a teacher herself. She supported us by teaching at various schools in England, and then, after Father died and I was able to be on my own, Edith got a position at that prestigious French boarding school. We went our separate ways for a while."

Now my curiosity was aroused. "Why isn't she still teaching at the French school? What made her leave, if she liked it so much?"

Edgar flushed and fidgeted nervously in his seat. "The spoiled daughter of a wealthy English nobleman made trouble for Edith. The girl thought she could get away without studying, and that Edith would excuse her, but when my sister was firm with her, the girl complained to her father, who, in turn, complained to the headmistress. Rather than lose such august patronage, the headmistress let Edith go on the pretext that her services were no longer required."

I shook my head sadly. "That must have been a bitter blow to Edith."

"Yes, it was. She is so proud and hated to ask me for help, especially since my clerk's salary is so meager, but after all my sister has done for me, I could not refuse."

Though his sister bullied and belittled him, Edgar could not find it in his heart to turn her away in her hour of need. While I deplored his spinelessness, I admired his consideration.

Now he brightened. "I'm sure she'll find another position soon. She is just too good a teacher to be out of work for long."

I couldn't resist saying, "She seems determined to find you new employment as well."

Edgar rolled his eyes. "My sister can be most embarrassing at times when she tries to convince people they should hire me. To tell you the truth, Miss—Cassandra, I am content at Westminster's, but I can't seem to convince my sister of it."

"It seems as though she has enough ambition for both of you."

"Edith has enough ambition for half the men in London, I think," Edgar agreed. "When Father was alive, the poor man never quite could measure up to his daughter's expectations. He was always such a failure to her. Now I suppose she sees me as just another failure, like poor Father."

My heart went out to him. "How can you say that about yourself, Edgar? You've got a fine position at the bank, and I'm sure that in time you'll move up through the ranks."

He shook his head and smiled. "You have greater faith in me than Edith."

"Everyone needs someone to believe in him," I said. Before Edgar could reply, I added, "And does Leonie believe in you, too?"

"Lady Lester has been most encouraging."

My years of meeting hundreds of people from all walks of life in Cairo had attuned me to their moods, their whims, their unspoken desires. Just the way Edgar spoke Leonie's name, and by the way his dark eyes softened, gave me the answer I wanted. I could tell Edgar Wickes loved Leonie, even if it was one-sided, but I said nothing, for I was sure that I would only embarrass the poor boy.

Before Edgar could say another word, there came a bold knock on the door, and Edith herself strode in.

"Ah, there you are, Edgar. I was wondering where you'd disappeared." Her face was alive with curiosity, as though she wondered what we could possibly have to discuss. "The carriage is waiting, and you're delaying its departure."

"I'm sorry if I've kept everyone waiting," Edgar said meekly as he bade me good night and headed for the door.

When he hesitated and said, "Coming, Edith?" she replied, "In just a moment. There's something I must discuss with Cassandra."

As it turned out, Edith wanted to ask me if I would mention Edgar's name to any financiers I happened to meet when I went to dine at Marlborough House. Perhaps one of them would agree to discuss a new position for him. I should have said I would feel rather awkward asking such a favor of a man I had just met, but I felt so sorry for Edith in her reduced circumstances, I couldn't bring myself to refuse her request, though in the long run it might have been better to have done so. I kept thinking of what Edgar had told me earlier, about their ne'er-do-well father and Edith's misguided ambition for him.

Against my better judgment, I promised her I would do as she asked. Just to see her face brighten with pleasure convinced me I had been right to agree.

When I retired to my room for the night, I was startled to find the gaslight on and yet another surprise awaiting me.

"Good evening, sister dear," Leonie said, without looking at me or rising from the corner of the window seat where she sat with her knees drawn up to her chin.

"Leonie," I said, stopping in the middle of the room. "You startled me. I would have thought you'd gone to bed long ago."

Now she looked at me and there was something in her manner that made me uneasy. "I couldn't sleep. That note upset me too much."

I started pulling the pins from my hair, wondering just why she had come to my room. "That was a sick, vicious thing for someone to do. Anyone would be upset by such a frightening note."

I shook my hair free and scooped up the night shift Sally had laid out for me on my bed. I was heading for the dressing room when my sister's next words brought me up short.

"Is that why you sent it to me my dear, *dear* sister?"

I stopped and spun around. "You think *I* sent that note to you? Leonie, I am appalled!"

She rose now, her gossamer nightdress billowing about her

with each step. "I can't think of a more likely suspect. You don't like me, you don't approve of my relationship with Edward, and you want my husband," she replied casually, as if she were reciting a list of new dresses to buy. "You can't bear to confront me directly, so you went behind my back to try to frighten me."

I knew if we didn't resolve this misunderstanding immediately, I would lose all hope of ever becoming close to my sister, which I desired above all else, in spite of the supercilious way she treated me. Animosity between us would continue to fester and grow, until there would be no hope of reconciliation. No, I had to find some way of convincing Leonie that I was not responsible for what had happened, and that she could trust me to help her.

I set my nightdress down. "I don't know where you got the idea that I would ever do such a thing to anyone, especially my own sister, Leonie. You cannot hold me in high regard, or even know me very well to accuse me." Now I faced her squarely. "And as for wanting your husband . . ." I shook my head. "That is the most absurd accusation of all. If I had wanted to marry, I could have had my pick of the suitors who fancied me in Cairo. No, I'm afraid I treasure my independence too much to fall in love with anyone, especially my sister's husband." Then I smiled and took a step toward her. "You are my *sister*, a part of me. No matter how much I disapprove of how you conduct your life, I would still never do anything to harm you. Can't you understand that?"

Her great violet eyes were dark with mistrust and doubt, and, for the first time, I saw something like fear in their depths. My poised, self-assured sister had never shown vulnerability before, especially to me, and it made her seem softer somehow, more human. It so moved me, I wanted to extend my arms to her and comfort her, as Cyrus's older sister had so often comforted me, but I held back. I knew it was too soon and would just alienate Leonie further.

She said slowly, "If you didn't, who did?"

I shrugged. "As Geoffrey said—"

"I don't believe him for a moment!" she snapped. "I think the culprit is someone right here in this house."

For a moment, I wondered if the events of the last few hours had somehow unhinged her mind. "Leonie! You can't mean that!"

Gliding to my bed, she grasped one of the carved bedposts, leaned back, and gently swung herself to and fro, much as a child would. "Oh, but I do. Geoffrey, Maud, even Mother . . . They all have cause to want to frighten me." Suddenly, she stopped and any look of vulnerability vanished. "And still you, Cassandra, always you."

I am a patient woman, but I was finding my patience sorely taxed. "Leonie—"

"You pretend you want us to be as close as sisters," she said, moving away from the bed and eyeing me with suspicion, "but I think it's part of a cleverly conceived plan."

"And what is that?"

"You want me to trust you and take you into my confidence, while all the while planning to steal my husband from me. You've got Sherborne panting after you, so why won't you content yourself with him? No, you must have what is mine. You want to destroy me!"

"Will you stop it! You're acting like a silly little girl with all this talk of my wanting to steal your husband." I was furious now. "I've told you a hundred times I have no interest in Geoffrey!"

She wouldn't listen. "Methinks the lady doth protest too much." She fell silent; then presently she asked, "Why couldn't you just have gone back to Egypt when you learned Geoffrey hadn't received your telegram?"

My mind raced, and I suddenly had the answer to something that had been puzzling me since my arrival. "You were the one who intercepted my telegram, weren't you? You're the one who didn't want me here."

Leonie smiled so sweetly. "Yes, and you should have taken your cue to leave."

Without another word, she floated off, leaving me angry, frustrated, and very sorry for her.

Chapter Ten

"**I**f the truth be known, you look lovelier than the mistress herself, though don't tell her I said so."

"Oh, Sally, do I really?" I straightened the tiny gathered sleeves of my gown and tugged at its fitted waist, while praying Mother's tiara wouldn't come tumbling down the moment I bowed my head. Then I turned a critical eye on the garland of white roses and leaves that was attached at the waist and trailed down the skirt to the floor. "Do you think these flowers make the gown look too fussy? I'm afraid they'll catch on something and be torn off."

"Miss, the flowers will be fine," Sally assured me. "You look elegant and refined."

My gown, of emerald green *mousselline de soie* and brocade, was a tribute to the skill of Madame deBrisse's seamstresses, and did make me look as elegant as the princess herself, but my constant fussing with the emerald necklace that Mother had lent me destroyed any illusion of refinement.

"The closest I've ever come to dining with royalty was dinner with a German prince in Cairo," I said to the maid, trying to control my nervousness. "I'm so afraid I'll do something gauche and embarrass Master Geoffrey."

"Miss, you couldn't embarrass anyone. Now, be off with you and have a splendid time." And the maid held the door open wide for me.

As I walked down the corridor past Leonie's room, I could hear the angry voices quite plainly through the closed door.

"—and this extravagance must stop!" Geoffrey bellowed.

The indignation in Leonie's voice matched his. "I am a— if not *the*—leading member of society, Geoffrey. I *need* every single gown and hat and pair of shoes I buy because I simply cannot be seen in the same dress twice in the same month. One would think you were as poor as Edgar Wickes, the way you niggle and begrudge me every penny I spend."

So, Geoffrey was taking his spendthrift wife to task again. I tiptoed away before I was caught eavesdropping and went downstairs to the drawing room, where my mother and Maud were waiting to see me off.

I hesitated for a moment to straighten the gown's heavy train behind me, then walked in without a word.

"Oh, Cassandra . . ." Mother crooned as she rose to look me over.

Maud just stared, her mouth agape. Finally, she said, "I would say Leo had best look to her laurels," and rose to lean over and give me a sisterly kiss on the cheek.

"Yes, a few borrowed jewels can transform anyone," came a bored voice, and Leonie herself glided into the drawing room. A moody, glowering Geoffrey followed in her wake.

Tonight, instead of her usual pink, Leonie wore a gown of shimmering white satin with a low, square neckline that enhanced her magnificent bosom. Her diamond necklace was elaborate, and she wore a diamond tiara instead of the plain gold fillet. With the flickering gaslight playing off the hard, brilliant gems and soft fabric, Leonie seemed to sparkle like an icicle in the sun.

When I asked why she wasn't wearing the fillet tonight, she gave me a condescending look and replied, "Since the princess will be wearing a tiara tonight, it's considered *très gauche* not to wear one as well."

That remark caused Maud to say, "And since you're wearing the Lester diamonds tonight, Leo, why aren't you wearing the earrings that match them? They're quite magnificent, if I recall, though I haven't seen them in a while."

"You know I never wear earrings, Maud," Leonie retorted.

And I could understand why. Since Leonie always drew her hair down to conceal her ears, any jewels would just sparkle unseen.

Maud's brows came down in a scowl of frank dislike, and she straightened to her commanding height. "My, my, aren't we in a foul mood tonight. Have another argument with your husband?"

"Maud, please . . ." Geoffrey warned.

As Maud shrugged and held her tongue, Leonie said impatiently, "Well, shall we be off? We mustn't keep Edward waiting."

Once in the carriage, Geoffrey went to one corner and Leonie the other. Each pretended the other didn't exist. When the uncomfortable silence dragged on and on, with no end in sight, I made a few attempts to draw them into conversation, but failed.

Suddenly, Leonie turned to me and became talkative. "There is something I must warn you about, Cassandra, before we arrive at Marlborough House. You must not look shocked if you see some dignified gentleman go sliding down the stairs on a silver tray, and if the footman should serve you a salad with chunks of soap in place of the cheese, you must laugh heartily and be a good sport about it. Edward hates boredom and loves guests with a great sense of fun."

I made a face. "I don't think finding soap in my salad would be very amusing, Leonie." Suddenly, I wished I had never agreed to come tonight, royal command or no. I was nervous enough without having to worry about becoming the butt of some jest.

Leonie's light, mocking laughter filled the carriage. "Oh, don't be such a spoilsport. Besides, this is your first visit to Marlborough House, so I'm sure you'll be left alone. Most likely the butt of the prank will be Christopher Sykes." She stifled a giggle with her fingertips. "He's the most ludicrous man. Edward can perpetrate the most outrageous acts against him, and he's so deferential, it borders on the hilarious."

Then she launched into a story of how Sykes had once got drunk at a house party and collapsed in front of all the guests. In retribution, the prince had had a dead seagull hidden in the man's bed. The prank was so well-received by the patient, good-natured Mr. Sykes that the next night, the prince repeated the jest, only this time placing a live, trussed-up rabbit between the sheets.

While my sister was convulsed with laughter, I was frankly shocked. "I'm afraid I can't really picture our future king doing such a thing."

Geoffrey glanced at me from the depths of his corner. "Few would suspect the heir to our monarch of being such a boisterous, madcap fellow, now would they?" Just by the tone of his voice, I could tell Geoffrey was not of the number who was amused by such royal antics.

"Oh, both of you are just a pair of old sticks," Leonie declared with a pout.

Geoffrey must have sensed that all this talk of pranks had increased my uneasiness, for he said, "In spite of their penchant for such antics, the people you'll be meeting tonight are quite interesting, Cassandra, and I think you'll enjoy yourself."

I prayed he was right.

We fell silent again, and before I knew it, the carriage slowed and drew to a halt. We had reached our destination, and my ordeal was about to begin.

Marlborough House itself, all cut stone and brick, was smaller than I had anticipated, but commanding enough to bring the butterflies back to my stomach. As we entered the hall, I examined my surroundings. There were several graceful marble female figures set among the tall potted palms, and I wondered if the prince had shot the leopards whose skins now graced the floor, for he was reported to be an enthusiastic sportsman. When I glanced at myself in the huge mirror over the mantel, I was surprised to find I looked rather calm and composed, considering that my apprehension had settled like a rock in the pit of my stomach.

"Don't worry," Geoffrey said with a smile as he took my elbow, and we fell in step behind a liveried footman. "You look—you are—beautiful, Cassa. Just be yourself, and everyone will be charmed."

The steady pressure of his fingers and the soft intimacy of his voice both sent my heart racing and paradoxically calmed me. With Geoffrey by my side, I knew I could conquer anything.

"If only Cyrus could see me now," I replied. "Imagine, Cassandra Clark dining with the Prince and Princess of Wales!"

"Your cousin would probably advise you to recommend the hotel to the prince."

How well Geoffrey knew Cyrus. I couldn't help but chuckle aloud, which caused Leonie to turn and glare at me.

By that time, we had reached the drawing room, were announced, and walked inside.

The prince, who had been standing with another gentleman before an oriental screen, came forward to greet us as soon as we were announced, his chest gleaming with medals and orders.

"Lady Lester-r," he murmured, kissing Leonie's hand as though she were just any other guest, but the gleam in his eye gave his feelings away. "You look lovely tonight, my dear."

"Thank you, sir," Leonie said with a shallow curtsey.

Then the prince turned to me, and his sparkling blue eyes assessed me with the expertise of a true connoisseur of women. When he smiled slightly in approval, I didn't know whether to be flattered or on my guard.

"And Miss Clar-rk," he went on, bowing over my hand. "How delighted I am that you could join us tonight."

"Your Highness," I said, curtseying low and praying my tiara would stay in place. "I was honored by your invitation."

He turned his attention to Geoffrey. "Lester-r," he said, informally grasping his hand, "we were sor-r-ry to hear of your accident. Most unfortunate. Some drivers can't control their own horses. But you've fully recovered, I trust?" There was no mistaking the warmth and sincerity in his voice and manner, and he seemed genuinely concerned as he asked Geoffrey details of his hospital stay.

As I watched them together, I thought there was something quite touching about His Royal Highness's concern for his mistress's husband. He would be our ruler, our king, and he needn't have given a damn about Geoffrey, yet he obviously did. It was almost as though he were trying to make amends for appropriating Geoffrey's wife, much like a disobedient child making up to his father. I recalled Maud's description of the prince as a naughty boy, and I decided it was apt after all.

"I've quite recovered, sir," Geoffrey was saying, "and I wish to thank you and the princess for your thoughtful notes and gifts." As always, his tone was scrupulously polite, but his heavily lidded eyes held no hint of acceptance.

"Think nothing of it." Then the prince turned and said, "Come. There are some people I would like Miss Clar-rk to meet."

We first paid our respects to our hostess, seated on a crimson upholstered sofa and attended by a distinguished man wearing a regimental uniform of dark blue. He was introduced as Colonel the Honorable Oliver Montagu, commander of the Blues, and he impressed me as being very attentive toward Alexandra. I wondered if she had found a knight errant of her own, and could hardly blame her, considering her husband's behavior.

Like Leonie, the princess was dressed entirely in white,

with seed pearls and brilliants covering a gown that displayed her slender, youthful figure to its best advantage. The high collar she wore was made up of at least fifteen rows of small matched pearls, and I wondered how she could incline her head without chafing her chin against it. She smelled deliciously of violets, and was by far the loveliest woman in the room, glowing with a serenity and inner beauty that surpassed physical attractiveness.

The prince leaned over and said, "Alix, my dear, you remember Miss Clar-rk, Lady Lester-r's sister, from the park?"

She smiled sweetly and nodded at me. "Of course. I understand that you come to us from Egypt, Miss Clark."

"Yes, ma'am," I replied, after curtseying deeply. "I run a hotel there, with my cousin."

I sensed Leonie stiffen by my side, so I knew I had committed a faux pas, but the princess didn't seem to think anything of it, for she leaned toward me and said, "Bertie and I have visited Egypt twice." Now she looked up at her husband. "Do you remember our quarters in the Ezbekiya Palace, my dear? The beds were made of solid silver, and the chairs gold!" Then she laughed, a light, girlish sound. "The poor khedive thought that we were accustomed to sleeping on silver beds and sitting on golden chairs." Now her soft blue eyes twinkled mischievously. "Then we visited the Sultan of Turkey and I was invited to inspect his harem, Miss Clark. While I was there, his wives dressed me in veils and hid me in my husband's rooms."

The prince chuckled indulgently. "I was quite fooled. I thought the sultan had made me a gift of one of his wives." Then he stopped smiling. "The only part of our Middle Eastern trip I didn't relish was that pyramid. I never-r should have let them persuade me to climb it. I thought I'd never-r get down!"

Considering the prince's considerable girth, I could easily understand why scaling the Great Pyramid had proved to be a formidable undertaking, but I laughed politely with everyone else, then we left the princess to Colonel Montagu and proceeded to the other guests.

As we went round the gold and white drawing room, I was introduced to a haphazardly dressed man who turned out to be Lord Hartington, and to his consort, the Duchess of Manchester, whom I had met when she had called on Leonie; to Lord Randolph Churchill and his beautiful American wife, Jennie; to tall, solemn Christopher Sykes of the seagull and rabbit; to one of the men Geoffrey mentioned had dissuaded him from taking Leonie abroad, Sir Francis Knollys, the prince's private secretary; and to Sir Edward Ponsonby. There were also various embassy officials and their wives, one of whom, I noticed, was in a corner, deep in conversation with the Marquis of Sherborne.

After the interminable round of introductions was over, I followed my sister as she flitted among the women present, and, though I managed to converse now and then, I did more listening than talking and received an eye-opening look at the workings of society. I learned from a marchioness that Alexandra's three daughters were so plain they were called The Hags, and another woman with slightly crossed eyes told her scandalized audience the rumor that the solemn, tawny-haired Christopher Sykes was on the verge of financial ruin because he spent so much entertaining his friend the prince. When an ambassador's wife admonished Leonie for not going to Cannes this year because "Tum Tum," as she called the prince, looked especially dashing dressed as a devil for something called the Battle of Flowers, I decided I could tolerate no more. I excused myself and went in search of Geoffrey and some more stimulating conversation.

Before I could reach him, dinner was announced.

Liveried footmen passed among the gentlemen present, discreetly informing them who their dinner partners would be. I was pleasantly surprised when the Marquis of Sherborne came up to me.

"I have the pleasure of escorting you to dinner, Miss Clark," he said with a mischievous smile as he bowed and offered me his arm.

"And how did you arrange that, pray tell?"

"Oh, connections in high places. Very high places."

As I walked into the dining room on his arm, and saw the long table sparkling with a daunting array of silver cutlery and no less than nine crystal wineglasses at each place, I mentally thanked Chef Henri back in Cairo for his strict tutelage in the etiquette of formal dining.

Lord Sherborne and I were seated near the center of the table, and, as I waited for the others to be seated, I unfolded my napkin and glanced at the menu, which was written on a little card set at every place. My eyes widened at the elaborateness of it. I counted no fewer than thirteen courses, with several choices for each, beginning with *consommé aux ailerons* and ending with a *bombe glacée*, each with its complementary wine. Reading the menu was enough to make me feel that if I ate everything set before me, I would surely burst my stays or explode from overindulgence. I could understand why the prince was so rotund, if he ate meals like this every day.

I looked round the table and saw that Leonie was closer to the prince, while Geoffrey was seated directly across from me. I had to peer around a decorative pyramid of golden apricots and blue plums to see him clearly. He looked as though he would rather be anywhere else in the world than at Marlborough House.

The princess nodded at the butler, and liveried footmen with white gloves began serving; one set a bowl of consommé on the silver service plate before me, and I had to concentrate on dining rather than Geoffrey.

Egypt intrigued Lord Sherborne, and he asked me questions about the country and its people. He said he planned to winter in Cairo rather than Cannes, where he usually rented a villa. I extolled the virtues of Egypt's hot, dry climate and the amenities of the Clark's Hotel, and I could envision Cyrus beaming at me in approval as he anticipated another successful season. When, however, the marquis learned that I might not be returning to Egypt, he abruptly lost interest and proceeded to tell me of his grand plans for adding acreage to his Sussex estate.

Even as I conversed with my partner, I kept one eye on Leonie, for it was the first time I had seen her with her royal paramour, and I was curious as to how she kept his interest. She was very attentive and smiled often, while keeping up an incessant flow of chatter, which I could not hear very well from where I sat. The prince appeared to say very little, but wore a look of utter contentment as he ate. Never once did I see him drum his fingertips against the table, which, Maud had once told me, was a sure sign of impending boredom. My sister obviously knew what was expected of her and played the role well.

As the meal progressed, I found myself actually relaxing and enjoying myself more than I ever suspected I would. The food, indeed, was delicious and served with great imagination and flair. Soft candlelight made every lady present look beautiful, even those long past their prime, while the spicy scent of carnations set in silver epergnes perfumed the air. Around me, dishes were tasted or devoured, as the diner's inclination directed, and, on occasion, a hand was discreetly waved to notify the footman that a particular course wasn't desired and shouldn't be served.

We had just finished the *soufflé de cailles au riz*, which I had skipped, and were about to progress to the *boeuf flamande en gelée*, when tragedy struck.

As Geoffrey's wine was poured, I should have taken note of Leonie's sudden silence and her pointed look at her husband, whom she had ignored all evening. I should have, but I didn't.

Geoffrey sipped his wine. Suddenly, he coughed, sputtered, and barely had time to put his napkin to his mouth.

The entire table fell silent; people turned and stared. Even the footmen stopped in their tracks, serving dishes poised in their hands.

"Is there something wr-rong with the wine, Lester-r?" his host boomed from the head of the table.

Everyone held his breath, waiting to hear what his response was going to be.

Geoffrey dabbed at his lips. "It has the unmistakable taste of vinegar, sir."

"What?" the prince roared, and immediately tasted the wine in his own glass. "I beg to differ with you, Lester-r. There is nothing wrong with it."

As the prince looked at each of us in turn, everyone followed his example, sipped his wine, and echoed the prince's pronouncement to his neighbor. I drank mine and looked at Geoffrey in puzzlement, for it was a rich, full-bodied claret. I didn't fully understand until I glanced down at Leonie.

She was trying so hard not to laugh that her shoulders were shaking and her pouting mouth began to twitch at the corners. In a flash of comprehension, I thought of Mr. Sykes and his seagull.

How could I possibly warn Geoffrey without causing a dreadful scene and antagonizing the prince?

The conversation had resumed, and the marquis further distracted me by asking if I had yet seen the Egyptian Galleries in the British Museum. The prince made a sign. A servant removed Geoffrey's glass and poured him another. The incident appeared forgotten.

This time, Geoffrey merely sniffed the wine's bouquet, then set it down untasted, and I knew this glass of wine was no better than the first. I prayed the prince would not call attention to it and let the matter pass, but, of course, that would have spoiled everything.

"Something wr-wrong with your wine again, Lester-r?" he said in undisguised annoyance. "You're not drinking it."

Conversation ceased abruptly, like the flow of water from

a tap suddenly closed. Not a fork clinked. Even silk dresses stopped rustling. I could almost hear all the heads turn in unison to stare at Geoffrey, and I held my breath along with everyone else, wondering what his next move would be.

Judging by the look that suddenly sprang into his eyes, I knew I had to do something to stop the situation from becoming ugly.

Placing a hand on Lord Sherborne's arm, I swayed and murmured, "My lord, I'm afraid I feel faint."

The man jumped to his feet and managed to catch me as I let myself go limp and pitch forward, praying I wouldn't land face down in my plate, and that my tiara wouldn't slip off.

My ruse worked.

"What is the matter with Miss Clar-rk?" I heard the prince demand as the flustered Lord Sherborne began fanning my face with his napkin and calling for female assistance.

I let my eyelids flutter and pretended to revive. "It—it must have been the carriage accident. I'm afraid I haven't completely recovered. All the excitement . . . Pray do forgive me for interrupting dinner."

Geoffrey must have understood immediately, for he rose and set his napkin down. "If Miss Clark isn't well, then she must be taken home at once. With Your Highnesses' kind permission, I shall escort her."

"That won't be necessary, Lester," the marquis insisted. "There's no need for you to spoil your wife's evening by leaving so soon. I can escort Miss Clark home."

I groaned inwardly, for the marquis's gallantry was spoiling my plan, but I hadn't counted on Geoffrey's determination.

"Most generous of you to offer, Sherborne," he said, with a warning glint in his eye, "but I can't impose. *I* shall escort Miss Clark home."

The entire table had fallen silent, and everyone was looking from one man to the other, wondering, I suppose, which would emerge victorious from this battle of wills.

Finally, I smiled brightly and said, "Gentlemen, please. I

refuse to be fought over. You are most kind, Lord Sherborne, to offer your assistance, but I'm afraid I cannot impose."

Since he would not contradict a lady, the marquis withdrew gracefully, albeit reluctantly.

When the princess insisted that I see her personal physician, I protested that all I needed was to go home and get some rest. Leonie managed to contain her fury and started to rise, but Geoffrey waved her back into her seat, insisting that there was no need for her to come with us and spoil her evening. Judging from the looks on the other guests' faces, I knew we weren't fooling anyone with this elaborate charade, but no one was about to challenge the veracity of a lady. With profuse apologies to our royal host and hostess, I leaned dramatically on Geoffrey's arm and he escorted me out of the dining room. Our carriage was brought around quickly, and we left Marlborough House.

Once inside, Geoffrey smiled and said, "That was quite a performance. Thank you for rescuing me."

I was trembling with rage. "How could Leonie be a party to such a prank, serving you vinegar instead of wine?" I found myself wishing my sister had come with us, so I could vent my spleen directly at her.

"Where's your sense of fun, Cassa? Didn't you think it amusing to watch me sputter, and choke, and make a fool of myself in front of everyone?"

"No," was my heartfelt reply.

"Well, my own wife obviously did." He was silent for a moment, then changed seats so he could sit beside me. "Do you think they expected me to drink the vinegar rather than insult the prince by contradicting him?"

"Perhaps. But I saw the look in your eyes. You looked as though you wanted to strangle someone."

Geoffrey's laugh was rueful. "I have a wicked temper on occasion, and, if the truth be known, I was on the verge of telling my future king exactly what I thought of him and his little amusements."

I shook my head at the narrowness of his escape. "That would have been disastrous."

"Leonie would never have forgiven me, though I don't think I really care anymore. As it is, she's probably apologizing to everyone for my atrocious manners right this very minute. How very thoughtless of Geoffrey not to go along with their little lark." Now he folded his arms. "But I am not Mr. Sykes."

"It was a cruel and thoughtless jest," I said, shaking my head.

"However, the prince did offer me some compensation for stealing my wife."

My brows rose. "Oh?"

"While you were talking to the other women, the prince was offering me a knighthood. It's his way of spreading balm on a sore wound, you see . . . an order, a medal, or an exalted position at court in exchange for a man's wife. If I had accepted, I would have become Sir Geoffrey Lester. It has a certain aristocratic ring to it, don't you think?" Suddenly, bitter self-deprecation was replaced by a wistful tone. "My father always dreamed of a knighthood for me."

"But I doubt that he would have approved of this method of winning one," I declared. I was silent for a moment. "Whatever did the prince say when you turned it down?"

"Well, he didn't threaten to have me beheaded, if that's any consolation. He was speechless, then he became very angry, though he suppressed it admirably. I don't think anyone has ever refused such an honor before." In the darkness of the carriage, I could barely discern Geoffrey's face, but I knew he was regarding me thoughtfully. "Don't you think I was a fool for refusing that knighthood?"

"Honor? It was merely a bribe, that's all. There's more honor in refusing it, even if it was offered by royalty."

I sensed him smile. "Ah, Cassa, so full of honesty and

good sense. Somehow, I knew you'd say that." Then I felt his hand close over mine, and before I could draw away, he put it to his lips. "Thank you."

At least the darkness kept him from seeing how much his touch affected me.

We sat there in silence for a while, and then Geoffrey said, "Would you care to dine at the Savoy tonight? You look much too beautiful to be taken home right away, and, since our dinner was so rudely interrupted . . ."

I was confused. "The Savoy . . . but I thought that is where the Gilbert and Sullivan operettas are performed."

"That's the Savoy Theatre. The hotel is right next door and was just built by Richard D'Oyly Carte, the theatre's manager. It's one of the new luxury hotels springing up in London, a bit more posh than Clark's of Cairo, but I think you'd like it." He paused for a moment. "Come, Cassa, will you join me?"

"Oh, I—I don't know. It is rather late, and, after all that food at Marlborough House, I'm not very hungry."

Geoffrey recognized a lame excuse when he heard one. "Oh, come now. It's not even ten o'clock, and, even if you're not hungry, we could have a sweet and coffee, if you prefer."

"No, Geoffrey, I really must decline. I'd appreciate being taken back to Upper Brook Street at once."

I heard him chuckle, and I knew he was regarding me with amusement. "My dear, I assure you you'd be much safer at the Savoy than you are at this very moment, alone with me in a carriage. If I wanted to, I could have Fred drive to some farm on the outskirts of London, and . . ." He left the rest to my imagination. "Your screams would go quite unheeded, I can assure you."

As soon as I recognized the undercurrent of laughter in his voice, I realized that my brother-in-law was only teasing me. "I'm being quite foolish, aren't I?" I murmured sheepishly to his shadow.

"Yes, you are," he replied. "You have nothing to fear from me, as I believe I have said to you on more than one occasion."

"Yes, I would like to go to the Savoy with you."

"Splendid."

When the carriage finally stopped and Geoffrey handed me down, I had to tilt back my head in order to look at the magnificent building that towered six stories or more. In the center of the courtyard was a fountain sending jets of water shooting into the air, as soothing as the sound of rain on a rooftop, and welcome after the brittle tension of Marlborough House. But the grand facade of this new hotel was insignificant compared to the elegance of the mahogany-panelled dining room inside, and I found myself noticing every detail, minor or otherwise, to report back to Cyrus. Since it was a balmy summer's night, Geoffrey requested that the head waiter seat us at a table on the balcony that extended off the dining room, where we could look out over the roofs of the city.

We said little to each other as we consumed a delicious confection of swirled meringue, hazelnuts, and raspberry sauce, but Geoffrey never took his eyes off me. Whenever I glanced up and caught him staring, he would quickly smile and call my attention to the beautiful glass chandeliers overhead, or the idiosyncrasies of one of the other diners. His scrutiny was beginning to make me feel uneasy, and I was relieved when we finally finished our coffee and it was time to leave.

"Now, that wasn't so bad, was it?" he said, when we were back outside in the night air, which had suddenly turned cool. Before I could say a word, he added, "But I have one more request to make of you."

"And what is that?"

"Take a walk with me along the Embankment. It's still too early to go home."

I knew if I refused, he would mock me again, so I readily agreed, much to his surprise.

We walked arm in arm from the hotel down to the Victoria Embankment, which, Geoffrey informed me in his best tour guide voice, was land reclaimed from the Thames and extended from Westminster to Blackfriars. So, instead of rising tides, there were grass, trees, and pathways for both pedestrians and carriages. That night there were just a few other couples strolling, and the odd policeman, who gave my jewels a stern, thoughtful look and warned Geoffrey to be on his guard for thieves and such. As we strolled on toward Cleopatra's Needle, the stone obelisk given to Britain by the Khedive of Egypt, I noticed even the cast iron benches were in an Egyptian motif, with winged sphinxes on either side. Most of these benches were vacant except for an old derelict lying on one because he had nowhere else to spend the night. Seeing the man huddled there in his rags, his bleary eyes staring hopelessly into space made me think of Maud and her good works. Geoffrey must have been thinking of his sister, too, for he approached the wary man, pressed a gold sovereign into his hand, and told him to find shelter before the police ordered him to move on. The man pulled his forelock, murmured his thanks, and ambled off, whether to shelter or an alehouse, I did not know.

As we crossed to the footpath on the river side, the night air was filled with the scents of the Thames—dampness, rotting garbage, and oil from passing barges and boats. Far down the river, we could hear a series of plaintive whistles and toots. One boat would sound its horn, to be followed by an eerie answering call that would linger over the water before fading away and dying altogether. I shivered and wished the mournful sounds would stop.

We leaned over the cold railing and looked down into the murky water, so black and implacable as it flowed to the sea. The night was filled with thousands of stars, and across the river, the lights of Southwark couldn't rival them in brilliance. It was a magical night made for lovers, and, for the first time in a long, long time, I yearned to belong to a special man, and he to me.

Geoffrey broke the silence by saying, "I can't remember when I've enjoyed an evening more, in spite of its disastrous beginnings." He looked over at me and smiled. "I think it has something to do with the company."

"I've enjoyed this evening very much, too. Thank you for taking me to the Savoy. I'm sure Cyrus will want to hear all about it when I return to Cairo."

This must not have been what Geoffrey wanted to hear, for he suddenly looked annoyed with me and fell silent. After a while, he said, "If the Thames were a wishing well, do you know what I'd wish for?"

The utter fancifulness of his mood quite caught me by surprise, and I regarded him with astonishment.

"I would wish that this evening never had to end." Then, as I watched, he reached into his pocket, took out another gold sovereign, and held it up for me to see. "Since this sovereign is worth much more than a penny, my wish is sure to come true."

As I looked into his eyes and saw the fires of desire in their depths, I realized too late what a fool I had been to trust him and that I never should have come with him tonight. All the times I had gone out of my way to avoid being alone with him, all my scrupulous attempts to keep him at arm's length crumbled and came to naught. I girded myself for another battle.

"I think I'd like to go home now, Geoffrey," I said stiffly.

Suddenly, he jammed his coin back into his pocket and glared down at me, and I involuntarily stepped back in fear, for I had never seen a man so angry, not even the German prince whose face I slapped as payment for his unwanted embrace.

"You are not going home until you hear what I have to say," Geoffrey said.

I turned defiantly and started to walk away, but was halted in mid-stride as a hand clamped down on my wrist. Before I could utter a word of protest, I was unceremoniously whirled around to face him, my wrists imprisoned in his hands.

"Let go of me," I managed to say quite calmly, and did not subject myself to further indignity by struggling against his superior strength.

"There is something I must say to you first," he replied, "and I will say it to you as I hold you here, or I will release you and then we'll talk. What is it to be?"

There was something in his voice that warned me not to cross him, so I had no choice but to relent. "All right, I'll listen."

He released me, and the anger drained out of his face. "I don't know quite how to say this, so perhaps I had better be as direct as possible." He took a deep breath. "Cassa, I'm afraid I've quite fallen in love with you."

From somewhere in the city, there came the steady chime of a clock striking the hour, and, once again, the mournful horn of a boat passing beneath Waterloo Bridge floated on the night air.

I was so taken aback by Geoffrey's declaration, that, for a moment, I was in a daze, unable to speak or even think another thought. But through the haze of shock, I knew this was a situation that had to be faced and handled delicately. I could not run away this time.

"Please don't say any more, Geoffrey."

The merciless white light of the electric lamp overhead drained the color from Geoffrey's face and distorted it. "It's true. I know I should have urged you to return to Egypt every time you threatened to go, but I couldn't bring myself to do it, not even for your own good. I'm a greedy, selfish man, and I enjoyed your company. And, as the days went on—"

"Stop!" I took a step away from him. "You mustn't say such things, ever again. You are married to my sister."

A look of incredulity twisted his face. "Marriage? Is that what you'd call our relationship?" He made no attempt to touch me, though I know the effort cost him a great deal, for he rocked back on his heels. "I call it a hell on earth."

"I'm sorry, Geoffrey, but there is nothing I can do to help you."

"You could tell me that you love me as much as I love you."

I turned away from him and ran my hands along my arms to warm them. "But I'm afraid I don't feel the same about you, Geoffrey. I—I treasure you as a close, valued friend, but nothing more. I'm sorry if that causes you pain."

He groaned as he came to stand behind me, and I sensed some great power within him being held in check against his will. "You're deluding yourself, my girl. You may think you don't care for me, but I've had enough experience with women to know otherwise."

I turned to face him, annoyed with his arrogance. "Credit me with knowing my own feelings, Sir."

That infuriating wry smile pulled at one corner of his mouth. "You think you know yourself, Cassa, but not as well as I do. I've noticed the way you look at me, especially when I was lying in that hospital bed and you were seated at my side, clutching my hand, so afraid I would die. Your face was an open book, my dear, for all to read."

My breath quickened, and I became less sure of myself, because I knew he spoke the truth. "Even if I did love you, we could never be together. You are married to my sister."

He drew my hands to his lips and kissed my fingers, while staring deeply into my eyes. "Leonie is a minor obstacle. There is a way, if you're brave enough to take it."

My brows rose in silent inquiry.

"You couldn't stay at Brook Street, of course, but there are other places—quiet, secluded places, right here in London, where we could be alone. I'm sure we could fabricate something to tell your mother. We could say that you decided to return to Cairo after all, but all the time, you would be right here."

I should have struck him for what he was suggesting, but I decided sarcasm was a more effective weapon. "Oh, I see.

So you plan to have me replace Mademoiselle de Vigne at the villa in St. John's Wood, is that it?"

His face fell, and he dropped my hands as if they were fire. "How did you know about Marietta? Did Leonie tell you?"

I shook my head. "That first day we rode in the park, I overheard some men discussing you and your *chère amie.*" I never knew I could sound so bitter and cynical. "When I first met you in Cairo, Cyrus insisted that you were a European gentleman seeking a diversion while away from his wife. How right he was. I'm disappointed in you, Geoffrey. I would have expected you to be more honest. You might at least have asked me to become your mistress right then, in Cairo, rather than give me some tale about my mother wanting to see me." My voice trembled. "What does love mean to you? A few stolen hours between going to the stock exchange and joining your wife for the Hyde Park promenade?"

His rage was steadily mounting, though he fought valiantly to control it. "You know I can't offer you marriage."

Suddenly, my own anger melted like the snow before the spring sun. "Geoffrey, when I do find a man I can love, I want to do so openly and proudly. I want to be with him always, not for just a few hours here, and a few hours there. I would want to have his children recognized, not stigmatized as bastards."

"Cassa—" he groaned and reached for me.

But I stepped neatly aside and evaded him, keeping him at arm's length. "And I don't wish to share him with another woman. I saw what my mother's infidelity did to my father, how it made him die inside. I know my mother felt she had to have the Earl of Knighton whatever the cost. Fine for her, but what about those she left behind, my father and me? We were left with scars that never healed, feelings of loss and rejection that I haven't overcome to this day. And I wouldn't hurt my sister, even if I did love you." I shook my head stubbornly. "I wouldn't want to be responsible for destroying someone else's marriage. I couldn't live with myself, if I did." I sighed, feeling suddenly weary and inexplicably sad. "Content yourself with your Mademoiselle de Vigne, Geoffrey. Fewer people will be hurt that way."

He placed his hands on the railing and stared out at the opposite shore. "I can't. Marietta has left me. She realized even before I did that I loved someone else, and she said it would be kinder to me if she dissolved our liaison. Extraordinary woman, my Marietta," he added.

I didn't know what to say to that.

Then he said, "If I weren't married to Leonie, Cassa, would you have me?"

"I don't know. Perhaps."

Then he reached into his pocket, took out the gold piece again, drew his arm back as far as it would go, and flung the coin over the railing with all his strength. I watched it rise in a sweeping arc over the railing and catch the light, flaring like a match in the darkness for one instant before plunging into the water.

I looked at Geoffrey in curiosity. "Why did you do that?"

"I made a wish."

"What did you wish for?"

A slight, enigmatic smile touched his mouth as he drew my arm through his. "But that would be telling, now wouldn't it? And then my wish would never come true."

But somehow, I knew what his wish was, and part of me wished it would never come true, for Leonie's sake as well as my own.

Chapter Eleven

Feeling that I owed the marquis an explanation for my behavior last night, as well as an apology for using him so shamelessly to extricate Geoffrey from further embarrassment, I called on him the next morning.

After a short walk to his house next door, which was even larger and more imposing than the Lesters' residence, I was shown by his butler into a spacious drawing room decorated in a simple, tasteful style favored nearly ninety years ago. I sat on the edge of a divan covered in striped yellow silk, noting the pale yellow walls, which made the room seem airy and bright, and furniture that glowed with the mellow patina of age and years of hand rubbing. I was sure each piece was an original Sheraton or Hepplewhite. More than anything, the marquis's elegant drawing room brought home to me most forcibly the difference between old-moneyed aristocrats and men, such as Geoffrey, of recent fortune. This room represented a reverence for the past, for traditions bred over hundreds of years into the bone and sinew of a man.

Suddenly, the doors flew open and Lord Sherborne himself came striding in, looking as though he had just awoken and dressed hastily. But his smile was welcoming and gracious as he said, "Good morning, Miss Clark. Do forgive me for keeping you waiting."

I rose. "It is I who should be asking your forgiveness, my lord."

"For what, Miss Clark? I should have risen hours ago." Stifling a yawn, he motioned for me to be seated, then seated himself in a chair opposite. He listened attentively as I explained that I had only pretended to faint last night in order to rescue Geoffrey from any more of the prince's "larks."

The marquis scowled, and for a moment, I feared I had angered him. "I am such a dolt! I should have realized that's what you were doing, Miss Clark." There was genuine regret in his voice when he said, "And I almost ruined everything with my stubborn insistence that I take you home. It is I who should apologize to you."

"No harm done."

"I have been the butt of several of His Royal Highness's larks myself." He shrugged. "But he is our future king, after all."

To me, that justified nothing, but I held my tongue.

As we sat there, an awkward silence suddenly grew between us, and I felt slightly ill at ease in the marquis's presence for the first time since meeting him. He was regarding me with an expression I recognized all too well from certain guests at the Clark's Hotel: a look of blatant romantic interest.

And here I was, alone with the man in his house. How could I have been such a fool as to call on a single gentleman at ten o'clock in the morning, without a chaperone? I mentally berated myself.

Then I rose hastily. "I'm—I'm sorry for calling so early my lord. I hope I haven't inconvenienced you."

He didn't detain me, as I feared he might. "Nonsense." Ever the gentleman, he seemed to sense the reason for my sudden discomfort. "Why don't you leave by the rear entrance, Miss Clark? Our gardens are adjoining, and there is a gate, you'll remember. I'll show you the way."

No sooner did I return to the Lesters' house than I had to get out again. I ordered a carriage and spent the entire morning browsing among the shops in the Strand. Throughout the entire time, I couldn't stop thinking of Geoffrey and his declaration on the Embankment last night.

Was he right, I wondered, as I looked idly at leather-bound books and delicate lace handkerchiefs? Did I really share his love, and was I refusing to acknowledge it, even to myself?

After spending fruitless hours shopping, I had Fred drive me to the British Museum in Grafton Street, and, as I strolled through its Egyptian Galleries, gazing in wonder at the black basalt Rosetta Stone and a large collection of statues and mummy cases, I wondered what Cyrus would have to say about my situation.

I could envision him, his large bulk seated behind his desk, the nearly invisible brows raised as I told him about my dilemma, and I could hear him as clearly as if he were standing right at my elbow. "Well, coz, if you really love this Lester fellow, I would say go after him and damn the consequences. Besides, from what you've told me, your sister doesn't seem very deserving of such a man. It would serve her right if she lost him."

Ah, but that was my point. Did I really love Geoffrey?

"You're no help at all, Cyrus," I said aloud, causing several ladies on a tour to look at me as though one of the mummies had just come to life and was strolling around the gallery.

After leaving the museum, I decided to visit Maud at the school, for I wasn't quite ready to return home just yet.

When I arrived, I received the shock of my life.

Maud looked up from her desk and announced, without preamble, "Geoff has asked Leo for a divorce."

I stopped where I stood. "What?"

She rose and grimaced as she cursed her stays. "I was as shocked as you are when he told me this morning before leaving for his club. I went to your room to tell you, but you were still sleeping, and I didn't have the heart to wake you." Then Maud took my arm and led me over to a chair, where I collapsed gratefully. Her smile was both triumphant and a trifle malicious as she said, "I couldn't be happier."

"Oh, Maud, you don't mean that."

"Oh, but I most certainly do." Her hazel eyes hardened and grew cold. "That woman has made my brother's life a living hell ever since she married him, not to mention making him the laughingstock of London. She's spent his money as though it were candy and treats him as though he isn't fit to kiss the hem of her gown. Geoffrey can't tolerate it any more, and I don't blame him."

"But a divorce, Maud? That's such a drastic step."

"Oh, it is, I grant you, but quite justified." Her face took on a zealous glow as she dropped down into her chair. "My brother is a *man*, Cassa, not some groveling sycophant willing to let another man take his wife whenever he pleases."

"What will the prince have to say about all this?"

"Who gives a damn what that spoiled little boy thinks?" Maud asked indignantly. "For once he'll see that he can't go helping himself to other men's wives like a third helping of *jambon de Prague!*"

This tirade caused me to wonder what had changed Maud from a passionate defender of the prince to his reviler. Then I had my answer. Maud always supported Geoffrey, even if it meant changing her stand on an issue. Her brother could do no wrong in her eyes. If Geoffrey accepted his situation with the prince, then his sister would, too, and if he decided not to tolerate it, Maud would reverse her stand and back him up as well.

"What did Leonie have to say when Geoffrey asked her for the divorce?" I asked, my curiosity getting the better of me.

Maud pulled the pins from her hair and fluffed it out with her fingers until it looked like a lion's mane. "He asked her this morning, just as she was sitting in bed, having her morning tea. She wasn't ecstatic, that's obvious. Geoff told me that first she just laughed at him and said he wouldn't be free of her until she was in her grave."

When I thought of the note with WHORE written in red, I shivered as though someone were walking over *my* grave.

"When he insisted he would have a divorce, she threw her teapot at him. Fortunately, it was empty."

"Well, if Leonie won't grant him a divorce, what's Geoffrey going to do?" I wondered aloud.

Maud smiled wryly, propped her elbow up on her desk, and cradled her chin in her hand. "Oh, Leo can refuse to cooperate all she likes, but the truth of the matter is, Geoff has a case against her, and she knows it. Our divorce laws are such that a man can divorce his wife if he can prove she's been unfaithful to him. Leonie's lover is the Prince of Wales and everyone knows it. One can't have more damaging evidence than that."

As I sat there, staring at the photograph of the queen on the wall behind Maud, I recalled Aunt Venetia telling me something years ago about the prince standing as a witness in the sensational divorce case of one Lady Mordaunt. The queen and Alexandra stood by him, presenting a united front in the face of so much public outcry against the loose morals of the upper classes, but the prince's reputation was damaged by his association with Lady Mordaunt, who was judged insane and the case dropped. For weeks afterward, the prince and princess were hissed as they rode through the streets of London.

Although the Mordaunt incident had happened nearly twenty years ago, I somehow doubted that the prince would welcome being summoned to the witness-box in another such case.

"If this case comes to trial, Maud . . ."

She shrugged it off optimistically. "I really don't think it will come to that, Cassandra. I'm sure Geoffrey will eventually make Leonie see reason and the prudence of agreeing to this divorce quietly. If he makes a generous settlement on her, knowing how Leonie loves money, I'm sure she'll agree to the divorce quite amicably."

Privately, I thought Maud was deluding herself, but I held my tongue.

Suddenly, she seemed to forget about her sister-in-law for a moment and told me that one of the instructors at the school was leaving, so there might be a position for Edith at last. "But don't tell her yet," Maud cautioned me, "because I still want to check her references. Even though she's a family friend, I can't be too careful when it comes to my school." Then she scowled at a paper in her hand. "How odd. Edith didn't list her last employer, the Ecôle Lafarge, as a reference. I wonder why?" I explained what Edgar had told me about Edith's dismissal, and Maud nodded. "That would explain it. But, as I was saying, Cassa, I think Leo will agree to the divorce quite amicably."

But I didn't think my sister would ever let Geoffrey go, and when I returned to the house later that afternoon, I soon discovered that my fears were justified.

As soon as I walked through the door, I found my sister pacing back and forth in the foyer as though waiting for someone. When she saw me, she stopped, and I was surprised to find not the virago I expected, but rather a strangely subdued young woman, her eyes puffy and red from crying.

"Cassandra, will you please step into the drawing room for a moment?" she asked, her voice soft and quavering. "I must speak with you."

Baffled by this sudden change, I followed her into the room and shut the door behind me. I decided I had best play the innocent. "What do you wish to speak to me about, Leonie?"

"You know very well." Her eyes suddenly filled with tears, and I steeled myself for an outburst. "You know Geoffrey has asked me—no, told me, he wants a divorce."

"Maud informed me a little while ago. I'm sorry."

"Sorry? Are you really?" She dabbed at her eyes with a handkerchief. "Please don't insult my intelligence by lying to me, Cassandra. I know all about you and Geoffrey."

I thought about the night on the Embankment, and felt

myself blush guiltily. But what did I have to be ashamed of?
"There is nothing between Geoffrey and me, Leonie."

Now she turned a painful, angry shade of red. "Do you
think I'm blind as well as stupid? I've seen the way my husband looks at you, the way he once looked at me."

"You're imagining it. Geoffrey sees me as his sister-in-law,
nothing more."

She sniffed loudly again, then walked over to one of the
tables and picked up a small china figurine of a prowling
tiger. Leonie ran her finger down its back and seemed to
study it for a moment as though debating whether to hurl it
at me. I took a deep breath and prepared to dodge, but she
just put it back on the table and turned to me with a reflective look.

"Perhaps I misjudged you. You may be the innocent party
after all," she said quietly. "It's Geoffrey who has pushed
you for a liaison, isn't it?"

"Leonie—"

"No, don't try to defend him. I know what a cruel, callous
man my husband can be. Any woman is fair game, and he
knows he has certain . . . charms that are irresistible to our
sex." Now she draped herself on one corner of the divan and
looked across at me, still standing in the middle of the room,
my hands folded before me as though I were a prisoner coming before a judge. "Don't you remember when you first
arrived, I warned you that he would try something like this?
Didn't I tell you that if he wanted you, he would stop at
nothing until he won you?"

Something inside of me, some sixth sense, warned me
that Leonie was just trying to undermine my defenses and
somehow get me to take her into my confidence and betray
Geoffrey. Even though he said he wanted me for his mistress, I couldn't tell my sister that.

"Geoffrey does not have designs on me, Leonie," I insisted.

A petulant look flickered across her face as she rose and

took a menacing step toward me. "Then why has he asked me for a divorce?"

Her naïveté astounded me. "You mean to tell me that you have no idea? Perhaps he's tired of playing the cuckold. And after that humiliating prank last night, can you blame him?"

"The only reason I instigated that lark was to make Geoffrey feel he was a part of our set, to let him know he was accepted by Edward and his friends. He is always so stand-offish with everyone, always acting as though he'd rather be anywhere other than socializing with royalty. And we probably could have cajoled him out of his black mood if you hadn't pretended to swoon like that."

I just shook my head.

Leonie continued. "Besides, would Geoffrey risk the scandal of divorce just because we had a lark at his expense? No, I can't believe that. And as for my affair, Geoffrey has never been blameless in that area, either. He's tolerated my relationship with Edward this long; why does he suddenly want a divorce?"

She was so self-centered, she honestly couldn't see what her behavior was doing to her husband's pride and self-esteem. I was suddenly filled with disgust, but I managed to control myself. "I don't know Geoffrey's reasoning."

"Well, I'm not giving him a divorce, and that's that," she said with great finality.

I was on the verge of pointing out that if they were both trapped in a loveless marriage and so very unhappy, what was the point in remaining shackled to each other? But I held my tongue. Leonie would only misconstrue my concern for interest in her husband.

She waited, as though expecting me to say something. When I made no comment, she went on. "He's told me he'd be most generous with a settlement. I'd have my own house, of course, horses, servants, and a large allowance, even more than I'm getting now." She shook her head. "It sounds so enticing, but no amount of money could compensate me for the social standing I'd lose. Why, I'd be an outcast in society, like poor Mother. None of my friends would receive me in their homes ever again. Surely Geoffrey expects too much of me."

"I'm sure your real friends would stand by you."

A furrow creased her brow, and, for a moment, the old Leonie reappeared, more haughty than ever. "Cassandra, you know nothing of the intricacies of society. I wouldn't expect my friends to stand by me through this. It would simply be asking too much of them."

Privately, I thought any friends worthy of the name would staunchly support her, but again, I kept silent.

Leonie shook her head resolutely. "No, I won't give up my friends and social position to become like Mama, ever an outcast, never going anywhere or doing anything interesting. Geoffrey owes me that much for all the suffering he's put me through. He can be so clever, that one. I think Geoffrey's silver tongue could convince the Almighty to let him into Heaven after all he has done to me."

"I don't think Geoffrey is quite the blackguard you paint him, Leonie."

Her smile was sharp and pitying. "Innocent Cassandra . . . so trusting, so quick to believe the best of people. I can't believe anyone could reach the advanced age of whatever you are and still be so ignorant of certain matters. Didn't that priggish aunt of yours ever warn you about men like Geoffrey?"

I resented her sarcastic tone, but I made allowances for her state and bit back the retort that was on the tip of my tongue. This was no time to argue with my sister.

All I said was, "The decision is yours to make, Leonie. Whether you decide to grant Geoffrey a divorce will be of no consequence to me."

How wrong I was.

After leaving Leonie, and asking Heffer to notify me the moment the master returned, I locked myself in my room and waited.

Around half past five, Heffer knocked and told me that Geoffrey was waiting for me in his study. When I went downstairs, I found him looking chastened and subdued. He didn't smile when he saw me, but his features softened and his expression was one of profound tenderness.

Before I could speak, he said, "First of all, I want to apologize for last night. Not for saying I love you, but for asking you to become my mistress. I misjudged you, and I'm sorry."

"I accept your apology." Why did I always feel like a schoolgirl in his presence? It was maddening in a woman of my age.

He indicated a chair in front of his desk. When I sat down, I said, "I have heard the most disturbing news, and I hope it's not true."

"It is," he said.

"But why do you want to divorce Leonie?"

"Why?" His mouth curved into a sardonic smile as he tugged on his tie to loosen it. "I thought that would be obvious. I want to be free of a burdensome, detested wife who doesn't—who never—loved me." Now his voice changed, losing its bitter edge to become soft and gentle. "Then perhaps you will consider me as a suitor."

I could not believe what I had just heard. "Are you saying you want this divorce because of me?"

He nodded.

"But why?" I asked again.

"It's the only way that I can have you." He was quiet, as though waiting for me to speak. When I didn't, he said, "Cassa, there is something I must tell you." While I watched, he rose, crossed the room to a window, and stared out, not looking at me. "At the time I first met you in Cairo, I was still very much in love with my wife."

"I know. Whenever you spoke of Leonie or showed me her photograph, your face glowed. I could tell that you loved her very much."

"I did until I returned to England and discovered what

had happened in my absence." His fingers flexed restlessly behind him. "But, through it all, I always held on to my belief that once the prince tired of her, Leonie and I could somehow put the past behind us and pick up our lives together." He stared down at the floor and shook his head. "Poor, deluded fool."

My heart went out to him, but I could think of no words of comfort.

"Then you came to us because you thought your mother needed you. You were disgusted with our benign tolerance of the prince's philandering and Leonie's part in it, and you made me ashamed of myself for accepting it as my duty. And when you helped Maud to recruit girls for the school . . ." He stopped and was silent for the longest time. "Everything you did showed me true, selfless love, something that Leonie sorely lacks. For the first time, I began to see what I was missing, and damn it, Cassa, I thought I'd go mad!"

I clasped my hands together to keep them from trembling. "I don't know what to say, Geoffrey."

He came toward me and stood there, his blond head bent, his gray eyes guarded, as though he was unsure of my response to what he was about to say. "I found myself falling in love with you, Cassa. oh, not right away, of course. Despite what you may think to the contrary, I did make a valiant attempt to resist you, for I did realize the impossibility of our situation. But when I woke up in the hospital after the accident, my first thought was of you. There I was, in pain and flat on my back, with no way of knowing whether you were alive or dead. In my dreadful fear of losing you, I realized how much I loved you, and that if, by some miracle, you had survived, I was never going to let you go again."

By mentioning the hospital, Geoffrey brought back feelings I had tried to forget—my fear that he might die, the sense of devastating loss that had overwhelmed me at the time—but, as I sat in this room, I resolutely told myself these emotions did not necessarily mean I was in love with Geoffrey. They couldn't.

He was speaking again. "Then, when I began seeing signs that perhaps you felt the same about me—oh, don't shake your head and deny it, Cassa, because you have betrayed your true feelings on more than one occasion—I knew the only course open to me was to divorce Leonie."

I looked over at him now. He was still standing by the window, filling the room with his strength and his presence, while the sunlight burnished his hair. Yet there was something very trusting and vulnerable about him that shook me.

With a sigh, I leaned back in my chair and closed my eyes, vaguely aware that he was walking toward me.

When he reached down to touch my shoulder lightly, it would have been so easy to take his hand and press it to my lips, but I forced myself to resist him. "Leonie is my sister, Geoffrey, and you are her husband. As I told you last night, I can't sacrifice her happiness for my own." I could not stop the tears from springing to my eyes, but I could keep Geoffrey from seeing them, so I rose.

Suddenly, he said, "Why are you denying that you love me, Cassa? Is there someone else who has captured your heart?" He paused. "The Marquis of Sherborne, perhaps?"

I whirled around. "The marquis? Of course not!"

Geoffrey's face suddenly relaxed, losing its anxious look. "That's reassuring. Not that I would blame you. Sherborne is one of the wealthiest men in England, titled, handsome. . . . Most women find him irresistible. And he's certainly interested in you. That was obvious at Marlborough House."

Embarrassed now, I turned away again. "The marquis is not interested in me." Even as I denied it, I knew there was some truth to what Geoffrey was saying.

Then he was behind me in one swift, silent movement, wrapping his arms around me and pressing me to him so I couldn't escape. His words were soft and mocking in my ear as he said, "You try so hard, but you can't resist me, because you love me as much as I love you. Surely you realize that we were destined to be together?"

I struggled, but could not break away. "You're wrong, Geoffrey," I said, praying for the strength to resist the treacherous closeness and warmth of him.

Now he whirled me around and held me by the shoulders, so I was forced to look into his eyes, which were filled with challenge. "You think so? Then why are you still here? Why haven't you fled back to Egypt and your Cyrus, or your proper Aunt Venetia?" He grinned. "And don't tell me you're still here because of your mother. No, I think I hold you here as surely as she does."

My heart was beating wildly now. "You do realize too many lives will be destroyed if you go through with this divorce."

He shook his head as his fingertips lightly trailed down my cheek. "You exaggerate, Cassa. All Leonie will lose is her social standing, and you and I will gain happiness such as neither of us has ever known. The prince needn't fear a scandal, as long as Leonie cooperates, and I'm sure your mother would understand."

In my own exasperation, I brushed his hand away. "But don't you understand? Social position is what Leonie values most. She will not grant you a divorce."

Before I could stop him, he grasped my hands in his. Suddenly, his face changed, and a look of cunning and calculation replaced warmth and concern. "I don't need Leonie's consent to divorce her. I have enough evidence of her infidelities to do that. Leonie likes to delude herself that she can manipulate people into doing what she wants, but I have bested opponents more formidable than a mere whining, spoiled woman." He dropped my hands and stood back, regarding me with a crafty smile that was so unlike him. "No, I will get what I want from my beloved wife, one way or another."

As I stared at him, something Leonie had once said to me suddenly flitted through my mind. She had once told me that Geoffrey had an air of violence lurking just below the surface. Now, for the first time, I knew what she was talking about, and I suddenly feared Geoffrey.

He looked at me long and hard, and I had to avert my eyes. "One day I shall have you, Cassa. That I promise you."

Then he held out his arms to me, but I managed to evade him and didn't stop running until I reached the safety of my own room.

Geoffrey's words had shaken me more than I cared to admit, and I decided not to go down to dinner that evening. I couldn't face the family, so I had Sally bring me up supper on a tray and I ate alone.

Later, there came a knock at the door, and I started. Was it Leonie, trying to convince me of Geoffrey's ruthlessness, or Mother, fearful for her daughter's marriage?

Much to my relief, Edith stood there, a grim expression on her handsome face. "Good evening, Cassandra. May I come in?"

"Certainly," I replied, standing aside as she walked into my room and looked about, a little enviously, I thought. I indicated a window seat. "Please sit down." When she did so, I joined her and said, "I don't think I need to tell you why I didn't come down for dinner tonight."

She knew what I was referring to immediately. "You were wise to remain here. The entire family was shocked and subdued by the news. Although Geoffrey and Maud were absent tonight, your poor Mama was red-eyed, and her hands shook so that she finally excused herself. I've never seen Leonie so upset."

"This has come as quite a shock to us all."

Edith nodded sagely and her hypnotic voice filled the room. "I am not a member of society, but by associating with Leonie and her family all these months, I've come to know something of its ways. And I can tell you the main rule seems to be: 'Thou shalt not be found out.' As long as everyone remains discreet, the upper classes may engage in the loosest moral behavior that would never be tolerated by lesser folk such as ourselves. But let one word of it become public knowledge . . ." She shrugged eloquently. "I'm sure if Geoffrey were to go through with this divorce, there would be a scandal."

Edith said, "There would be such a scandal, it would rock society to its very foundations, and the prince would lose his great popularity with the people. I'm certain he, in turn, would cast Leonie off." She sighed. "And I know my former pupil well enough to know she would rather die than face social ostracism."

I looked at her. "Aren't you being a trifle melodramatic, Edith?"

Her straight back sagged and she leaned against the window. Then one of her large, bony hands grasped my wrist, and I recoiled from its coldness. "I am going to tell you something in the strictest confidence, Cassandra, because you are Leonie's sister, and you have a right to know. But you must promise me you won't tell another soul." She shook my arm. "Anyone. Understood?"

I don't know whether it was the chill from her hand or the intense sense of danger in the air, but I suddenly trembled. "Of course. You have my word."

Now she leaned forward and lowered her voice so it was at its most mellifluous, drawing me in. "I'm afraid Geoffrey will try to harm Leonie if she doesn't allow him to have his own way in this matter." She removed her hand, but the cold remained, encircling my wrist like a bracelet.

I tried to rub some warmth into it and failed. "I can't believe that, Edith. I don't believe Geoffrey is capable of harming anyone."

Her eyes narrowed, as though assessing me. "But you've only known him for so short a time. Leonie has confided in me that she fears him."

"But what has he done to warrant such fears on her part?" I demanded, folding my arms for warmth.

"She said he threatened her when he first heard of her

liaison with the prince. She said he told her that a man of his means could hire someone to do anything—even murder—and get away with it."

The cold returned. I reached over and unlatched the window, but even the warm evening breeze had turned chilly. I closed the window.

"I don't believe that," I said stoutly. Suddenly, movement in the garden below caught my eye, and I sought to divert Edith from this morbid conversation. "Look. There's someone in the garden."

It was Leonie, standing with a man directly beneath my window, and though it was still light enough to recognize my sister, the man had his back turned toward us and was in shadow. As we watched, Leonie slipped her arms around his waist and buried her head in his shoulder, and from where we watched, he did not appear averse to her embrace.

Beside me, Edith drew herself up like an indignant pigeon, and a scowl of frank displeasure formed between her brows as though she had caught a pupil cheating and was about to reprimand him.

"It's Edgar," she muttered disapprovingly between pursed lips, "and Leonie is blatantly encouraging him. That stupid brother of mine!"

So, my intuition had been right on target. Edgar was in love with my sister after all, and eager to comfort her in her time of trial.

Edith went on with, "It may surprise you to know that my brother has been Leonie's adoring slave ever since she so graciously welcomed us into her home. Sometimes I think he would—" She caught herself. "Never mind." Then she rose and seemed in a hurry to leave, and I suspected she was determined to go downstairs and break up Edgar and Leonie. "Well, I must leave now. They will be wondering what has been keeping me."

She was just at the door, when suddenly, she stopped and said, "By the way, Cassandra, did you have an opportunity to discuss Edgar's career with any of the prince's banker friends when you dined at Marlborough House the other night?"

I grimaced, then flushed in embarrassment. "No, I'm sorry, Edith. I'm afraid I forgot all about it."

She sniffed, and I could tell I had hurt her. "Oh, I see." I felt so guilty, I apologized profusely, but Edith brushed it off, wished me a chilly good night, and left me to watch the shadows grow longer and darker in the yard below.

In the days that followed, the tension and animosity intensified as Geoffrey and Leonie engaged in a terrible battle of wills. I often heard them arguing violently as I passed Leonie's bedchamber or the drawing room, but, for the most part, they could not bear even to be in the same room with each other. If one of them should happen to enter by chance, the other would wordlessly rise and walk out. Geoffrey never accompanied his wife to social functions any more, even the park promenade at five.

But that didn't stop the determined and irrepressible Leonie. Life, to her, went on in spite of Geoffrey. She did her shopping and paid her calls during the day, and every evening, the Wickeses would come to dinner, at which Geoffrey was usually conspicuously absent. Then a brougham would call for her, and she would go to meet the prince somewhere, though he never again made one of his nocturnal visits to Lester House. If anything, it seemed as though Geoffrey's estrangement from his wife was making it easier for her and her royal lover to keep up their liaison.

Except for Leonie, no one in the household was unaffected by this battle. Mother, who seemed to age ten years almost overnight, lost interest in anything except sitting in the garden with her pot of lemon grass tisane and staring into space. Though Maud kept herself busy with her school and other philanthropies, she became quite irritable and no longer even pretended to be civil to her sister-in-law, often lashing out with a wicked, cutting tongue.

And then came the dinner party none of us would ever forget.

London was in the midst of a light summer shower when Leonie returned from the regatta at Cowes, which, she had informed me just before leaving without her husband, was the last great social event of the season before all of society deserted the hot, dusty streets of London for their cool country estates.

When she was all unpacked and settled, she summoned me to her sitting room. She looked fresh, well rested, and even more beautiful, and if the emotional upheavals in the house were preying upon her mind, she gave no outward sign. She was as confident and condescending as ever.

As I sat across from her chaise and watched her nibble delicately on a chocolate bonbon, I wondered if she had summoned me here to quiz me about my imagined relationship to Geoffrey once again, but she had not. She merely wanted to invite me to a dinner party she was giving in two days, making it very clear that she didn't particularly crave my company, but needed an extra woman to make an even number at the table.

I agreed to attend, then left her to her bonbons.

The dinner party began innocently enough. Although Maud, Geoffrey, and the Wickeses were absent, Mother was there, and I soon felt at ease among the friendly, glittering people who congregated in the drawing room. I recognized no one from that disastrous dinner party at Marlborough House, so my initial trepidation soon left me, and I began to enjoy myself.

I was seated on the divan, talking to a lively young woman with a nonstop tongue and impossible carrot-red hair, when she suddenly saw someone she just had to speak to at once, and excused herself. No sooner had she flitted off than Lord Rushton eased himself smoothly into her place. Most women, whether young or old, couldn't seem to take their eyes off him, and even I had to concede that, in his form-fitting black evening attire, Adam Rushton looked as handsome and dangerous as one of his favorite poet's heroes.

"Miss Clark," he murmured, sitting too close, as was his custom, "how lovely you look this evening."

I couldn't resist saying, "'She walks in beauty, like the night'?"

His gypsy eyes twinkled as he purposely stared deeply into mine, a tactic designed to turn my will to butter, I suppose. "Ah, the lady mocks me. But I am not offended. I like spirited women, especially those with such enchanting green eyes."

I glanced around the drawing room and was dismayed to find his wife not far away, speaking to a man with a military bearing and eye patch. Even though Lady Rushton appeared engrossed in conversation, I knew her attention was focused on her husband and me.

Now Lord Rushton was leaning closer, as though what he had to tell me were confidential, and I was thankful that I had my fan to keep between us. "It's been weeks since you've ridden in the park, my Night Beauty. I know because I search the lanes for you every morning. Why don't you ride there any more?" Now his leg was pressed against my knee with unbearable familiarity, and he was so close I could smell the cologne he used so liberally, a heavy, cloying scent. "Or do you have someone else who occupies your time now?"

I knew he was referring to Geoffrey, but I snapped my fan shut and challenged him. "And what, sir, do you mean by that?"

He pulled away and held up his hands as though to ward me off, but before he could speak, his wife swooped down on us like an enraged eagle protecting its young from a vicious predator.

"Adam, my love, Major Burlingame would like to speak to you. Will you excuse us, Miss Clark?"

The coldness in her voice was like a knife blade pressed

against warm skin, and I was as glad to relinquish her husband as she was to get him away from me. Lord Rushton smiled secretively and left.

Then my mother came to me with a uniformed young man she introduced as Lieutenant St. James Cavendish, who, as it turned out, had just returned from a tour of duty with his regiment in the Sudan. He sat down next to me, and soon we were talking about Egypt as though we were old friends. Then Leonie announced that it was time to go in to dinner.

I must confess I enjoyed the meal more than I had expected, thanks to the attentive Lieutenant Cavendish. While Leonie's friends were discussing all the yachts at Cowes and the appearance of the prince's nephew, Kaiser Wilhelm, with an escort of German gunboats, the lieutenant and I talked of the serene splendors of the desert. Before I knew where the time had flown, the sumptuous meal was over, and Leonie was rising and collecting eyes. We women rose and, leaving the men to their port and cigars, returned to the drawing room.

Just as we were about to enter, Heffer approached his mistress holding a large box tied with a scarlet ribbon.

"Madam," he said, "this just arrived for you."

As she took the box, Leonie's face froze for just an instant, and I knew she was thinking of the time that she had also been interrupted by a messenger.

"I wonder what this can be?" she murmured, as all the women flocked around her, craning their necks to see.

"A gift from another admirer, no doubt," the girl with the nonstop tongue said.

While we all watched, Leonie slowly untied the ribbon to build suspense. "My goodness. What *can* it be?"

As I watched with as much curiosity as anyone, I saw my sister's face turn from expectation to horror. Her eyes widened, and she blanched as she stared into the box. Then she flung it away and screamed, clutching her hands to her mouth in fear. When it hit the floor, something came rolling out and landed at my feet. For a moment, I thought I was looking at Leonie, as a tiny china face with blond hair and one blue eye stared back at me, and as I bent down for a closer look, I realized it was a doll's head. But one side of its face was a gaping black hole where someone must have crushed it.

Leonie's scream brought the men running from the dining room, and as the other women saw the doll and recoiled, Leonie suddenly collapsed into a dead faint. Luckily, Adam Rushton was near enough to catch her before she hit the floor.

Suddenly, amid the babbling, shoving, and shrill cries of consternation, Geoffrey's voice came booming down from the top of the stairs.

"What is going on here?"

Everyone fell silent, and looked up at his tall, imposing figure standing there. The moment he saw Leonie unconscious in Lord Rushton's arms, he flew down the stairs to his wife's side.

"What happened?" he demanded again. When everyone just looked at each other and didn't answer, he snapped, "Doesn't any of you have the wits to speak?"

I stepped forward with the doll's head. "Leonie saw this and fainted." I handed the gruesome thing to Geoffrey. While he scowled and examined it, I said, "It came in a package for Leonie. She thought it was a gift, but when she opened it and saw what was inside . . ."

"My word! It looks as though half the face has been crushed!" Major Burlingame exclaimed, peering over Geoffrey's shoulder.

"Who could have sent such a dreadful thing?" one of the women exclaimed.

Another added, "What can it mean?" and soon everyone was buzzing with speculation.

"Take Leonie into the drawing room," Geoffrey commanded Rushton, and when my sister was placed on the divan, with a cushion beneath her head, Mother came forward to wave smelling salts under her nose.

Just at that moment, when Leonie's eyes flew open, I thought of the doll's head with its one blue eye, and I shuddered.

She struggled to sit up, her hair in disarray and her pretty face pale and distorted by terror. "Oh, my God! It's happened again!" She was shaking uncontrollably now and seemed on the verge of hysteria. "Who could be so insane as to send me that horrible, horrible thing?" Now Leonie recoiled from Geoffrey, who was kneeling by her side, and by the wild look in her eyes, I knew with dismay that she wasn't going to be rational.

Leonie's voice rose to a wail as she stared at her husband. "Why are you doing this to me, Geoffrey? What have I done to deserve this?"

He rose, his face hard as he glowered down at her. "Don't be absurd, Leonie. I didn't send it."

She shrank away from him in fear, and her frightened gaze alighted on me standing at the foot of the divan. "Or was it you, Cassandra?"

With a growl of impatience, Geoffrey whirled around and turned toward the assembled guests, who were all exchanging looks and muttering among themselves. "Get out of here, all of you! My wife has had a shock and is not herself." And then he moved toward the throng as though he would bodily push them out of the drawing room. Everyone scrambled to leave, and in moments, the drawing room was silent, except for Leonie's sobbing.

It was past midnight by the time the doctor and the police left, but Maud, Geoffrey, and I were still too keyed up to follow my exhausted mother upstairs to bed.

Maud, who had returned from a housing committee meeting to find the house still ablaze with lights and crawling with men from Scotland Yard, looked from her brother to me. "Who could be doing this? First that note, and now the doll's head . . ."

Geoffrey closed his bloodshot eyes and sighed wearily as

he buried his face in his hands. "Before Leonie could be taken to her room and given a sleeping draught, she accused me and Cassa of doing it."

Maud bristled. "You? How absurd! Why would you want to do such a thing?"

He raised his head and looked at his sister. "Because Leonie won't give me the divorce I seek."

Maud turned pale beneath her freckles. "Did she tell this to the police?"

"No," I replied. "By the time they arrived, Leonie was asleep and the guests had all gone."

Maud cradled her chin in her hand. "What do the police think?"

"The inspector felt, as I do," Geoffrey said, "that some religious zealot sent it as a warning to Leonie to mend her ways. He doesn't think she is in any real danger, though she feels certain someone wants to harm her, namely me."

"That's preposterous," Maud scoffed, rising and placing a comforting hand on her brother's shoulder.

But I thought of Edith's warning that Geoffrey had once threatened Leonie, and I found myself filled with fresh doubts.

The clock in my bedroom chimed three o'clock, and I still hadn't fallen asleep. It had begun to rain steadily, but I couldn't blame the sound of water beating against the glass for my sleeplessness. Whenever I closed my eyes, I would see that crushed doll's head, its one blue eye staring up at me. Finally, I flung back the sheet, rose, and went to the window seat.

As I sat curled there, my cheek against the cold glass to revive me, I forced myself to think about Geoffrey dispassionately. I had always been a little cynical about men and especially distrustful of those like the Earl of Knighton, who stole other men's wives, or Lord Rushton, who regarded all women as nothing more than conquests for his own pleasure. And there were all those who came through the Clark's

Hotel, year after year, seeking, as Cyrus said, "a diversion." But there was something different about Geoffrey. Perhaps it was because he appreciated me for qualities that had nothing to do with looks.

Had he discovered a way out of an intolerable marriage? Did it include frightening his wife half out of her wits so she would capitulate and give him what he wanted? If a man thought nothing of defying a prince, what else could he be capable of?

Lightning cracked and snapped, causing me to jump in time to see it stab at the horizon like a pitchfork. Like the light suddenly illuminating the darkness, the answer should have come to me in a blinding flash, but it didn't. I wanted to be able to say with certainty, "Geoffrey is innocent," but I could not. I knew Leonie feared him. Perhaps it would be more prudent if I feared him, too.

I sat huddled there until the storm passed, and all was quiet once again. I rose and went back to bed.

The following day, I awoke around noon, and after dressing and starting downstairs, I received another shock. Just as I reached the landing, I saw Geoffrey and the prince walking down the hall toward the library. Both men looked grave, and the prince was puffing away nervously at his cigar.

When I entered the dining room and saw Mother sitting there with her tisane, I said, "Was that the prince I just saw?"

She nodded and rubbed her red-rimmed eyes. "He just called a few moments ago, asking for Geoffrey. I suspect he's already heard what happened to Leonie last night. News travels so fast in their set."

"I wonder what he wants?" I murmured, as I helped myself to eggs and toast. "Geoffrey hasn't spoken to him since he asked Leonie for a divorce."

"I suspect we'll soon find out."

"And how is Leonie this morning?" I asked, as I sat down beside her. "Have you seen her?"

"She's still sleeping," Mother replied. Then she shook her head and looked worried. "I just hope and pray that everyone realizes her hysterical accusations last night were just that, and no one takes them to heart. Society is such an insular group. Rumors can run rampant in a matter of hours. I'd hate to have anyone think that Geoffrey sent that horrible doll to his own wife."

We were to learn that rumor had already done its insidious work. When Geoffrey finally joined us in the dining room, he looked drained and strangely defeated.

He stood before us and rested his fingertips lightly against the table. Taking a deep breath, he said, "His Royal Highness has requested a personal favor of me. He's asked that I reconcile with Leonie, at least for the time being, to quell any unpleasant rumors that may result from last night's incident." Geoffrey looked squarely at me, his gray eyes begging me to understand. "The prince said any scandal could make him unpopular with the people, and he implored me not to let this happen."

"And what did you say?" Mother asked, though I suspect she already knew the answer, for Geoffrey was an honorable man.

He was silent for a moment, then he looked down at the table, where he was tracing some formless design with his fingertips. Finally, he said, "I told him I would do so, but only for appearances' sake, and only temporarily. I told him I do plan to divorce Leonie eventually. He suggested that we go down to Punjab House, to get away from London, and I agreed. He also graciously consented to forgo his usual trip to Germany to join us there, just to put any rumors to rest once and for all." A muscle in his jaw twitched, and he could not look at me. "Now, if you ladies will excuse me, I'm going to my club. I'll be there for the rest of the day."

Chapter Twelve

As our carriages made their leisurely way toward Punjab House, I felt my initial fears and misgivings gradually melting away. The gently rustling leaves of ancient oaks and elms arching in a bower over the narrow road, the steady rhythm of clopping hooves, and the fragrances of fruit trees from nearby orchards conspired to soothe me. I leaned back and just enjoyed the glimpses of our destination in the distance, flickering between the trees like a beguiling candle flame.

Maud, who was riding with me while the others rode up ahead in the first carriage, said, "My hectic schedule has taken its toll. I really do need several weeks in the country to refresh myself and recuperate."

Maud did look exhausted and enervated. She was very pale, and there were deep circles beneath eyes that had lost their usual sparkle and enthusiasm. She slouched more than usual, like some drooping lily.

She took a deep breath and closed her eyes as she exhaled. "I do so love it down here in Kent. The very air is a tonic. Do you know you can tell what season it is just by the way the air smells? In the winter, there's the heavenly smell of log fires, and in the spring, fruit blossoms. Now, in the summer, it smells of the sun on warm meadows, and when the hops are harvested and dried in autumn, there's a lovely bittersweet tang to the air. That's when I love it best, I think."

I breathed deeply and caught the faint fragrance of wild honeysuckle growing by the side of the road. "I'm glad I came." As I watched the carriage bearing Geoffrey, Leonie, Mother, and Edith up ahead, I said to Maud, "Do you think your brother and Leonie will reconcile?"

"That will never happen," she insisted.

As if to belie her words, Leonie's musical, lilting laughter floated back to us on a summer's breeze, and I could see Geoffrey laughing, too.

Maud caught my expression and said, "He only agreed to come down to the country to quell any rumors that might damage the prince's reputation. But, Leonie's got what she wanted."

"What do you mean?"

Now Maud gave me one of her level, assessing looks, and I could tell she was on the verge of giving me some sisterly advice, whether I wanted it or not. "Surely you realize by now that Leonie is nothing more than a spoiled, rebellious child playing at grown up. When she has her way, she's sunshine and sweetness itself, but when she doesn't, she resorts to tears, hysterics, or childish tricks. Those accusations she made against Geoffrey the night of that disastrous dinner party? I doubt that she seriously believed my brother sent that package, but by accusing him in front of all her friends, she suggested to others that he might have. Her clever ploy put him into the position of having to prove he didn't." Maud sat up straight and squirmed in her seat. "If you want my opinion, I suspect the doll's head was a little scheme engineered by Leonie herself."

I stared at her in disbelief. "Oh, Maud, you can't mean that! What reason would she have?"

Maud looked at me, her thin mouth set in an uncompromising expression reminiscent of her brother. "Leonie wants to delay Geoff's filing for a divorce because she thinks that the longer he holds off, the better her chances of keeping him. She's already succeeded in garnering sympathy for herself by making everyone think someone is seeking to harm her, and that her life is in danger. And she *has* kept him from filing thus far."

"I can't believe she could be that heartless."

Maud rolled her eyes, losing patience with me at last. "And I can't believe you're as naive as a baby! Haven't you noticed that ever since Geoff suggested we go down to Punjab House and invite the prince for the weekend, your sister has conveniently forgotten about the doll's head?"

I blushed at that, for Maud had a point. Leonie seemed to have quickly forgotten about that horrible night.

I shook my head. "And I thought the Egyptians were masters of intrigue."

Maud chuckled at that. "Yes, Leonie fancies herself another Machiavelli, but what she doesn't realize is that she isn't clever enough. We all see right through her pathetic little strategems."

I said, "What do you think will happen when the prince leaves?"

Maud looked out over the lush fields that surrounded Punjab House, and her brows came together in a scowl of speculation. "He may go to some spa in Germany to try to undo some of his gastronomic excesses, or perhaps he'll go directly to Scotland for the shooting. If I know Leo, I think she hopes to convince Geoff to accompany them 'for appearances' sake,' and the divorce will be forgotten. But if I also know my brother, his mind is made up and there's precious little Leo will be able to do."

Suddenly, my gaze met Geoffrey's as he stared back at me from the carriage ahead, and for a moment, I felt his yearning. I quickly looked away.

We turned down a wide lane bordered by hedges, and I could see the house in more detail as we drew closer. I recalled Lady Quartermain's assertion that Punjab House was a strange, heathen-looking place, and from where I sat, it did look unlike any other English house I had ever seen. The entire house was white, whether from white stone or white-wash, I couldn't tell, but it gleamed in the morning light and seemed to glow with a warm translucence. I could envision the neighboring yeomen leaning on their rakes and shaking their heads when they saw what their new neighbor had erected among their very English rolling fields and fruit trees.

As we drew closer, I exclaimed, "Why, it reminds me of the mosques in Cairo!"

And it did. Now I could see the magnificent onion dome that dominated the entire house, as well as delicate minarets too small and narrow ever to have known a muezzin's presence.

Maud smiled indulgently. "I've always thought it resembled the Brighton Pavilion myself, but it's not as large. I remember when Papa was having it built, I pleaded for a modern house, but he would indulge his fancy for all things Indian. He wanted to be a nabob so badly, you know. He was always studying Indian culture and entertaining East India Company veterans who had spent their lives there. He was eventually admitted to membership in the Oriental Club on the strength of his enthusiasm, though membership is usually restricted to those who have served in the East." Maud shook her head and smiled at the memory of a father she obviously loved. "But, I suppose I really can't complain. In spite of its exotic exterior, you'll find it's really quite modern and comfortable inside. I'm forever grateful that Papa didn't decide to erect one of those drafty, pseudo-Gothic dwellings that were all the rage years ago."

When the carriages came down the circular drive and rolled to a halt, I could study Punjab House up close. There were pointed archways over all the doors and windows, just as one sees on buildings in Cairo. Many of the windows were covered with filigree grilles.

When we stepped down from the carriage, Geoffrey came

up to me and said, "Welcome to Punjab House, Cassa. What do you think of it?"

"It's beautiful," I murmured, staring up at it. "I feel as though I'm back in Cairo."

Leonie joined us and placed a proprietary hand on her husband's arm as though all were well between them. "Wait until you see the Avenue of the Bulls and the Pavilion of Surya, the sun god."

Geoffrey stepped away from her, ostensibly to talk to Heffer, who, along with most of the servants, had been sent on ahead to prepare the house for occupancy. It was a gesture of rejection strangely reminiscent of the one I saw the night I had watched him caress her shoulders, and she had shrugged him off. I saw a flicker of annoyance cross Leonie's face, but she did it admirably by pretending to be concerned for our welfare.

"Well, shall we go in and get settled? There will be plenty of time to show you the estate later."

I was a little disenchanted when I went inside and discovered that the exotic shell hid a conventional English country house, with a large foyer panelled in oak and with numerous fireplaces, but, as Geoffrey pointed out, England isn't India, and certain harsh realities of English life couldn't be ignored when building a house. Fireplaces might not be necessary where the climate is warm year round, but try surviving an English winter without one. And, though filigree grilles made lovely patterns on the floor when the sun shone through them, glass windows were still necessary to keep out pouring rain, bitter cold winds, and driving snow.

The bedchamber to which I was shown was not much different from my room in the London townhouse. I was surprised to find a brass holder outside my door, and my name written neatly on the little card it held, but there would be a number of other guests also unfamiliar with Punjab House, and it was prudent to take a precaution that would prevent confusion. It didn't occur to me then that perhaps there were some guests who would want to go to another's room on purpose.

As I entered mine, I was disappointed to find there was no window seat, as there was in the Green Glass Room, but I could see Maud's skillful hand at work in the Morris wallpaper and graceful furniture.

Later, after Sally had unpacked for me, and I had rested, I was shown to the dining room, where we gathered for luncheon.

"Is your room to your liking?" Geoffrey asked as he assisted me with my chair.

"Most satisfactory," I replied.

"It's just a relief to get away from the grime and heat of London in August," Leonie declared. "Absolutely no one stays in London after the season is over—except for my dedicated sister-in-law, of course. Don't you, Maud?"

Maud was still rather hostile and abrupt with Leonie. "I have work to do, Leo, and it doesn't stop just because the season ends."

"So dedicated," Leonie murmured, but by the tone of her voice, she plainly told everyone she didn't think it enviable at all.

Now Maud turned to her brother. "How many guests will we be having come Monday?"

Geoffrey replied, "The prince and his retinue, of course. I understand that the princess will not be accompanying him this time and sends her regrets."

"How convenient," I heard Maud mutter under her breath.

Then Geoffrey went on to rattle off the names of most of the people I had met at the Marlborough House dinner party, as well as Lord and Lady Rushton and a few others whose names I didn't recognize.

"It must be an honor to have the Prince of Wales come to your house for the weekend," I said.

"Honor!" Maud grumbled. "A frightful expense is more like it. History is rife with loyal subjects who went bankrupt entertaining royalty. There are extra servants to be hired, a chef from London to prepare His Royal Highness's favorite dishes, suitable entertainments to arrange so his royal personage won't be bored . . ."

She was in full career now and could have gone on and on, when Geoffrey cocked a warning brow at her. "Maud . . ."

Her temper flared and she sat up straight. "Well, I'm sorry, Geoff! When I think of all the money we've spent to entertain the prince—"

"Oh, I can't believe you, Maud!" Leonie snapped, flinging her napkin on the table and joining in the fray. "We can afford it. I can't believe you'd begrudge a few guineas to entertain the man who will one day be your sovereign!"

"Please, please, no more fighting," Mother declared, holding up her hands to restore order. "Let's have no more of this squabbling, shall we? The prince is coming, so we may as well enjoy it."

Everyone fell silent at the table. Suddenly, Edith said, "I can't thank you enough for inviting Edgar and me. We've never been to a country weekend before, let alone with such august company as the Prince of Wales."

I found myself wondering if Edith would use this opportunity to promote her brother to Geoffrey's financial friends, and I could see by Maud's pained expression that she was wondering too.

"Why couldn't Edgar come down with us today?" Geoffrey asked.

"Well, as a working man, he can't absent himself whenever he feels like it," Edith said. "He will join us on Thursday night, though. I appealed to his superior myself and said that Edgar was needed on Friday and Saturday to settle an urgent family matter, and the man graciously allowed him the holiday."

When luncheon was finished, Geoffrey turned to me and said, "Cassandra, would you like to tour the estate?"

Before I could open my mouth to reply, Leonie said, "Oh, what a splendid idea! I'm sure Edith would like to join us as well, wouldn't you, Edith?"

Mother and Maud politely declined, and the three of us rose to accompany Geoffrey.

After a brief tour of the inside of the house, where many of the rooms still bore Maud's tasteful stamp and remained untouched by Leonie's penchant for heavy furniture and clutter, the four of us went outside to a wide flagstone terrace at the back of the house.

Geoffrey leaned on the low balustrade, looking down a grassy path lined with tall, slender cedar trees that must have extended for nearly a half-mile from the house.

"The Avenue of the Bulls," he announced.

As Leonie and I gathered our skirts and slowly started down the avenue, I soon saw where it got its name. On pedestals at either side of the entrance stood huge bulls carved from gray stone, each taller than Geoffrey.

Seeing my look of astonishment, Geoffrey said, "They are Brahman bulls, sacred to the Indian people, and my father thought they'd be a nice touch. Actually, he wanted to put a stone bull between each pair of trees, but Maud dissuaded him. She pointed out that he would have needed at least forty such figures to reach all the way down to the temple, and carving them would have taken years. Father saw reason and decided to have just two bulls, guarding the entrance as it were."

"There are temples in Egypt like that," I said, recalling the row of ram-headed sphinxes at Karnak and thinking suddenly of Cyrus.

"Well, that is Egypt and this is England," Leonie declared in her bored drawl. "Personally, I think the bulls are hideous eyesores. This area would look so much prettier with classical statues of white marble. Diana, perhaps, or Aphrodite."

"The bulls will be here long after we're gone," was all

Geoffrey said, and by the tone of his voice, I knew Leonie wasn't going to have her way in this matter.

"I think the bulls are rather . . . imposing," Edith said diplomatically, "and rather complement the house."

The three of us strolled in silence to the temple at the avenue's end, where we examined the small pavilion, a tiny replica of the house complete with dome and minarets. Farther on, the stables were built around a huge courtyard paved with cobblestones, and there seemed to be stalls for at least fifty horses. Grooms rubbing down their charges and polishing bits tipped their hats to the master as we passed, and an old hound lying in the shade of a building wagged his tail in feeble greeting, and raised his head, but made no move to follow us. I breathed deeply, savoring the honest country smells of green hay and horses.

In the fields beyond the main buildings, horses of every size and color were grazing placidly together, and while I am no judge of horseflesh, even I could tell these were thoroughbreds of the finest quality. One in particular caught my eye, a handsome chestnut who had a high fenced paddock all to himself.

"That's Anarchist," Geoffrey said as we passed, and the animal whistled and pawed the earth. "He makes Westwind look like Bittersweet."

As if to give credence to his words, the horse suddenly rushed the fence, and for one horrifying moment, I thought he was going to go sailing over it in one magnificent leap. We all stepped back involuntarily, but he had to stop, for the fence was just too high and the paddock too small for him to get up the speed needed to clear it.

"The animal seems dangerous," Edith said, her hand to her breast as though to quell a rapidly beating heart.

"He is," Geoffrey replied, leading us away. "You'd do well to stay away from him. He nearly killed one of my grooms when I first bought him, but his bloodlines are impeccable and he breeds true. That's why I keep him." Then he glanced at Leonie and said, rather maliciously, I thought, "Perhaps I'll let Lord Rushton have a go at him."

Leonie just tossed her head and replied, "I'm sure Lord Rushton would succeed where others have failed."

"Perhaps," was all Geoffrey said. "There is just one more place to show you, and then we can return to the house."

We followed his lead through a shady grove of trees, and when they thinned out at the top of a small rise, we came upon a beautiful scene that caused Edith and me to gasp in delight.

Below us stood a large round pond. Its glassy surface, reflecting the blue of the sky, was broken only by three black-necked swans swimming idly across it. A wide pier jutted out into the water, connecting the shore with a little summerhouse that stood almost in the middle of the pond itself.

"How very lovely!" Edith exclaimed, and I echoed her sentiments.

"We can bathe here if the weather gets too sultry," Geoffrey said, starting down the slope and heading for the pier.

"I'm afraid I will only be able to watch the rest of you," I said. When Geoffrey gave me a quizzical look over his shoulder, I added sheepishly, "I'm afraid I don't know how to swim."

He looked surprised. "Not swim? Now you're jesting with us."

"No, it's the truth. I never learned to swim because none of my Clark cousins ever had time to teach me."

"Never learned to swim!" Leonie echoed. "In that case, you'd better not go in the water here, because, except for this part, the pond is very deep. It's man-made, but it's fed from an underground spring." When we reached the pier, she continued with, "Since it is so far from the stables or the house, the bathers have a great deal of privacy. See, it's as if we were all alone, in the middle of nowhere."

Bathers or lovers, I wondered as I stepped out onto the wooden path?

The pier extended all the way round the summerhouse, enabling us to walk in single file to the front and look out over the placid water. There was no railing to prevent one from falling from the narrow walk, and, as I stared into the water, I involuntarily recalled the fortune teller's prophecy and Cyrus's admonition. Yet, how could I deny myself the pleasure of enjoying such a beautiful, serene spot? I would just have to remain in the summerhouse or watch from the pier while the others bathed.

As I turned and peered into the summerhouse itself, I noticed the windows did not have glass panes, but shutters, like the Clark's Hotel, and inside, there were fixed to the walls benches on which one could lounge or sit.

Geoffrey noticed my look and said, "Those shutters can be closed so the guests can change into their bathing costumes right here, rather than having to traipse down from the main house."

"Convenient," Edith murmured in approval as she walked around, inspecting everything with a touch of envy, I thought.

Leonie opened the door and invited us inside. The benches were strewn with large, soft pillows, and I found myself wondering if my sister had ever used this private, out-of-the-way dwelling for an assignation.

Her next words added to my suspicions. "It's so nice to come here on a summer's evening and watch the moon rise over the water."

I caught Geoffrey giving her a quick scowl, and knew he was thinking the same thing.

"Well, shall we be getting back, ladies?" he asked, a bit too sharply. "I'm sure you're all quite fatigued and would like to rest."

That Monday, the prince and his entourage—including the Marquis of Sherborne—arrived.

I had never seen anything like it. First, every carriage Geoffrey owned, plus, I suspect, several borrowed from neighbors, was dispatched to the station to bring the guests back to Punjab House, and then, once empty, sent back to collect the servants and mountains of monogrammed luggage. I watched in amazement as an army of valets and maids, guarding their mistresses' jewel cases with their lives, descended on us like locusts. I overheard the servants grumbling about all the extra work. One muttered about having to share her small quarters with a hoity-toity duchess's maid. I was beginning to share Maud's view that a royal visit was more drudgery than honor for everyone concerned.

After my dinner at Marlborough House, I was not looking forward to another meeting with the prince, but when I was presented, he said only, "Miss Clar-rk, I see you are now in the pink," with a knowing twinkle in his eye.

In fact, I was amazed to find that he seemed to relish my company. Leonie monopolized him, of course, but he insisted that I be seated next to him at dinner that evening, despite the injunctions of protocol, and, afterwards, when I confessed that I did not know how to play card games of any sort, the prince said he would teach me to play whist. I caught on quickly, and our table was soon engaged in a spirited game.

As the evening wore on, I found myself gradually drawn into the prince's orbit. Everything Maud had said about him was true. One could not help but like the man, in spite of his excesses. He was charming, witty, interesting, and made me feel as though I were his prime concern all evening. He took a child-like delight in the games of hide and seek and charades we played after cards, and his jolly laughter was infectious as it rang throughout the room.

Finally, Heffer appeared bearing a huge silver tray laden with silver candlesticks, and I found myself actually regretting that the evening was drawing to a close. The debonair Lord Rushton lit a candle for me, and, as I yawned and trudged upstairs to find my bedroom, I could finally see why everyone let the prince do whatever he wished.

The next morning, when I went down for breakfast, I was dismayed to find that I was not the first. Lord Rushton rose from his chair as I entered. "Good morning to you, my Night Beauty," he said smoothly, his dark eyes roving approvingly over me. "I see you are an early riser, as am I." He glanced at the sideboard. "The servants haven't even put the food out yet, lazy dogs."

I moved as far away from him as possible. "It's not yet nine-thirty. I'm sure they'll bring in the dishes at the proper time."

He came forward to hold my chair, though I tried my best to beat him to it, then he dropped down beside me and looked crestfallen. "Will you please tell me what I have done to earn that cold tone in your voice? Have I unwittingly offended you in some way?"

I flushed slightly, but more in annoyance than in embarrassment. "You've done nothing to offend me, Lord Rushton."

An arrogant look crossed his dark gypsy features. "Or are you cold to hide your true feelings for me?"

"I assure you, sir, I have no hidden feelings for you."

If I thought I would daunt him, I was mistaken. The tips of his fingers touched my sleeve, and he moved his head closer to mine, perhaps so I could get the full effect of those dark eyes.

He looked about to say something further, when suddenly, I heard the door open and a maid appeared, bearing a covered silver dish. "Ah, here's breakfast," I murmured as though it were my salvation, and rose.

It was fortunate that I did, for following the line of servants was Lady Rushton herself, looking bilious in a dress of a regrettable shade of green. When she saw her husband and me alone together, she gave me a look that could have made me feel guilty merely for being alive.

"Good morning, my dove," Lord Rushton said, rising and giving his wife a peck on the cheek. "How lovely you look this morning. That shade certainly becomes you." Then he said, "I've been waiting for you."

I don't think she believed him at all, and even though she was scrupulously polite to me, I could sense her disapproval all through breakfast, though Lord Sherborne soon joined us and never left my side. Throughout the rest of the day, I could feel Lady Rushton's hard stare boring into my back. When we all went for a stroll in the gardens after luncheon, I kept as far away from her husband as possible and remained exclusively in the marquis's company, yet I could sense Lady Rushton watching me through hedges or from behind rosebushes. Then, during the afternoon, when our group went riding, her horse was never very far from my own, and once I suspected her of purposely trying to cause an accident.

A group of us was riding down a wooded path that bordered a deep, wide ditch, when suddenly Lady Rushton's horse broke into a canter and veered into mine, pushing us perilously close to the edge. Fortunately, by throwing my weight to the right and hauling on the reins, I was able to steady my frightened horse and make him push back until Lady Rushton's mount relented and drew away. Once I was safe, everyone stopped and crowded around, demanding to know what had happened. Lady Rushton offered the lame excuse that her horse had suddenly bolted out of control, and everyone seemed to accept it. The incident was forgotten, and we continued on our ride. I, however, knew she had run into me deliberately, hoping to cause me serious injury, so I kept a watchful eye on Fiona Rushton from then on, determined not to give her another such opportunity.

I had Leonie to deal with as well. She was colder toward me than ever, and I suspect it was because she felt the prince was paying far too much attention to me, her insignificant sister. I caught her staring at me with the intensity of

Lady Rushton several times, and I was decidedly uncomfortable.

The dawn was just a wash of light pink and blue as I skipped noiselessly down the terrace steps and hurried along the Avenue of the Bulls, unmindful of the dew-drenched grasses that soaked my slippers and the hem of my skirt. But I had promised myself some time alone this morning, before the activities of the day began, and it was a promise I was going to keep.

When I reached the temple, I seated myself inside and waited, shivering and slightly out of breath. The cool country air smelled of flowers, grasses, and earth rather than the pungent smokiness of London, and I breathed deeply, savoring the mélange of scents. I closed my eyes and suddenly felt myself transported to the Cotswolds of my childhood. If I concentrated, I could hear Cyrus shouting for me to be careful as I boldly clambered over high, dangerous rocks, or childish voices squealing in delight when one of us was caught in a game of blind man's buff. My eyes flew open, and those childish voices receded into the past and died altogether.

Suddenly, the sky grew lighter, and I knew the sun was beginning to rise behind me.

I rose now and stood in the center of the temple. "Come forth, oh Surya!" I intoned, like some pagan priestess, my arms extended over my head, "and bring the morning to us." Then I dropped my arms and giggled at my own fancies.

As if in answer to my prayer, the sun's first rays slowly began to touch the topmost minarets, gilding their white surface.

"Your prayer is answered," a voice said from behind me, and I spun around to find Geoffrey standing there, dressed for riding and holding the bridle of a strapping gray horse.

"I thought I was alone," I murmured lamely, folding my

arms against the shiver that suddenly racked me, though it had nothing to do with the weather.

Geoffrey dropped the reins so his horse was free to graze, then he slowly climbed the temple's steps to join me. "I just returned from an early morning gallop myself. I too wanted some time alone before the day begins. It's amazing how we think alike."

His fair hair was wind-tossed, his cheeks were slightly flushed, and there was vigorous sparkle in his eyes. As he stood there, tapping his crop against his boot, I was once again aware of his intense masculinity. "How are you enjoying the house party so far?"

I sat down on one of the stone benches and drew my cashmere shawl more closely about me, relieved that he was going to keep the conversation pleasant and light. "Now I know why Mother insisted I have so many gowns. Why, I must change dresses three times a day. One in the morning, a tea gown for tea, then a formal gown for dinner."

Geoffrey smiled absently at that as he sat down beside me. "It's always been a mystery to me why women need so many clothes. A man wants a flesh-and-blood woman, not a dress-up doll."

I knew he was thinking of his own wife, so I tried to draw him off a subject I knew was sure to lead to a discussion of his battle to divorce her. "Everyone seems to be enjoying himself, even my mother and Edith."

Although Mother was never received in society because she was a divorced woman, here, as mother of the hostess, she could hardly be snubbed by her own guests. Last night at dinner, as I watched her converse with the guests and join in the various entertainments, I caught a glimpse of the vivacious, charming woman who must have captivated the Earl of Knighton all those years before. I found myself wondering if she ever missed being a part of society. Perhaps sharing Leonie's successes was enough for her.

Geoffrey said, "I think Edith fits in less with this set than I do, but Leonie insisted that she come, as usual."

"Everyone has been very kind to Edith," I said. "Even the prince seems to enjoy her company."

They shared a mutual love of Paris, and to everyone's surprise, Edith managed to keep our royal guest entertained with her stories of the city, told in that hypnotic voice that seemed to intrigue people.

We fell silent, and as I stole glances at the man seated by my side, I could see Geoffrey was deeply troubled and preoccupied. Yet, while he appeared resigned to his situation, there was always a spark of defiance deep in his sleepy eyes.

"One day, I shall be free of Leonie," he declared, pulling off his pigskin gloves.

"Please, Geoffrey," I murmured with a groan, "let's not discuss it any more, shall we?"

He didn't seem to hear me. "I remember my father returning once when I was a boy, from the Oriental Club with a story he had heard from one of the nabobs newly returned from India. It seems that some local maharajah had taken a fancy to one of the officer's wives. He risked war to kidnap her and held her captive in his palace until she returned his love." He looked at me now, and his eyes twinkled. "Perhaps that is what I should do to you."

I gasped at the impropriety of such a suggestion, then said, very sternly, "Don't be absurd, Geoffrey. This is England, not India."

With a sigh, he leaned his head back against the temple's wall. "More's the pity. It was just a fanciful thought, but then, you make me want to do impetuous things."

And sometimes you make me wish I had never met you, I said to myself. It's just too painful.

Suddenly, I felt strong fingers grasp my own. "You must have faith in me, Cassa. One day, I shall be free of Leonie."

"Even if you were free—"

"Look, sun goddess. Your prayer has been answered."

As I followed his gaze, I saw the white surface of the house bathed in a bright orange light, seeming to set the building afire, but I could not share Geoffrey's optimism about the omen. As he went to get his horse, and I stepped out of the temple, I had noticed a solitary figure standing on the terrace suddenly turn and disappear into the house. I could tell it was a woman, but I was too far away to tell who it was. Whether it was Leonie or Lady Rushton, I suspected, it boded ill for me.

I didn't have another chance to get away from all the other guests until later that afternoon, when the other women had retired to their rooms to nap or read before tea.

I decided to take advantage of the warm, balmy afternoon to write Cyrus another letter while the men were out somewhere shooting or displaying their prowess in other masculine endeavors. I took my writing paper and started for the pond.

As I walked down the path toward the stables, I found myself thinking of Adam Rushton and his advances at breakfast the other morning. I wondered what it must be like to be married to such a philanderer, so in love with him one suffered agonies whenever he looked at another woman. I like to think that if I were in Lady Rushton's situation, I would have left the man long ago.

So absorbed was I in thinking about the Rushtons that I hadn't realized where I was until a voice shouted, "Miss, watch out!"

Snapping out of my daydream, I realized I had wandered too close to Anarchist's paddock. From the way the horse's neck was strained as far as the high fence allowed, I could tell he would have reached out to savage me with his teeth if he could.

I never took my eyes off him as I jumped back and warily hurried past. Most horses have soft, liquid brown eyes, but not this one. They were black and filled with malice.

Once I was away from the stableyard, I found myself a shady knoll, spread my skirts on the grass, and began a letter chiding my cousin for his tardiness in answering my first one. Above me, birds were chirping in the trees, and in the pond, the three stately swans went silently gliding to and fro.

Ten minutes must have passed before I realized that the birds had fallen silent, and when I looked down at the water, the swans were nowhere to be seen. An uncanny, expectant hush enveloped me, as though something unexpected was about to happen. I suddenly felt as though someone were watching me.

My heart hammering wildly, I rose and looked around.

There was Anarchist, standing in the trees.

For one terrifying moment, I froze. The horse and I just stared at each other, and the minutes seemed to stretch into hours. As soon as the stallion began pawing the earth, I knew he intended to kill me.

I flung my half-finished letter away and ran for my life.

There were perhaps fifty feet between me and the pier, but it looked miles away. If I could only reach it in time, perhaps I could stay in the summerhouse until help came.

Holding my skirts up with both hands, I forced myself to take huge strides, willing my legs to move. Behind me, I heard a snort, and when I felt the earth begin to shake under my feet, I knew the half-crazed stallion was running me down. Terror propelled me forward, faster and faster, giving my legs strength I never knew I had, and I saw my goal drawing closer, ever closer.

Then it happened.

I felt something catch at my toe, like a hand rising from the earth, throwing me off balance, tripping me deliberately. With a choking sob of anguish, I went down on my knees and waited for murderous iron-shod hooves to come crashing down on my back.

But, to my amazement, Anarchist had stopped, perhaps baffled by my abrupt fall. It gave me the few precious seconds I needed to scramble to my feet and race the few remaining steps to the safety of the pier. In the brief time it took the animal to realize his mistake and resume his charge, I had run to the end of the pier and was safe inside the summerhouse.

For one agonizing moment, I thought the horse was going to come charging right down the walkway, but as it put its front hooves on the wood, the hollow sound they made as they struck the boards deterred him. He stood for a moment, bewildered, as though debating what to do. Then he moved away to solid ground, where he continued to stand guard, watching my every move the way a cat watches a mouse hole.

Gasping and out of breath, I flung myself against the cushions and let my heart return to its normal rate. How the horse had got out of its paddock in the first place was the furthest thought from my mind. My main concern was getting out of this predicament.

I did not have long to wait. Suddenly, Anarchist stopped, threw back his head, and listened. Through the shutters of the summerhouse, I could see two horsemen approaching from the opposite direction.

Rushing from the summerhouse, I called out, "Anarchist is loose!" just before the stallion saw them also and bounded away.

Halting his horse at the end of the pier, Geoffrey scowled after the animal, then turned to me, "What happened, Cassa?"

I couldn't stop shaking with relief as I ran toward him. "He—he got loose and—and chased me. I managed to—to run into the summerhouse. He didn't follow me, thank God!"

Geoffrey was out of the saddle in an instant and drawing me to him. "Are you all right?" When I nodded and buried my face in his shoulder, he seemed to remember that Lord

Rushton was watching and gently put me away, albeit reluctantly.

"I wonder how the horse got loose," Rushton murmured.

"Grooms a bit careless, old man?"

Geoffrey did not appreciate the taunt. "If they were, it's the last time they'll work for me." But his concern was less for his runaway prize stallion than for me. "I'm going to take you back to the house."

"Miss Clark can ride with me," Lord Rushton offered, with a glint in his eye I did not trust. "I'm sure you'll want to go to the stables and see how this terrible accident happened."

"Thank you for your generous offer," Geoffrey replied, swinging effortlessly into the saddle. "I'll look into this matter later."

He took his foot out of the stirrup and reached down for me. Taking his hand, I swung up behind him and encircled his waist with my arms, soothed by the solidness of him. Ignoring Lord Rushton's narrowed eyes, we rode back to the house.

I went right to my room, threw myself down on the bed, and tried to block out my narrow escape. Every time I closed my eyes, I could see the powerful stallion standing in the trees, watching me with that hateful look in his eyes. I could still hear his snort of triumph and the thundering of hoofbeats as he chased me, and my skinned palms and knees were burning reminders of the narrowness of my escape. Finally, when the shaking subsided, I was able to rise and bathe my wounds in warm water, brought to me by a maid.

I was just patting them dry, when there came a knock at the door, and Mother, Leonie, and Maud came trooping in.

"Geoffrey just told us what happened," Mother said, looking pale and worried. "Are you all right, Cassandra?"

"I just skinned my hands and knees when I fell," I replied.

"I've warned Geoffrey that animal is just too wild," Leonie said with a shake of her head. "Why, you could have been killed! Perhaps now he'll listen to me and sell the brute."

"But how did this happen?" Maud demanded, her brow furrowed. "The paddock fence is too high to jump, and the men are scrupulous about keeping it locked. They know that horse is dangerous."

I sat back on the bed with a sigh. "I don't know, Maud. Geoffrey's investigating now. I'm sure he'll come up with some answers soon."

Mother shivered. "Well, whatever the reason, you're safe now, my dear. It was just a freak accident, and I'm sure it won't happen again."

By the time we all went down for tea, every guest had heard about my narrow escape, and it livened up an otherwise lazy country day. Everyone, from the prince himself to Edith, expressed his gratitude for my providential escape without serious injury. Most of the women listened wide-eyed and horrified as I described my furious run down the hill, but Lady Rushton seemed rather unmoved by it all. While she murmured solicitous comments with everyone else, her voice lacked sincerity and her sharp eyes held no warmth or sympathy for me. Most of the men offered their own theories as to how the horse escaped in the first place.

Geoffrey listened patiently to them all, then said, "Somehow, the latch became undone, and when the horse threw his weight against the gate, it opened. Apparently no one noticed that he was loose, and Miss Clark had the misfortune to get in his way. I can assure everyone that additional precautions have been taken, and such an accident will never happen again."

Satisfied with that explanation, our guests turned to other topics, and my unpleasant episode was soon forgotten by everyone except the marquis.

Later, when I was returning to my room, he stopped me in the upstairs corridor. He looked quite pale beneath his beard, and he was visibly agitated, fidgeting nervously where he stood and stroking his beard with his fingertips.

"My lord, is something wrong?" I asked.

"That horse could have killed you, Cassandra!" he exclaimed, his voice shaking with emotion.

"But it didn't," I said with a soothing smile. "Fortunately, the summerhouse was there."

The marquis took a step toward me, reaching out. Before he could take me in his arms, his sense of propriety intervened and he stopped himself just in time. "You must forgive me for being so forward, but I am just so relieved that you weren't harmed. I—" He groped for the right words. "—I am pleased you are all right."

"Thank you for your concern."

He smiled, bowed, and strode away down the hall.

As I walked back to my own room, I couldn't stop thinking about my odd meeting with the marquis. It was obvious he had been frightened for me with an intensity that went far beyond the casual concern displayed by the other guests. I hoped he didn't fancy himself in love with me, for I had enough worries without numbering the Marquis of Sherborne among them.

After dinner, I excused myself on grounds of fatigue, and escaped a game of hide-and-seek that was to precede the prince's favorite entertainment of cards. No sooner did I have Sally dress me for bed than a knock sounded at my door.

It was Maud.

"I must speak with you," she said as she came marching into the room. Her hazel eyes were troubled, and her lips were compressed into a thin line.

"What is it, Maud?" I asked as I dismissed Sally and closed the door behind me. "You appear worried."

Indeed, I had never seen my friend look so disturbed. She

was pacing the room at a furious rate, and when she stopped suddenly, the diaphanous silk of her dress kept moving.

She hesitated for a moment, as though about to change her mind, then blurted out, "No, I must tell you. No good will come of keeping it to myself."

"What is it, Maud?"

She took a deep breath. "I think someone let that horse loose deliberately."

At first, the full impact of her words didn't register with me. My laugh was shaky as I said, "What are you saying, Maud?"

"I'm saying someone tried to harm you!"

When I saw that she was deadly serious, my knees turned to rubber, and I had to sit down on my bed and lean against the post for support. "Oh, Maud, you can't mean that."

"But I do. Geoff told me that he questioned the men, and they all insist they kept the paddock locked. They are good, honest men, all experienced, and the head groom never allows anyone near that paddock. Only one man handles Anarchist, and he's been with our family since I was a child. He assures us the latch was secure."

"But anyone could have brushed by the latch and—"

"No, Cassa, it can't be done. If that latch was undone, it was undone deliberately." Then Maud looked at me. "And anyway, who would want to? All the guests have been warned how dangerous that horse is. They've been warned to stay away from him." Maud came over to me and looked down from her great height. "I didn't tell Geoff this yet, but this afternoon, when all of the ladies retired to their rooms to rest before tea, I saw you leave the house. And I also saw Leo follow you, then return a little later."

We just stared at each other. "You don't think—"

"I don't know what to think, Cassa," she replied, her voice low and serious. "All I know is that I saw Leo leave the house after you. She returned. Then later, Geoff came riding up with you and told me the horse had got loose and chased you."

"I'm sorry, Maud," I said, rising with a shake of my head. "Why would my own sister want to harm me? She's the one who received that note and the doll's head, not I."

"I should think that's rather obvious."

I blushed. "Geoffrey?"

"Geoffrey. She knows how he feels about you, and he's asked her for a divorce. Perhaps this is Leo's way of warning you to back off."

"But Maud, that horse could have *killed* me!"

"And then it would have looked like an accident, and Leo's objective would have been achieved." When she saw my look, she softened her tone a bit. "Perhaps Leo only planned to frighten you after all." Now she headed for the door. "Well, I must be getting back to our guests. I'm engaged in a spirited discussion with the prince about housing for the poor, so I must press my advantage. I'm just telling you what I saw, Cassa. It could all be just a coincidence. Your sister could have been going for a walk. But still, I would be on my guard, if I were you."

Needless to say, after Maud's visit, I could not sleep very well. Had my own sister tried to harm me? I found it difficult to believe that even someone like Leonie was capable of such an act.

Still, I resolved to follow Maud's advice to be on my guard from then on.

Chapter Thirteen

Punjab House's large ballroom was a symphony of light and sound. The twin chandeliers blazed, though the jewels some women wore rivaled them in brilliance, and the lively strains of the orchestra in one corner made one want to dance, or at least tap one's toes in time to the music.

There must have been well over a hundred people present that night, members of the Marlborough House set mingling with the neighboring Kentish gentry who had come from miles around at Geoffrey's invitation to rub elbows with London society and meet the prince. I could tell the locals at once, for their clothes were not so elegant, though some women tried, and the men looked distinctly uncomfortable and in awe of the prince, who kept passing among them with a wide smile, a hearty handshake, or a pat on the back. Soon, even the most awkward country squires were laughing with him quite unselfconsciously, for such was our future monarch's great charm.

From my place beside a potted palm, I could see Mother being whirled around the dance floor in a frantic waltz, while Maud had buttonholed some distinguished-looking man and appeared to be talking his ear off, no doubt about one of her charities. Leonie was by the prince's side, where she had been since the ball started, and Geoffrey was off in a corner, the prisoner of some old dowager whose mouth never stopped moving.

I was hot and breathless from dancing a quadrille and three waltzes in a row, and needed a brief respite. Evading the graceless son of a local squire who seemed smitten with me, I slipped out unnoticed onto the terrace.

It was still too early for most of the guests to have tired of the dancing. I discovered I had the dimly lit terrace all to myself. I shut the French doors behind me, muffling the music and the voices, and giving full attention to the summer sounds of enthusiastic crickets, frogs, and other nocturnal creatures I was glad I couldn't see. Before me stretched the Avenue of the Bulls, its way lit with fairy lamps, and the Temple of Surya had also been illuminated, so that it was like a beacon beckoning to those who wished to dally in private.

I was leaning against the balustrade, breathing deeply of the fresh country air, when I sensed someone approach. I turned, and there was Edgar, who had just arrived from London a few hours before the ball.

"It's a beautiful night, isn't it, Miss—Cassandra?" he said as he stood next to me. I noticed Edgar's one threadbare suit had been replaced by regulation evening dress, and I wondered how a man of such slender means could afford it.

I smiled at him. "Isn't it, though? Are you enjoying the ball?"

A pained expression flitted across his face as he ran his finger beneath his collar to loosen its stranglehold. "Well, to tell the truth, I'm feeling a little awkward in my borrowed finery," he said ruefully. "One of Geoffrey's guests was my size and graciously lent me these clothes for the evening." Leave it to Geoffrey to see that no one was slighted or made to feel out of place.

"Oh, I think it makes you look most distinguished," I assured him.

He smiled shyly and thanked me, looking for all the world like a lost little boy caught trying on his father's clothes. Then he turned to look back into the ballroom, just at the moment Leonie and her royal lover came strolling by the doors. "Doesn't she look beautiful tonight?" Edgar said wistfully, his eyes following her.

"She always does."

Now he turned to me, his dark eyes troubled and his face a study in anguish. "Then why does she do it, Miss— Cassandra? Why does she let that—that *pig*—"

"Edgar!" I glanced quickly around, lest any members of the prince's entourage overhear such an insult. "You're referring to the Prince of Wales, remember. A little discretion, please!"

He breathed deeply, as if to bring himself under control. "I'm—I'm sorry," he said, passing his hand over his eyes. "I don't know what came over me. It's just that—that I—"

"Love Leonie yourself?" I suggested gently.

He swallowed hard and nodded dismally, his eyes suspiciously bright.

I slipped my arm through his and drew him over to the farthest corner of the terrace, where no one could overhear us without my seeing him. "I don't know why Leonie ever became involved with him. My sister is a very complex person, Edgar, very difficult to know, and I doubt if I'll ever understand her myself. But, even if she didn't have the prince, she is still married to Geoffrey."

"Oh, I know it's hopeless. I know that, even if Leonie were free, she wouldn't marry a penniless clerk from the Westminster Bank. But that doesn't make it easier to bear the pain."

"I know, Edgar."

He looked at me. "You really do understand, don't you? I think you've known about my feelings for your sister from the very first day we met."

"Yes, I'm afraid I have. You're not very adept at hiding your feelings for her, you know."

He winced. "I was afraid of that." Then he said, "Have you ever loved someone desperately who couldn't love you?"

I didn't know how to answer him, so I looked toward the French doors, which had suddenly opened to allow more people to come outside, and said gently, "I owe someone a dance and must go in now."

Edgar's face fell, but he said, "Yes . . . yes, of course. We must go back inside."

The moment I went back into the ballroom, Lord Sherborne stepped up to claim the next dance. Like all the men present, he looked especially distinguished in black formal attire, and, as he took me into his arms and we whirled away in perfect time to the music, I wasn't surprised to discover he was an excellent dancer. But then, the marquis seemed to excel at everything.

Except racing horses, I reminded myself.

I had never been so physically close to him as I was now, and, as he held me in his arms, I became aware of a pleasant glow enveloping me. Mutual respect, admiration, and pleasure in each other's company flowed between us. With the instincts of a man who has known many women, the marquis was just as aware of the attraction as I.

He smiled. "You look especially beautiful tonight, Cassandra." He had slipped into the use of my Christian name ever since my narrow escape from Anarchist, but he had not invited me to call him Horace.

When I thanked him for the compliment, he said, "But then, I have thought that ever since the moment I met you in the garden, with your mother. There you were, striding across the yard like a man, yet so deliciously feminine. And the first time I stared into your green eyes . . ." Before I could stop him, he drew my hand to his lips. When I blushed and quickly glanced around to see if Geoffrey had noticed, the marquis said, "I'm not embarrassing you, am I?"

"A little," I confessed. "My Aunt Venetia always said that beauty can hide a black and sinful heart, so it's best to discover what a person is like inside before making judgments."

"Modest as well as lovely," he murmured. "I find it difficult to believe that your beauty could conceal a black heart."

Why, I thought as we whirled across the dance floor again, *I think he is falling in love with me.*

I suppose I shouldn't have been surprised, but I was caught off guard and stunned into silence. I noticed that Geoffrey was staring at us from the sidelines, a slight scowl creasing his brow as he conversed with Christopher Sykes. I wondered how long he had been observing us.

Suddenly, the dance ended, and the marquis asked softly, "May I have the next dance as well?" knowing that to dance with the same lady twice was to invite speculation about a romantic involvement.

But when I consulted my dance card, I discovered to my dismay that I had promised the next dance to Lord Rushton, and, before I could disappear once again, he sought me out and cornered me.

"I believe the next dance is mine, my Night Beauty," he said, bowing, "and all the others after that."

As he led me out onto the dance floor, I shook my head. "Just this one, Lord Rushton; otherwise people will talk, and your wife will be upset with me."

When he slipped his arm around my waist, I knew he was going to hold me too close, which he did, but there was no escape, for the music was starting up again.

"Do you know what Byron said about the waltz in *Don Juan?*" he asked, his dark eyes becoming the only constant as people whirled around us in a blur of color and light.

"No, Lord Rushton, I don't, but I'm sure you'll tell me."

"He says it's the only dance that teaches girls to think."

"Pardon my ignorance, but what did he mean by that?"

My partner grinned. "Damned if I know, but it sounds profound."

So, Lord Rushton was one of those people who quoted poetry to impress others. I was not surprised.

His grip increased upon my waist, and despite my best efforts, I could not keep from drawing even closer to him. In

the crowd of spectators, I could sense his wife's eagle eyes
on me, even though I was dancing much too fast to catch a
glimpse of her.

"You are the most beautiful woman here tonight, Cassandra," Lord Rushton said softly, his gypsy eyes roving
over my face boldly. "You even eclipse our fair hostess."

"Thank you," was all I said.

Judging from the irritated look that passed over my partner's face, I had the feeling he expected more from me, a
flirtatious smile, perhaps, or coy words. He chuckled. "So
cool, so contained, aren't you? But I know you, Cassandra,
better than you know yourself. I know the Cassandra of legend was a prophetess of doom, but I see you as a cool marble
statue just begging to be brought to life. And if you will
allow me to be the one who—"

Suddenly, the music slowed, then stopped. The dance
ended, and before Lord Rushton could go on, I stopped,
smiled up at him, and said, "Thank you for the dance, Lord
Rushton. It has certainly taught me how to think." Then I
turned and swept away from him before he could stop me.

I managed to evade him for the rest of the evening by
keeping my dance card filled, and during those few dances
when I wasn't spoken for, I sat the dance out and fanned
myself rapidly, all the while proclaiming how weary I was.
But, even though I danced with others, I could see Lord
Rushton watching me, and I wondered why I had suddenly
become the object of his unwanted attentions. Oh, he had
always flirted with me whenever we met, but this was somehow different, more intense and more in earnest. It was as
though the Byronic lord was determined to make a conquest
while here, and that conquest was to be me. I suspected
rejection only heightened his ardor, so great was his conceit.

Then, when it seemed as though the ball had just begun,
it ended.

Those who weren't staying the night began drifting off,
one by one, and soon, there were only a few couples left on

the dance floor, serenaded by yawning musicians. The rest of the guests had wandered off to go strolling through the garden, while others sat on the stairs to talk. Mother was deep in conversation with Lord and Lady Churchill, and Maud was nowhere to be found, so I decided to escape to the terrace again, but when I went outside, I discovered someone else had the same idea.

"Good evening, Your Grace," I said to the Duchess of Manchester.

She turned her head slightly. "Ah, Miss Clark. Tired of dancing already? But you're so young!"

"Oh, the dancing is nearly finished, and besides, my poor sore feet couldn't tolerate one more waltz. I just came out here for a breath of fresh air before retiring."

"So did they," she said, nodding in the direction of the Avenue of the Bulls.

I first saw the orange glow of a cigar tip in the darkness and the portly shadow of the prince. By his side was Leonie, holding his arm and leaning toward him. I recognized her, even in the dim glow of the fairy lamps.

Thinking of Edgar's agonized question, I said to the duchess, "Forgive me for speaking out of turn, but you are a good friend of His Royal Highness, so perhaps you can answer a question for me."

Her brows rose as she looked at me. "If it's not _too_ personal, of course."

I moistened my lips and steeled myself for a rebuke. "What does the prince see in my sister? What is it about her, of all the women in England, that attracts him to her?"

The duchess did not take offense, or think me too bold, as I feared she might. She just sighed. "I've seen his favorites come and go over the years, Miss Clark, so I know whereof I speak. I would say that His Royal Highness is attracted to Lady Lester for her youth, vitality, and considerable beauty. And, as much as we have had our differences in the past, I will grudgingly admit that your sister is good for him. Not only is she a capable mistress in the bedchamber, if you'll pardon my frankness, but she is a discreet one. I've never known your sister to use her position of considerable influence for her own—or her friends'—gain. Oh, many powerful men have come to her thinking they can appeal to her vanity and ask for favors, but she just laughs at them all and sends them on their way."

So, that's why Leonie hadn't gotten Edgar Wickes a new position through her royal lover. She refused to take advantage of her exalted status as his favorite for another's benefit.

"Leonie never ceases to surprise me," I murmured.

The duchess chuckled at that. "Yes, she has her good points and bad, as do we all." Then she turned to the house and said, "Look. The butler is coming round with the candles, and I think that's our signal to retire."

"Good night, Your Grace," I said, and she wished me good night before disappearing inside to find Lord Hartington.

I stayed on the terrace alone for a little while longer, watching the two figures as they reached the temple. They were clearly illuminated for a moment as they embraced, then they extinguished the lights, one by one, leaving the temple in darkness and solitude.

I turned and went inside.

Later, long after everyone had retired for the night and the house was quiet, a noise awakened me. My eyes flew open, though my mind struggled to throw off the shackles of sleep that still held me.

There was just enough moonlight shining through a window to turn everything in the room into distinct, definable shapes, whether it was the armoire across the room or the night stand beside my bed. As I lay still, hardly daring to breathe, my eyes searched the darkness for whatever it was that did not belong among these other things. And then I saw it.

There was someone standing at the foot of my bed.

Now I was fully awake, straining to pick out the person's features, but failing. It was just too dark. I sat up, bravely ready to confront whoever had dared to intrude on my privacy.

"Who's there?" I demanded, clutching the sheets about me and trying to keep the panic out of my voice.

A soft chuckle answered me. "Why, it's Adam, of course. Whom else were you expecting?"

He moved now, coming slowly around the bed toward me, and just as I saw him sit on the edge, heard the mattress creak, and felt his weight on it, I flung back the sheets and bounded out the other side, away from him.

"Get out of my room this instant, Lord Rushton!" I snarled, wishing he could see my furious face in the darkness.

"My darling Cassandra, this is no time to be coy with me. I will be denied no longer."

I sought to deflate him by saying, "Does your wife know you're here?"

He chuckled again. "Dear Fiona thinks I am downstairs, playing cards till all hours with some of the other men. She won't suspect a thing."

I was glad I couldn't see his face, glad I heard only a voice coming from a shadow.

"How did you know which room was mine?"

"Why, by the name plate on the door, of course. That's why they're there, my innocent, to make sure lovers like us don't wander into the wrong room by mistake. It wouldn't do for H.R.H. to find himself in your room instead of your sister's, now would it? Or me in the Duchess of Manchester's room instead of yours."

"If you don't leave this instant, I'll scream the house down, and your wife will know you haven't been playing cards."

The shadow stood up and slowly began its progress around

the bed, toward me. "Now, why would you want to do that? Screams would only bring people running, and I think it's best we be alone for what I have in mind, don't you?"

Now he had reached the foot of the bed, and I could discern his features a little better. Lord Rushton was grinning, giving him a look similar to a statue I had once seen of a lustful satyr in pursuit of a terrified wood nymph. I could also see that he wore trousers and a dressing gown.

"I think you had best leave now, Lord Rushton," I warned him, hoping my voice sounded strong and determined.

"Now, Cassandra, you don't want me to do that. Please, why don't you light your candle so I can see what you look like?"

I knew he wasn't referring to just my face, but his mentioning of the silver candlestick inspired me. I reached behind me, never taking my eyes off him, and fumbled around the night stand until my eager fingers found it. Just as they curled around cold metal, Rushton made his move, lunging so quickly and quietly I barely had time to blink.

"Don't come near me!" I cried, filling my lungs to scream.

He stopped within almost an arm's length of me. "Why the pretense of shyness?" He was breathing heavily now. "I can assure you I won't hurt you. I will be very gentle. At first."

Just as he reached for me, I raised the candlestick and aimed for his head, propelling it with all my strength. I felt it connect with a soft thud, and with a grunt of surprise and pain, Lord Rushton crumpled and fell to the floor, where he lay in an undignified heap at my feet.

As I stared at him lying so very still, I suddenly wondered if I could have killed him, and panic and fear almost rendered me senseless. Then my trembling fingers struck a match and, without another glance at the unconscious intruder, I lit my candle and went running for help.

My feet seemed to have wings as I flew down the silent

corridor, hurriedly scanning the names on every door until I came to Geoffrey's. I prayed he wasn't playing cards with the other men as I turned the knob and ran in, hurrying over to his bed. Much to my relief, he lay sleeping on his back, one arm across his forehead.

"Geoffrey!" I cried, shaking his shoulder urgently. "Please wake up! Please!"

His eyes flew open and for a moment, he stared at me in a daze, without comprehension. "Cassa, what—?"

I took a deep breath and babbled, "Lord Rushton came to my room and tried to—to force himself on me. I hit him with this candlestick and knocked him unconscious." My hand flew to my mouth and the flame wavered. "Good God! I think I may have killed him!"

Now Geoffrey was fully awake and taking command. He took my trembling free hand and spoke slowly. "Get me my trousers from the chair over there, Cassa, and wait in the hall while I dress. I'll join you in a minute."

"But I—"

"Do as I say. And don't panic. I doubt if you seriously hurt Rushton. His head is as hard as those granite bulls outside."

That brought a smile to my lips as I left the room and waited for him in the hall. In seconds, Geoffrey was by my side and we were hurrying toward my room.

When we arrived, my heart sank, for Lord Rushton was still lying where he had fallen, but I was relieved to hear a soft groan coming from his supine form. Geoffrey knelt down beside him, turned him over, and examined Rushton's head. I blanched when I saw an ugly raw scrape where the candlestick had hit him.

"I don't think you did him serious injury, Cassa," he told me, "but Rushton will have a nasty bump and one very sore head tomorrow. It's the very least he deserves, under the circumstances."

Then Geoffrey shook him and slapped him in the face none too gently to revive him.

I felt profound relief flood through me when Lord Rushton's eyes fluttered open, and he groaned and struggled to sit up. He sat there, rubbing his head gingerly for a moment, and when he fully regained his faculties, he remembered what had happened and glared menacingly at me.

"Why did you hit me?" he snarled.

He looked so ferocious, I stepped back behind Geoffrey for protection. "Because you came in here and tried to force yourself on me. I had to defend myself."

Now Geoffrey rose, crossed his arms, and regarded Rushton with a look of pure contempt. "Do you always go to a lady's room uninvited, Rushton?"

Rushton, who looked less like a gypsy prince and more like a clown with his legs akimbo, growled, "I *was* invited, Lester."

I felt the blood stream into my cheeks. "Liar! I never asked you to come to my room."

Geoffrey's arms fell to his sides, and his hands balled into fists. "Rushton?"

"Well, she never invited me outright," he admitted slowly, "but it was made very clear to me by someone else that she wanted me to come to her room tonight but was too shy to ask herself. I was told if I came here tonight at a certain hour, my advances would be welcome."

I was shaking now and had to hold on to the bed post lest my legs fail me. "Who told you such a monstrous lie?"

He rose shakily to his feet, swayed slightly, then regained his balance. "I cannot say. My honor as a gentleman—"

Geoffrey's arms shot out, grasping Rushton by the front of his dressing gown. "Do you need further persuasion, my friend?"

Rushton's eyes fell away, and he mumbled. "No need to get hot under the collar, old man. It was your wife."

"Leonie told you Cassa desired your advances?" Geoffrey demanded, his hands falling to his sides in surprise.

Rushton nodded. "The same. She told me that ever since Miss Clark and I were introduced, she has been attracted to me, but was too shy to tell me outright. Leonie said Miss Clark was inexperienced with men, and unskilled at flirting, so I was not to be put off by her sharp words and cool demeanor. They were merely her way of encouraging me. Then Leonie told me tonight would be the night to make my move, at one o'clock."

Geoffrey just gave Rushton a look of disbelief and shook his head. "And you believed her?"

"My sister lied to you, Lord Rushton," I said. "I assure you my sharp words of rebuke were just that. I have no desire whatsoever to form a liaison with you."

The thought of a woman scorning his advances was more than Lord Rushton's considerable pride could bear, and he reddened, regarding me with frank dislike now, and I knew I had made myself an enemy.

Geoffrey said, "I think we should return to our rooms and forget this ever happened."

Rushton adjusted his robe, then looked from me to Geoffrey. "Splendid idea. We have the lady's reputation to consider."

I suspect Lord Rushton was thinking more of his own reputation and his wife's wrath, but I said nothing and murmured my acquiescence. He smiled in relief, bowed, and left hurriedly, before his wife discovered that he hadn't been playing cards all night after all.

"Blackguard," Geoffrey muttered after him. Then, when we were alone, he turned to me, and the harshness of his face startled me. "Leonie is going to have quite a bit of explaining to do in the morning."

I shivered. "Why would she do such a thing to me? She knows I dislike Lord Rushton."

"I don't know, but I'm certainly going to find out."

Suddenly, the full extent of my sister's perfidy rocked through me like a bolt of lightning, and I felt the need to flee, to be alone and away from this house.

"We must talk, Cassa," Geoffrey said gently, seeing my pain and humiliation."

"Tomorrow, Geoffrey, tomorrow. I can't talk now. It's been too upsetting. Please go, before you are discovered and I'm compromised further."

He looked about to speak, then just bowed and left me. I waited until he was gone before leaving the house.

The grass was damp with dew beneath my bare feet, and the small moon high in the night sky illuminated my way as surely as if it were the middle of the day instead of the middle of the night. A fresh breeze wafting from the north cooled my skin through my night shift, for I was hot with humiliation and treachery.

How could my own sister have done this to me, I asked myself for the thousandth time as I darted across the lawn and past the garden? How could she have deliberately misled Lord Rushton into thinking that I burned to have him as my lover when she knew I detested the man? And it was plain she had been feeding him such lies for weeks now.

My breath was coming in short gasps, but I didn't slow my pace, for movement seemed to purge my pain. And why had Leonie done this? If it was to embarrass me, she had succeeded, and the thought of facing Lord Rushton over the breakfast table made me blush in mortification. But I couldn't believe her actions were designed merely to cause me shame. Knowing my sister as I did, I suspected she had a more sinister motive for tonight's machinations, one designed somehow to hurt Geoffrey. But I couldn't figure out what it was.

Finally, I arrived at my destination and hesitated for a moment to catch my breath. Before me lay the pond, its silvery, glassy surface still and unbroken, and the summerhouse looked like a confection of white icing in the moonlight. As I walked down the knoll toward the pier, I thought for one fleeting second of my mad dash to escape Anarchist, but I knew he was locked safely in his stall tonight with the other horses, and I banished my fears as I walked out onto the pier, the wood smooth against the soles of my bare feet. When I went around the house and came to the end of the pier, I sat down well away from the edge and rested my back against the wall of the summerhouse.

The night air was warm, and as I sat there, it soothed me and took away the tensions of the confrontation with Lord Rushton. But nothing could erase what my sister had done to me. First Anarchist, and now this. Why was my own sister trying to harm me, especially since I had always tried to be kind to her? Did she really hate me that much?

I lost all track of time; I don't know how long I had been sitting there alone with my tumultuous thoughts, when I heard footsteps on the pier. I wasn't afraid, because I knew at once they belonged to Geoffrey. I had become quite adept at sensing his presence even before I saw him, whether in a crowded ballroom or sitting by myself.

"I thought I'd find you here," he said, as he rounded the summerhouse and stood beside me. "As soon as I went back to my room, I realized that I couldn't leave you alone tonight after what happened. When I returned to your room, I found you gone, and when I looked out the window, I saw you running across the lawn. I followed you. I hope you don't mind."

I didn't look at him, just listened to the water lap softly against the pier and watched its ripples fan out across the pond to the other side.

"From here," I said, "it looks as though the moon is floating on the surface of the pond, doesn't it?"

Geoffrey said nothing. When he did speak, his voice sounded strained. "Do you know what a moonraker is?"

I scowled down at the water as I tried to remember the old legend Uncle Harry had once told us children gathered wide-eyed around a warm winter fire. "The moonraker sees the moon floating in the water and mistakes it for cheese, if I recall, so he goes out in his boat and tries to rake it in. It always eludes him, of course. Some say he's mad, and some say a fool."

"Sometimes I feel like that moonraker," Geoffrey said heavily, and I knew instantly that he was referring to his own hopeless love for me.

All I said was, "I came out here to be alone and think."

"About what?"

"About what Leonie did to me tonight, and what I'm going to do about it."

"And what have you decided?"

I kept my gaze fixed on the shimmering moon in the water. "I've decided to do what I should have done from the very beginning. Return to Cairo."

Geoffrey reached down, grasped my waist lightly in his two hands, and pulled me to my feet as if I were a feather. I had to face him now. Then he held me by my shoulders, but his touch was gentle this time, not cruel. "You know I'd never allow that. You're never going to leave me, Cassa."

"It's for the best," I said dully, turning my head away to avoid looking into his eyes. "It would be best for all concerned if I returned to Cairo and the hotel. It's where I belong."

"You belong here with me."

"You can't force me to stay, Geoffrey."

He laughed, and his grip on my shoulders tightened ever so slightly. "No, I can't," he agreed with false amiability, "but I don't think you really want to go back to Cairo. Oh, you think it's the noble thing to do under the circumstances, but deep in your heart, you want to remain here with me."

"You are so sure of yourself, aren't you?"

He smiled and nodded slowly. "If you can look me in the eye and tell me you don't love me, Cassa, then you'll be able to return to Cairo. But I wager that you cannot."

Now the shock of what Leonie had done was fading, and my head was clearing. For the first time, I could really see

Geoffrey, and I caught my breath at his magnificence in the moonlight. He looked as though some Renaissance sculptor had chiseled him out of fine white marble, from his fair hair to the broad, craggy planes of his face. Since Geoffrey was shirtless, his torso was bare, and I let my eyes rove over his broad, muscular shoulders. I fancied that, without his trousers, he would look like some old Greek god come to life, with slender hips and muscular thighs. Such an immodest thought left me shaking.

If his body was cool stone, his eyes were not, and burned with some inner fire, while his lips were softly curved in a knowing smile.

Geoffrey reached for me, but sanity returned just in time, and I resisted. "Please don't. My mind is quite made up. Leonie has shown me that she will stop at nothing to hurt you, and I can't be responsible for that."

His arms came around me. "Say it, if you can, Cassa. Say you don't love me, and I'll never touch you again."

"I—I don't . . ." But the words wouldn't come. I couldn't lie to Geoffrey, even to save myself.

"You see," he said simply, taking one of my dark curls between his fingers and caressing it gently.

When his lips touched mine, feather light, I no longer pulled away or tried to resist him, but sighed in surrender as I went to him willingly. Geoffrey had been right all along. I loved him and could no longer deny it. I didn't even want to.

As I sought the strength and shelter of his arms, I felt as though a magic circle had been drawn around me, and not even Leonie could harm me here. When Geoffrey kissed me again with renewed passion, I responded as though my sister, Cairo, and tomorrow no longer existed, and we had an eternity of discovery stretching out before us.

When we finally parted, breathless, Geoffrey moved away from me, and instantly, I felt cold and abandoned, missing the closeness of him, so I had to reach up and lightly place my hands on his shoulders, just to maintain contact. He smiled at my sudden possessiveness, and, in response, I stood on tiptoes and boldly kissed him, invading his mouth instinctively.

"Wanton," he gasped, startled. "I must let you go long enough to do this—" And he began untying the ribbons of my nightdress with one hand, his other arm around my waist. I could have pushed him away and begged him to stop, but I didn't want to, though I knew what was going to happen next. Now, rather than the revulsion I had felt with Rushton, I felt only the sweetest anticipation.

When he gently pushed the loosened garment from my shoulders, letting it float down to my ankles, and lowered his head to my breasts, I gasped and my submission was complete. I leaned against the supporting arm that encircled my waist, savoring the languorous pleasure of his caresses.

When I thought I would just melt away, he scooped me into his arms and took me inside the dark summerhouse, setting me gently down on the cushions.

As he towered above me, his face inscrutable in the shadows, he murmured thickly, "Cassa, are you sure?"

"Do you even need to ask?" was my soft reply.

I heard him breathe as his clothes fell to the floor. Then he was lying beside me, warming me with his length, letting his lips brush my face, glide down my throat, and rest in the hollow between my breasts.

"You are the most beautiful woman I have ever known."

He made love to me tenderly and with agonizing slowness, as though he were afraid I was made of porcelain and might break if he handled me too roughly in my initiation into love's mysteries and awakening to the delirious delights of my own body. Then, after I had known ecstasy, he turned to me again, only this time with fierce, unrestrained passion that was both exciting and a little frightening.

Later, as we lay clasped to each other, his damp face against my shoulder while he dozed, I felt as though I had awakened from a long sleep, and now that I was awake, I had become a different person. I loved Geoffrey. I no longer wanted to return to Cairo, ever, unless it was with him.

Yet even in the afterglow of euphoria and bliss, my practical mind couldn't escape thinking of consequences, always consequences. I turned my head enough to look through the shutters toward the eastern sky and fancied it had lightened.

"Geoffrey," I whispered, gently shaking him, "it will be morning soon. Perhaps we should return to the house before someone sees us here."

He nestled closer to me and mumbled, "Stay, Cassa. Nothing to worry about."

I foolishly believed him and closed my eyes.

When I next opened them, I could just see the rim of the sun rising above the line of trees across from the pond. It was morning. The stablehands would be feeding the horses. The guests would be rising and going down to breakfast. Perhaps one of them would decide to go for an early morning stroll past the summerhouse.

"Geoffrey," I cried, shaking him awake. "It's morning. If we don't get back to the house this instant, someone will see us!"

He grumbled sleepily and reached for me again, but I managed to wriggle out from under his heavy imprisoning arm, spring to my feet, and dress hurriedly in my nightdress. When he realized I was gone, he stirred, opened his eyes, yawned, and ran his hand through his hair.

"Cassa, what's the matter?"

"It's morning, and I'll have much explaining to do if someone sees me wandering around the grounds in my nightdress."

"You're right, of course," he said soberly, reaching for his trousers. "I should have thought about that sooner."

He seemed so angry with himself that he had compromised me, I had to take his hand and say, "I don't regret what happened."

He reached for me and drew me into his arms for one last kiss. When he reluctantly released me, he said, "Neither do I, but we must be prudent." Then he sat down to tug on his boots. "You go back to your room through the servants' entrance. No one will see you. I'll go to the stables and borrow a shirt from one of the grooms. I'll look as though I've just returned from a morning ride. Don't worry, my dearest. The servants will be discreet."

"It's not the servants I'm worried about," I replied as I left the summerhouse.

There must be a patron saint for new lovers, for I managed to return to the house unobserved. I went through the day as though nothing had happened and was even able to face Lord Rushton when he finally appeared at lunch looking green around the mouth and a little worn around the edges. He pointedly ignored me, as though the bump on his head were somehow my fault. At least it was hidden by his hair, and no one would know where he got it. Somehow, I couldn't even feel angry with Leonie for her part in sending Lord Rushton to my bedchamber, for, if she hadn't, then Geoffrey and I would never have found each other.

And then, just before tea, Mother summoned me to her sitting room.

The moment I saw her standing there, hands tightly clasped together before her and her face as gray as her dress, I knew something was terribly wrong.

"Mother, is something the matter?" I asked, closing the door behind me. "You look quite ill."

Her voice cracked as she said, "You've played right into Leonie's hands, my girl."

As I stared into her green eyes, I knew at once what she was referring to. I took a deep breath to stave off the feeling of disaster that was rapidly surrounding me. "She saw Geoffrey and me in the summerhouse last night."

Mother squeezed her eyes shut as though in pain and nodded.

I stumbled over to the nearest chair and slid down into it. "How—how did this happen? How did she find out?"

"She's been watching you carefully for days, hoping to catch you and her husband together in a compromising situation. Then, last night, she saw you leave the house and Geoffrey follow you, so she tracked the two of you to the summerhouse. She saw . . . everything, Cassandra."

I understood all too clearly now. Leonie had sent Lord Rushton to my room, not to compromise me, but to serve as a catalyst between Geoffrey and me. That's why she had told Lord Rushton I wanted him to come to my room at precisely one o'clock, so she would know exactly when to watch Geoffrey and me. Perhaps she had thought Geoffrey would stay in my room that night to comfort me, and, when he hadn't, she waited and followed.

Suddenly, anger gave me strength and I rose. "I won't apologize for what happened between Geoffrey and me, Mother. We love each other. And who is Leonie to criticize me? Her own behavior has not exactly been exemplary. She has been unfaithful to Geoffrey many times."

"My dear, dear child," Mother said with a touch of annoyance, "don't you *see?* You have given your sister the weapon she's needed to use against Geoffrey. If he presses for this divorce now, she is going to tell him that she will name you as co-respondent in court." Mother bowed her head wearily and placed her hand to her forehead. "She even has a witness."

"A witness? Who, Mother?"

"Fiona Rushton. When Leonie saw what was happening, she got Lady Rushton out of bed and the two of them followed you. Since Fiona has the idea that you fancy her husband, she was only too willing to oblige."

Obviously, Lady Rushton hadn't known about Leonie sending her husband to my room, and I told my mother all about my unwelcome nocturnal visitor.

Mother just shook her head. "You should have seen Leonie's face when she told me. Such malice, such a look of triumph . . . I hardly recognized my own daughter."

Now I could feel all the defiance drain right out of me, and I fell back in my chair, cursing myself for a fool. Leonie had set a very clever trap for Geoffrey, with me as bait, and I had led him right into it. I felt heartsick as tears of frustration slid down my cheeks.

Mother came over to me, slipped her handkerchief into my hand, and put her arm around my shoulders as she must have done when I was a child. "I tried to dissuade Leonie, but she wouldn't listen to me, as usual. I'm afraid she's going to tell Geoffrey what she's planning to do." She was quiet for a moment as she scanned my face. "You love him, don't you?"

I sniffed and nodded. "I love him with all my heart, Mother, even though he is my own sister's husband. I've tried to fight what I feel, because I know it's wrong, but I haven't been very successful at it." I squeezed her hand and cried even harder. "I—I just can't seem to help myself."

She sighed. "I know that feeling all too well and where it can lead."

I looked up at her and knew she was referring to her love for the Earl of Knighton. Now, for the first time in my life, I could understand why my mother had left my father for another man. My loving Geoffrey was just as wrong as Mother's having loved the earl, but since it had happened to me, I felt as though I were a blind person suddenly granted the gift of sight. Now I could understand an irrational love that knows no conventions or boundaries. I knew what it was like to be swept away by a passion so strong it would let nothing stand in its way.

And then I recalled a quotation from the Bible that my moralistic Aunt Venetia so conveniently forgot. *Judge not, that ye not be judged.* What right had I to withhold forgiveness or understanding from my mother, when I was no better than she?

"Oh, Mother," I cried, throwing myself into her arms. "I'm so, so sorry for being so harsh with you. Can you forgive me for being such a fool all these years?"

She smiled through her tears, nodded, and held me to her as though she had finally found something that had been lost a long, long time ago and was doubly precious to her for all that.

I had found, in a single night, not only Geoffrey, but my mother as well.

I didn't see Geoffrey again until twilight, when I happened to go out on the terrace and noticed his tall, straight figure striding down the Avenue of the Bulls. When I caught up with him, he was standing in the temple, his back toward me.

"Geoffrey?" I said, as I walked up the steps.

At the sound of my voice, he turned, his face mirroring the rage and frustration I felt at being Leonie's dupe.

We looked at each other in silence, and when he was about to speak, I said, "I know. Mother told me."

Geoffrey pulled me into his arms, heedless of who might be watching from some upstairs window or some nearby path. As he held me, his cheek hard against mine, he said, "She says if I attempt to divorce her, she'll name you as co-respondent. She says she'll make sure we're never granted a divorce. If she has to lose everything she cares for, she'll drag us down with her. She's out of her mind, Cassa."

I moved away and touched his cheek, while looking up into his tormented eyes. "I don't care, Geoffrey. Let Leonie do her worst. As you said to me that night on the Embankment, there are ways we can be together if we're only brave enough to take the risk. If you still have that villa in St. John's Wood—"

"That's not good enough any more, Cassa." He smiled bitterly. "Isn't it ironic that, when you're freely offering to become my mistress, I don't want it any more? Now I want you for my wife." He stroked my hair lovingly.

I shook my head. "That may be impossible, so I would suggest that we seize whatever happiness we can."

"No," he insisted stubbornly, "there must be another way to get around my beloved Leonie."

Then he stared broodingly out at the rolling fields beyond, and when he spoke, he didn't look at me, as though there were something in his expression he didn't want me to see. But his voice betrayed him anyway. There was steely determination there as well as pure hatred.

"I will be free of her one day, Cassa," he said. "That is my promise to you."

When he turned to me, I saw the face of a ruthless, diabolical stranger, a man I didn't recognize and would run from if I met him on the street. He was not the same Geoffrey Lester to whom I had given myself willingly, and who had made such tender love to me in return. I crossed my arms to keep from shivering, for I was suddenly afraid.

"What are you going to do, Geoffrey?" I demanded, searching his face for any sign of the man I had once known. There was none.

"I'm going to make her see reason," he replied, striding away from me, "if it's the last thing I ever do."

Chapter Fourteen

I am a temperate person by nature, preferring calm, rational discussion to violent outbursts of anger, but Leonie's deceitful machinations had finally worn my patience paper-thin, and I decided that a confrontation with her was long overdue.

She was in the sitting room off the solarium, humming to herself and calmly arranging fresh summer flowers in a vase as though blissfully unaware of all the turmoil she had caused around her.

"Leonie," I said, walking in and closing the door so no one could wander in or overhear us. "I must talk to you."

She looked up but did not smile. "Yes, sister dear, what is it?"

"You know very well." I hid my hands in my skirts so she wouldn't see them shaking with anger as I faced her. "Did you let Anarchist out of his paddock the other day?"

"Now why on earth would I want to do something like that? Anarchist is dangerous. He could have killed you."

"For the same reason you intercepted my telegram to Geoffrey," I replied. "You want to frighten me away."

Now she casually snipped off the stem of one bloom with a pair of sharp shears and acted as though she didn't have a care in the world. "Getting fanciful in your old age, Cassa? Mind playing tricks on you, is it? I never went near that paddock."

I sighed. "Don't lie, Leonie. Maud saw you follow me, then return."

"I was merely taking a walk, that's all. It's not a crime to walk my own property, is it, or do I have to ask Miss Maud Lester's permission for that, too?"

I could see I was getting nowhere with her. "Perhaps I can't prove you let the horse out, but I do know that you purposely misled Lord Rushton into thinking that I desired a liaison with him. He even came to my room last night at one o'clock, just as you instructed him to."

Now she fluttered her long lashes in surprise. "My dear Cassandra, I'm sure if Adam went to your room last night, it was at your express invitation."

I longed to shake the truth out of her, but gritted my teeth and restrained myself. "You know that's not true, Leonie. You know I've despised the man ever since I met him that day in the park."

"I know no such thing. I always thought you rather fancied his Byronic looks."

"You astound me, Leonie, you really do. I've caught you in a lie, and you blithely deny it. Lord Rushton told both Geoffrey and me last night that you were the one who led him to believe I would welcome his advances. He said you told him I wanted him to come to my room precisely at one o'clock, which, of course, I did not."

"Then he must be lying to save his own reputation."

From the adjacent solarium, I thought I heard the sound of a chair scraping against the wood floor, but when I listened for it again, there was nothing except the snipping of my sister's shears.

Now Leonie's tone became self-righteous as she stuck a lily into the vase. "You're such a hypocrite, sister dear. You condemn me for supposedly misleading Lord Rushton, which is absolutely preposterous, but at the same time, you're not above trying to steal my husband. Do you recall all those times you denied it, hmm? If anyone should be furious, it is I." Now she looked at me. "And what were you and Geoffrey doing in the summerhouse last night, Cassandra, hmm? Discussing the weather, perhaps? I think not." Her smile was one of triumph and self-satisfaction.

I knew it would be pointless to deny that Geoffrey and I had been together, so I didn't even try. "Geoffrey turned to me because he's tired of your selfishness, your lies, and your infidelities."

Aside from an almost imperceptible pink flush that crept up Leonie's neck, she showed no outward signs of having been goaded by my words. "Do you know what I loathe most about you, Cassandra? Your priggishness and self-righteousness. Right from the very first day you appeared on our doorstep, I knew just what kind of a person you were, and I detested you. Always thinking you were so far above me, always so disapproving of my relationship with Edward. Well, sister dear, how does it feel to be just like me, a whore, because that's what you are, my girl."

Her words stung, as she had intended, but I didn't let her see how much. "If you've lost Geoffrey, you've no one to blame but yourself, Leonie."

"Well, that may be," she replied blatantly, "but you'll never be together now." She stuck another flower in the vase, studied it for a moment, then pulled it out. "By the way, did you enjoy it? Geoffrey's lovemaking, I mean?"

I smiled. "Yes, very much."

It was not the answer she had been expecting, and she glared at me, her pouting mouth pursed in displeasure. "Well, I'm glad, because I have all the proof I need that he has his own infidelities as well, so there will be no question of a divorce now. Unless, of course, he wants a bitter tale from me, with your name dragged into it. And he won't because he's such a gentleman, my Geoffrey."

She had goaded me at last. "You are the cruelest, most unfeeling—"

"Are you quite through with your little tirade, Cassandra, because even if you aren't, I'm quite tired of listening to you. Good day."

"Oh, but I'm not quite through with you, Leonie. Someday you're going to pay dearly for what you've done to other people, especially Geoffrey and Mother, and I hope I'm around to see it!"

Her light, mocking laughter filled the room. "Why, my dear sister, are you actually *threatening* me?"

"Not at all," I replied, stepping into the doorway that connected the sitting room to the solarium, and turning to face her. "I'm just warning you to fear the wheels of justice, Leonie. They turn slowly, but when they do . . ." I shrugged and turned to leave.

No sooner had I stepped into the glass-enclosed room filled from floor to ceiling with plants that screened out a good deal of sunlight, than I glanced to my left and blushed in dismay. There, seated in a chair close to the door, but hidden from view, was Lady Rushton herself, and her hawk's eyes were filled with malice.

She had heard everything. She now knew that her husband had come to my room, and, judging by the look on her face, she did not believe Leonie had sent him there. I knew excuses would be useless, so, without a word, I hurriedly exited through the solarium and the garden door into the bright sunshine.

That night, my confrontation with Leonie kept running through my mind like a Gregorian chant, over and over, refusing to let sleep come. Finally, around midnight, I put on my dress and went outside.

I found my way through the garden easily, thanks to a full moon, but as I glanced over my shoulder, I noticed storm clouds were rapidly approaching from the opposite direction. I mustn't stay out too late tonight, or I would be caught in the rain.

As I passed the stables, I heard the horses neighing and stamping in their stalls, as restless as I. Looking around at the silent buildings, I shivered, for there was something in the air, and even the animals sensed it.

I quickened my step as I approached the grove of trees through which I would have to pass before reaching the summerhouse and pond. The trunks and limbs seemed darker, and as the upper branches creaked in a breeze that suddenly sprang up, the trees seemed to be whispering among themselves, telling secrets to the night. I looked back over my shoulder nervously.

"Cassa," I murmured to myself, "Leonie was right; you are getting fanciful in your old age."

After walking defiantly through the grove as noisily as I could, I came to the top of the slope and stopped. An owl's "who-o-o" overhead made me jump, challenging my right to be here, but I ignored him and continued on.

Suddenly, as I marched down the slope toward the summerhouse, I heard the distinct sound of twigs snapping underfoot, of someone walking through the underbrush away from me. I stopped and looked around, but saw nothing or no one. I waited. There was no more sound. If anyone had been there, they were gone now. The summerhouse was all mine.

My footsteps had a hollow, eerie ring to them as I walked down the pier. When I reached the building and looked inside, my heart gave a queer little lurch. Someone had righted the cushions Geoffrey and I had left strewn about last night when we became lovers. I thought of him and sighed in pleasure at the memory.

I sat for a while in the summerhouse, then leisurely rose and started for the entry facing the pond. As I glanced down, I noticed a lady's lace handkerchief on the floor, in the doorway. When I picked it up, the faint scent of geraniums filled my nostrils.

Leonie had been there.

Out of the corner of my eye, I saw something move, and I whirled around, looking about wildly, lest whoever had gone moving through the underbrush should return. Nothing. Then I stepped out onto the pier, and found Leonie.

She was floating on her back in the water, her arms at her

sides, her dress billowing out about her, buoyed by the water. Her pale hair, silver in the moonlight, fanned about her head and shoulders, moving in a macabre dance, as though the strands had a life of their own. The rest of her was still. Her eyes were closed, as if she were sleeping. But I knew she wasn't asleep. She was dead.

I was so paralyzed by shock, I didn't hear the boards creak to herald someone's approach. I just flung myself back against the walls of the building and tried to scream, but only short whimpers passed my lips.

"Well, Miss Clark . . . ."

At the sound of my name, I jumped, my hand flying to my mouth, and turned to see Lady Rushton standing there.

"Waiting for my husband, are you? I suspected my Adam would—"

And then she saw Leonie, and her eyes widened as she knelt down to look into the black, silent depths of the pond, while I stood, still speechless with horror.

"Leonie!" Then Lady Rushton slowly rose to face me. "You've killed her. You've murdered your own sister."

Her words were like a dash of cold water. "You think I did this?" I shook my head. "But I swear to you, I didn't! I just came down to the summerhouse because I couldn't sleep, and I found her here."

I could tell the woman didn't believe me, and it would be a waste of my time even to try to convince her. I had to tell Geoffrey.

"We must go back to the house to tell the others," Lady Rushton said, and turned, with me hurrying after her.

To my astonishment, when I returned to the house and ran as fast as I could upstairs to Geoffrey's room, I found him awake, dressed, and sitting in a chair, reading.

He closed his book when he saw me and smiled. "It's rather late, Cassa. Shouldn't you be in bed?"

"Geoffrey, you must come at once." I tugged at his arm. "Leonie is dead." When he just stared at me in disbelief, I stamped my foot in impatience and cried, "She's *dead*, Geoffrey! She drowned in the pond."

Suddenly, a thought leaped into my mind, and I had to stifle a giggle of hysteria. "*I* was supposed to die by drowning, not my sister. A fortune teller in Cairo said I would die in water, but she got it all wrong. All wrong! She didn't mean me, she meant Leonie. My sister!"

Geoffrey turned white, leaped to his feet, and grasped me by the shoulders. "Cassa, control yourself. Now, tell me exactly what's happened."

While we rushed to the door, I explained in a halting voice, but my words came out all jumbled, not making any sense. By the time we arrived downstairs, Lady Rushton had roused several other men, the marquis among them. They stood in trousers and nightshirts to accompany Geoffrey to the pond. I would have gone, too, but he told me to find Maud and then to wake my mother.

The rest of the night was nothing but a long blur in my memory. After I managed to wake Maud and tell her about the catastrophe, she took charge with her usual calm efficiency, waking some of the servants to prepare coffee, for it was sure to be a long, long night for everyone. Then we went to break the news to Mother.

She took the grim news better than I had feared she would, sitting up in her bed, so pale, and clasping my hand as though it were anchored to sanity. She was in shock and couldn't cry at that moment, but merely rang for her maid and said she must get dressed and go downstairs to see to our guests. I never realized what a strong woman my mother really was until that moment.

Several of the women, the Duchess of Manchester among them, who had been awakened by the commotion, joined us in the drawing room, and we all stood vigil, waiting for the men to return from their grim task. Lady Rushton just stared at me, but I didn't need to guess what she was thinking. I already knew.

The men soon came filing into the room, white-faced and

grim. Everyone surged around Geoffrey, demanding to know what had happened. He quickly confirmed the fact that Leonie had drowned, and they had brought her body back to the house. After saying he had sent one of the servants for the doctor, he told us there was nothing more we could do tonight, and for all of us to go to bed. I wanted to go to him, for he looked devastated, but I knew I mustn't.

Just as I was returning to my room, Lady Rushton stopped me in front of my door.

Her smile was shrewd and malicious as she said, "Well, Miss Clark, Leonie's death will certainly alter your plans now."

"What do you mean?" I demanded, resenting her tone.

"Isn't it ironic that by Leonie's death, Geoffrey is lost to you?"

"I still don't have the faintest idea what you're talking about, Lady Rushton. Now, if you'll excuse me . . ." And I reached for the doorknob.

She spoke quickly, as though she feared I would disappear before she had a chance to sow her poison. "Why, I'm talking about the law, of course." She licked her lips in relish. "The law that prohibits a man from marrying his deceased wife's sister. You do know about it, of course. But then, living abroad as you have . . ."

Through the shocking events of that night, I dimly recalled some neighbor of Aunt Venetia's who had wanted to marry his sister-in-law, after the woman had selflessly spent years nursing her sick sister, but was prohibited from doing so because his wife had died. I recalled it at the moment, but its significance didn't dawn on me until much, much later.

"No, I didn't," I replied wearily, which was a foolish admission to make to someone like Fiona Rushton.

I should have known that Lady Rushton's smile boded no good for me. Then she wished me a pleasant good night and left me.

* * *

The prince and his servants left quickly and quietly at dawn the following morning, and it was as though they had never visited Punjab House. For him to be in the same house where his lovely mistress had met with an untimely death would cause a scandal, so he was spirited away before anyone was the wiser. The rest of the guests remained, however, to answer any questions the police might have about Leonie's death.

We all gathered in the drawing room around dawn, just after the prince departed, and, judging by all the haggard faces and bleary eyes, no one had gotten much sleep last night, least of all Geoffrey. But we all wanted to hear the results of the doctor's examination and learn the cause of my sister's death.

Dr. Jones-Burrows, a skinny man who wore his spectacles poised on the end of his pointed nose, read the results of his findings in a solemn voice.

After examining the body, he discovered what looked like a blow to the back of Leonie's head. He proceeded to explain in esoteric medical jargon how he had determined the cause of Leonie's death, and, when we were all about to go mad from impatience, he summarized his findings by saying she must have tripped, been knocked unconscious when her head struck the edge of the pier, fallen into the water, and drowned. His verdict was accidental death.

One could almost hear the collective sigh of relief that filled the room, but then Lady Rushton, looking a bit garish in dark purple taffeta, rose and commanded our attention.

"I have something to say that might dispute your verdict, sir."

Everyone stared at her as a ripple of astonishment passed through those gathered here. I looked at Maud, who just rolled her eyes and shook her head.

"Lady Rushton," Geoffrey said, "if you know anything about this matter, please speak up."

She went to the front of the room and addressed the two dozen people assembled. "I was restless last night, so I went for a walk," she said, looking straight at her husband, who fidgeted in his seat. "I discovered Miss Clark already at the summerhouse, staring at Leonie's body in the water."

"And I told you I had just discovered the body myself," I said.

"So you say."

Geoffrey scowled at her. "Are you doubting Miss Clark's word, Lady Rushton?"

She smiled, and all I could think of was a hound running a hare to ground after a long, exhausting chase. "Ordinarily, I wouldn't, but, as one of Leonie's best friends, I feel I must speak out." She looked around the room. "I think you all should know that yesterday, I heard Miss Clark threaten her sister."

Now Lord Rushton, who had been sitting on the divan, glared at his wife. "Eavesdropping again, Fiona?"

She looked at him as though he were some loathsome insect, and continued speaking. "I was in the solarium, enjoying the plants, and Leonie was in the adjacent sitting room, arranging flowers. I heard Miss Clark come in and accost her sister in a most belligerent manner. I happened to overhear Miss Clark make all sorts of wild, incredible accusations to Leonie, and when she denied them, Miss Clark told her that someday she was going to pay for her cruelties." Now she looked around the room again as though seeking sympathizers. "I'm sure I don't need to tell anyone here that our host and hostess were not on the best of terms. In fact, we all know that Geoffrey wanted to divorce his wife so he could marry his sister-in-law!"

I heard several gasps of astonishment and indignation arise around me, for Lady Rushton had committed the cardinal sin of mentioning in public someone else's personal life.

"Fiona, that will be quite enough!" Lord Rushton boomed, jumping to his feet. "You're making a damned fool of yourself, and me as well."

"Oh, you do that quite well yourself, without any help from me, my love," she retorted. I could see Lady Rushton had finally reached the point where her husband had been unfaithful to her for the last time.

"Lester, old man," Rushton was saying to Geoffrey, "you don't need to listen to her."

Geoffrey held up his hand and faced Lady Rushton. "Are you saying that I killed my own wife?" Geoffrey asked, his eyes as cold as gunmetal.

An unbecoming flush mottled the lady's face. "Of course not."

"I know I needn't dignify your comments with a response, your ladyship, but there is something I will say." Geoffrey addressed his guests as though he were in the witness-box. "My wife's death came as a bitter shock to me, and it's also something I never wanted. True, we haven't been close in recent months, but I wanted her alive, so I could divorce her, and—yes, I will admit it—marry the woman I really love." He glanced at me, and my heart seemed to turn over. "I won't make a secret of my feelings for Cassandra."

"But Miss Clark didn't know about the law that forbids a man from marrying his deceased wife's sister," Lady Rushton persisted. "She as much as admitted it to me last night, when I confronted her about it."

Geoffrey said, "Lady Rushton, are you now accusing Miss Clark of murdering her own sister? Madam, you astound me!"

His voice was so menacing, she actually recoiled from him a little. "But she could have! She hated her sister and threatened her. By killing Leonie and making it look like an accident, Miss Clark, who didn't know about the law at the time, thought she would free you to marry her."

Now Maud rose, her indignation matching her brother's. "I have never heard anything so preposterous in my life, Lady Rushton. Cassa would never harm a flea, and you are a malicious person to say so!"

Mother, sitting beside me, reached out to place her hand protectively on mine. "I don't believe for one instant that my daughter killed anyone, especially the sister she had been trying to get close to for weeks."

Even Lord Rushton had had enough. "Fiona, your jealousy has really gone too far this time."

Now that the initial shock of Lady Rushton's unfair accusation had worn off, I was moved to anger. I rose and faced my accuser, who was staring at me with pure contempt. "I know you've always disliked me because you suspect me of leading your husband astray, Lady Rushton, but for you to try to take your revenge by accusing me of murder is contemptible." Then I turned toward Lord Rushton, still fuming, looking decidedly uncomfortable for all his Byronic airs. "If you'll ask Lord Rushton where he received that lump on his head, I'm sure he'll clear up any misconceptions you may have had about our relationship. But, aside from that, I resent your accusations that I would harm anyone. True, Leonie and I were not on the best of terms, but that didn't give me any reason to kill her."

When no one jumped to her defense, Lady Rushton's furious eyes searched the faces of those she had once counted as her friends. "So, you're going to close ranks and protect this—this murderess! You're not concerned that justice is done, just that you're not involved in a scandal."

"You're hysterical, Lady Rushton," Geoffrey said, "so we'll excuse you for your outburst. Lord Rushton, I would like to see you and your wife out of my house by noon today. I won't tolerate guests who accuse me or my family of murder."

While Lord Rushton turned an ugly shade of red, his wife raised her head proudly and flounced toward the door. "Nor do I wish to remain with people who twist the law to their own ends." She stopped and faced us all squarely. "I am going to see that everyone knows about this."

She left, her husband trailing behind.

She had done her worst. Now, as I looked around the room, some of those present avoided my glance, while others, such as Lady Churchill and the Duchess of Manchester, met my gaze with candid speculation of their own. I knew they were wondering if perhaps Lady Rushton hadn't been speaking the truth about me. They might not say aloud that they thought me a murderess, but I could see the doubt and mistrust written on their faces, which were no longer as open and friendly as they had once been.

Aside from my family, only the Marquis of Sherborne was sympathetic. At least he hadn't lost faith in me.

But if the rest of these strangers doubted me, why should the police believe my protestations of innocence?

Later, after the local police came, questioned me, and seemed satisfied with my answers, I escaped to the Temple of Surya, to be alone and to wrestle with my tumultuous thoughts.

Leonie's death had had a powerful effect on us all. The entire house was silent, as though its very walls were numb with shock, and guests talked among themselves in hushed whispers, while the servants moved about on silent feet, not daring to make a sound. Even the birds in the trees along the avenue had ceased their chirping, as if in respect for death.

How could Lady Rushton make such a foul accusation against me, I wondered as I sat down on a stone bench inside the temple. She was a vindictive, jealous old harridan, as Leonie had once said, and this was her way of tormenting me for what she thought was my affair with her husband. Her threat to spread it all over London that I was a murderess frightened me, not for myself, but for Geoffrey and his family.

Like everyone present in the drawing room today, I wondered what had really happened to Leonie. Had she merely tripped, as the doctor claimed, hit her head, and drowned? What was she doing at the summerhouse anyway? So many puzzling questions, and no answers.

I sighed as I stared out at the sky, which had suddenly become overcast, giving the landscape a dull, gray look. I recalled the rustlings I had heard in the bushes last night, the sounds of someone hurrying away from the pond. A man? A woman? I couldn't tell, for the sound had been neither heavy nor light. Had someone else found her body, then fled in panic, or was it the murderer himself, fleeing before he could be detected?

Who could the culprit be?

Lady Rushton herself, perhaps? She could have learned that Leonie had been filling her husband's head with tales about me, and it was she who sent him to my room that night. Or had Lord Rushton finally realized that Leonie had been playing him for the fool and gone to confront her himself? Then, of course, there was shy, gentle Edgar, hopelessly adoring Leonie. Perhaps he had met her at the summerhouse last night to declare his love and persuade her to give up the prince, and when she laughed at him and refused . . .

I pressed my fingertips to my temples, my head bursting with suspects. The truth was, many people had reason to want Leonie dead, even Geoffrey.

As if my thoughts had conjured him, Geoffrey himself was walking toward me, his step heavy and his head bowed. On this gray, misty day, his golden head shone brightly, like a beacon. When he reached the temple, he stopped and regarded me solemnly. Dark circles beneath his eyes made them look bruised in his lined, tired face, and his mouth was set in a grim line. I just wanted to put my arms around him and hold him.

"I'm sorry Leonie is dead," he said, his voice ragged as he sat next to me and cradled his face in his hands. "I'm sorry for the love we once had, before it turned sour somehow."

"I know. Even though she was often unkind to me, I'm sorry for what happened to her." I shivered, suddenly cold again. "I can't believe Lady Rushton accused me of murdering her."

"No one believed her."

"Oh no? You didn't see the looks on your guests' faces. Lady Rushton evidently made a strong case." I was silent as

I watched a hawk swoop and dive in the sky high above.
"And that policeman today . . ."

"They questioned everyone, not just you, Cassandra, and
they've accepted Dr. Jones-Burrows' statement about
Leonie's death."

"But Lady Rushton said she's going to tell everyone in
London that I'm a murderess!" I cried.

Geoffrey placed his hand on mine. "The prince will see
that she doesn't, believe me. If Fiona Rushton defies him,
she'll find herself ostracized from society and doors closed to
her. It's the least he could do for his former love. No, His
Royal Highness wants to avoid scandal at all costs."

Yes, I was sure Fiona Rushton would do as the prince
wished, even if it meant not having her revenge.

Suddenly, Geoffrey said, "I won't be a hypocrite, Cassa.
Leonie's death has freed us to be together."

I rose now, impatient and more than a little angry. "Free
us? How can that be? You know the law."

Now he rose as well, and there was a trace of exasperation
in his voice. "From the way Lady Rushton was talking, I
don't blame you for thinking there would be a constable
waiting to arrest us at the altar. True, it is against both
church and civil law for us to marry, but the law can be cir-
cumvented, Cassa. Others have done it. If no minister in
England will marry us, then we'll go to France. We could
live as exiles, if we had to."

His words surprised me. I looked back at Punjab House,
its onion dome silhouetted majestically against the sky, and
wondered how anyone could leave such an enchanting place.
In exile, there would be no long strolls down the Avenue of
the Bulls, no graceful Temple of Surya where one could
await the dawn. And there would be no autumnal air redolent with the scent of harvested hops. This was the sacrifice that Geoffrey was laying at my feet.

"But England is your home. You could live with the prospect of never seeing Punjab House again, just to be with
me?"

He nodded solemnly. "I would give up everything to be with you. But, don't you see? We wouldn't have to. We could return to England without fear of prosecution. We would, however, be ostracized by society. There would be no more dinners at Marlborough House. Former friends would cut us at the opera." His voice was heavily ironic as he said, "It seems a high price to pay, doesn't it?"

Suddenly, my heart sank to my shoes. Geoffrey's words to Lady Rushton rang through my brain like bells: "I wanted Leonie alive, so I could divorce her and marry the woman I love." But, as he had just admitted to me, Leonie's death was no obstacle. And, since it didn't matter, couldn't Geoffrey have killed his own wife? Was his speech in front of all those witnesses designed to provide himself with an alibi? I recalled the sounds of someone fleeing through the underbrush last night, and my surprise at finding Geoffrey dressed and reading a book when I went to tell him the dreadful news. Could he have hit Leonie on the head, then fled just before I got there? Perhaps there wasn't enough time to change out of his clothes and pretend he had been sleeping. And what about Leonie's insistence that he had sent that note and the doll's head, trying to frighten her into agreeing to a divorce? Had I been too blind to see the danger? Had my sister been right all along?

My suspicions must have registered on my face, or perhaps I had drawn away from him involuntarily, for Geoffrey was looking at me oddly. Then he knew.

"Cassa, no—!"

I had to turn away so he couldn't read my thoughts.

"You think I murdered Leonie, don't you?"

"Geoffrey, I—" But I couldn't say any more, couldn't go to him, couldn't deny what I was thinking, even to ease his anguish.

I wanted so desperately to believe in his innocence, tears filled my eyes.

"Look at me, Cassa."

He stood very still and silent behind me, not attempting

to touch me or take me in his arms. I knew I had to turn of my own accord and go to him. I tried to make that leap of faith, but I kept seeing my sister's lifeless face in the water, and I couldn't move. Tears stung my eyes as I shook my head.

I waited to receive the full force of Geoffrey's wrath, but what he did was even more devastating than bitter words or raised voice. All he said was, very calmly, "Your betrayal has hurt me more than anything Leonie ever did." And then he started walking away, only to stop and turn. "Why don't you marry Sherborne? He's flawless, unlike me, and he obviously loves you."

As I watched Geoffrey's proud, erect form retreat down the avenue, I knew that I had lost him forever. How could a man forgive someone who thinks him capable of murder? No apologies, no denials, no entreaties for forgiveness, could ever heal such a breach of trust.

The damp air suddenly turned colder, and a soft rain started to fall, or it could have been my own tears wetting my cheeks. I shivered and pulled my shawl tightly about me, but it was no substitute for the warmth and security of Geoffrey's arms as I followed in his wake toward the house.

Thanks to the influence and invisible hand of the prince, Leonie's funeral was a simple, dignified one, unmarred by hordes of brassy, curious journalists clamoring and digging for the story of Leonie's death. I suspect my sister would have preferred a grand funeral, with hundreds—nay, thousands—of weeping mourners clutching their picture post card portraits of Lady Leonie Lester as they filed past her coffin, but it was not to be.

The simple service was performed in the local church in Kent, rather than in the large churches of London, and my sister was laid to rest beside Geoffrey's father in the family crypt on the estate. No one had bothered to consider that Leonie might have wanted to be buried beside her own father in Northumberland; since she was married, Mother thought it fitting that she be laid to rest with her husband's family.

So the death of the Prince of Wales' greatest love went unobserved and unmourned except for family and a few close friends.

Mother held up rather well, but it was Edgar who seemed the most affected by Leonie's untimely death. He bowed his head into his hands and sobbed silently throughout the service, while his sister kept giving him disapproving looks as though he were somehow less of a man for displaying such strong emotions so openly. But I didn't blame him. I better than anyone knew how much Edgar loved my sister.

Throughout the service, I could sense Geoffrey surreptitiously watching me, but I never raised my eyes to meet his. He hadn't spoken two words to me since that time in the temple, when I wordlessly accused him of killing Leonie, and he had read my mind. There were details of the funeral to be taken care of, people to see, condolences to accept, so I'm sure no one thought it odd that he didn't say very much to his sister-in-law.

Much later, when the graveside service was finally over, and all the black-clad mourners had supped on funeral meats, Mother and I were alone at last.

She was sitting quietly in her room, dry-eyed and sipping her tisane, when I went to her.

"Mother," I said softly, as I approached her sitting in a chair near a window, "is there anything I can get you?"

She dabbed at her nose with her handkerchief and patted the seat next to her. "You can come talk with me, if you would. There's something I must say to you that I've been putting off for too long."

When I sat down, she seemed to pull herself together by sheer force of will. "Do you remember when you first arrived, I told you there were certain things about your father that I had to tell you?"

I smiled and squeezed her hand. "Now is not the time, Mother. We can discuss it later."

She shook her head stubbornly. "No, now is the time. I've already lost one daughter, and I don't intend to lose another."

"Mother—"

"No, Cassandra, hear me out. I know you loved your father very dearly, and you may not believe what I am going to say, but I must tell you my reasons for leaving him. You may believe, or choose not to believe, if you wish." Then she took a deep breath and settled herself in.

"When I first met your father, I knew he was a soldier, and, blinded by love, I thought I could adjust to his life because I did love him dearly, despite what your Aunt Venetia always thought. His first assignment was India, where you were born." Mother turned pale at the memory. "I hated it so—the heat, the people, the strangeness of it—but most of all, I hated the aching loneliness. Every time I would make a new friend, her husband would be transferred, and she would leave with him. Or else she would leave a widow.

"Whenever I tried to explain my feelings to your father, he would just pat me on the shoulder and tell me to be his good little soldier and forbear. But I couldn't. God help me, I couldn't!" Mother's voice broke, and for a moment, she couldn't speak. Finally, she regained her composure enough to continue. "I can't tell you how happy I was the day your father was transferred back to England. As soon as we arrived, I resolved never to leave my home again. I tried to persuade your father to resign from the army and go into trade, but he wouldn't listen." She looked at me warily, as though she couldn't gauge my reaction when she said, "He could be a very selfish man, you see."

This time, I did not bristle at any implied criticism of my father, for I think I was beginning to realize that he was not perfect, either.

Relieved that I was accepting her words so calmly, Mother said, "And then came the day his regiment was posted to China. I could envision the loneliness engulfing me again, because, even though I was married to your father, his first love was the army, not me. He never understood me, Cassandra, just as I never understood him. Then you got sick, so I stayed with you. Your illness was a blessing in disguise." She shrugged. "I've already told you how I met Reginald."

As I sat back, I thought about my father and his visits to the Grange, how few and far between they were for a man who supposedly loved his daughter so desperately. Perhaps I, too, had taken second place to the army.

Mother sniffed into her handkerchief. "Everything was fine with Knighton at first. Finally, at long last, I wasn't lonely any longer, and we were blessed with Leonie. But soon, even Knighton turned away from me."

I recalled what Lady Quartermain had said about the Earl of Knighton and the pistol by his plate.

"Leonie was the only joy left in my life, but then, she changed and was lost to me. It was as though God had punished me for leaving your father by decreeing I should forever be lonely."

I rose, stood by her chair, and placed my arm around her shoulders. "You have me, Mother," I said quietly, tears springing to my eyes. "You'll never have to be lonely again."

As I held her, I felt a great sense of peace envelop me at long last.

The day after the funeral, all of the guests packed up and departed quietly for London, except for Edith and the Marquis of Sherborne. Although Edgar had left to go back to work, his sister remained behind with us at my mother's express invitation. She seemed to take comfort in Edith's presence and asked her incessant questions about Leonie's years at finishing school, as though such information could give her a more complete picture of her daughter.

I was soon to learn why the marquis had hesitated to depart with the others.

After watching the last carriage roll down the circular drive and disappear, I went out to the garden for a solitary stroll down its orderly pathways. I hadn't been there ten minutes when I saw the marquis leave the house and walk toward me. Like all of us dressed in deepest mourning, he looked sober in his black frock coat, but I sensed his preoccupied air had little to do with Leonie's death.

"Lord Sherborne," I murmured in greeting.

"It would please me greatly if you would call me Horace, Cassandra," he replied.

He was paying me a great honor, I knew, for this request to call him by his Christian name signified that he considered me much more than a friend.

"Horace, then," I said. "Tell me, why haven't you left with the others? I believe you'll miss the train."

He took a deep breath. "There is something I must say to you before I leave. Will you walk with me?"

"Certainly. There's a path leading down to the fields." I didn't want to walk down the Avenue of the Bulls, or to the summerhouse, for both places held such painful memories of Geoffrey. Horace nodded, and I could tell at once that he understood.

We strolled through the garden, down past the stable, and toward the fields, green, tranquil, and fragrant with wild-flowers. Horses raised their heads and whickered in greeting, then returned to their grazing when they saw we had no apples or sugar for them.

"It's such a beautiful day," Horace said unnecessarily.

"Yes, it is."

Soon, we were truly alone.

The marquis began, "Cassandra, in the short time we've known each other, I've come to feel as though I've known you forever." He hesitated. "And I've come to love you as well."

I stared at him, my cheeks coloring. "Horace, I—I don't know what to say."

He smiled ruefully. "I know I have taken you by surprise with my sudden declaration, but surely you have guessed the depth and sincerity of my feelings for you?"

"Yes, Horace, ever since the night of the ball."

"I've never met anyone quite like you, Cassandra. In all modesty, my wealth and social position have made me quite an attractive marriage prospect. I've had ample opportunity to meet scores of beautiful, wealthy women, but none of them can compare to you. You're warm, spirited, generous—"

He would have gone on forever with this recitation of my virtues, if I hadn't stopped him with, "Horace, please . . ."

"Well, you are. What man could help but fall in love with you?"

I stared at the grass. "I don't know what to say."

"Say you'll make me the happiest man in the world by agreeing to become my marchioness."

Now I had to look up at him. His eyes were warm with love and tenderness, and by the expression on his face, I had no doubt that he cared about me and wanted me for his wife.

"We would have a wonderful life together, Cassandra," he continued. "I have enough worldly possessions to give you whatever you desire. You would never want. And I would also love and cherish you as no woman has ever been loved or cherished." Then he smiled. "Think of what splendid children we would have."

I knew he was right. If I married him, we would have a wonderful, perfect life together. What had Geoffrey called him? Flawless. Like a diamond. Horace was handsome, well-mannered, and always did what was expected of him. Any sensible woman would accept his proposal without hesitation.

But then I thought of the lemon-yellow drawing room and the centuries of tradition it represented. I, too, would become as much a part of the Sherborne history as the mellow Sheraton furniture. Every day of my life would be dedicated to preserving what had existed for centuries.

Then I thought of Geoffrey. With him, I would never know what the next day would bring. He made me feel as though life were an unexpected adventure, and we were the first of a new breed.

I swallowed hard. "Horace, there is something I must tell you."

"I'm sure whatever it is won't change how I feel about you. True, you have led something of an unconventional life in Egypt, but once you took my name, no one would dare criticize you."

"I don't mean to hurt you, Horace, because I am quite fond of you as a friend." I looked at him, my eyes begging him to understand. "But I'm afraid I don't love you."

Suddenly, his face fell and all the warmth in his eyes died, to be replaced by utter disbelief. Not heartbreak, or disappointment, but pure astonishment. "You can't mean that, Cassandra! I am the Marquis of Sherborne! Dozens of women would be honored to become my wife, and here you are, daring to refuse me!"

I just looked at him, dumbfounded.

Then, because he was flawless, he quickly realized that his outburst made him look like a fool and was a gross lapse of manners. Collecting himself, he became the perfect gentleman once again. "I see. Well, if that's the way you feel, Cassandra, there is nothing I can say to change your mind, I'm sure."

Since he would never leave a lady standing alone in the middle of a field, he added, "Come. Let me escort you back to the house. I think there is still time for me to catch my train."

"Please go ahead without me, Horace. I wouldn't want you to miss it on my account."

"As you wish." Then he bowed, and, without even one last lingering look for remembrance, turned and said, "Good-bye," over his shoulder.

As I watched him hurry away, out of my life forever, I tried to feel sadness or regret, but all I could do was compare him to Geoffrey. Geoffrey was a man of passions, and he never would have let me go so easily. He would have come storming back, his gray eyes dark as thunderclouds, angry and hurt that I had rejected him. And he would love, cajole, and bully until he had won me back. Geoffrey would willingly give up his life for me, but I was certain Horace would never forsake so much as his lemon-yellow drawing room for any woman.

But now even Geoffrey was lost to me.

I stood in the middle of the field for the longest time, feeling the hot sun on my face and listening to the buzzing of industrious bees as they went about their work, oblivious to my pain.

What was to become of me? I knew Mother wanted me to remain with her, but could I possibly live in the same house as Geoffrey, after what had happened? I had doubted him and thought him capable of murder. Even if I apologized, I wondered if it would ever be the same between us again.

My answer was to return to Cyrus and Cairo, but somehow, I doubted if I could ever pick up the threads of my former life. Still, it was all I had.

Chapter Fifteen

S everal days after the marquis had departed, Geoffrey made a startling announcement at the dinner
table.

"Maud and I are leaving for London tomorrow," he said,
casting a glance in my direction. "There's some business
there that demands my immediate attention."

"The London dock workers have just gone on strike,"
Maud added. "I'm going to try to organize a relief effort for
their families."

Mother stopped eating and regarded them with raised
brows. "How long will you two be gone?"

"Only two or three days," was Geoffrey's reply.

Edith said, "Perhaps I should go with you. I think I've
overstayed my welcome as it is."

"Nonsense," Mother said. "You're welcome here for as
long as you like, Edith. In fact, I was hoping you'd stay the
rest of the summer with us."

"Thank you, but I couldn't possibly impose. After all, my
brother needs me to cook and keep house."

"Oh, I think Edgar will get along just fine without you for
a few more weeks," Mother insisted. "Besides, fresh country air will do you a world of good."

"Well, if you insist . . ." Edith demurred.

"I do."

Now Geoffrey addressed me, his tone one of polite disin-
terest. "And will you be remaining here as well, Cassandra,
or are you planning to return to Egypt?"

Before I could open my mouth to reply, Mother interrupted. "There is no question of Cassandra's returning to Egypt yet. She's staying right here with us."

Geoffrey said nothing, while Maud gave me a puzzled look, and we finished the meal in silence. But I could not help thinking that Geoffrey was not looking forward to my presence here.

The next morning, shortly after breakfast, Geoffrey and his sister departed for London, and, without them, the house seemed unnaturally quiet and empty. I went riding by myself through the fields and past orchards heavy with fruit, though I avoided the summerhouse, while Mother finally finished embroidering Maud's velvet coat and began another piece, as though she couldn't bear to have her hands unoccupied for a moment. She and Edith were constant companions, incessantly talking of Leonie's years at finishing school. I never joined in, for I always felt as though I were intruding.

Once I strolled down to the temple, to think about the last time Geoffrey and I had been together. Could he have murdered his own wife? The evidence certainly appeared overwhelming. Some part of me refused to believe him capable of such a crime, but another part was still consumed by doubt. If I doubted Geoffrey, could I truly love him? And if he refused to forgive me for these doubts, could he truly love me? The times I tried to apologize to him, the words stuck in my throat, and he certainly never approached me to try to reconcile.

As I listened to a pair of sparrows squabbling beneath the temple's eaves, I wondered if the police were still investigating Leonie's death, or whether the prince had used his considerable influence to close this particular case. I could understand his fear of being implicated, but it didn't seem fair that my sister should die without anyone ever knowing what had really happened to her that night she had gone out to the summerhouse alone. But then, I was old enough to know that life is often unfair and cruel. Murderers often went free, and beautiful princesses didn't necessarily live happily ever after.

Two days after Geoffrey and Maud's departure, while Edith and I were sitting down to tea, Mother came to us with a surprising request.

"I have decided to go through Leonie's clothes and have them put away in the attic. Would you two mind helping me?"

"Mother," I began hesitantly, "don't you think it's too soon to do that? Perhaps you should wait a little longer, until you've had time to properly mourn Leonie."

Her eyes were sad and filled with pain, but her voice was strong and resolute. "Leonie is dead, Cassandra. Nothing will bring her back to me, and seeing her clothes enshrined in a dressing room won't make it any easier for me to bear the loss."

Edith rose and set her cup down. "I think that's most sensible of you," she said gently. Then she turned to me. "Coming, Cassandra?"

"Of course." And I went with them up to Leonie's room.

Putting away her daughter's dresses was an emotional time for Mother, more so, I suspect, than even the funeral itself. As we went through Leonie's spacious dressing room, taking gowns off their satin padded hangers, tenderly folding them, and wrapping them in tissue paper to protect the delicate fabrics and laces, Mother would relate some anecdote about the event Leonie attended in a particular gown. Her memories flowed as freely as her tears, and sometimes, overcome, she had to leave the room to collect herself.

Soon, dusk was beginning to steal upon us. We lit the lamps and continued our painstaking work. Finally, we were finished with our sad task and the dressing room was stripped bare, as though no one had ever used it. We had packed a total of eight large trunks that were then carried upstairs to the attic by footmen.

Mother dabbed at her eyes and looked around the empty room in satisfaction. "Well, I'm relieved that's over and done with." Then she spied a large box sitting on Leonie's dressing table. She opened it, examined the contents, then turned to Edith and me. "This is Leonie's jewelry case. All of her expensive pieces are in a London bank vault, but the lesser jewels are in here and all strewn about with their chains and clasps tangled. Would you mind going through it, ladies? Choose anything you'd like to keep as a memento of Leonie, and the rest we'll give to Maud. I'm sure she can sell them at a charity bazaar or auction." Mother smiled wryly. "There must be many people willing to pay for a piece of jewelry once owned by Lady Leonie Lester, the prince's favorite. I, meanwhile, am going to see about dinner."

When Mother left, I looked at Edith. "Well, shall we? We should finish by dinner, if we work together."

We sat on the bed and put the box between us. It was rectangular in shape, covered in rich, embossed oxblood leather, and closed with an ornate decorative clasp. When I lifted the lid, I uttered a gasp of dismay at the chaos that greeted my eyes. "I stand corrected. We'll be here all night."

As I reached in and pulled out a handful of brooches, bracelets, and necklaces and gave them to Edith, I thought of Leonie. These jewels had all been dumped indiscriminately into the box, probably because they were inexpensive pieces not worth taking care of, in Leonie's eyes. What were a few small diamonds compared to the magnificent necklace she had worn the night we dined at Marlborough House? As I fingered a delicate brooch set with a large, oval carnelian, I knew that if any of these jewels had been mine, I would have treasured it as if it had been worth thousands.

"What could Leonie have been thinking of?" Edith muttered in exasperation as she attempted to pick one necklace's thin chain from the clasp of a bracelet. "You'd think she would have taken better care of her things rather than just piling them in here helter-skelter."

"That was Leonie," I said.

We must have been untangling chains for the better part of an hour, our activity punctuated by sighs of frustration and groans of exasperation, when I came across a large, engraved silver locket. As I examined it, I wondered if Geoffrey had given it to his wife, and whether she had just tossed it carelessly aside, as she had his love. Or perhaps it had been a gift from some early suitor.

Suddenly, the thought of seeing a photograph of one of Leonie's early loves—her lost viscount, perhaps—teased my curiosity. I sought to pry open the locket with my thumbnail. It sprang open without much resistance, but there were no photographs, no faded lock of hair curled inside. There was just an engraved inscription.

I squinted as I sought to read the tiny script. It said, "To Leonie, with love everlasting. E.W."

E.W. Edgar Wickes.

I sat back and stared at it in surprise. "Edith. Look at this."

Did I imagine it, or did my companion turn quite pale when she took the locket from me?

"It's from Edgar," I said. "Your brother must have given it to Leonie."

Edith scowled at the inscription. "Obviously."

"Did you know about this, Edith?"

She shook her head and handed it back to me, her face expressionless.

I stared at the locket, turning it over and over in my hands. "It's a fine piece of workmanship and looks expensive. A bank clerk would have to work six months to be able to afford such a gift."

Edith's hypnotic eyes held mine. "What are you implying, Cassandra?"

I didn't reply at first, just rose, walked over to the window, and stared out at the red-orange horizon. I thought of Edgar comforting Leonie after she had received the message with WHORE written on it. How tenderly he had held her in his arms. He did love her, and it was all unrequited, his gift unceremoniously dumped into the farthest recesses of a jewelry box and forgotten.

Could Edgar have killed my sister? Who would ever suspect such a shy, self-effacing man? And yet, I was a witness to his rage when he saw Leonie and the prince together at the ball. He could have easily met her at the summerhouse that night to plead with her to end her royal liaison, and when she refused and mocked him, he struck her. Then Edgar panicked and ran.

"I know what you're thinking," Edith said from across the room, "but you're wrong. My brother couldn't kill anyone."

I turned. "But this locket . . ."

Her look was most condescending. "So he gave her a locket that cost him a great deal. That doesn't prove he killed her."

Edith made sense, as always. I sighed as I returned to the bed. "You're right, and I do apologize for suspecting Edgar. I'm afraid I am so anxious to prove Geoffrey didn't murder Leonie that I'm too willing to fix the blame on anyone else."

Edith smiled. "That's understandable, in light of your feelings for Geoffrey. But, believe me, Cassandra, I know my own brother." Now her tone was heavy with sarcasm. "Shy, retiring Edgar, who would move out of the way if a fly threatened to light on him? He's incapable of killing anyone." Then she peered into the jewel case. "Now, shall we finish and go down to dinner? I don't know about you, but I'm starved."

I returned to the bed, scooped out the last of the jewels, and handed some to her. "Well, we've come to the bottom, and— What's this?" Now that the case was empty, I noticed that the jewelry had been resting in a sort of satin-lined tray that fit snugly into the bottom, forming what I suspected was a secret compartment.

"What is it, Cassandra?" Edith demanded sharply.

"Why, I think there's a false bottom in this case. There seems to be a wide gap between where this tray ends, and the actual bottom of the case itself." I struggled with the tray and finally managed to lift it out.

There, hidden, was a slender book bound in fine purple calfskin. As I lifted it out and examined it, I recalled the day I had once been summoned to Leonie's room and she had been writing in such a volume as I entered. She had quickly hidden it beneath her pillow, as though she hadn't wanted me to see it.

I could feel my eyes growing wide as I read the first page. "Why, this is a diary. Leonie's diary."

Edith and I stared at each other for what seemed like hours, each reading the other's thoughts. Finally, she said, "Do you think it might give a reason why someone wanted to kill her?"

"I suppose we'll have to read it to find out."

Suddenly, before I could open the book again, Edith snatched the diary away from me, rose from the bed, and reached for an oil lamp on the side table.

"Come," she said, her eyes glittering with anticipation. "Let's go somewhere where we can read it without being interrupted. Ah, I have it! The summerhouse."

I had no choice but to follow her, for she went sweeping out of Leonie's room before I had had a chance to protest. As I followed her swiftly moving form down the corridor and hurried to catch up with her as she trotted down the servants' stairs, I tried to convince her that we could just as easily tell Mother about the diary and read it in her presence. I was sure she would be interested as well.

"No!" Edith snapped as we walked outside into the warm evening. "If this diary proves that my brother murdered Leonie, I want to be the first to know about it, Cassandra. I want time to accept it and decide what to do."

I fell silent, for I understood how she felt. If the diary proved Geoffrey was guilty, I wanted to be the first to know it as well.

I was thankful that Edith had thought to bring the lamp with her, for there was barely a candle's worth of light left in the sky, and the way was dark and perilous. Once I stumbled when the path suddenly dipped, and another time I stubbed my toe against a rock and nearly went sprawling in my efforts to keep up with Edith, who sailed determinedly ahead with rapid strides.

Finally, we came to the summerhouse.

As we stood on the rise for a moment, a knot of apprehension formed in my stomach. The moon had not yet risen, so the little house was still and dark, a vague shape sitting on the water's surface. Not a leaf rustled, not a cricket chirped. It was as though the very trees were expecting something to happen here tonight. I rubbed my arms nervously.

"What's the matter?" Edith taunted, her voice booming out at me. "Are you afraid of Leonie's ghost?"

"Of course not," I replied, and we walked down the hill together.

When we reached the pier and I hesitated, Edith stopped. "Oh, for goodness' sake, Cassandra! This is no time to be faint of heart. Don't you want to learn who killed your sister?"

She spoke to me the way she must have spoken to lazy students, or her brother, and her tone spurred me on. I shrugged off my feelings of foreboding and strode purposefully down the pier, with Edith trailing behind me. When I reached the summerhouse itself, I opened the door, which creaked softly. Suddenly, I felt a sharp blow between my shoulders that expelled the breath from my lungs while throwing me off balance and propelling me into the summerhouse. As I cried out in alarm and fell staggering inside, the last sound I heard before losing my balance and falling was the tinkling of glass. Then I cracked my head against the opposite wall and everything went black.

Smoke. The stinging, acrid odor revived me more quickly than smelling salts. Even as I longed to slip back into warm, comforting darkness, away from the pain, something forced me awake. My head hurt and I groaned as my senses sprang to life. I was lying on the floor, the wood hard and smooth against my cheek, and I was conscious of heat, light, and smoke.

Fire!

I was wide awake now, struggling to my knees, crouching against the wall like a frightened animal as I stared at the barrier of flame leaping higher and higher. As I staggered to my feet, coughing and choking on the smoke, I somehow managed to rush out the door facing the pond. For a moment, I gulped fresh air, letting it clear my lungs and head, then I rushed along the pier, praying the fire hadn't yet cut me off from that wide wooden walkway leading to shore and safety.

As I rounded the corner of the building, flames suddenly spurted out, driving me back. My heart pounding in terror, I looked around wildly for any means to escape, and the only way open was through the water. But I couldn't swim. I would surely sink and drown before I even reached the other side, which must have been over thirty feet away. To me, it might as well have been a mile.

And where was Edith?

"Edith!" I screamed. "Help me! I'm trapped!"

Through the leaping, crackling flames and shimmering heat, I saw her standing on the shore. She just stood there, watching me and making no attempt to save me. When I saw her smile, I understood all too well.

Edith had pushed me into the summerhouse, then flung the oil lamp at the pier to make it burn. That was the sound of breaking glass I heard just before losing consciousness. In the few minutes that I had lain senseless, the flames had taken the dry wood greedily, and the fire spread quickly, isolating me, trapping me in the inferno.

Standing there numb with shock, I realized that if Edith had done this to me, she was no doubt the one who had killed Leonie. I was sure that the proof was in the diary. As soon as Edith saw it, she realized she would be incriminated, which was why she snatched it from me and pretended she needed to read it alone. She was crafty and quick-thinking. While we were walking to the summerhouse, she was probably already formulating a plan for my destruction. Then she would destroy the diary and concoct some tale about my going out here alone and knocking the lamp over. And everyone would believe her. I cursed myself for a fool.

But I had no time to concern myself with Edith. My own survival was uppermost in my mind. The flames were snapping furiously as they began enveloping the summerhouse. I had perhaps only minutes before they reached me.

I looked around frantically. Someone at the stables must have noticed the fire by now. The sky was sure to be glowing a vibrant orange over the trees, and the smell of smoke was heavy in the air. But this was the dinner hour. Mother would be getting ready to sit down to dine, and I suspect the servants were rushing about to prepare and serve the meal. Even the stablehands would be eating. No one would think to look at the sky. By the time someone noticed, it would be too late for me.

I whimpered as a scorching wave of heat billowed at me, and I looked down into the black, bottomless depths of the pond. Time. I needed time! If I could just manage to stay alive a little while longer, I felt certain I would be rescued.

Then I had an idea. I stripped off my dress, my flying fingers making short work of buttons, and was soon down to my camisole and drawers. Then I knelt down, grasped the edge of the pier for dear life, and eased myself into the water, gasping in shock as I lowered myself to my neck. As I tried to tread water, I had to fight the panic I felt when my feet touched nothing.

Time seemed endless as I hung on to the pier with fingers that were rapidly becoming numb from the strain. Luckily, a breeze had blown up and was pushing the black, billowing smoke away from me; otherwise I would have choked to death. As it was, I could smell charred wood and hear sparks and cinders hiss and sputter as they flew into the water. While the flames drew ever closer, I averted my eyes, for the searing heat was intense, and I held my breath as I ducked my head below water several times to wet it.

As I clung to my corner, I scanned the shore for any sign of life, but even Edith had disappeared by this time, satisfied, no doubt, that I could not possibly survive this inferno. The flames leaped higher and higher, and, in moments, I would be forced to let go of the pier and drown, or cling to it and be burned to death.

I thought of the old fortune teller in Cairo, her leathery skin wrinkled and her face contorted, her eyes glazed as she intoned what the future held for me.

"Well, Cyrus," I murmured, as tears of hopelessness filled my eyes, "she was right after all."

Then I closed my eyes and prayed, for, in one more minute, I would be forced to choose the manner of my own death. I looked out over the pond, red with reflected light. I had heard somewhere that drowning was actually a pleasant way to die, if you didn't try to resist the water as it filled your lungs and smothered you.

"Cassa!"

Now, in my extreme exhaustion, I was imagining I heard Geoffrey calling to me. There it was again, louder this time.

"Cassa!"

I raised my head. I wasn't dreaming after all. There, on

the edge of the pond, specks of light floated and bobbed, growing larger as they kept coming toward me. I could see a group of men carrying lanterns, and they were searching for me.

"Geoffrey!" I cried with the last of my strength.

A familiar figure detached itself from the group, paused only long enough to strip off his coat and shoes, and dove in with a resounding splash. In seconds, Geoffrey's head broke above the water, inches from mine, and he gasped for breath.

"We haven't much time," he said, his voice urgent as he glanced at the burning summerhouse. "Let go of the pier, Cassa, and roll over on your back. I will get you away from here."

I was suddenly paralyzed with fear. "I—I can't!"

"You must trust me, Cassa!"

And I did trust him, with my life. I felt calm and strangely buoyant. As soon as I let go, I felt Geoffrey's arm, strong and secure, encircling my chin, and suddenly I was being towed through the water. I closed my eyes and let myself go limp, telling myself I was floating through a dream. I panicked only once, when water suddenly washed over my face, stinging my eyes and choking me. I suddenly stiffened.

"Don't fight me, Cassa, or we'll both drown!"

His words frightened me into relaxing once more. Before I knew it, several pairs of hands were reaching for me, pulling me out of the pond that was to have been my grave. As I sat there, coughing and sputtering, shivering with cold, shock, and relief, I watched the final flames envelop the summerhouse in triumph, then the building collapsed upon itself in a great swoosh and hiss of steam. The place where Geoffrey and I had become lovers was no more.

If I was not aware of my state of deshabille, Geoffrey was, for he bellowed at the men circling us. "Why are you all standing there gawking? Get some buckets and put out that fire!"

When the men scattered, he wiped the water from his face and stared down at me, his eyes darting from my bare legs to my breasts, accentuated by the wet, clinging camisole. His mouth twisted into a leer as he reached for his coat and draped it over my shoulders. Then he collapsed beside me.

"I really shouldn't blame them for gaping. You're too much of a distraction for any man, Cassa," he murmured as he held the back of my head still with one hand, and his lips came down on mine. His kiss was bruising, but it revealed how very frightened Geoffrey was of losing me.

Finally, after a long, blissful moment, he reluctantly released me. "As much as I long to go on kissing you, I'm afraid there are matters we must attend to."

"Edith?" I inquired, suddenly missing the warmth of his mouth. "She's the one who tried to kill me, she—"

"Hush, my darling. I know." His arms were around me now, crushing me to him as though he'd never let me go, his cheek pressed against my wet hair.

"And she must have killed Leonie."

"I'm almost certain she did."

"But why?"

"Edith was blackmailing her."

"Blackmail!"

I pulled away, a question on my face, but Geoffrey rose. "Come, Cassa. I'll explain everything when we return to the house. You're barely dressed, and, as much as I prefer you that way, I don't want you to catch your death out here." He glanced at the summerhouse, now a charred ruin, then swung me into his arms and carried me away from this place of death.

By the time we reached the house, Edith had been taken into police custody. She refused to speak to any of us.

Later, when I was dried off, dressed in a warm nightdress, and sent promptly to bed, Geoffrey and Mother came to my room. He was carrying a box, which he set down on my dressing table, then began explaining how he knew about Edith.

His gray eyes were tired and grave as he stood to address us. "Actually, Maud was the one who first suspected Edith. She always wondered why Leonie insisted on cultivating Edith in the first place. But what really made her suspicious was the fact that Edith's employment references didn't list anyone from the Ecôle Lafarge, and she thought this quite odd. When Maud contacted some of Edith's former employers, they damned her with faint praise, saying she was an excellent teacher, but implied she wasn't quite right in other respects. Finally, Maud decided to go to Paris and speak with the headmistress at the French school. That's where we were, by the way, not London.

"And I have always wondered how my wife could spend so much money on clothes. Her accounts weren't balancing, no matter how hard she tried to pad them. Also, no one had seen Leonie's diamond earrings in months. That's when I started wondering if someone was blackmailing her." Geoffrey was silent for a moment, as he looked from Mother to me. "Maud's discussion with the headmistress proved most enlightening. She told her that Edith had been dismissed because she had made improper advances to several female students."

Mother and I gasped in unison.

"So, my sister and I wondered if perhaps there were more to Leonie's relationship with Edith than a mere teacher-student one. We returned to London, and, with Edgar's assistance, searched their house. We found this." Geoffrey went over to the table for the box. "It contained over two thousand pounds, the diamond earrings, and these."

Then he handed me the box. Sitting up in bed, I lifted the lid with trembling fingers. There, inside, were letters tied with a blue satin ribbon, and a wad of picture post cards. "These are all of Leonie," I said incredulously, flipping through them. "Edith must have bought every single one of them!"

Then I put the cards back and took out one of the letters. I hurriedly opened it and read it aloud. "My dearest, darling Edith. These days that I have spent away from you have been hell for me, and I long to feel your loving arms around me once again as soon as I return."

I couldn't read any more. Revulsion rose in my throat like bile as I saw my sister's signature scrawled at the bottom of the page. "These letters were written to Edith by Leonie. Love letters. They were—were lovers, weren't they?"

My heart went out to Geoffrey as a look of anguish flitted across his face. "It certainly would appear to be so."

Mother turned white, then buried her face in her hands and sobbed.

I stared at Geoffrey. "But why did Leonie allow Edith to blackmail her? Why didn't she go to you for help in exposing her?"

"We'll never know for certain until Edith confesses," he replied, "but we think Leonie feared there would be a scandal if those letters were ever published. They are most incriminating. You must remember she was beginning her affair with the prince at this time and perhaps she feared embroiling him in some scandal." Then his voice became both bitter and ironic. "Obviously, my own wife was afraid I wouldn't understand."

Mother managed to control her tears. "But why did Edith have to kill my daughter?"

Geoffrey shrugged. "We don't know yet, Persia. We think it's because Leonie finally threatened to expose her."

"And she had to try to kill me tonight," I said, "because of the diary we found hidden in the bottom of Leonie's jewel case." While they listened, I told them about the locket and the diary. Then something occurred to me. "The initials in the locket . . . I thought they stood for 'Edgar Wickes,' but they must have been Edith's initials. She's the one who gave Leonie the locket."

"She could have been the one who sent Leonie that upsetting note and the doll's head," Geoffrey added.

Mother shook her head sadly. "She never would have got away with it."

"Perhaps," Geoffrey said. "But with the money Edith collected, she could go anywhere in the world to start a new life. It would be so easy to disappear."

"She's a sick, sick woman," Mother declared with a shudder.

I laid back against the pillows, suddenly exhausted. "Where is Maud now?"

"In London, comforting Edgar," Geoffrey replied, taking the box from me. He looked down at it. "As soon as we found this, I caught the next train down here to warn you about Edith." He looked at me, and the tender, fiercely possessive look in his eyes made my heart stop. "I was just in time."

Mother sighed. "Well, this has been an evening of revelations. I, for one, think we should all get some sleep." and she turned to leave.

Geoffrey leaned over to lightly kiss me on the mouth. "I'll see you in the morning, Cassa. There is much we have to discuss."

The following morning, a constable came around with a copy of Edith's confession for all to read. She still refused to see any member of our family, though Mother begged that she be allowed to visit. Her request was denied.

The confession corroborated what Geoffrey and Maud had suspected all along, that Edith had been blackmailing Leonie and threatening to take the love letters to certain unscrupulous newspaper editors for publication. Edith also confessed to killing Leonie for threatening to expose her. Then, when I discovered the locket and the diary, she had to eliminate me as well.

In one last stunning piece of irony, the diary made no mention of Edith or her blackmail scheme anywhere in its pages. So, Edith's attempt on my life had been quite unnecessary. If she hadn't panicked, she probably could have quietly disappeared to America or Australia with her blackmail money, and no one would have ever found her.

Just before leaving, the constable handed me a letter. It was from Edith, and all it said was:

> *I thought you would like to know that your sister and I were never lovers, much as I might have wished it. She was merely infatuated with me. Girls sometimes idolize their teachers, you know, and fancy themselves in love with them in all innocence. However, Leonie imprudently wrote me letters that could be misinterpreted if they fell into the wrong hands. I have always been so poor, and Leonie always had so much, I couldn't let such an opportunity pass me by.*

I felt as though a great weight had been lifted from my shoulders. At least Edith had had the decency to set our minds at rest. I went in search of Mother to show her the note.

Later, as I stood on the terrace basking in the gentle August sun, thankful to be alive, I heard the distinct tapping of heels on flagstone. Even without turning my head, I knew that it was Geoffrey.

Leaning against the balustrade, I smiled and murmured, "The temple is so beautiful, so pristine, in the sunlight." My voice caught and the smile died. "I thought I'd never see it again."

"Hush, Cassa," Geoffrey said, drawing me to him, his arms encircling me protectively.

I sighed as I rested my head against his shoulder. "It's all over at last."

"No," he replied, "it's only the beginning."

I reluctantly drew away from him, for there was much that still had to be said between us. "Geoffrey, can you ever forgive me for my horrible suspicions about you?"

He smiled as he slowly caressed my cheek with his thumb. "There is nothing to forgive my love. I know I must have looked guilty often enough because I had the most to gain by Leonie's death."

"Still, I shouldn't have doubted you."

"Oh, I agree," he said with a grin, his voice light and teasing. "At first, I was furious with you when I saw the mistrust in your eyes, but then I realized it would be too much to ask of someone to believe in my innocence against such damning evidence. I decided the only thing I could do would be to unmask the killer and allay any doubts you might have had about me. Then my wonderful Maud came to me with her suspicions and said she wanted to go to Paris to substantiate them. Since Edith was staying here, we thought it best not to say anything to anyone about our real destination."

Suddenly, Geoffrey was staring at me with such intensity, I felt myself blushing. With a groan, his mouth came down hard on mine, and, for one eternal moment, I forgot Edith, the fire, my brush with death.

When our lips parted, he still held me close, murmuring, "Cassa, you don't know the agonies I endured when we were finally certain Edith was the murderer. The train ride down here seemed to take days. I had this terrible premonition that something was dreadfully wrong, and when I arrived and saw the sky lit up like a sunset . . ." Words failed him, and he could not go on. "Cassa, I would die if I lost you."

I slipped my arms around his waist and just held on to him. "I'll never leave you, Geoffrey. Never."

When we parted, he said, "I wish my wife had trusted me a little. I could have dealt with Edith, and perhaps Leonie would still be alive today."

"I know. She was trapped in a prison of her own making."

"She hurt many people with her selfishness, Cassa."

"I won't deny that. But she truly loved the prince. She

tolerated Edith's blackmail because she wanted to protect him."

"Perhaps it's the one selfless act of kindness she ever did." Now he grasped my hand and pressed it to his heart. "You will marry me, Cassa."

"But the law—"

"Oh, to hell with the law! I've endured a loveless marriage for two years, and now that I've finally found a woman I can share my life with, nothing is going to stand in my way. Where would you like to be married, my love? We'll have to wait until after Edith's trial, of course, but then we can go where we please. I rather fancy Cairo myself, with cousin Cyrus as my groom's man and Maud as your attendant. The old girl needs some time away from her good works, don't you think, and, who knows? Perhaps she and Cyrus would suit. Your mother will come, of course, then we can have a reception at the Clark's Hotel that will set all of Cairo on its ear. That's only fitting, don't you think? Cassa, why are you crying?"

"Because I'm so happy, why else?"

As Geoffrey gave me his handkerchief, he suddenly grew somber and reflective. "I'm not saying our life will be easy. I'm warning you again that we'll be shunned by all decent, law-abiding folk."

"I suppose I shall be 'living in sin.' Aunt Venetia will never speak to me again when she finds out."

He caught the laughter in my voice and smiled. "I'm afraid not." Then he stopped speaking long enough to kiss me again. Abruptly, Geoffrey set me away from him, and, for the first time, seemed unsure of himself. "But what about Sherborne?"

"What about him?"

"You've no regrets about not accepting such a flawless specimen?"

Someday I would tell Geoffrey about the lemon-yellow drawing room and Horace's proposal, but not right now. I smiled up into his eyes and stood on tiptoe to reach his lips. "Why don't you just forget all about Horace Reeve, Marquis of Sherborne? I already have."

Geoffrey chuckled. "With pleasure."

After a kiss that seemed never to end, I looked down the Avenue of the Bulls to the temple and felt excitement and anticipation taking hold of me. I finally knew what my mother had experienced with the Earl of Knighton, a love so consuming, so complete, it knows no rationality or bounds. I was soaring. I felt that I finally belonged somewhere, and to somebody.

"And I love you, Geoffrey, more than life itself." As we stood side by side, our fingers entwined, I thought of that night he had declared himself to me after the Marlborough House fiasco. "The wish you made on the Embankment that night, when you threw the gold sovereign into the Thames . . . did it ever come true?"

"It just has, my love," he replied.

And we walked together toward the temple and our future.